Unforgettable Novels of th...

BANDIDO CABALLERO: Once a Confederate spy, Tom Fallon has found a new career stealing gold from the French and giving it to another rebel cause in Mexico. He's becoming a legend on both sides of the border as the mysterious gunslinger Bandido Caballero . . .

THE HARD LAND: Though Jess Sanford left Simon Bauman for dead, the man is still alive. And there's one thing more relentless than the law: a shamed son with all the wealth of the Bauman family behind him . . .

IRON HORSE WARRIOR: Hunting for his brother's killer, Chance Tenery takes a job on the Union Pacific Railroad and begins a long fight for his honor, his life, and the woman he comes to love . . .

ANGEL FIRE: When Kurt Buckner agrees to escort a woman to the Colorado Territory, he finds that hostile Indians are no danger—compared to the three men who want her dead . . .

POWDER RIVER: Case Gentry is no longer a Texas Ranger. But the night a two-bit gunhand rides up to his cabin, he has to bring back every instinct to survive . . .

GUN BOSS: Raised by an Apache Tribe, Trace Gundy must call upon the fighting spirit he learned as a boy to avenge the loss of his beloved wife . . .

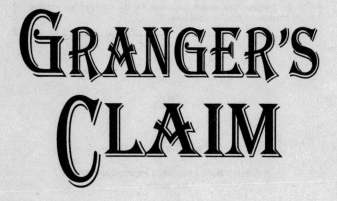

GRANGER'S CLAIM

JACK BALLAS

BERKLEY BOOKS, NEW YORK

GRANGER'S CLAIM

A Berkley Book / published by arrangement with
the author

PRINTING HISTORY
Berkley edition / July 1998

The Penguin Putnam Inc. World Wide Web site address is
http://www.penguinputnam.com

ISBN: 0-425-16453-5

BERKLEY®
Berkley Books are published by The Berkley Publishing Group,
a member of Penguin Putnam Inc.,
200 Madison Avenue, New York, New York 10016.
BERKLEY and the "B" design
are trademarks belonging to Berkley Publishing Corporation.

PRINTED IN THE UNITED STATES OF AMERICA

10 9 8 7 6 5 4 3 2 1

To Jack D. Weidenfeller of Missoula, Montana, and Ted and Rosalie Ostendorf of Miles City, Montana, I wish to express my deep sense of gratitude for the historical and geographical information each of you have provided about your area of the beautiful state of Montana. My friends, I thank you.

1

COLT GRANGER, ONE-TIME scout, rancher, and soldier, stood shivering outside of William Palmer's saloon in Nevada City, Montana Territory. He tried to ignore the enticing smell of wood smoke boiling from the chimneys of the shacks surrounding the town. Only a few minutes ago, he'd looked at the thermometer at the side of the door outside Lott Brother's store. The temperature hovered at thirty below zero.

Not ten feet in front of him stood Palmer's buckboard, a frozen body in its bed.

A hard, cold knot in his stomach, he heard the silent voice in his head build to a scream, asking the Lord to not let it be who he thought. He peered closer and tried to penetrate the frost coating the body's face, again hoping against hope the face he looked upon did not belong to the one man in this town too decent to die in such a manner, a man he'd taken in as a boy of eighteen.

He pushed closer to the wagon, close enough to see the bullet hole over Nicholas Tbalt's left eye, and the rope burns around his neck.

The knot in Granger's stomach tightened. The voice in his head stopped. Behind the tears, his brain exploded to a red, all-consuming anger, then cooled to an ice-blue flame. A controlled resolve pushed all else aside. He'd find whoever had done this and make him wish for a Comanche death rather than face what he had in store.

Unconsciously, his right hand pushed inside his coat to massage the walnut grips of his Colt. Someone had killed his best friend—almost a son—and dragged him by the neck to a place of concealment. Now, with the body found, it had been brought here for people to gawk at.

One by one, sometimes by twos and threes, men, mumbling curses, walked to gather in a close-knit crowd around the buckboard. Then, from the frozen silence, ugly, angry rumblings came from the throats of the throng. Their numbers grew. Upon hearing the news, miners dropped their picks and came toward the saloon. This sort of thing happened all too often in the settlements along Alder Gulch.

Granger tried to swallow the knot in his throat, tried to think where to start looking for his friend's killer, tried to think how to break the news to Molly, Nicholas's sister, a girl he thought of as his daughter. His mind muddled around in the quagmire of pain and anger until he became aware of a group of horsemen riding toward the gathering from the upper end of the gulch.

"Who found the boy?" asked a burly miner by the name of Benning, apparently the leader of the posse. Several of those standing around the buckboard pointed to Palmer. "Take us where you found him," Benning said.

Granger stopped only long enough to pick up his 12-gauge, sawed-off Greener and fill his pockets with buckshot, before he climbed on his horse and followed the posse.

The saloon keeper led them to a ravine about a mile outside of town and wordlessly pointed to its bottom.

Granger stared at the scrubbed-out snow where the body had slid down the incline. He turned his gaze on Palmer. "What happened then?"

The saloon keeper's face flushed with anger. "I rode to that ranch over yonder an' tried to get help getting him up here an' into the wagon. There's a bunch o' men stayin' in that house, none of 'em fit to 'socciate with. Cy Skinner, that saloon keeper over from Hell Gate, wuz one of 'em. He said as how killin's wuz too common round here to worry 'bout one more body. Said for me to just push snow over what wuz left of young Tbalt here an' forget it, we could worry 'bout it come spring thaw.''

Several in the posse nodded in agreement, and reined their horses as though to head back to town. One by one, Granger locked gazes with every man there. ''Tell you what I'm gonna do. I'm ridin' over yonder, an' I'm findin' out who did this. Every damned one o' you can go back to your warm fires—but I'm goin' over there.''

''I'm going with you,'' said Ted Benning, who sat his horse next to Granger. His words triggered the rest of them to swing their ponies back alongside.

When they approached the ranch house, the ex-scout assumed leadership. He pulled his horse to a stop. ''Don't want to go bustin' in there. Don't want none of you hurt if they're of a mind to keep us out.'' He twisted in his saddle and swept the surrounding area with a look. Next he glanced at the saddle scabbards of the riders. They all carried rifles.

''Barton, take two men an' set up the other side of that knoll over yonder. Benning, you an' a couple more come to rest just over the lip of that ravine. Smith, take up the other side of the house behind the barn.'' He paused. ''I want the rest o' you close to the house. I'm goin' in an' bring out that slime who refused to help Palmer load the body—then we're gonna ask 'im a few questions.''

''What you figurin' on doin', Granger?''

''When we get Cy Skinner out o' there, we'll make up our minds, depending on what we find out.''

When close to the house, Granger waved his hand for the remaining men to circle the shack. He climbed from his horse, broke the breech of his sawed-off Greener, checked the loads, and stepped to the porch.

He had drawn back his foot to kick in the door when it swung open. A man poked his head around its edge. Granger knew him from having to run him off someone else's claim. ''What you want?''

Granger kicked the door back into the claim jumper's face,

pushed his way into the room lighted with several coal-oil lamps, stepped to the side, and swung the shotgun in an arc to cover all in the hot, stinking space, smelling of unwashed bodies, stale whiskey, and tobacco. A glance showed him seven men; five sitting around a table playing poker, one lying in a bunk hung from the wall, and the man he'd kicked the door into, nursing a nose streaming blood.

Every man at the poker table swept a hand toward his side.

"Any willin' to digest a gut full o' buckshot go ahead." He waved the man holding his face with both hands toward those playing poker.

Holding the shotgun like a pistol, Granger covered the room. "Any o' you figure I'll miss blowin' your guts all over this room?"

Every poker player placed his hands palm down on the table. One of the men in bunks raised his hands to grasp the wooden supports holding the bunk. The other rolled as though to come from under the blankets. A pointed object pushed the blanket up about where the man's waist would be. Granger swiveled the 12-gauge and fired into the blanket where he suspected the man's revolver was pointed at him.

The full load ripped into the man, picked him up, and knocked him against the wall. Without another look, Granger swung the gaping maw of the gun back to the others. "Got one more load here, an' six slugs in my forty-four. Any o' you feel lucky?"

They sat as though frozen.

Colt knew Cyrus Skinner only by name, a man with a shady reputation. "Which one o' you is Skinner?" No one answered.

"All right. I'll take you all; we can hang the bunch of you. Now, which of you is Skinner?"

Still not a peep from any of them, but one man glanced at the player next to him. Granger assumed the man receiving the glance was the man he wanted.

He swung the shotgun to center on the poker player's chest. "Stand up, scum. Reach for your side gun, I'll cut you in two."

"Aw now, mister, I ain't done nothin'. What you takin' me outta here for?"

"Gonna ask you some questions. Depending on how you answer will determine what we do with you." He pinned the others with a gaze. "Shuck your hardware. Use your fingertips and throw your guns here at my feet."

He stepped closer to the door and yelled over his shoulder. "Got everything in here under control. One of you come collect this hardware."

The handguns gathered and tossed into the yard, Granger had a posse member search the cabin for other weapons and take them out. "Now, Skinner, let's go."

Before Granger could clear the door behind the claim jumper, one of the men at the table asked, "What we gonna do with Slim there, the one what you jest killed?"

Granger had been hoping for that question. He tipped his hat to the back of his head and, with a smile he forced through the anger freezing his brain, said, "Well, now. Why don't y'all throw a loop round his neck an' drag 'im over yonder to that ravine. Slide 'im into it, push some snow in to cover 'im, then when spring thaw comes, figure out what you want done with his stinkin' carcass." He tipped his hat. "Gentlemen." He backed out the door, broke the shotgun, pulled out the fired shell, and pushed in a fresh load.

Back in town, the posse took Skinner to Palmer's saloon, and pushed chairs and tables against the wall, except a lone chair. They sat the renegade on it in the middle of the floor. Then Granger told the saloon keeper to clear the saloon of everyone who hadn't ridden with the posse.

"Hell, man, you do that an' I'll lose a lot of business."

Granger stared at the saloon keeper a moment. "Palmer, do it my way, or you're gonna lose a lot more'n that. I'll take target practice at all them pretty bottles behind the bar."

Palmer looked at the tall man standing there. He knew of Granger's reputation with a gun, and out at the ranch he'd seen that the ex-cattleman didn't bluff. He had an idea the hard-faced man standing in front of him would do exactly as he said. He swung his look to cover those who hadn't ridden with them. "All right, clear the building."

When the last man left the room muttering something like "Shore wish I could stay an' see what's gonna happen in here," Granger bolted the door. He walked over and stood in front of Skinner. "Now we gonna find out who killed the boy."

The hardcase cast a sullen look around the room. "Don't know who killed 'im. Ain't seen Tbalt since last week."

Granger took Skinner's jaw between his thumb and forefinger and squeezed hard enough to pucker the hardcase's lips. "You saw what I did to your friend in the cabin? Well, I ain't gonna do that to you. Gonna use my forty-four on you, an' I'm gonna shoot off one toe at a time till you decide exactly where and when you seen the boy last, then tell us who killed 'im."

He looked over his shoulder. "Smith, pull his boots and socks off—if you can stand the smell." He turned his attention back to the hardcase. "You got lucky. I could've taken any one of that scum you run with. They all know what happened, but I chose you to be the hero and spill your guts."

Granger backed off a few feet, eyed a knot in the floor, only a couple of inches in front of Skinner's big toe, and, in a smooth, lightning move, drew his handgun and fired. The knot disappeared. "In case you figure I missed your toe and ain't very good with this forty-four, think again."

He slipped the cylinder out and slipped a full one into the Colt. He pinned the hardcase with a stony look, then grinned. "Want to make sure I got enough shells to finish all five toes on that foot."

"Aw hell, Granger, you ain't really gonna do this, are you?"

Without aiming, the tall man thumbed off another shot. Skinner's big toe punched a bloody hole in the floor. The hardcase stared at his foot a moment, moaned, and passed out.

One of the men standing at the side stepped forward. "Man, you cain't do this. It ain't human."

"Ain't tryin' to be human. Gonna get some answers outta this hardcase. Now stand back 'fore I lose my patience."

Skinner stirred, his face the color of bread dough. He opened his eyes and stared at his mangled foot. "Granger, they'll kill me if I tell."

The tall, hard-faced man opened the gate on his Colt and carefully counted to five. "Way I cipher it, Skinner, I got five shells left here, an' four left in my other cylinder, considerin' I had my revolver ridin' on an empty an' I fired once. That leaves me nine shots, an' you got nine toes left. Reckon it comes out even. Fact is, you an' Clubfoot George Lane gonna have somethin' in common—only you're gonna be one up on 'im." He thumbed back the hammer. "You gonna let us in on your little secret?"

Skinner shook his head. "Cain't."

Granger slipped his thumb off the hammer. The hardcase had another bloody stub.

When someone poured a shot of raw whiskey down his throat, Skinner mumbled, "Cain't stand no more o' this. George Ives wuz the one who done it. He kilt the boy for the horse he wuz ridin', then lit out for Bannack."

Granger scanned the members of the posse. "You men go after Ives. Bring 'im back here. We gonna keep this legal. Try 'im, then hang 'im. Ain't gonna be like all those other trials where we turn 'im loose tellin' 'im to leave the country, then have 'im show up back here in a couple of weeks an' nobody seeming to care." While talking, he thumbed fresh loads into the two cylinders. Then, his voice soft, he said, "Somebody's gonna have to tell Molly, Tbalt's sister. Reckon I'm the one's gotta do it, sorta took those two kids to raise when I found them huddled by the side of their folks' burned-out wagon after a Sioux attack."

Benning once again assumed command of the posse. "All right, men, we got a long, cold ride ahead of us. Let's go."

Granger glanced at Skinner. "Gonna lock you up nice an' safe somewhere until Ives's trial." He told Palmer to bring him a glass of whiskey, then again looked at the claim jumper. "Lockin' you up is gonna do two things. First, it'll keep you from headin' for parts unknown; second, it'll keep you alive, 'cause when your friends find out you spilled your guts, they'll be hard-pressed to keep from killin' you."

Granger had a couple of men carry Skinner to Kinna and Nye's store in Virginia City, only a couple of miles down the road, and lock him in the cellar, where they had a doctor attend to his foot. From there, he headed for the cabin he had helped Molly and Nicholas build after they staked their mining claim.

The closer he got to the cabin, the slower he walked. He studied the piled-up gravel along Stinking Water Creek, looked at the sluice boxes sitting idle along the frozen stream, pulled his neck deeper into his sheepskin, and smelled the scents of cooking food mixed with the pungent smell of wood smoke. "Damn! How can I tell Molly about Nick?" His words were swallowed by the thick wool collar pulled up in front of his mouth.

Molly, now twenty, was a strong woman. She'd had rough times, had weathered those storms, and now had to face the brutal killing of a brother only two years her junior. Granger swallowed, then swallowed again. Yeah, she was strong, but this was the toughest thing she'd faced since her parents were killed four years before.

He looked up the hill at the sturdy little cabin they had built. Smoke streamed from the metal chimney, then bent and lay close above the ground. He squared his shoulders, wiped moisture from his eyes, and walked up the hill.

2

EVEN THOUGH HE shared the cabin with Molly and Nick, he always knocked before entering, not wanting to catch Molly in some state of undress. He knocked now.

"C'mon in, Colt. I saw you coming up the hill. Nick's not back yet, so we'll eat and I'll keep his food warm on the back of the stove."

Granger shrugged out of his coat and hung it from a peg on the wall, only dimly aware of the spicy scents coming from the stove. How was he going to tell Molly about Nick? He stood staring at the neat row of pegs. Nick had helped him whittle them from small limbs. He squeezed his lids tight over tears trying to form. He didn't want her to see him cry, but he had to tell her, and putting it off wouldn't help. He blinked his lids again, and decided that straight out was the only way to do it.

He walked to her and grasped one of her shoulders in each of his big hands. "Little one, there's something I have to tell you, an' puttin' it off ain't gonna make it any easier."

Tall for a girl, she still had to tilt her head to meet his eyes. She waited, quiet, but Granger felt her stiffen, ready to accept whatever he would tell her. "Molly, Nick ain't comin' home—not ever. George Ives killed 'im, shot 'im in the

head. I've sent men to find the bastard and bring 'im back
here.''

Tears welled into her eyes. Her face stiffened, looked on
the verge of crumpling. She closed her lids as though to hide
the tears, blinked, and stood back. She showed no emotion.
She'd hold her sorrow inside until she could be alone, then
she'd drown it in tears. Colt wanted to wrap her in his arms,
say things to ease her pain, but he only stood there, thinking
back to the day he'd found her and her brother, seeing her
and Nick clinging to each other beside their parents' burned-
out wagon, both holding onto all they had left of the world
they had known.

Molly looked at him straight on. ''You gonna kill Ives,
Colt? If you don't, I will.''

''I thought to do it that way, girl, but that would be too
quick, too easy. I figure to have a trial, an' if that don't result
in gettin' 'im hung, I'll hang 'im myself.''

''Promise me that, Colt? Promise you'll make 'im hurt
before he dies, then I'll stand aside, let you do it your way.''

Granger dug in his pocket for his pipe, packed and lit it
before answering. He blew a great cloud of smoke to the
side so as to not choke her. He again looked at her. ''Molly,
I love you like I would my own daughter if I had one. I felt
the same about Nick. The two of you are my children even
though I'm not much older than you, only seven years.
You're twenty now, ain't you?'' He choked trying to get out
the words. ''Yeah, you're twenty, 'cause Nick was only eighteen.'' He lapsed into silence. Only seven years between
them, but in his life he'd been through the War Between the
States, fought Indians, and punched cows among other
things. He'd grown up fast, grown up hard. The life he'd led
made him feel at times a hundred years older than the two
youngsters he'd found on the prairie. He was older, much
older than the few years separating them. They were his kids;
he'd treated them as such, and he vowed to himself, no matter what happened, no matter the circumstances, he'd always
treat Molly like his daughter. He'd let no man court her until
he knew the man could live up to what he thought a proper
husband should be, and to his mind that man had to be a

whole lot better than him. He broke out of his thoughts, and pinned Molly with a hard look. "You don't have to ask me to promise, but I do—Ives is gonna pay for what he done. He's gonna pay in spades."

Molly turned her head to the side and sniffed. "My bread!" She grabbed a dish towel from the back of a chair and pulled the oven door open. "Thank goodness. It didn't burn." Squatted in front of the oven, she looked over her shoulder. "Know you don't feel like it, I don't either, but we've got to eat. Sit up to the table. I'll dish up."

Pride in this girl-woman put a knot in his throat that made it hard to swallow. The hurt inside her would be long in softening, but she'd hold her head high and play the hand life dealt her; she always had.

When they'd eaten and had steaming cups of coffee in front of them, Granger told her what had happened, and how he'd found out who did it. "A posse's headin' for Bannack right now to bring Ives back."

"You think a jury'll hang him? For that matter, where'll you find a lawyer to try him?"

The muscles in Granger's face pulled tight. "Molly, if none o' that's available, reckon I'll be judge, jury, an' hangman. Ives ain't gettin' away with this. It's time we put a stop to the robberies an' killin's around these diggin's."

Molly studied him a moment longer, sipped the last of her coffee, and stood. "Better get things cleaned up an' get to bed. Sounds like we got a busy day ahead of us."

Molly climbed the ladder to the loft to make ready for bed. Colt insisted she sleep up there because it was the warmest place in the cabin. In summer months he swapped places with her so she'd be cool.

When she had the covers pulled up around her ears, her chin quivered, tears slipped from under her closed lids, and she pushed the quilt tight against her mouth to stifle the keening, grieving sounds squeezed from her throat.

Wracked with sobs, her sorrow tore at the roots of her soul until there were no more tears. Finally, weak, devoid of all feeling, she lay staring at the rough rafters not more than two or three feet above her head.

Now only Colt was left to her. Sometimes, most of the time, she looked on him as a big brother. At other times, when she was alone like this, she thought of him as the kindly man who'd taken her and Nick in and raised them as her own father would have. She didn't know what she'd do if she lost him. But as she'd grown older, become a young woman, her thoughts of him had changed. She didn't want him as a brother, or father. She wanted the other half of being a woman.

She had studied him, and knew that even now he thought of her as the girl child he'd taken under his wing. She'd watched his eyes to see if at any time he looked on her as a woman—but could only see that in his mind she was still the young girl he'd found after the raid. Regardless how he looked on her, she'd not be able to stand losing him. Having any part of his love, even parental, was better than nothing.

Finally, emotional exhaustion folded her in its arms. She slept.

Two days later, a light snow fell through the pall of smoke streaming from the chimneys of the hundreds of cabins lining the banks and hillsides of Alder Gulch. Through this, necks pulled deep into sheepskins, the posse rode down Wallace Street, the frozen, rutted main street of Virginia City. George Ives, bound hand and foot, lay across a saddle in their midst.

Benning pulled his horse alongside the killer, bent, cut the ropes tying him to the cinch rings, and dumped him to the ground in the middle of the trail.

The first man to come through the door of the saloon was a man Benning knew. "Hey, Whitey, stand here and hold a gun on this baggage while we get a drink and thaw the ice outta our bones. I'll fetch 'im then. Anybody tries to help 'im, blow a hole in them. Got it?"

Whitey nodded and took the rifle from Benning's hands. The posse leader led his frozen platoon to the Champion Saloon and ordered a glass of whiskey for each. The big, redheaded bartender put Benning's drink in front of him and asked, "You boys find Ives?"

"We found 'im. He's lying out yonder in the middle of the street."

"Dead?"

"Nope, but he sure as hell better wish he was. 'Cordin' to Granger, we're gonna hang 'im sort o' slow like. He figures to try Ives legal, then hang 'im."

Red shook his head. "You ain't gonna find a lawyer in this town to prosecute Ives. The bunch he hangs around with have already bought off the services of every shyster in town."

Benning grinned. "Won't do 'em no good. We brought a skinny, lanky young fellow name of Wilbur Fisk Sanders back with us from Bannack. He's a lawyer; young but good. He's itchin' to get his teeth into tryin' one of the bunch what's been robbin' an' killin' us miners. 'Sides that, I figure Granger'll hang 'im if we don't. That cowboy set a heap of store by young Tbalt. He'd sort of taken the youngster an' his sister to raise."

The trial began early the next morning. Every ruffian in the territory gathered in the saloon, obviously thinking to intimidate the honest, hardworking miners and townspeople— but the ruffians were outnumbered, and outgunned. Every honest man in the Gulch who could crowd into Con Orem's Champion Saloon on Jackson Street stood there, all carrying weapons of some sort—shotguns, revolvers, rifles, and huge bowie knives.

Sanders ordered that no drinks be dispensed until a verdict was reached. Granger smothered a smile. He figured the weather being what it was, and the crowd being what they were, lack of drinks would force a quick verdict.

The lanky Sanders, in the face of almost sure death if he got a verdict of guilty, skillfully prosecuted the case. The twenty-four-man jury sentenced Ives to "hang by the neck until dead."

Granger watched it all, and when the verdict came in, he volunteered to do the hanging—his way. He got the job, and immediately requested there be no gallows: He wanted more than a hanging; he wanted information. They turned Cyrus Skinner loose, figuring he'd head for his saloon in Hell Gate.

The evening of December 21, 1863, Granger stood under the loading arm at the livery; a new manila rope had been strung through a block and tackle about twelve feet above his head.

By his estimate two or three thousand men, braving the cold, crowded the area. Many sat on rooftops or hung out of second-story windows; the rest pushed and shoved to stand where they could see. The tall cowboy had been to hangings before. In the West it was a form of entertainment.

He stood in front of Ives, stared him in the eye, and placed the noose around the killer's neck. "Ives, you were sentenced to die by hangin'. Nobody said how you was to hang, so I'm tellin' you now. You can make it easy on yourself, or as hard as you like. I want to know the name of every man who has robbed, killed, and terrorized the folks in this community."

Ives stared back, venom shooting from his gaze. "Ain't tellin' you a damn thing, cowboy. You're even dumber'n these miners. You worked for thirty an' found. 'Sides that, you dug your own grave when you killed one of us."

Granger took the slack out of the rope, forcing the sullen killer to rise to his toes. "Names, Ives, names."

"No."

Granger pulled the bitter end of the rope a couple of feet and let Ives dangle there a few moments. When his face turned blue, Granger lowered him until his feet touched the ground. "You gonna tell me what I want to know?"

Ives shook his head.

Granger pulled the rope again. This time he watched until Ives feet kicked the thin, cold air in agony, then lowered him. Someone in the crowd yelled, "My God, Granger, you cain't do this. It's flat-out savage."

The cowboy swept the crowd with a hard glance. "You don't like what you see, go home." The knot in his stomach hardened, and with it he felt his guts roil. He didn't know whether he could finish the job he'd volunteered for, then he remembered Nick's laughter, and his kidding. His heart hardened. They needed to find all the men guilty of crimes here.

He turned his attention back to Ives. "Names now, Ives. I ain't messin' with you no more."

Ives shook his head. Granger pulled the rope taut and lifted the killer until his feet twitched an inch or two above six feet from the ground, an inch short of flapping above Granger's head. He tied the bitter end of the rope to a hitching post at the front of the stable. Four men, all of the same stripe as Ives, rushed toward the post; one held a bowie knife in his hand.

Granger stepped in front of them. "Any man touches that rope, I'll kill 'im."

As one, they drew up short. The man in the lead, Messer by name, studied Granger a moment. "Hear tell you been a gunfighter among other things. When the time's right, I'm gonna make you prove it."

Granger, his face feeling like cardboard, smiled thinly at the man. "No time like right now, Messer." He pulled his sheepskin back from over the walnut butt of his Colt.

Messer's face turned putty-colored under the red flush caused by the cold. "Ain't talkin' 'bout right now. Talkin' 'bout when I get ready."

"I'm ready now, you worthless bastard. You yellow? Gonna back down after makin' your brag?"

Granger waited, and took a breath of cold, scentless air, willing his nerves to relax. Messer wiped his hands on the front of his coat and took a step back, obviously knowing he'd pushed his bluff too far, but more afraid of being branded a coward. He went for his gun. It came free of its holster. Only then did Granger draw and thumb off a shot.

Messer, knocked back a step, caught his balance and tried to bring his weapon up. He fired into the ground at his feet, lifted his revolver, and looked at it as though he couldn't believe it failed him. His look shifted to the small black hole in the center of his chest. Blood seeped from it. At the same time trickles of red drooled from the corners of his mouth. He toppled forward onto his face and lay still.

Before the would-be gunfighter hit the ground, Granger moved his eyes to watch the other three. "Any o' you want to join 'im?"

"Dutch" John Wagner stood rooted in front of the tall ex-rancher. "Tell you somethin', cowboy. Ives had a lot o' friends around here. You better keep lookin' over your shoulder, 'cause you're gonna get it. Front or back, don't make no difference, you gonna get it." He spun on one foot and led the other two ruffians from the crowd.

Many in the crowd, their lust for gore satisfied, went home to their cabins. Most of those who had served on the posse went with Fisk Sanders and Granger to Con Orem's saloon. Orem, a prizefighter, didn't drink, but he told his redheaded bartender to set up a round for the posse. "Them drinks is on the house, and as many more as you want. You earned 'em with this day's work."

Sanders shook his head. "Thanks, Con, but we have a lot more work to do." He looked at each of the men with him. "I want to have a meeting, in private. Drink your drink and come to Kinna and Nye's Store. We'll meet in the basement. I've already spoken with them about it." He tugged at Colt's sleeve. "C'mon, I want you to know what I've got in mind."

Granger knocked his drink back and followed the lawyer.

In the basement of the general mercantile store, amid bales of jeans, bags of coffee, leaf tobacco strung from the ceiling with leather thongs, saddles, and guns, Sanders looked at Granger. "Colt, we have to do something about this riff-raff, something permanent."

Granger would normally enjoy the scents surrounding him. Now he ignored them. He nodded, feeling the hair on his neck stand out. He had an idea what was coming. "You thinkin' vigilance committee, Fisk?"

His face solemn, Sanders looked Granger in the eye. "If we're to have any sense of security, any comfort in which to work our claims, any chance to live a normal life, we must get rid of the criminal element around these camps— Bannack, Hell Gate, Gold Creek, anyplace there's gold being ripped out of this earth, and especially here in the Gulch." He spread his hands, palms up. "I know of no other answer."

Granger frowned, then nodded. "I agree with the idea, and will back you in any way I can, but I won't ride with you."

At the startled expression Sanders showed, Granger shook his head. "Don't get the wrong idea. I would go with you, but in the last three days I've made enemies of the very men you'll be hunting. Sanders, they'll be comin' for me. If I'm with you, and Molly's alone, they might try to get to me through her. No tellin' what they might do. Ain't lettin' that happen."

Fisk toyed with his pipe stem a moment, staring at the bowl, then he looked at Granger. Colt was startled to see the haunted look in the young lawyer's eyes. "Mister, I've been a believer in the legal way in which things should be done. I've studied Blackstone's book to try and make things happen under the law—but I'm afraid we're past that." He packed and lighted his pipe. "I'm convinced the people we're going after are well organized. They're scattered about every mining camp in the territory, but one thing I'm certain of is, there is one man responsible for leading them, and perhaps another informing them when someone is about to move his gold. Anytime a miner draws his dust from safe-keeping and heads for the States, they seem to know about it. I see no answer but speedy justice. We don't have time for trials, stuffed juries, and softhearted judges. We have to find who they are and rid the earth of them." He puffed life back into his pipe, studied the red glow in its bowl, then looked at Granger. "I understand you not riding with us, but I want you here at the meeting, every meeting, to support me if you will."

Granger nodded. By then, members of the posse had begun to trickle in. Finally, Sanders made a count. He looked at Benning. "Everybody here?" Benning nodded.

The young lawyer laid out his plan. While he talked, Granger studied the expressions of the men present. He saw reluctance on the faces of a few, whether from fear of the bandits, or unwillingness to be part of a group taking the law into their own hands, he was unable to determine.

He stepped forward. "Sanders, may I say a few words?"

Sanders nodded. "I yield the floor to Granger."

When Colt stepped to the front of the group, he deliberately let his gaze rest on each of them. He let his eyes stay longer on those in whose faces he'd seen doubt. "Men, there's not a one o' you what ain't worked like a dog to make enough to set you up good back in the States. We're talking 'bout makin' it safe for you to get there with your hard-earned money 'stead of having it taken from you an' leavin' you to die in some coulee. We intend to find every man responsible for these robberies an' hang 'im high.

"There's gonna be some who'll criticize what we're doin'. Most of them'll be newspaper reporters back in the States—an' they'll sway public thinkin', but they ain't livin' out here. They ain't workin' their collective asses off draggin' the nuggets and dust outta freezin' water; they ain't payin ten times what the market allows for clothes an' food; they ain't gettin' shot an' robbed. There'll be them right here in the Territory who'll criticize what we're doin', but damn their criticism. Let them come out here an' work beside us—then they'll have the right to have their say."

He stared at the floor a few moments. "There's some here who'll say I ain't got a right to voice my opinion when I tell you I ain't gonna ride with you." He nodded. "That's right, I ain't, but I'm gonna join you, an' I'm gonna do my part in relievin' this territory of outlaws. I gotta do it my way because of Molly. Since I shot the man in the cabin, and the other one at the hangin', an' pulled the rope to hang Ives, I'm a marked man. I don't mind that, but I have the responsibility of protectin' Molly, an' that I intend doin'." Again he looked at each of them. "Reckon I'll turn the floor back to Sanders."

It took another couple of hours for them to draw up rules by which they would operate, another hour for them to hear arguments for and against some of the rules, and another hour or so for them to hear Kenna and Nye justify the prices they had to put on their store's goods. They, too, were victims of the bandits. Their freight wagons were being robbed, and the drivers killed.

There were a few who argued against letting Confederates join the committee—and Confederates who were reluctant to ride with Unionists. Again, Granger took the floor. "Gonna tell y'all somethin'. I've scouted for the Union Army. I grew up in Texas, a Confederate state, but they ain't a damned one o' them from either side here to put a stop to these killin's. Personally, I don't care who wins even one battle of their war, a war fostered on people like you an' me by a bunch of self-serving politicians. Politicians who, on one side want states rights, and on the other side want a strong central gov'ment to tell us how to live when it ain't none o' their business. Like in most wars, the little man does the fightin' the rest ain't got guts enough to do for themselves. If you want to let a war what ain't none o' your business cause you to get killed—or robbed—so be it. Most o' them men, on either side fightin' that war, never owned a slave, most o' them never shipped a bale of cotton at the exorbitant rates charged by the railroads. If you feel so strongly 'bout what they fight for—go join up an' help 'em fight.''

One member of the group cleared his throat. "Don't you b'lieve in nothin', Granger?''

Colt felt heat rush to his face. He turned his gaze on the man who'd spoken. "Mister, I'm gonna say this right now—once. I make up my own mind what I b'lieve in. Nobody tells me how to think. This territory is my home. I'll fight for it, an' its people. If the Union, or the Confederacy, helps me, then I'll help them. I got no stake in either of their current problems, an' I don't choose my friends by which of those two sides they are loyal to. Got it?''

Several of those present grumbled under their breath, but none spoke out, and when he sat, several gave him hard looks, but there were many who nodded in agreement.

Finally at a quarter of one in the morning, Sanders called a vote and swore each of the members to secrecy. The Montana Vigilantes were now an organization.

The first order of business? Collect those persons with Ives when he was captured. After selecting the members who were to go after Ives's friends, the meeting broke up.

Granger stepped from the doorway of the store, looked up and down the quiet street, then headed for home. He'd taken only a couple of steps, steps that took him away from the nearest member of the newly formed Vigilantes, when he felt a burning and tug at his coat sleeve, then heard the sharp crack of a rifle.

He threw himself to the ground behind a horse trough filled with a solid block of ice. His gaze swept the empty street. Those leaving the building had disappeared back inside.

From where he lay, he studied much of the street and the buildings on the other side of the frozen trail. No movement. He couldn't tell where the shot had come from. He didn't move for fear of drawing another shot. Someone inside the store's doorway said, "You hit bad, Granger?" He didn't answer. Then the hard ring of hoofbeats broke the stillness. He lay there another few minutes, then stood and walked toward his cabin.

Fearful something might have happened to Molly, he quickened his steps. He'd not been home since early afternoon.

3

GRANGER PULLED HIS sheepskin away from his shoulder, looked at the crease the bushwhacker's bullet had made, saw that it hardly bled, and walked the frigid mile to the bottom of the hill. He looked up. A lighted lamp sat on the windowsill. Molly always left a lamp burning "to guide him home," as she put it. Tonight the thought didn't leave him with the feeling of warmth he usually felt. It could be a trap, and if so, what had they done to Molly?

He squinted against the cold wind blowing in his face and looked at the cabin a long moment. Smoke shredded when it escaped the chimney into the wind, the lantern's glow painted a golden swath across the snow, the snug logs chinked against the weather, the cabin itself gave the landscape a tranquil, sheltered, warm look—but things were not always the way they seemed.

He lifted his sheepskin, slipped his .44 from its holster, put it in his coat pocket, and inched his way up the steep hillside, cringing as each step broke through the thin frozen crust, causing noise he thought might be heard all the way to town. He'd slipped up on Comanche camps with less racket, but then he'd not had this kind of weather.

The cabin had only one window, which was to the left of

the door; the back of the cabin was built into the side of the hill. Within forty yards of the swath of lantern light, Granger went to ground, and lay there a few moments to see if his approach had been noted.

No one came to the window. The door didn't swing open. If anyone had looked out, they couldn't have helped but see him. The snow gave off a light of its own, brighter than moonlight. He tried to shrink within his bulky clothes, tried to become smaller against the white background.

His stomach knotted; his neck muscles tightened. He wanted to stand and walk to the door as he had every other night—but this wasn't every other night. Those nights, he hadn't killed any of the bandit gang. He hadn't drawn return fire from them. Now they'd be looking for him, and get him anyway they could, even if they had to kill Molly to do it.

Keeping his eyes glued to the window, Colt snaked his way closer. Snow pellets felt grainy under his hands, freezing them, stiffening them, perhaps too stiff to pull a trigger. It couldn't be helped—working his way up the hill he had to use his hands.

Finally, he reached the base of the wall under the window, pulled his legs under him, and inch by inch raised his head until he could look into the room.

Molly sat in front of the stove, a lamp at her side. She knitted some garment she'd worked on for several days. The entire room came into view, except the corners on each side of the door. He stood there a moment, hoping Molly would look up, but even if she did, the lantern light between them would block her sight.

She glanced toward the window, stood, came over, and turned the wick up. Then she looked out. "For heaven's sake, Colt, what in the world are you standing out there in the cold for? Come in the house this minute and warm up."

His muscles turned to water, made him so weak he could hardly reach for the latch string. At the same time he felt like a fool. But no. Taking the precautions he'd taken had kept him alive many times. He'd do it again if he thought Molly might be in danger.

She handed him a cup of steaming coffee as soon as he

closed the door behind him. "Now tell me why you stood out there in that freezing weather." Her eyes shifted to his left shoulder. "Now, how in the world did you tear your—" Her eyes grew wide; her lips pursed. "That's . . . that's a bullet hole."

He eyed her a moment. "Molly, things ain't like they've always been. The bunch what's been causing all the trouble around here tried to shoot me. They'll try again, an' I'll tell you right now, they'll hurt you to get at me." He sipped his coffee, blew on it, then sipped again. "I was standin' out there tryin' to see if there was anyone in the cabin with you."

She placed hands on hips, squared her shoulders, and looked at him straight on. "Colt, when are you gonna trust me to take care of myself? I can handle a gun. I keep one with me all the time. Now let me take a look at your shoulder."

He let her fuss over him only a few moments before he answered her question.

He nodded. "I know you're right good with handgun and rifle, but if they come bustin' in here, you might not have a chance to get hold of either. Gonna tell you right now, little one, from here on out, you're gonna be with me wherever I go."

She shook her head in wonder, then looked at the table. "I bet you haven't eaten a bite. Sit down. I'll feed you."

While eating, Granger glanced toward the spot they'd dug back into the hill where they'd buried the doeskin sacks holding almost fifty thousand dollars in dust and nuggets. They'd hit it rich for awhile, then the daily take began to dwindle. Now they were lucky if they got three or four dollars' worth of the precious grains during a long day's work.

Finished with supper, he poured another cup of coffee for each of them, then looked at Molly. "Been thinkin'. Our claim's 'bout worked out. Figure come spring we'll pull stakes, go up there around Hell Gate Canyon, see what them streams'll give us."

She grinned. "Colt, those streams won't *give* us anything. We'll have to work just as hard there as we have here." She sobered. "The real reason you're talking about leaving is, you want to get me as far from danger as you can—right?''

He frowned, studied the dark liquid in his cup, then nod-ded. ''Reckon you're mostly right, but there's other reasons. When Father DeSmet an' Father Ravalli come through Hell Gate Canyon, they seen there was gold in them creeks, but didn't let the word out because they figured it would bring a flood of whites into Indian country. They didn't think the Indians were ready for that.''

He packed and lighted his pipe. ''I also hear tell Lewis, Clark, an' their men seen plenty of evidence of gold. The clay the Indians made their pipes from was speckled with gold dust, but that expedition wasn't interested in gold, nor were the Indians—it wasn't what they were there for.''

Molly steepled her work-worn fingers in front of her face, then looked over them at Granger. ''When we leavin'?''

''After spring thaw. We got us a nice comfortable cabin here; better'n most, so we'll winter here, till it's warm enough to snake logs off the cliffs around whatever creek we decide to stake a claim on. We'll want to build close to our claims. An' we gotta think 'bout movin' that dust we got cached back there; gold we done sweated our skin off for is another problem.''

Molly stood to red-up the dishes. ''We'll talk about it later; we gotta get some sleep now.'' He helped clean up the mess made by his supper. By the time they finished, daylight pushed its way through the window. Granger stoked the fire while Molly climbed to the loft.

Afternoon shadows stretched long across the frozen land when they awakened. They again had talked well into the night. They talked about the good times the two of them and Nick had had, and the bad times. Part of their talk helped purge the grief of losing Nick, but mostly it showed the friendship each felt for the other.

The next afternoon, the posses returned, empty-handed from their search for the men with Ives. They called a meet-ing.

Granger left Molly with her friend at the dressmaker's shop and headed for the meeting. Members of three different groups of the posse compared notes and found that each had met someone named "Red" Yeager on the trail. He told each group a different story about the whereabouts of Ives's henchmen. The longer the posse members talked, the madder they became. Finally, Fisk Sanders held up his hands to quiet them. "In my opinion, men, it's obvious Yeager is part of the bunch we're looking for. Let's find him."

Granger stood. "Wait a minute. This is a big territory. I figure he's at one of the ranches that bunch hangs out at. My bet is the Rattlesnake outfit. Try that one first."

"Why that one?" Benning asked.

Granger frowned. "Way I see it, judgin' from where each of your groups saw 'im, the Rattlesnake Ranch is not far from any of those spots. In this weather I figure he'd head for the closest warmth where he knew he'd find friends."

Several of the riders nodded. "Makes sense," Sanders said. "We'll head out there in the morning. You're all cold and hungry. Get food under your belts, a good night's sleep, and we'll meet back here at daylight."

Soon after the meeting broke up, Granger collected Molly and headed for their cabin. He'd reached for the latch string when he noticed it was a new strip of leather. He put his fingers to his lips. Molly nodded.

Colt put his lips close to her ear and whispered, "You replace the latch string?" She shook her head.

"Way I figure it, we got company—unwelcome company." He sucked in a breath, swallowed to try and rid his throat of the knot swelled there, pushed Molly to the side where she wouldn't catch lead, and drew his .44. "Stand back." With those words he kicked the door in.

Two men sat at the table in the dark. Granger thumbed off shots as fast as his thumb would work. Each man had a revolver on the table in front of him, but by the time they could realize what had happened, they'd each taken two bullets to the chest.

Granger hit the floor, rolled, and scanned the darkened corners of the room. The two men he'd put lead into were the only ones present. He stood and walked to the table.

Both men, hit hard, stared at him while trying to take hold

of their guns. Granger swept their weapons to the floor and squatted by the table, punching fresh shells into the chamber of his Colt.

"What's this about? Why're you here in my cabin? Who sent you? Who do you work for?"

Both stared at him, fear and shock showing on their faces. The man on the right worked his mouth a couple of times, then, his voice hoarse, he whispered, "Never figgered you'd come in shootin'. We'd've got you if you hadn't." He stiffened, blood gushed from his mouth, and he fell to the floor.

Granger glanced at the other ruffian. His eyes stared at the long trail to tomorrow—a trail he'd never travel.

Colt glanced at the door. Molly stood there, studying him. "You all right, Colt?"

"They never got off a shot. Yeah, I'm all right. 'Cept I better get busy an' fix that door I wrecked."

She drew in a quavery breath, then blew it out slowly. Granger figured she was trying to get her nerves under control. She squared her shoulders and pinned him with a look. "Colt, get them outta here. I'll clean up the mess you've made and start supper, then you fix the door."

He looked at her a long moment, mentally shook his head, and marveled at the way she took things in stride. Inside, her guts must have been churning, her chest tight, but she never showed the fear she must have felt, or the revulsion she must now be experiencing when she looked again at the bodies.

He dragged the two gunmen to a snowdrift about fifty yards from the cabin and left them there, figuring that on the morrow the posse who'd gone after Yeager would be back, and he'd then tell the town fathers to bury his latest contribution to ridding the territory of the likes of these two. He went back and repaired the door. By the time he'd finished, Molly had supper ready.

True to Granger's guess, the next afternoon the posse returned with Red Yeager. Now even more concerned with Molly's safety, Granger thought of leaving her at the sheriff's office, where she should be safe, until they could question the outlaw. He frowned. For some reason he didn't trust

Sheriff Henry Plummer. He couldn't quite put his finger on it, but the law officer was too smooth, and to all appearances got along well with the riffraff. He shook his head and took Molly to stay with the preacher's wife.

Walking away from the preacher's house, Granger studied the reasons he didn't trust Plummer. Yeah, he seemed too cozy with the trash, but the one the sheriff seemed to have the most in common with was Quirt Clinton, a hog of a man, so fat he peered at the world from small rodentlike eyes buried behind cheeks puffed up to the point of hiding them. And Colt's reason for suspecting Clinton of being cut from the same bolt of cloth as Plummer was that the hog always, in some way, ended up with title to the mining claims of murdered miners. Maybe he only took advantage of the situations the outlaws left him, but then again maybe Plummer and Clinton had something going between them. Maybe Plummer was closer to the outlaw gang than anyone suspected. That thought caused him to stop in the middle of the frozen, rutted trail. Could there be a Plummer-Clinton alliance—one running the outlaws, and covering it up by being the law, the other sweeping the leavings up, gathering in the abandoned mining claims when he knew from the sheriff the claims were available? Granger continued walking to the meeting, determined to give that angle a lot closer study. He'd make it a point to keep a close watch on the two.

The vigilantes again met in Orem's saloon. The door hadn't swung shut behind Granger before Sanders approached. ''Colt, Yeager won't tell us anything.'' He smiled. ''But having seen the persuasive way you had the last time we wanted information, we thought to turn him over to you.''

The cowboy's face hardened. He didn't want this job, but maybe he could get it done with threats; he was damned if he would shoot a man's toes off again. He looked across the room at Benning. ''Set the room up like we had it at Palmer's saloon.''

When they had the room cleared and Yeager sitting in the chair in the middle of it, Granger stood in front of him. ''You hear how we got answers from your friend?''

Yeager's face took on a sheen. Sweat oozed from every

pore. "Yeah, I heard." Then, his voice pleading, he said, "You ain't gonna do that to me, are you, Granger?"

Colt turned his look on Benning. "Take his boots and socks off."

In a few moments, Colt drew his .44, taking so long to do it that several of the posse downed a couple of drinks in the interim. He thumbed the hammer back and eyed Yeager's feet.

Yeager strained against the rope holding him in the chair. Despite the chill in the room, the outlaw sweated profusely. His shirt soaked it up until it would hold no more. Granger slipped his thumb off the hammer. The heavy slug tore into the floor between the outlaw's two big toes.

Granger shook his head. "Damn. Figured I could get both toes with one shot. Hate wasting cartridges. Hold your feet together so I can make up for the one I wasted."

Yeager, his face the color of new snow, shook his head frenziedly. "No—please don't. What you want to know?"

"We figure to have every name o' that bunch you travel with, every name of those who've robbed or killed any of the miners, or teamsters."

"All right. All right."

When Yeager got through spilling his guts, he'd named Sheriff Henry Plummer as the head of the gang, and Clubfoot George Lane as the informant about gold shipments. Lane's shoe repair shop was in Dance and Stuart's store, where miners stored much of their gold. And on the list Yeager provided, there were as many as twenty others in the gang.

Granger looked at Sanders. "Reckon we got what we wanted. Two of them on that list are lying up yonder by my cabin. They broke in an' were waitin' to bushwhack me. It didn't work. Have the town bury 'em."

Sanders nodded. "I'll see that it's done, Colt, then in the morning we'll head back to Bannack. Plummer hasn't been seen here in several days. I believe we'll find him and a few more of his men there." He stepped toward the door, then turned back, a thin smile creasing the corners of his lips. "I suppose what you did up at your cabin is what you meant when you said you'd side us, but you'd do it in your own way?''

Granger pushed his hat back, gave the lawyer a head-on stare, then nodded. ''Fisk, I wish I could say that's the end of it, but I know different. Them two are just more evidence they ain't gonna let me be.'' He gripped Sanders by the shoulder. ''Come, let's have a drink before we go out in the cold.''

Benning edged up to the bar beside them. ''What next, Sanders?''

The young lawyer seemed to shrink a little. He swallowed a couple of times. He hated what they were doing as none other, but it had to be done, and he could think of only one other man who could lead his vigilantes: Colt Granger. He looked at Benning. ''First, take Yeager out and hang 'im. We'll cut 'im down in the morning before we head for Bannack—that's where I think we'll find several whose names Yeager gave us. We'll hang them where we find 'em.''

January 10, 1864, in Bannack, the posse found Plummer, Ned Ray, and Buck Stinson, all on the list Yeager gave them. Plummer had built a scaffold there. Sanders figured it right accommodating of him in that it saved them from having to find a place from which to drape the three bodies. They hanged them where they found them.

Benning took a long look at the three, who had quit kicking twenty minutes before. He turned his look on Sanders. ''You find it sortta odd we took these men without a fight?''

The young lawyer shook his head. ''Nope. We're the only ones who know who we are, and what we're doing. We made a good decision when we decided on secrecy. This way we can walk right up to one of Plummer's bunch without causing alarm. Last night, catching Plummer alone, I walked to him, stuck out my hand as though in greeting, and shoved my revolver in his stomach with my other hand. Three of our men helped get him to jail, where we held him until we got the other two. You didn't have trouble with them, did you?''

Benning shook his head. ''I hear Pizanthia is holed up in his cabin just outside o' town. Figure we gonna have trouble takin' him 'cause by now he's had time to think on what happened to his cohorts. We better be prepared for a fight."

Sanders thought on it a moment. "We'll go out there in the morning. Tell the rest of the men to be ready at sunup."

The first gray light of dawn saw the posse members mounted and ready to ride. A horse snuffled, another stomped a shod hoof—the only sounds breaking the stillness. Not a breath of wind stirred the limbs on the trees surounding them.

Sanders squinted through the dim light at his men, then toed the stirrup. "Pizanthia's cabin's in a grove of trees just over that knoll. We'll split and surround him. I'll call for him to surrender. If he doesn't, and I don't think he will, open fire. Be careful to keep your aim away from any of us. And, Benning, have two men lie behind that pile of boulders on the side of the hill. They'll be able to see the entire periphery of the cabin from there."

They rode a bit closer, then dismounted where the hill hid the horses from view. His gut rolling with fear, Sanders slipped from tree to tree until he was about twenty-five yards from the front door. He pondered trying to get closer, then decided to take cover behind the bole of a large pine tree.

He cupped both hands around his mouth and shouted, "Hello the cabin. Pizanthia, come out. Leave your firearms where they are and come out with your hands above your head."

The sharp crack of a rifle answered him. The shot's echo had not died before every gun in the posse fired. Splinters flew from the door and two windows. Sanders signaled his men to cease fire. "Pizanthia, there's too many of us for you to fight; come on out."

"Go to hell. I come out you hang me. I stay in here, warm, my gut full, an' after awhile I take a bullet. I ain't got a chance either way, but I reckon a bullet's the easy way."

Sanders sighed, then thought he'd give the outlaw another option. "How you feel about us burning that cabin down around your ears? You'll be a helluva lot warmer than you are now, and while it burns, we'll draw in close enough that we'll be warm too."

"You done made up your mind to hang me like you done to them others. Reckon I'll take the fire."

"We'll give you a fair trial. Come on out."

"Fair trial, hell. Come an' get me."

Sanders waved one of the men toward him. "Circle to the back of the cabin. Gather a couple armfuls of pine straw, a few limbs, stack them against the back wall, and put a lucifer to them."

The miner stared at him a moment, shook his head, and said, "Damned if you ain't as hard as Granger, Sanders."

Sanders's jaw muscles knotted. "We set out to clean up this area. You know a better, softer way to do it, say so."

The rawboned man stared a moment longer, shook his head, and muttered. "Reckon it's the way we gotta do it, but it ain't easy." He reached toward the ground and raked up a huge clump of pine straw.

Thirty minutes later, the group stood around the burning cabin and watched the roof fall in, sending showers of sparks into the clear sky. One of them voiced the epitaph that reflected the feelings of all of them, which showed in their eyes. "Joe 'The Greaser' Pizanthia, you died like a man. That's the most any of us could hope for."

4

ON THE WAY back to Virginia City, the posse came across Dutch John Wagner, also on Yeager's list. They "tried" and hanged him. Then it was Virginia City's turn.

January 14, the town, ringed by miners and vigilantes from up and down the gulch, collected Clubfoot George Lane and four others. They tried the five in a building at the corner of Wallace and Jackson streets. Sanders acted as prosecutor.

After the trial he looked from one end of the street to the other. "Still no gallows?" He turned to Granger, who had been standing at his elbow during the trial.

Granger shook his head. "No gallows, Fisk, but there's an unfinished buildin' down yonder at Wallace an' Van Buren. Reckon we could use one o' them exposed beams."

Sanders packed and lit his pipe, stared in the direction Granger mentioned, then nodded. "Colt, we'll use that unfinished building. Tell you the truth, I don't have the stomach to watch them hang one at a time, and one's all the loading arm down at the livery can handle." He took a couple of puffs on his pipe. "Benning, take about ten men, go to Hell Gate, collect all on the list you find there, try them, then hang 'em. I hear that's where Cy Skinner went after Granger shot his toes off. Should be a few more on the list there."

He sighed, a feeling of completion permeating his chest. Sadness and shame that he'd violated every belief he had in the legal system threatened to choke him. He swallowed past the lump in his throat. "Except for a few dregs, we should be about through with all on this list."

Granger took Sanders by the shoulder and shook him gently. "Fisk, this had to be done, by you or somebody else. You the only one with the guts, brains, an' book learnin' enough to do it. Come, I'll buy you a drink, an' tell you 'bout Molly's an' my plans to move to Hell Gate. Our claim's about worked out. It's time to move on.

"Figure there's still men out there who'll try to take advantage of lone miners and their womenfolk, but if we're careful, we can protect ourselves. It's taken you almost two months to clean up that den of rattlesnakes. You've whittled 'em down to where it'll be right hard for them to reorganize."

A few days later, word reached Virginia City that Cy Skinner and seven others had been hanged at Hell Gate, and a couple of days later Bill Hunter was hanged alongside the Gallatin River. That brought to twenty-two the number of outlaws cleaned out.

Granger looked across the supper table at Molly. "Don't get the idea you can leave that handgun in the drawer. We still gonna have to be right wary o' strangers."

Molly glanced at him, then down at her plate. "Colt, you worry about me too much, but, yeah, I'll keep my revolver with me." She looked at the windowpanes rimed with ice. "You thinkin' about leaving here sometime in late April?"

He smiled. " 'Bout then. An', little miss, you better get your muscles in shape 'cause you gonna have to help me pull a crosscut saw. We'll need a lot o' timber for our cabin."

"Colt Granger, I'll pull that saw as long as you will." She sipped her coffee, set the cup down, rolled it around on its base, picked it up, and studied the wet ring it made. She worried about the next question she wanted to ask, afraid of the answer, but wanting to hear his say on the subject. "Colt, you reckon we're ever gonna settle down? Seems like we up and move every time we have a pretty nice place built.''

"Molly, we never had enough money to sit back an' sprout roots. Figure we do now. If it looks like settlers are gonna move into that Hell Gate area, we'll build our cabin to stay, buy a few cows, hogs, sheep, an' set up to be there awhile. Don't know what size place Hell Gate is, but it'll have two more people when we get there.''

Molly's heart swelled. It was the first time Colt had said anything that sounded like he meant to keep her with him. She didn't want to be like those poor, hungry, Canary children she'd read about in Virginia City's *Montana Post*, a paper one week old when she read it.

The eldest, Martha Jane, twelve, had been carrying a baby, about a year old, while her sister, about ten, hung onto her slip, the only garment she wore. They had been going door to door begging for food. When asked where her parents were, Martha Jane said her father had left for the Nevada Territory to gamble and she hadn't seen her mother in three days.

Molly knew she wouldn't end up like that, but she could end up with no one to care about her. She studied Colt from under almost closed lids. Taller than most men, he stood well over six feet; black hair, blue eyes, and the flat planes of his face made him the most ruggedly handsome man she'd seen—and he didn't seem to know she was in the world as far as women were concerned. She sighed. Well, maybe someday.

April 27, 1864, Granger put the last bit of furniture on the wagon he'd traded their cabin for. Before loading it, he and Molly transferred the bags of dust and nuggets to its bed while the night shrouded them in smoke and freezing mist. Then the gray light of dawn gave Colt light enough to build a false bottom in the buckboard.

Finished loading, he walked into the now-empty cabin. Molly stood in the middle of the floor, tears threatening to spill down her cheeks. "Oh, Colt, our poor dear cabin, it looks so forlorn without everything in it. I . . . I suppose it takes people and their furnishings to make a place a home.''

"More'n that, Molly. It takes laughter, tears, and memories.'' He walked to her and wiped her eyes with his bandanna. ''You're doin' right well with the tears, an' we'll always have the memories. Now, let's go before the day gets away from us.''

He helped her to the rough wooden seat, then climbed aboard; they had their saddle horses tied to the tailgate. ''You strap your handgun to your thigh like I told you?''

She nodded. ''And I slipped my throwin' knife and its sheath down the front of my skirt.''

He slapped the reins against the backs of the four-horse team. ''Good. Hope we won't need 'em, but travelin' alone . . .'' He let his words trail off.

Molly looked at him from head to toe. ''Where you have your extra handgun?''

''Stuck inside my belt in the middle o' my back, an' we got our rifles by our legs. I packed the guns we took off that riffraff I shot. Hell, little one, we could fight a war with the weapons we got. Now you take them two quilts we left out an' bundle up real good. Don't want you gettin' the grippe.''

About mid-morning, Colt noticed Molly's face looked blue around her chin. They'd made only about four miles, but he pulled the wagon off the trail into a copse of pines.

''Gonna fix a pot o' coffee. You're gettin' mighty cold.''

Molly laughed through chattering teeth. ''Like you aren't?''

Colt chuckled. ''Yeah, reckon me, too.''

The coffee ready, he poured each cup about half-full of whiskey. ''You're mighty young to be drinkin' whiskey, young'un, but this weather calls for it.''

''How old do I have to be before you'll figure it's all right for me to take a drink, Colt?''

He laughed. ''Oooh, 'bout a hundred, I reckon.''

She shook her head, but let the subject drop.

Warmed by the small fire and spiked coffee, Granger shoveled dirt over the flames and they moved on.

Their third night out of Virginia City, Granger woke to the sound of water dripping from the snow-laden trees. He grinned into the darkness, then glanced across the fire at the lump under Molly's blankets. She had covered her head and couldn't hear the ice-melt.

He had mixed emotions about the Chinook wind whining and moaning down the mountain slopes, a warm wind that broke the intolerable cold, but that in only a few hours would make a quagmire of the trail. He shrugged. A man couldn't have everything.

The next day, their nooning saw them shed sheepskins for lighter jackets, and that night they made camp beside the Beaver Head River. Bare, skeletonlike cottonwoods surrounded them, their branches reaching toward the heavens, as though imploring the Great Spirit to bring an early spring.

Granger gathered wood and built a fire, larger than he would have liked. Deep into the night it would be chilly enough to warrant a blanket and he didn't want Molly to get chilled. He didn't worry the fire would attract Indians—they were close to the friendly Flatheads—but he worried about road agents. The Vigilantes had done a good job of clearing the territory, but smaller gangs remained.

Molly fixed supper while Granger cleaned and oiled their weapons. They put the firearms and knives back on their persons before they sat for supper. After eating, huddled close to the fire, and seeking the warmth of the granite coffee cups clutched tightly in their hands, they sat in silence, enjoying relief from the bumping, jolting wagon.

A twig cracked somewhere in the darkness outside the circle of firelight. "Molly, we got visitors," Granger whispered. "When I say go, make a dive for that brush over yonder."

Before they could move, a gravelly voice spoke from the shadows. "Hold it right there, Granger. You too, missy."

To move or draw a gun would get them both killed. "Sit tight, Molly. Don't do nothin' to get yourself hurt." If he'd been alone, Colt might have tried to draw and fight his way out of the fix they'd gotten themselves into. But not with weapons pointed at Molly. He cocked his head as two men walked into the ring of firelight. He'd seen them around Virginia City, and Nevada City. Bull Madden and Spike Delon.

"Well, what brings you two out in the cold? You figure to take a man's goods 'stead of workin' for a livin'?"

Madden, a hulking brute of a man, walked over, looked into the stew pot simmering at the edge of the fire, then slanted a look toward Granger. "Don't smart-mouth me, cowboy." He glanced toward Delon. "Tie 'em up, Spike. Take Granger's side gun an' that bowie knife, then we'll eat some o' this fine-lookin' stew missy fixed for us."

"If I'd made it for you, it'd have a batch of rat poison in it." Molly's eyes looked like chips of blue ice.

Delon stood back, cocked his head, and raked her from head to toe with a nasty, vile look, his eyes undressing her with each downward glance. "Well, now, missy, don't look like yore man's slapped you around enough. You got a mighty smart mouth too."

"Any man puts a hand on me, mister, I'll kill 'im. Don't know how I'd do it right now, but I'll get it done."

Delon went to his saddle, pulled a handful of rawhide pigging strings from where they were tied at its side, jerked her hands behind her, lashed them together, pulled her legs out straight, and tied her feet. Then he pulled Granger's hands behind his back and did the same. After tying Colt's feet, he pulled on the lashings a couple of times to make sure they were tight, then took Granger's .44 from its holster and slipped the bowie from its sheath. He glanced at Molly, shook his head, and said, "Nah, she wouldn't be packin' a gun."

When Delon was through with that task, Madden, obviously in charge, told the skinny bandit to bring the horses in and strip the gear from them. Finally they sat close to the fire eating Molly's stew.

"You eat like an animal, Delon—slurping, belching, smacking. Didn't your folks teach you anything about manners?"

"He never had folks, Molly. Somebody dug 'im out from under a rock."

From where he sat, Madden backhanded Granger across the face. " 'Nother smart remark like that, cowboy, an' I'll blow your brains out."

"Don't think so, Madden. You ain't found whatever it was you come here for."

They finished eating, left the stew pot simmering at the side of the fire, then turned their attention on Granger. Delon—dirty, unshaven, rail thin—eyed the tall ex-rancher a moment. "Where's the gold?"

Granger frowned. "So that's what you think. You're here 'cause you think we got a gold cache somewhere."

Madden cut in. "We don't *think,* cowboy. We know. Before the Vigilantes hung Clubfoot George Lane, he told us all the while you two and her brother been pannin' that stream, none o' you ever put even an ounce of dust in Dance and Stuart's store. You got it with you somewhere in that wagon."

"Why you think we're movin' on, leavin' a good cabin if we took more'n eatin' an' tobacco dust outta that stream?" Granger kept talking, trying to keep their thoughts off of Molly. He wouldn't put it past them to take advantage of her.

After the two helped themselves to coffee, smoked, and took a couple of cupfuls of Granger's whiskey, they settled back. Delon eyed Molly.

Apparently reading his skinny partner's mind, Madden tried to head him off. "Right nice-lookin' gal, but too bony for my taste," he said. He eyed his blanket roll still tied behind his saddle. "Better get some shut-eye. In the mornin' we'll decide what to do with these two."

Granger sighed. Good. He'd need time to make his escape plan work. Delon cut into his thoughts.

"Right with me, Bull, but I'm gonna have me some o' that girl right sudden like."

Madden pinned Delon with a look that went right through him. "Tell you now, you ain't messin' with that filly. I done a lot o' things, but ain't gonna be party to mistreatin' no female critter."

The skinny bandit eyed Madden, and slid his hand toward his holster. "You ain't tellin' me what to do with no female. I want a piece now. Gonna have it."

Madden grinned. Neither his lips nor his eyes showing

humor. "Delon, don't b'lieve your mama raised a total damned fool. You reach for that gun, I'll put three holes in you before you get it outta the holster—an' you reach for that girl, I'll put six holes in you."

Madden stood and, keeping Delon under his gaze all the while, took the quilts off the wagon, then untied bedrolls from behind their saddles.

Then he swept the buckboard with a glance and shrugged. "We'll wait till mornin' to unload that wagon, too late now. Their dust is in there somewhere an' we might miss it in the dark. Come daylight, we'll find it."

Granger kept his eyes on them. Molly had her knife and handgun, he had his extra revolver. He hoped against hope Molly wouldn't try to take them on with her Whitney .36-caliber Navy without his help, but he had to get close to a puddle of the melted ice, and he needed cover over him to keep his hands out of sight.

The outlaws rolled up in their blankets close to the fire. Granger got the idea then. "Madden, let us have at least one o' them quilts. We can huddle close enough so's we'll only use one o' them."

Madden eyed him a moment, frowned, shook his head, and stood. "Don't give a damn if you freeze to death—after you tell us where you got your dust stashed." He picked up one of the quilts. "Scrunch over close to her so's it'll cover the both o' you. Don't reckon you'll mind gittin' close to yore piece one last time."

Blood rushed to Granger's head. The idea that this cow dung even thought of anyone in bed with Molly made the hair stand out on his head. He wanted to strangle the uncouth brute so bad he could feel Madden's windpipe under his thumbs, but the thought that Madden had defended Molly squelched some of his anger. He swallowed, and worked himself closer to Molly, but used care to lie close to one of the puddles. Madden threw the quilt over them and went to his blankets. Before crawling between them, he pulled his six-shooter, lay it beside him, and grinned at Delon. "Just in case you get any ideas 'bout shootin' me an' taking the girl an' the gold, you sleep across the fire from me." He lay back, his eyes open, pinning Delon with a look.

The skinny bandit tried to fake sleep. His snores were so phoney, Madden laughed. "Gonna take more'n them fake snores, Spike. Been with you too long. I know how you sleep." He pulled his covers up, then said, "Yeah, been with you too long. Come mornin' we split the gold—an' we split. Don't never want to see you again."

Some of the tension flowed from Granger. Madden was an unexpected help. Maybe he could keep the skinny bandit off of Molly long enough for Granger to get his hands loose. His stomach knotted. He needed time. A whiff of smoke. He coughed.

Molly grunted, strained at her bonds. "Not yet," he muttered.

"What you talkin' 'bout?"

"Madden, that bunch you rode with never told nobody 'night,' but I always tell Molly 'night.' That's all I was sayin' "

Madden grunted. "Shut the hell up from here on out." He pulled his blankets around his chin and settled in. Spike already snored. And the snores apparently sounded genuine to Madden this time. He slid farther into his blankets—and Granger worked his hands and wrists into the puddle of snowmelt.

He soaked the rawhide while he waited for Madden to breathe deeply, with an occasional snore. He strained at his lashings and whispered to Molly, "Now."

He didn't believe for a second that Delon was asleep. With what the filthy bastard had on his mind, he'd not sleep before he'd ravished Molly's young body until exhaustion put him out. But Delon had shut his eyes, and was too far away to hear Granger shifting against his bonds.

Certain that Madden slept, Granger kept his eyes on Delon while he sweated and strained at the now-soft rawhide. Under his breath, he told Molly what he figured to do. "See if you can loosen yours the same way."

After what seemed an eternity, the rawhide stretched—a little. Granger strained harder. A little more. His right hand slid free of the slippery leather. He pulled his .44 from the back of his trousers. Madden snorted. Granger held his breath, and eased the hammer back, the ratcheting sound pounding his ears like a hammer blow. Every nerve in his body was stretched to its limit. After a moment, Madden continued snoring.

Colt let his breath out, then holding his revolver in his right hand, he rolled on his side to face Molly. "Gonna get your knife outta your dress." Even under the circumstances, he felt shame that he had to touch Molly inside her skirt, but he got the knife. He cut her hands loose then pulled his legs higher and sawed at the lashings on his feet; then he cut those holding Molly's feet. He felt her pull her skirt above her knees and take her handgun from its thigh holster.

As he was about to throw the quilt off them, Granger saw Madden raise up and look toward them. The outlaw's eyes widened. He opened his mouth to yell. Granger fired through the quilt. A hole appeared above Madden's left eyebrow. The bull of a man fell into the fire. Colt swiveled his revolver to fire at Delon.

Too late. Molly stood between them. She grabbed the handle of the stew pot and upended the steaming pot over the filthy, skinny lecher's head, waited a moment for agony to contort his face—then shot him, shot him again, then again.

"You dirty scum. Gonna take from me what I been savin' for my husband someday?" She fired into him again.

"Hey, hold on a second, little girl. You can only kill 'im once." Granger went to her, put his hand over her smaller one, and, being careful not to hurt her, took her weapon. She stood trembling, staring at the skinny gunman. Colt pulled her to him and held her tight until she settled down. "There now. No need to be scared anymore. They're both dead."

She stood back from him, hands on hips. "Scared? Scared? Colt Granger, I ain't scared. I'm mad enough to spit. I lay there that whole time thinkin' what he figured to do to me. The longer I thought on it the madder I got." She looked at the body she'd filled with lead—and laughed. "Wish I could've known how much he enjoyed bathing in that boiling stew before he died."

Her laugh, and continuous talking, told Granger her nerves

were stretched tight as a fiddle string. He picked up the half-empty bottle of whiskey Madden had set by his blankets and poured about three fingers in her cup. "Drink this, little girl. It helps after a gunfight."

"You gonna have one, too?"

"You can bet your prize pony on that." With those words he tilted the bottle and poured himself a half-cupful. The cup almost to his lips, he looked at the quilt Madden had thrown over them. Smoke curled from around the hole he'd blown in it. He grabbed the quilt off the ground and, using the butt of his hands, smothered the smoldering fire.

"Molly, lay some tinder on them embers after I get what's left of Madden outta the fire. I'll drag the two of 'em into the woods. We'll have a cup of coffee, then get some sleep." He lifted the cup in a toast. "Here's to a damned good team, Molly. You're the best partner a man ever had."

She took a swallow of whiskey, coughed, blushed, and lowered her gaze. Colt blamed her blush on the whiskey.

5

MAY 28, 1864, four weeks and three days since leaving Virginia City, Granger pulled the wagon to a stop along the banks of Gold Creek, which flowed into Hell Gate River from the north.

Not waiting for Colt to help her from the wagon, Molly jumped to the ground. "Oh, Colt, this has to be the most beautiful place in the world. Pine, fir, tamarack trees, wild roses, berries. And the scent, clean, pure, sorta like a baby after his bath, better'n any of those perfumes they sell in the stores. Back there along the canyon, where the roses grew over the trail so as to form an arch, made it seem almost like heaven. What possessed anyone to name the canyon Hell Gate?"

Granger grunted. "From what I hear, the Indians started it, they called the canyon 'the place of ambush.' You could've painted the canyon in Indian blood there were so many fights here. The story goes that the *voyageurs*, the French, picked up on the Indian words an' called it *Le Porte du Infer*, 'Door to Hell,' then the Americans—trappers, mountaineers, an' explorers—put the English meanin' to it. It's been Hell Gate ever since."

"Well, I think it's a downright shame so pretty a place has so cruel a name."

Granger grimaced. "You'd have a hard time convincin' those Indians who lost family and friends in tribal wars of that." He wrapped the reins around the brake handle, climbed down, looked first up- and then downstream. "It was along this stream that two Stuart brothers found color, so what do you say we give it a try?"

"I thought you were gonna work me like a horse building a cabin first."

"No. Figure it'd make more sense to pan until we find the richest pockets, stake two claims, one for you and one for me, then find a place for our cabin."

Molly nodded. "Makes sense, but even if we have to take a little less gold outta the creek, let's try to find a place where we can have our cattle and other livestock."

Granger picked up a pinecone, turned it in his hand, studied it, tossed it aside, and looked at her straight on. "What's your aim, Molly—you want to get rich, or you want a nice comfortable home?" Before she could answer, he added, "Now, I ain't sayin' we gotta have one an' not the other. We might luck out an' have both. What I am sayin' is, if we have to make a choice, which would you rather have?"

She looked him straight in the eyes. "Colt, I reckon in the first place, we already have more money, even splitting it two ways, than I ever figured to have." She nodded. "Yep, if I have to make a choice, I'll take the home every time."

Granger shook his head. "Not splitting our dust two ways. We split it three ways. You get Nick's share. But even at one-third, I agree with you. A third of it's more'n I thought to have, an' I always wanted a home, ain't had one since I was a button."

She climbed back to the wagon seat. "We better ride some more. Let's find a place where we got room." She nodded. "A cabin we gotta have, and we need good grass, water— then we'll see what the creek offers in the way of gold."

Granger climbed up and sat beside her. " 'Nother thing we gotta think 'bout."

"I reckoned we'd thought of everything."

Colt wouldn't look at her. He looked at the trees, the creek, and where it looked like the high-water mark might have been in years past. Finally, he gazed at the ears of the horse directly in front of him. "Molly, one o' these days you gonna be a woman full grown. You gonna want yourself a man, a family, a town where you can go to dances once in a while, a town where you can buy the frilly things a woman wants, a town where you'll have other women to talk to. From what I hear, that town of Hell Gate's 'bout sixty miles west o' here. Every foot of it through this canyon. That'd be mighty hard travel every month or two so's you could see folks. You ain't gonna see nobody but me for months on end. You reckon you could stand that?"

"Long's you're there, Colt, reckon I could stand anything."

The absolute certainty with which she answered him, the trust in him to do the right thing, brought a knot to his throat, making it hard to swallow. When he could trust his voice not to betray him, he said, "Tell you what, little one. Why don't we take Hell Gate Canyon west? It comes out in the Bitter Root Valley.

"The Flatheads like that valley. It's been home to them for hundreds of years, but if they ain't already lost it an' been forced onto the reservation they're 'bout to be. Whites're pushin' 'em off their land. Ain't sayin' it's right, but that's the way it is. We might like it, too. Then, that town o' Hell Gate's right there at the mouth of this canyon. Let's take a look at it before we put our backs into work buildin' a cabin here so far from people."

Molly glanced toward the sun. "It's almost time for a nooning. I'll fix somethin' to eat and we'll talk about it." She climbed back to ground and walked around the buckboard in time to trap him at its side. "Colt, whatever you say to the contrary, I know you suggested going on for me. Well, I'm sayin' right now, if you like where we pick, I'll like it."

Granger smiled. "Looks like we already talked all we need to. Let's eat, then head west. At most, that town's not more'n another week o' travelin'."

Heading west was easier said than done. The river, swollen out of its banks by snowmelt, tumbling, roaring down the deep cut of the canyon, made staying on the trail next to impossible. For hundreds of years, Indians had used the canyon to go east from their permanent camp for the annual buffalo hunt, or to the creek where they found flint for their arrows, or to the place they called the Lodge of the White-tailed Deer because of the abundance of those animals at the eastern end of the canyon.

Granger found early on that the Indians had not stayed in the canyon all the way.

The swollen stream filled most of the gorge, then the walls pinched in so as to allow only room for the river. He pulled the team to a halt, studied the steep cliffs, and glanced at the roiling stream not ten yards to his side. There was no way to continue along the river's banks. "Sit tight, Molly, I'm goin' ahead a ways an' see if there ain't some way to get up the walls o' this here canyon. If we cain't, we gonna have to backtrack an' find a different trail to that town."

After scouting the cliffs ahead of them, Colt decided to give it a try. With Molly's help, he pushed and pulled, and, with backbreaking work, sometimes using a block and tackle to either pull the wagon to the top of the canyon, or again lower it foot by foot to the bottom, they finally pulled free of the canyon. By this time they were convinced Hell Gate was an appropriate name. Instead of the one week Granger had estimated to get to the town, it took them two and a half weeks. They'd had to ford Flint Creek, Stony Creek, numerous smaller streams, and Hell Gate River several times.

To call Hell Gate a town was to use a misnomer. "Small settlement" was a better term, but Granger didn't care about the size; he was glad to get there.

He and Molly sat on the wagon seat and looked the town over, studied the cluster of log buildings. It was not a town that had a look of any permanence to it, but judging by the signs painted on the building fronts, it was a town where a family could get the necessaries for living. There was the Worden & Company Mercantile Store, a building Granger judged to be about sixteen feet by eighteen feet; then there was the Higgins Residence, the Jenkins Saloon that still had a sign over the door naming it the Bolte Saloon. Cy Skinner had bought it and suddenly gone out of business when he got himself hanged. And there was the Buckhouse Blacksmith shop, the Woodward and Clements store, and Shockley's Boardinghouse. "Well there she is, Molly. Ain't much, but you think it's enough of a town to keep you from gettin' tired o' lookin' at me?"

Molly looked him straight in the eye. "Colt Granger, I don't reckon there's a thing you, or anything, could do to make me tired of looking at you."

Granger felt his face flush. It just wasn't right for her to talk like that; it almost sounded as if she looked on him like something more than was downright proper. Why, hell, she was a young girl, almost a daughter to him. A daughter just flat had no right to feel that way about her pa.

Not letting himself look at her, he looked beyond the town, out across the basin surrounded by shining mountains. Streams cut across the wide stretches of meadow and prairie. Clumps of trees dotted the grasslands. He changed the subject. "Hell Gate Ronde is what they call this valley, Molly. Reckon it's 'bout the prettiest place I ever seen. Cain't you just see our cattle dottin' them rollin' hills, an' our cabin settin' yonder against the side o' that mountain?" He shook his head. "Didn't figure there was any such place on earth."

He looked back at Molly. She looked like a spanked child; her shoulders slumped, and she had an expression in her eyes that seemed to acknowledge defeat. He wondered what he'd done to take the sun out of her day. He put it down to being tired.

"Come, let's get acquainted with some o' them folks."

On talking with a couple of the townspeople—Frank Worden and Christopher Higgins—who, it turned out, were partners in the mercantile store, they found that the permanent population of the town had been fourteen until only a few weeks ago, when the Vigilantes paid the town a visit and there had been some hangings. Nine people had died, at least two by gunshots. "But I don't want you young folks to get the wrong impression," Worden said. "Most of those hung were wont to hang out here after they'd done their deviltry around Bannack and Virginia City.'' He laughed. "The Vigilantes made certain they 'hung' out here forever. And we do a lot of business with folks traveling from east to west. Some stay, build cabins, and break ground for crops. The Indian agencies give us right smart business, too. It's a lively little town,'' he said and nodded. "Yes sir, a right lively little town. You folks thinkin' about settling in these parts?''

He cocked his head, studied Granger, and, not giving him a chance to answer, continued. "Four men, hardcases if I read them right, come through here about a week ago. Their description of the man they figured to meet up with fits you right close, young fellow.''

Granger nodded. "Yep. You read them four right. Reckon they think I done some o' their bunch wrong. They figure to get even. An' yeah, me an' this girl I taken to raise as my daughter, we figure to settle here if we can buy squatters' rights. Gonna start us a ranch. Hear tell them Durham cattle do right well in these parts.''

Worden frowned. "Watch your backside, young'un. Those were dangerous men.''

"Mr. Worden,'' Molly cut in, "the reason there's four of 'em is because Colt isn't anyone to mess with either. It'd take all four of them to take him—and me.''

Worden's look took them both in. He studied them a moment. His face solemn, he nodded and said, "See what you mean, young lady.'' He slipped a side of bacon into a gunnysack along with other purchases Molly had selected. He turned his attention back to them. "Talking about Durham cows, don't know of any in these parts, but you might get somebody from the coast to drive you in a herd. And if you ride up to the Jocko Indian Agency, they can probably tell you how to go about gettin' squatters' rights in this area.''

After they talked awhile, they finished replenishing their supplies and headed for the base of the mountain Granger had spotted as a good place for their cabin.

Molly didn't have much to say while they rode, but she kept casting glances at her partner. She squirmed about on the hard seat and finally said, "Colt, when you gonna look on me as grown up? Seems like when it comes to workin', fightin', or cookin', you figure me full grown, but when it comes down to lookin' at me, or lettin' me feel like a woman, you squash that thinkin' sudden like.'' She shifted about on the bumping, jolting wagon seat to look directly at him. ''Look at me, Colt. I'm not a little girl anymore.''

Granger's face stiffened. He stared straight ahead. ''Don't want to look on you as grown. Might let some young drifter start visiting you. Might let the wrong man have you. Wouldn't be doin' you right to let that happen.''

''See, that's what I mean. You don't trust me to have the common sense to make my own choice.''

Colt pulled the wagon to a stop and twisted to face her. ''Molly, I trust you. I know you got a lot o' sense in that head of yours. I . . . I don't know, reckon I'm just scared to give you free rein, scared I'll lose you. Don't think I could stand that. I took you an' Nick to raise, figured it was the right thing to do. You were both almost full grown even then, but mighty dumb in the ways of the frontier. You both come a long way in these four years. Reckon I want to get the job done right.''

Molly studied the backs of her rough hands, looked across the horse's backs, then placed her hands on Granger's. ''You do it your way, Colt. I won't hurry you. Just look at me once in a while as full grown.''

Granger's hands holding the reins tensed. Lord, if she only knew how hard he tried to keep from looking at her as grown, how hard his sense of decency fought with the man in him to ignore the fact she wasn't the same skinny, knobby-kneed, freckled girl he'd taken off the plains. He took a deep breath and looked toward the mountains, forcing his mind back to what they had come this way for.

He reined the team across a shallow stream, edged closer to the base of a butte, drove around it to the south side, and saw what he looked for. He knew it was the place when Molly gasped.

''Colt, this is it. Don't know if there's any gold nearby, but that backdrop of pines and firs, that bluff to back our cabin up to, well, when I've stared at the rafters in the middle of so many nights this's where I've pictured our cabin. It's where our home ought to be.''

Granger chuckled. ''All right. You pick the spot you want it to sit on an' we'll get started.'' He tied the reins to the brake yoke and climbed down. The bluff, about a hundred feet of sheer pink-and-gray granite, looked down on the tops of trees, and from a crack in its face a strong spring flowed. Scattered across the greening prairie, clumps of aspen stood, their spring growth trembling in the slight breeze.

Molly walked along the cliff's base, studied the trees, the springs flowing from the cracks in the rocks, and how high the ground stood above the creek at the bottom of the hill. Finally, she stopped and faced Granger. ''Reckon right here's a good spot.''

He smiled. ''Looks like you watched pretty close when Nick an' me picked spots before.'' He stood, cocked his head, and studied the cliff's face, checked for cracks that might let tons of rock fall on them. Except for the small openings from which water flowed, it looked solid. His gaze swept the surrounding area. He nodded. ''Good field of fire, water from that strongest spring we can run right through our cabin; fact is we'll build a room right into the face o' that bluff so's it'll take in the water supply. We'll first put in a trough to flow the water through, then when the mercantile can order us some, we'll buy piping and channel that water to where you'll be wanting to wash things up. Won't freeze in the winter that way.'' He turned a big smile on her. ''You did good, little girl.''

''Well, if I did so good, reckon we better set up camp and get busy cuttin' and draggin' logs. I don't want any trees cut here close to the cabin, except to thin them some.''

Granger unloaded the wagon and spread the tent in which they'd live until the first room stood tight against the weather. ''Reckon we'll build the kitchen an' livin' area first. Gonna have a stone fireplace so's we can sit of a night an' watch the flames dance while they comfort us.'' He smiled. ''Then, we gonna put up a bedroom, built just the way you want it so you won't have to climb to the attic durin' the cold months. We'll build me one later.''

"You mean I'm gonna have my own room, Colt? Well, what do you know. Never expected that. Looks like we're gonna stay awhile."

"You can bet your favorite pony on that, little one, but before all that we got a lot o' work to do. Let's get started." He pulled saws, files, ropes, chains, and other gear from the back of the wagon, then stopped and looked at Molly wrestling with a chair being stubborn about coming off the buckboard. "The first thing we gonna do is set the foundation outta a whole bunch o' them flat rocks. I figure to put in a puncheon floor soon's we get the rest o' the cabin finished." He flipped his hat off his sweating brow. " 'Nother thing, we gonna need to place them foundation rocks up against the cliff, so's nobody would notice, but there's gotta be a way to get outta the cabin in case of fire, or maybe attack."

For weeks they moved rocks, carefully fitted them together, and pulled the crosscut saw until by nightfall they were so tired it was all they could do to help each other prepare supper and drag themselves to bed. Many nights Molly went to sleep at the table. On those nights, Colt picked her up, put her to bed, and covered her with one of the quilts she'd spent many months of the last four years putting together. She'd awaken in the mornings ashamed for being so "puny," as she put it.

"Little one, don't feel that way. I'm just sorry you have to do the work you're doin'. One of these days we'll have it finished an' you'll be able to sit out yonder on the porch we gonna build an' rock yourself to sleep."

Finally, the logging done, Colt used his adze to notch the ends of the logs to fit snuggly to one another where the walls joined.

Well past the middle of summer, Molly moved close to him one day and said, "Rider comin'."

Colt laid the adze next to the log he worked on and picked up his rifle. "Get inside."

When Molly disappeared through the door of the living area they'd finished only two weeks since, Granger shaded his eyes and peered toward the approaching rider. "It's all right, Molly. It's Worden from in town."

He stood there, rifle lying in the crook of his arm, and waited for the storekeeper to ride up.

"What brings you out our way, neighbor? Climb down an' set a spell." Over his shoulder, he said, "Molly, set coffee on the stove."

Out of breath from his hard ride, Worden slipped from the saddle. "Left Higgins with the store. Thought you oughtta know, those four hardcases who asked about you earlier are back askin' more questions. Somebody's gonna tell them where you've settled."

Granger shrugged the kinks out of his back. "Might's well." He nodded. "Gonna have to face 'em sooner or later."

Molly came to the door. "I've set some victuals on the stove to warm. Wash up and come on in."

"Can't stay long. Gotta get back to the store before sundown."

Molly smiled. "Don't worry about it. I'll have you fed and outta here before you know it. While you eat, you can tell us all that's happened in town."

The only news Worden gave them was that a man by the name of William Cook had orderd a wagonload of whiskey, figuring to reopen the saloon. He thought to open it in the fall, cater to travelers, townspeople, make it a sort of meeting place. "More people are comin' into the valley all the time. I'm thinkin' of movin' my store out farther into the valley, to a sort o' central location so's people from all over the valley can come trade."

Molly squirmed a moment, then looked at him. "You know, Mr. Worden, it would be downright nice if we women had a place to meet and visit."

Worden cleared his throat and looking a bit embarrassed. "I'll take that up with some of the women in town soon's I can."

Molly didn't look satisfied with his answer but went to pour the coffee. They talked among the smell of strong coffee and herb-seasoned stew until Worden finished his coffee and stood. Granger thanked him for the long ride on his behalf. Worden headed back to town.

Granger looked at the sun, shrugged, and said, "Reckon we've 'bout wore the sun out for today. We'll put the tools away; tomorrow's gonna be a ridin' day. We're goin' to Hell Gate."

Molly stood still, not moving a muscle, then, almost under her breath, she said, "You're gonna face those men who're lookin' for you."

Granger studied his hard, calloused hands, then turned his eyes on her. "Reckon that's the only way I know, girl. Trouble don't go away, it comes to meet you, an' gets worse in the comin'. B'lieve if I get to where they are 'fore they get started, it might give me an edge."

"You dealin' me out, Colt?"

A slight smile broke the corners of his lips. "Didn't reckon to. Thought maybe you'd cover my backside."

Molly's grin was acceptance of the part she'd play.

That night after going to bed, Granger pondered the life he and Molly had ahead of them. Those four who awaited him in town would not be the end of the fighting. There were several more who would be hunting him, and each time he had to defend himself Molly would be in danger—he could think of no way to keep her out of it. She just flat had too much spunk to stand aside and let him do the fighting.

Too, the work she was having to do was man's work, there was no way around it, though she never complained. She bent her back to a job as hard as any man, and he didn't like her having to do it. He'd seen too many women on too many trails, heading west, and all of them were faded, sun wrinkled, old before their time. He couldn't stand the thought of Molly giving up the bloom of youth trying to help him get their place started.

Before letting sleep fold him in its arms, he decided that when winter set in they'd be through with the cabin, and Molly'd be through with the man-killing work.

6

GRANGER AND MOLLY rode into Hell Gate in time for their nooning. Each wore a holster and handgun. Each carried a Henry .44 rifle in the left hand. Some would wonder how a young woman could handle the weight and recoil of a Henry .44, but with the work she did, and the hardships endured, she could handle a firearm of that size with ease.

The smells of baking bread and broiling meat drew them to Shockley's Boardinghouse, where the owner greeted them at the door. "Have a seat at that long table over yonder. We feed family style. What's on the table's what you get." He stepped back and eyed their weapons. "Looks like you young'uns're loaded for bear."

Showing no humor, and not feeling any either, Granger locked gazes with him. "No, sir, we figure to hunt varmints today."

"Don't start shooting in here. The words gone around town there're four gunmen huntin' you, Granger. They ain't in here."

Granger nodded. "Thanks, I'll find 'em." His words were braver than he felt. His stomach muscles pulled in so tight he could hardly breathe.

They ate, and Granger paid Shockley fifty cents for their

meal. He turned to Molly. "You stay here. When I see who they are, I'll signal you from the door. And, young lady, all I want you to do is keep 'em off my back. Shockley called 'em gunmen. There's a lot o' difference between a gunman an' a gunfighter. A gunman'll shoot you from front, back—anywhere long's his hide ain't in danger. A gunfighter'll always be lookin' you in the eye. There's them down around Texas, New Mexico Territory, an' Kansas who've put the tag 'gunfighter' on me. Didn't want it, but it tells you I can handle most o' them you might call a gunman, long's I see 'em first."

He pulled the door open and stood there a moment, eyes scanning sod rooftops, spaces between buildings, parked wagons—anyplace a gunman might hide. Then he stepped to the boardwalk. "Stay where you are, Molly."

With those words, he edged along the front of the boardinghouse. At its corner he again checked spaces between the buildings across the rutted trail, areas he'd not been able to see from the door; then, using the oldest trick known, he removed his hat and stuck its brim and part of the crown around the gray, weathered corner of the hostelry.

A shot split the air. Granger's hat flew from his hands and landed in the trail. With the sharp sound of the rifle, he threw himself around the corner into the dirt at the side of the building, eyes seeking, and finding, the gunman. Another bullet kicked dirt in front of his face, but his .44 spit lead in one continuous roll of shots. His first shot pushed the second button on the gunman's shirt into his chest, his second glanced off the outlaw's belt buckle and opened a hole in his gut, and his third punched a black hole through the ambusher's shirt pocket. Each shot knocked the gunny reeling, until he sprawled on his back.

Every time he squeezed the trigger, Granger rolled to the side, frantically seeking others who might be looking for his scalp. No more shots. The sound of horses' hooves against the rocky soil replaced them.

Like they had a grizzly swiping at their tails, three men rode down the backs of the buildings, and when they came into the open, they fired wildly toward where the tall man

lay in the dirt. Granger fired his last two loads, and in a
smooth movement put a full cylinder in his handgun. But it
was too late; they had gotten away.

He stood, his face a frozen mask. He felt no more emotion
than he would have if the man lying on the ground in front
of him had been a rattlesnake. He walked to his victim, and
looked at him a moment before nudging him with his boot
toe. Dead.

He stooped, removed the cartridge belt, and picked up the
man's revolver where he'd dropped it. He went through his
pockets, removed three heavy doeskin sacks, probably dust,
and looked over his shoulder at Molly, who ran toward him.
"You hurt, Colt? You hit anywhere?"

He shook his head. "We ain't through with 'em, little one.
The other three rode outta here—in the direction of our
cabin. I'm goin' after 'em. You stay here."

Molly planted her feet in the rocky soil, placed hands on
hips, and eyed him. "Colt Granger, I'm not stayin' anywhere. You go, I go."

He studied her stance, and knew it was useless to argue.
"Get the horses."

They picked up tracks of three horses at the edge of town.
"Figure the cabin's where they planned to try for me in the
first place. They were surprised when we came to them.
Didn't have time to get set."

"Colt, if they find our home, they might set fire to it."

While riding, and thinking of what Molly said, he punched
out spent cartridges from his empty cylinder and pushed in
fresh ones. He rode closer to her. "Don't think they'll burn
us out. That cabin's pretty sturdy built, an' we located it
where it is because of the field of fire. Figure they'll fort up
in it an' shoot at us from there. They'll feel safe from us
burnin' our own home, an' lookin' at it, they know ain't no
bullet gonna penetrate them logs. Reckon they gonna think
we got a Mexican standoff."

"You sound like you got another idea about that standoff."

He grunted. "Got the beginnin' of a idea. Gotta think on
it a while."

He led them around piles of boulders, and copses of trees, staying out of rifle range. "Them jaspers mighta left one behind to see if he could pick us off 'fore we got home."

They topped a land swell. A shot sounded from well out in front of them. The bullet kicked up dirt about seventy-five yards ahead of where they sat their horses. "Get off your horse. I'll see if he's right serious 'bout gettin' us, or if he's just tryin' to scare us off."

He rode slowly, then stopped just beyond rifle range and sat there waiting for another shot. It didn't come. He nodded to himself and rode closer, his stomach muscles pulled tight as though to ward off a lead slug—if it came. No shot. Then he urged his horse to below the crest of the hill from which the gunman had fired at them. He stepped from his horse, crawled to the top, and peered over. He didn't take his usual care, having figured, when only the one shot came at them, that the gunman had fled.

The rifleman in the distance rode, his horse belly to the ground, toward their cabin.

"Reckon he don't want no part of us all by himself. He's gone to join his partners." Granger's words were more to steady his nerves than anything. He stood and waved for Molly to come ahead.

They talked while drawing nearer to the cabin. The tracks they followed didn't veer from a straight course except to go around rocks and trees or cross small streams.

Still out of rifle range, but within easy sight of the cabin, Granger pulled his horse in, stepped from the saddle, held his hand for Molly to dismount, then tethered the horses, knowing there was little chance a bullet would find them at that distance. His eyes swept every inch of approach to the cabin, and to each side of the sturdily built log structure. "Yep, we done us a helluva good job of settin' that there home of ours where nobody could get at it. But then, didn't figure on us bein' the ones tryin' to get at it."

Molly moved up beside him. "You think we might get close at night?"

He frowned. "Don't b'lieve so. We got us a bright moonlight night, and what with no side windows, all they gotta do is watch the front. They feel pretty safe in there. Course there's somethin' they don't know.''

Molly shifted from foot to foot. ''All right, tell me what they don't know that's got you so smug.''

Granger let fly a shot toward the cabin, knowing there wasn't a ghost of a chance he'd hit anything, but wanting to keep the renegades' attention focused toward him and Molly.

He looked at her, the shadow of a smile crinkling his eyes. ''Never figured to use it for anything except to get into the horse shed when snow had us covered in, but now we gonna use it for somethin' else.''

''What in the world are you talkin' about?''

Looking toward the cabin, he nodded. ''If I'm right, they ain't had a chance to really study the inside o' our cabin. They ain't seen that little flap of a door I put in the back, through them rocks, down about ground level. Remember I also put it there so's we could escape in case the cabin caught fire and we were trapped inside. Fact is, don't reckon they'll see it in dim lantern light, an' maybe not in daylight 'less they know it's there. I figure to use that little door to surprise 'em.''

She shook her head. ''You can't do it. You'll get yourself killed when they hear you crawlin' through that little space.''

He laughed. ''Naw, now. Don't reckon they gonna have a chance to get a bead on a little old sound like my clothes scrapin' 'long the ground when you gonna be raisin' 'nough hell out here to keep 'em busy.''

''What you talkin' 'bout?''

Before answering, he pointed to a pile of boulders, within rifle range of the cabin. ''Run like a Comanche's on your tail. Run a zigzag course. Get in behind them rocks, then I'll tell you what I got in mind. I'll stay in front o' you.'' He took off running and headed for the boulders, Molly right behind. They dived and hunkered behind the largest rock.

Granger pulled his Henry from its scabbard and leaned it against the boulder. ''See that there Henry Volcanic repeatin' rifle?''

''Of course I see it. You think I'm blind?''

He shook his head. ''No. Now, listen here a minute. You

know them rifles hold sixteen shells in the magazine, an' one in the chamber. Come sundown, I'm leavin' it with you. It, an' yours, give you thirty-four shots.'' While he talked, he checked the magazine to make sure it was fully loaded, then again leaned it against the rock. "Give me time to circle around an' get to the base o' our cabin, then start your own war. Put bullets through the window an' door fast as you can fire. That gun'll put them bullets through four inches o' wood at four hundred yards. We both know hittin' them logs we cut ain't gonna put lead inside. Them shots you throw through the door an' window's gonna keep them gunnies so busy staying low they won't be payin' no mind to the little ole sounds I make pushin' that trapdoor up an' gettin' into the cabin. When I get in, I'll start my show. Till nightfall we'll send a shot their way once in a while to keep their attention. Our horses'll be safe back yonder where I tethered 'em.''

She placed hands on hips. "Have you lost your mind? While I'm firing there'll be three men with guns in that small room with you, all figuring to shoot you unless I get mighty lucky an' nail one.''

"Don't want no argument outta you, woman. That's the way it's gonna be.''

"So now I'm a woman,'' she said and bristled, then slumped. "Aw, Colt, I know that's maybe the only chance we got to get 'em outta our home, but . . . but, well . . .'' Tears threatened to spill down her cheeks, then, her voice cracking, she finished her sentence: ". . . you take care, you hear.''

He laughed and pulled her to him. "Steady, little one, steady. I ain't lettin' nothin' happen to me. 'Sides, we gotta finish that cabin 'fore winter sets in. They gonna be so busy keepin' a whole hide they ain't gonna see me till I put holes in at least two of 'em, maybe all three. I'm takin' that forty-four Colt I took offa that gunny this afternoon. It, along with mine's, gonna give me 'nough shots for four times as many men as we got in that one room.''

Every few minutes, Granger threw a shot toward the cabin door or window, the slight breeze blowing the acrid smell of gunsmoke back into his face. With luck one of the shots would find flesh. The sound of the sporadic firing was the only thing that broke the afternoon silence, and the faint smell of wood smoke now coming from the cabin's chimney broke through the scent of ripening grass, and dust. An afternoon to enjoy if it weren't for men like those in the cabin.

Though it was mid-summer, the closer the sun sank toward the western peaks, the chillier it got. Molly shivered.

Granger pulled off his coat and wrapped it around her shoulders. "Gonna get you back in that cabin soon's possible. Don't want you catchin' a chill."

She stared at him. "Don't want *you* catching lead."

The large red orb finally hid its last fiery glow behind the peaks. Darkness pushed light to higher elevations, then the sun's light left the mountains. The moon already stood high in the sky to the east. Colt once again checked the magazines in the two rifles. "Every once in a while, fire, like we been doin' all afternoon. I'm gonna circle around and come up to the side o' the cabin. When I get ready to start the dance, I'll strike a lucifer. They won't be able to see it 'cause of the blind side o' the cabin. When you see its flare, start shootin'. I'll be usin' that time to get through the trapdoor. All right?"

Molly, her eyes wide, stared at him and nodded, then so low he barely heard her, she whispered, "*Vaya con Dios,* Colt."

He gave her a jerky nod, thinking how often God had been with him during the past years. "Goin' now, little one. If I don't come to the door an' swing the lantern twice when you hear the shootin' stop, get on your horse and hightail it back to Hell Gate. Get help to clear out your cabin and come back."

"All right, but without you here, there won't be nothin' to come back to."

He patted her on the shoulder, dropped to the ground when clear of the boulders, and dragged himself at a right angle to the bluff with his elbows.

Even with the sharp chill in the air, he soon sweated, not all of it caused by his exertions. Not many feet after he broke a sweat, the skin on his elbows wore through, and despite the pain, he dragged himself a few feet, stopped to catch his breath, then pulled himself farther.

The moon now bathed the grassy flat in front of him in a silvery sheen. He held low to the ground, figuring the dark of his body furnished only a small shadow in the lighter cast of the grassy surface. Finally, far enough to the side, he angled toward the cliff, and when broadside to the cabin, he stood, rubbed his raw elbows, and walked to the bluff's base. The sound of Molly's rifle cracked again.

Now, despite what he'd told her, his stomach tightened. A sick, brassy taste came to his throat. Every nerve in his body protested in sympathy with his knowing he might be shot full of holes in a few minutes. If he died, what would become of Molly?

He swallowed a couple of times and pushed that thought aside, breathed deeply, until his nerves relaxed a bit but remained taut. Then he reached in his pocket and pulled out the oilskin in which he kept his lucifers. While removing one from the packet, he continued to suck deep breaths into his lungs, and to let the air out slowly.

He felt along the cliff to the shadowed back corner of the cabin, located the flap door, pulled his revolver from its holster, and scraped the match along his trousers. It flared. He waved it twice before rifle fire erupted from the rocks well out in front of the cabin.

He dropped to his knees, then felt for the six-shooter in his belt, to make sure he could reach it when the one in his hand went empty. Then he pushed on the flap door. Because it was hung from leather straps, he had no fear of it squeaking. It swung smoothly inward.

He stuck his head inside the room and searched for the bandits. They all three lay on the dirt floor, folded into knots trying to avoid the ricocheting bullets Molly sent through the door and window. He thought to yell for them to drop their guns and flatten out belly-down on the floor. Now, that was a damned fool thought.

He slipped his thumb off the hammer and sent the nearest outlaw to perdition. The other two rolled, came to their knees, and, both firing as fast as they could fan the hammer, sprayed bullets everywhere except where he lay. Granger stood pat. Only his head and shoulders stuck into the room.

Lead whacked into the walls. Molly continued to fire. Her bullets mixed with Granger's and the outlaws', ricocheted, and whined about the room in a swarm. Granger's gut felt tight enough to break his ribs. One of the outlaws divided his fire between the window and the room. He fired blindly in every direction, then stumbled toward the center in front of the fireplace.

Dancing flames from the fire threw out light enough to turn the room into a scene from hell. Granger put another shot into the man knocked from the window, knocking him back to fall across the windowsill. Granger shifted his aim to the only remaining outlaw. His hammer fell on empty. He made a border shift, thumbed back the hammer on the now-fully-loaded gun in his right hand, and put lead into the gunman standing upright in the corner closest the door.

Granger's slug knocked him against the wall. He slid down the rough logs, and triggered off two more shots toward where Granger lay. One shot knocked dirt into Colt's eyes, the other splintered the trapdoor only inches above his head. He flinched. Fired again. The bandit slipped to the hard-packed dirt, and strained to bring his six-shooter level, only to have it rotate around his trigger finger, then fall to the floor.

Granger didn't move for a moment. He studied the three still figures lying in front of him—one on his back in the middle of the room, another slumped against the wall in the corner, and the last draped across the windowsill. He trained his Colt's muzzle on one, then another.

When none moved, he slid into the smoke-filled space. His eyes watered. He stifled a cough from the acrid stench of gunsmoke. Through teary eyes he checked each man, keeping his gun on the other two while doing so. All dead. Granger marveled that he hadn't missed a shot. There were twelve holes in the three bodies. The first one had gone down easy—one shot. One of the others had five holes in him, most in the chest, and the other had digested six slugs—two in his gut, three in his chest, and one beside his nose.

Granger listened to the deadly silence a moment. Molly had quit firing. With shaking hands he lighted a lantern, went to the door, stuck his hand out, swung the lamp twice, and stepped outside.

In only a few moments, Molly, riding her Appaloosa and leading his, rode to the front of the cabin. She launched herself from the saddle, ran to him, and threw her arms around his neck. "I was so scared for you, Colt. Are you all right?"

"Not a scratch, little one." He pulled her arms from his neck. "Gotta clean up the mess I made in here though. I'll drag this rubble out somewhere where that mama coyote an' her pups can find them. You clean the cabin while I'm gone."

He went to each body, went through the man's pockets, and took his guns, belts, rifles, and several bags of gold dust. He hung the weapons from pegs on the wall and tossed the dust to the table. "We come into a good bit of firearms tonight, little miss. That, with their horses and the gold dust they was carryin', made this a profitable night's work." Putting on a sober face, he said, "You reckon we oughtta forget huntin' gold an' seriously get to huntin' outlaws?"

She shook her head. "Honestly, aren't you ever gonna grow up? Don't think I ever want to go through anything like this again."

"Me either, little one." He smiled. "But cain't no one ever say we didn't get our home started right. You reckon anyone else has their cabin anchored down with lead? All the bullets stuck in these walls oughtta hold it down in a pretty stiff breeze."

He hooked up the wagon and hauled the bodies about a mile from the cabin, where he dumped them in a slight swale. He listened to the mama coyote sound her call, and headed back. He was satisfied that by morning there would be little left on the bones of the three. What the coyotes didn't eat, ants and other insects would.

When he walked through the doorway, Molly brushed by him with a bucket of water. The dirt floor showed signs of having been swept, the table had been scrubbed, and pots and pans washed.

The sound of water thrown from the bucket barely preceded Molly's question. "What'd you do with them?"

He eyed her a moment. "Left 'em for the varmints. We won't get any smell here."

"You figure to go out an' bury what's left in a day or two?"

"Nope. I'll rake up the bones an' stick 'em in a hole somewhere."

She stared at him a moment and shook her head, apparently used to not arguing when he let the hardness in him override the softer side he usually let her see.

She went to their beds and proceeded to check whether the outlaws had made themselves at home enough to use them.

"Leave 'em alone. Them varmints ain't had time to stretch out in 'em—we kept 'em too busy for that. Don't worry 'bout supper either. You've had a hard day. We'll get a night's sleep an' eat a good breakfast in the mornin' "

"We'll do no such, Colt Granger. We need all the strength we can get if we're gonna get done the work around here. Now, you just sit still while I fix us some victuals."

Relieved at her decision, he helped put the meal together, along with a pot of coffee, then stoked up the fire in the huge stone fireplace.

Sitting, drinking her second cup of coffee, Molly sighed. "I'm glad it's over. Now maybe we can get on without having to look over our shoulders, or make a check of the surrounding hills, for somebody to gun us down."

He stared into the flames, wondering if he should tell her. He didn't want to spoil her moment of peace, but he couldn't have her let her guard down. "Molly, we ain't through with them. There were six of that bunch in the cabin we took Skinner out of. None o' them was among those hung by the Vigilantes, an' ain't none o' them five the ones who showed up here. Buck Drago was one of 'em in the cabin. He ain't one to forget."

7

HER FACE STIFFENED, and her eyes widened with only a flicker of fear. She stared into the bottom of her cup a moment then looked at Colt. "You mean we'll have more days like this, more shootin', more times I'll run to you wondering if you took a bullet somewhere that'll kill you, more worry about just walking out the front door, afraid a gunshot'll end our happiness?"

" 'Fraid that's the way it's gonna be, little one. Till the last one of 'em's dead, or in prison, an' there ain't no prisons hereabouts, we gonna have to have eyes in the back of our head."

He drank the last of his coffee and stood. "Let's red-up the dishes and go to bed. 'Fore we start on the rest o' this cabin, I figure to ride in to Hell Gate. I seen a few chickens peckin' round there, a few milch cows, an' several hogs. Reckon whoever owns 'em might let us buy a male an' female of each to get us a start."

"But, won't varmints kill 'em off?"

"Yep, 'less o' course I build a pen that'll keep 'em out. I figure to do just that."

The next morning, he fashioned a henhouse out of long, slim saplings fitted close together, and built the floor up off the ground with more saplings, such that an animal couldn't burrow under the sides. He put together a hog pen also, and thought to let the cow graze out yonder on the flat until milking time—or until a bear, wolf, or some other hunting animal made a meal of her.

Sundown, four days later, he announced they would go to Hell Gate on the morrow.

The morning dawned without a cloud—crisp, cool. The mountains, still snowcapped, looked etched against the deep blue of the sky. The ride into town went without incident.

After questioning Christopher Higgins at the mercantile store, Granger found the men who owned the livestock, and they were willing to part with a boar and sow.

The lady who owned the chickens sold him a rooster and eight hens, saying at least five of the hens were laying. "You'll have plenty of eggs for breakfast now an' again, and still have enough to put under a settin' hen so's you'll have a bunch of chicks. That ole rooster'll take care of fertilizing them eggs for you."

Granger bought the sow, boar, and two shoats. He looked at Molly, grinning. "Figure them shoats'll give us some mighty tender pork. Be a good break from venison, fish, an' pronghorn."

They visited around town a while, getting acquainted, making friends, and enjoying the holiday from backbreaking labor. While Molly visited one of the town's ladies, Granger went to the boardinghouse to talk with Shockley.

As soon as he walked in the door, he could smell cooking foods—he couldn't tell what, but it smelled like broiled venison enough to make him hungry. The innkeeper wanted to know if the gunmen had given Molly and him any trouble, so Granger took time to tell him what had happened, then he eyed Shockley straight on. "That brings me to why I come to see you."

"Well, young man, let's have it, but I'll have you know right now, I don't want any shootin' here in my boardinghouse—outside's okay, but not in here."

"If I left Molly here under your protection, would you see she stays safe till I get back?"

Shockley backed up as though Granger had hit him. "Why you gosh-danged right I would. Jest 'cause I don't want no shootin' here in my establishment don't mean I'd let harm come to a young lady. Why you ask?"

"'Cause I'm goin' after what's left o' that bunch. Ain't gonna live in fear they'll shoot Molly tryin' to get me, an' I don't want 'er stayin' out at the cabin alone."

Shockley's eyes twinkled. He chuckled. "Son, watching that girl when you was gonna meet that gunman the other day, I'd say you gonna have more trouble keepin' her here than you will with what's left of the gunmen."

Granger clamped his jaws together, then growled, "I'll keep 'er here."

The innkeeper was right. Molly raised holy hell. She stood in front of Granger, hands on hips, eyes spitting blue flame. "So you think I'm gonna stay here an' let you go riding off to face five of that bunch. Ain't gonna happen that way, Colt Granger." From the start, her face flushed with anger, then turned redder. "I'm sidin' you, gonna cover your backside."

Despite his own anger, he chuckled. "Little one, you get any madder, you gonna bust a gut." His face hardened. "You'll stay here. Ain't gonna have to worry 'bout you when I find 'em."

They stood in the middle of the rutted trail running through the middle of town. Colt glanced to the side. People stood on the boardwalk in front of the mercantile, staring at them. He took a deep breath and, not wanting to air their family laundry before the whole town, looked toward the boardinghouse. "Let's get somethin' to eat. We'll talk *quiet-like* over supper." Without waiting for her, he walked away.

Three days later Molly swept her small room in the boardinghouse with a glance. She couldn't stand being cooped up like this. Worry about Colt, worry about the cabin, worry about things that needed doing at home would drive her mad if she didn't keep busy. She grabbed a handful of clothes and threw them in a gunnysack. If Colt wouldn't have her with him, she at least could be of some use by keeping things safe at the cabin.

Yes, he had finally convinced her he would be safer, more able to take care of himself in a gunfight, without having concern about where she stood and whether she'd catch a bullet if lead started flying. She'd agreed to let him go alone. But she hadn't agreed to stay with Shockley all the while.

Over the innkeeper's protests she had a couple of men staying in the hostlery fashion a pen for the chickens and one for the hogs, and load them into the wagon bed. She tied the cow to the tailgate and headed for home. Colt had taken out, leaving the animals to be taken care of by the people from whom he'd bought them. Now she'd take them home.

Letting the team pull the wagon at their own pace, she checked the two rifles and 12-gauge Greener lying in the boot; they were fully loaded. Today, she wore her handgun at her side.

When she pulled the wagon to the side of the cabin where Colt had built the chicken house and hog pen, she saw only the tracks his horse made when he'd come for his bedroll, extra cartridges, and another handgun and rifle.

After parking the wagon and taking care of the team, she walked into the cabin, stood in the middle of it, and looked around. Colt was wrong. It took more than laughter, tears, and memories to make a home. For her to feel like this was home she needed Colt with her, no one but him.

She went back out, penned the chickens and hogs, and turned the cow out to pasture.

The next couple of days she kept busy. She cleaned the cabin from floor to roof, swept the dirt floor and drew an oval pattern in it that she tried to make look like a rose. She washed clothes and dishes, milked the cow, penned her for the night, churned, and still looked for more chores. Then she went outside and chopped firewood, even though Colt had stacked enough to last the winter. When she first went out, she thought she smelled woodsmoke, but put it down to perhaps some of the scent from her breakfast fire lingering in the calm air.

She stopped, wiped sweat from her brow, and smiled. She could hear her dead mother's words as plain as though she stood at her side: "Ladies don't sweat, they perspire."

Then talking as though her mother could hear, she said, "Mama, you should see me now, that stuff I just wiped off was pure-dee *sweat*, so maybe I ain't a lady." She picked up the ax and pulled it over her shoulder, then eased it back down to the stump she used for a chopping block. She'd seen movement out along the brow of the hill to her right. She swallowed the lump in her throat. Where are you, Colt? she thought. I need you now. You'd know what to do.

Trying to act natural, she buried an inch or two of the ax bit into the block, picked up her rifle, and walked slowly to the door. She slipped into the cabin, dropped the heavy wooden bar into its slots, and pulled in the latch string.

Her heart felt as though it would pound through her breasts. She tried what she'd seen Colt do when in a tight spot: she sucked in one deep breath after another and let each of them out slow like. Yes. That did seem to make her relax a bit, but not enough to make her feel better about her predicament. Then, she stood to the side of the window and studied the crest of every land swell, every boulder, every coulee. Nothing to cause fear. She continued her search. Still no movement.

She didn't use curse words, but she'd heard Colt mutter them one time or another and they seemed to make him feel better. Her heart still pounding, she tried his remedy. "Oh damn, what do I do now?" The words didn't help, and she got no answer about what to do.

She stood there until dark, searching for sign of life. When night shrouded the cabin, she dropped the wooden shutter over the window, lighted the lantern, and, taking her Henry every place she went, prepared supper.

It wasn't very satisfying to cook for only herself. She wanted Colt there to enjoy the meal with her—and now to fight for her—but she ate, choking the food past fear.

After cleaning the kitchen area, she blew out the flame in the lantern and went back to the window to peek through the cracks. The wind picked up slightly, perhaps the harbinger of a thunderstorm. She sat still. The night sounds, the creek and groan of the cabin, each made her chest tighten, her neck hairs tingle.

After her eyes adjusted to the dark, she again searched the skyline along the hills. On her second swing across the area, she saw the thin glow from a fire flicker just over the brow of the hill, out close to where she'd fired the rifles so Colt could slip into the cabin.

She pulled her chair close to the door and sat. She couldn't go out to see who was there. She could fire toward where she saw the glimmer of light, but her chances of hitting anything were slim. She wouldn't waste the ammunition. She didn't dare saddle her horse and ride to town for help on the morrow. If whoever was out there meant her harm, she'd never make it. What was she to do?

She dozed, jerked awake, dozed again, jerked awake, and finally gave in to sleep.

When she awoke, tired, more than a little angry, she decided she couldn't sit there day after day until Colt returned. He might be gone three, four weeks, or more. She picked up her rifle, opened the shutter, cupped her hands around her mouth, and shouted, "Whoever is out there, show yourself." She waited another few moments and repeated her words.

About where she'd seen the fire flicker the night before, a short, skinny warrior stood and held his hands high.

Indians. Colt had told her the Indians here in the Bitter Root Valley were friendly. What did this man want of her? She trained her rifle on him.

Still holding his hands high overhead, the warrior walked toward the cabin. She let him come until well within rifle range and her ability to hit him. "What do you want of me?"

The Indian squatted, hands still above his head. "Woman Tbalt, I am Little Bear Who Runs, sub-chief of the Flatheads. Shockley, man who runs lodge for many people, send message for me to come see him. He asked me to see no harm comes to you. Say he give tobacco and food. To do that I have to know where you are, see you if I can. I wish to be your friend. Flatheads friend to good white men."

Molly studied him a moment. What he said fit the way Colt described the Flatheads, but he hadn't said they were starving, and this young Indian was hungry. Too, it was typical of what Shockley might do to safeguard her. "Why didn't you let me know you were out there?''

The warrior grinned. "I let you know, anybody watch cabin know. Better stay where can move around, not get caught in white man's box.''

Molly lowered the rifle, but still held it pistol-fashion. "I'm Molly Tbalt. My man is gone, come back anytime now.''

"Little Bear Who Runs know what Shockley tell. Your man be gone maybe three weeks. He say, keep you safe.'' He grinned. "Don't think Woman Tbalt need Little Bear keep her safe.''

Molly felt shame to admit it, but she swallowed her pride. She looked at the ground, studied a rock at her feet, then eyed the warrior. She'd test him. "I feel much better knowing you are here to keep me safe, Little Bear Who Runs, sub-chief of the Flatheads. Welcome to my lodge.'' If he started toward the cabin, she'd not accept his explanation. She'd not trust him.

He shook his head. "Little Bear happy you welcome him, but stay here in open where can see all. Nobody come near 'less you say me let in.''

Any doubt Molly had about the Indian dissolved with his words. He was there to keep her safe.

When she wakened the next morning, five lodges stood on the open ground between the cabin and the rocks from which she'd furnished cover fire for Colt. Little Bear Who Runs was making certain no harm came to her.

Granger rode into Bannack a week after leaving Hell Gate, remembering every face in that ranch house from which he'd taken Cy Skinner to be questioned by the posse. He'd know them, and would bet his saddle they'd know him. He reckoned it got down to who saw who first. His face hardened.

The bunch he looked for seldom hung out in saloons. They took their whiskey and card games to one of the several cabins or ranches the Plummer gang owned. This wasn't going to be easy, but what ever was?

Long since, his sheepskin hung across the saddle in front of him, so when he reined in in front of the Miner's Rest, the first saloon he came to, he took the opportunity to tie it to the back of his saddle, while studying the street stretching a good half mile along the trail. He figured on a few questions, then a ride toward Virginia City, unless he got the information he wanted.

Thinking a drink would be good, he pushed through the batwing doors and stepped to the side to await his eyes adjusting to the dim light. After a few minutes, he swept the room with a sharp, penetrating gaze, studied every face, then walked to the bar. He knew no one in the room.

He ordered a whiskey. When it came, he wondered whether to just flat-out say what he wanted and why. If he did, the word would soon get to the bunch for whom he looked, and they'd be likely to await a chance to dry-gulch him. There was only one of that bunch who would face him. He shrugged. Might as well take the chance. He had to have some idea where to start.

Granger tossed a coin on the bar to pay for his drink. When the bartender picked it up, he asked in a low voice, "Buck Drago been around lately?"

The bartender, a big man, all muscle, raked Granger with an unfriendly look. "Mister, we don't let his kind in this saloon. You a friend of his?"

Granger laughed. "Friend? Naw, I wouldn't say so. I'm lookin' to give 'im, or some o' that bunch he trails with, a chance to kill me while I'm lookin' at 'im. Don't cotton to gettin' shot from behind."

The bartender's attitude changed like from night to day. He smiled. "Seems you know 'em." He frowned. "Should I know you, mister?"

Granger shook his head. "Might a heard o' me. Name's Colt Granger, stuck a few pans in Stinkin' Water Crick over at Alder Gulch. Claim give out." He took a swallow of his drink and settled his holster more comfortably at his side. "I'm over at Hell Gate now, but some o' that bunch what ran with Plummer tracked me there. Figure to give what's left o' them a chance to get me from in front."

The big man behind the bar nodded. "Yeah, I heard o' you, Granger. Word is, you ain't a man to cross." He smiled.

"Tell you right now, I'm glad I ain't one o' that bunch."
He scratched his head, a slight frown puckering his eyebrows. "Yeah, to answer your question—heard tell Drago
was seen hereabouts maybe three, four days ago. Only one
of that bunch he runs with was with 'im. Don't know where
the rest of 'em are, an' ain't heard nothin' outta Drago in a
couple of days. Reckon he mighta gone back to Virginia
City."

Granger knocked back his drink, nodded, and thanked the
bartender for the information. "Reckon I'll look around town
a day or two and then take a look along the Stinkin' Water."
He tipped his hat. "Much obliged."

Out on the street he scanned the town. It looked like some
of its citizens intended to stay once the diggings gave out.
There were a few brick buildings.

He walked the length of the main street, scanned every
face he passed, then looked for a place to eat. Drago might
be back in Alder Gulch, but Granger wanted to give Bannack
a good look before he headed east.

He ate, asked the same questions of the cook, and got the
same answers. Then he went to the livery to stable his horse.
When he rode through the wide doors, he breathed deeply.
The mingled smells of hay, horse droppings, and leather were
among those he liked.

He stripped the gear off the Appaloosa and rubbed him
down before he turned to the gaunt, bewhiskered old man
inside. "Seen Buck Drago last day or two?"

The old man chewed a couple times, puckered his lips,
and let fly a brown stream at a horse apple off to his side.
He hit it dead center. "Ain't been lookin' fer 'im. Why?"

Granger felt the blood start up his neck, but he squelched
his rising anger, packed his pipe, and lit it. He had no reason
to get angry with this spindly, dried-up old man, who after
all was only trying to protect his own ass, and at the same
time he decided to trust the man. "Mister, I figure the Vigilantes didn't quite finish the job. Figure to sweep up their
leavin's. If you know where Drago might be, I'd 'preciate
you tellin' me."

The stable hand studied him a few moments. "Got a pot

o' hot coffee back yonder on the stove. Just made it yestidy. Oughtta have pretty good body to it. Want a cup?''

Granger had had all the coffee he wanted after he ate, but he had a hunch. ''Yeah, gettin' a mite chilly. Reckon a cup might put a little warm to the evenin'.''

The old-timer limped toward the back of the stable. He took his used-up chew from his mouth and tossed it aside before opening a door and ushering Granger into his living quarters. He poured them each a cup of mud, and allowed Granger might make himself comfortable on a sawed-off stump in the room's corner. Then, taking his time, he cut himself another chew, settled it comfortably in his jaw, and held out the plug to Granger, who shook his head and re-lighted his pipe.

The old man squinted at him. ''Now you wuz askin' bout some dog droppin's I mightta seen round here?'' He took three quick chews at his cud. ''Yep, I seen 'im an that there sidekick o' his. Ain't seed hide ner hair of 'em last day or two.'' The old-timer must have seen disappointment in Granger's face. He shook his head vigorously. ''Now, don't you go gittin' all down in the mouth.'' He squinted at Granger, a knowing look around his eyes. ''Gonna tell ye, young feller, figure I know where they done holed up fer a few days. Might not be there, unnerstan', but then they might be.''

Granger leaned forward. ''I'll take that chance, old-timer. Where you think they are?''

The gimmpy liveryman frowned, studied the ceiling, chewed his cud a few times, nodded, then looked at the cow-boy. ''If my reckon is right, I'd say they's at the old cabin where I took 'em horses a few times.''

Granger squirmed, but figured he had as much chance of hurrying the old man as a buffalo calf fighting off an old lobo wolf. He'd tell what he suspected in his own sweet time, so Granger only nodded to encourage his host to continue. ''Now, I reckon you be gonna ask me where that there cabin's at. Well, I'm fixin to tell you. They's a weathered-out cabin danged near due east o' here. It's a-settin' right on the banks o' Grasshopper Crick. Reckon it'd slide right down the bank if'n somebody hadn't cut two poles an' propped it up a mite. That's the way you gonna know you found the right one—them two poles.''

Granger nodded his thanks and went from the livery to the mercantile store, wondering what he might get the old man—something he'd like. He bought a box of Brown Mule chewing tobacco and took it to him. Again he offered his thanks and left.

A glance at the sun told him he could make a few miles before sundown. He tightened the cinches, toed the stirrup, and headed east.

Granger stayed to the woods as much as possible. Drago might not have heard he was on his trail, but news traveled fast when you didn't want it to.

That night, a cluster of boulders provided a good campsite where he could look down on the trail. Before building his fire, he walked to the wagon road, looked toward his camp, went down the road a piece, and again studied the rocks where his camp lay. Satisfied no one riding late could see the reflection of his fire off the piled-up boulders, he prepared supper.

He ate, then leaned against his saddle and drank coffee. The scent of pine, and fir, and the aroma of coffee, gave him a sense of peace, a feeling not justified—yet.

There was a bit of unfinished business needed taking care of. Then he could get back to Molly and the building of their home. He missed her, wanted to look across the table at her, wanted to feel her presence in the room, wanted to breathe the scent of her perfume—her clean woman scent.

He threw out the grounds in the bottom of his cup, banked the fire, and crawled into his blankets.

The next morning the sun still had not shown itself above the peaks of the Ruby Mountains when he rode from camp, keeping the Appaloosa to a ground-eating pace.

By mid-afternoon, he topped a hill above Grasshopper Creek. A long, searching look, both up- and downstream, showed no cabin, but for some time now the scent of wood-smoke had ridden the breeze, faint at first, now stronger. That cabin was close, maybe around the creek's bend, or Indians or whites might be camped somewhere close-by.

Staying to the woods, Granger rode toward where the water sliced its way around the bottom of a hill. He kept the roiling, dancing, stream in sight, whenever trees didn't interfere.

Not far around the curve in the stream, he saw first poles leaning at an angle toward something up the bank. Then the weathered old shack the liveryman had described came into view—and smoke spiraled from its metal pipe of a chimney.

Granger pulled farther back into the trees. He'd have to ford the creek to approach the cabin from cover. Two horses stood hipshot in a lean-to at the side of the shack. Saddles, with empty rifle scabbards, hung across the lean-to's rails. From the side on which he stood he could see no window. He reined his horse deeper into the trees and rode south along the stream's course.

Out of sight of the cabin, he crossed the shallow water, tethered the Appaloosa, pulled his rifle from its scabbard, and shadowed his way from tree to tree toward his target.

Now, standing behind a tall cottonwood not fifty yards up the bank from the cabin, he studied its front, and the side he'd not seen from across the Grasshopper. A door with a window beside it made up the front. He circled a few yards to better see the wall he'd not seen before. A single window broke the drab gray surface, about halfway toward the back.

As he squatted against the bole of the cottonwood, Granger's lips crinkled at the corners, his eyes wrinkled at the edges. "Sure would tickle my funny bone to tie a rope round them poles and pull 'em out from under that shack," he mumbled. "It'd be downright amusin' to see it tumble right into the middle o' that crick with them scramblin' to find a way out." He shrugged. "Reckon I'll have to let that go for now." But how was he to attack Drago and his henchman without getting himself killed?

He glanced at the sun. Still mid-afternoon. He'd have to get this settled before dark, or wait until morning to put any plan into action.

Sitting up here and throwing bullets into the cabin might work. Go busting in the front door, firing as fast as he could trigger, was another way, or set fire to the shack and shoot them when they came out would do it, but it'd probably set fire to the woods. He shook his head. "Ain't gonna do that. But gotta be able to cover the front and that side window at the same time."

He slanted another glance at the sun. "Hell, three, four hours o' daylight oughtta be 'nough time to take the Alamo. Reckon I'll try it. 'Sides, they might decide to leave, then I'd miss 'em." Alone, he'd taken to talking to himself, as he had many times when scouting for the army, or riding night herd.

He stood, putting a pine between him and the cabin, and sucked in a deep breath. He let it out slow like, felt his gut tighten, and the familiar lump come to his throat. Hell, cain't live forever, he thought. Then he yelled, "Drago, Colt Granger here. Got you boxed. Wantta come out an' face me, or you gonna sit in there an' let me pepper that cabin till I get you."

A few moments passed. "You think you can take us both, cowboy?"

Granger moved a bit so he could see the shack better. "Yep, that's my thinkin'. Come on out. I'll give you an even break."

"Reckon you're gonna have to do it the way things stand."

Granger didn't wait. He fired through the door, the front window, and the side window, in three staccato, Gatling Gun–type shots. He pulled back behind the tree, shoved three more loads into the Henry, peered around the tree bole, didn't see a rifle sticking out the windows or door, and triggered three more shots. Then he got serious. Figuring the walls wouldn't even slow his bullets, he peppered them at floor level. Then did it again.

"Hold up, Granger. You hit my partner. I'll face you."

Granger grunted, thinking, to hell with him, he'd given the outlaw his chance. He had no way of knowing he'd hit that scum anyway. He stepped from behind the tree and threw another fusillade of shots into the shack, then again moved behind the tree to reload.

Heavy fire came from the cabin. Granger stayed put until the firing stopped, then again stepped into the open, figuring they'd fire, duck to reload, and again raise to fire out the window. His bullets again sprayed at floor level. This time he knew one of the rabble took a hit. A muffled groan came to him. "Which one o' you I hit, Drago? Hope it was your sidekick. Want you lookin' at me when I do you in."

A moment passed, then Drago yelled, "You got my partner, cowboy. I'll be out, even break."

"Naw, Drago. We gonna keep this goin' like it is. Only way you gonna take me on now is to drag that pile o' cow dung out where I can see 'im. An' I'm tellin' you now, soon's you get 'im out where I can see 'im, I'm puttin' lead in 'im where I know he ain't gonna give me no trouble."

"No dice, cowboy. See if you can get us from in here."

The afternoon dragged on. A pall of gunsmoke hung heavy about the cabin and tree. The still air barely stirred the smoke. Granger occasionally swept the cabin with shots. He figured he'd hit Drago's partner, but not bad, or the surly bandit would have come out.

Sun sank behind the western peaks. Night was closing in, and Granger had no way of knowing what damage he'd done to the two. He didn't want this going into full darkness. They'd get away, or sneak up on him. He could accept neither.

He fired another batch of shots and scampered to a tree farther downhill, toward the side with the lean-to on it.

Slugs peppered the smaller tree behind which he now stood. He waited until they stopped firing, then he stepped out into the open, and waited for a rifle barrel to show above the windowsill. He had not long to wait.

A hat, then a rifle, showed. Granger waited until a face took form alongside the long gun's stock. He fired. Part of Drago's partner's face blew back into the room along with his hat. "Drago, that leaves only you. Wanta come out now?" He got no answer.

Thinking the outlaw would take time to check his partner, Granger left his tree and ran to the lean-to. The burly bandit would have to try for his horse if he hoped to get away.

Granger worked his way silently between the horses, not wanting to spook them and have them warn the outlaw. When he got to the wall, he checked the loads in his revolver and the spare cylinder. This would be close work.

8

DRAGO OPENED THE loading gate to his handgun and shoved cartridges in. Then he pulled the spring from his rifle's magazine, pushed cartridges into the tube, cursed, and slid down to lean against the wall, separated from Granger only by the thin wood. Granger read his every move by the clink of metal on metal and the scraping of cloth down the wall. All he had to do now was sit still. The bandit would get tired of waiting, and try to reach his horse. Now that full dark had set in, Drago would come from the front. Granger gave that his attention.

A slight noise, cloth against dirt, sounded about a foot to his side, toward the back. He twisted to see what might be behind him.

A door, similar to the one he'd built into his and Molly's cabin, swung silently up. Head and shoulders slid through. Granger waited until the outlaw's hands were busy trying to drag himself free of the framing, then stuck the barrel of his Colt against the side of Drago's head and thumbed back the hammer. His thumb slipped only enough for him to feel the hammer about to fly toward the chamber. He shook his head. Something just didn't feel right.

"Nice o' you to come out to greet your company, Drago.

Don't reckon I need tell you I'm gonna blow your head off if you make one wrong move." He pushed his .44 harder into the side of the outlaw's head. "Now, real careful, drag yourself free o' that little door."

Drago slid a few inches at a time into the lean-to. Finally, lying between a horse's legs, he cocked his head to look toward Granger. "Thought you were still out yonder by that tree. All right, I'm clear of it. You gonna shoot me now— or gimme a chance?"

Granger couldn't help the surge of respect for the bandit's courage. He stared at the big, beefy form in front of him. "Crawl on outta this shed while I think on what to do with you. Go belly down, an' put your hands behind."

When the bandit had done as he said, Granger stood, groped along the bandit's saddle skirts for pigging strings he thought might be there. He lucked out, pulled a couple from their lashings, and tied the big man's hands and feet. Then he dragged him into the cabin. As soon as he got inside, he wished he'd stayed out. The stink of stale sweat, stale whiskey, and stale tobacco smoke gagged him. "Didn't either o' you bastards ever take a bath?"

Drago nodded toward the body of his partner. "T'was him. Never could get him to bathe. Said it'd give a man his death of peemonia."

Granger scrubbed the outlaw down with a hard look, then nodded. "Yep, you look like you passed close to water in the last few days." His glance went from Drago to his dead partner, bent and checked Drago's bonds, then grabbed the skinny bandit by his heels. "Gonna drag 'im out in the woods a ways. You lie still."

"Ain't you got respect for the dead, Granger?"

The tall man shook his head. "Only for dead humans."

When he got back from disposing of the body, he led his Appaloosa to the lean-to, and brought his saddle, bedroll, and provisions inside. He dumped them in the corner and stood over the big man a moment before he went to the door and each window and opened them. "Let this place air out a while 'fore we spend the night here."

Drago said again, "What you gonna do with me?"

Granger threw wood on the fire, stood looking into it a moment, then looked at the beefy man. "Figured when you an' me met, it'd be in a stand-up gunfight." He shook his head. "Never figured to have this problem, but reckon however we met, still gonna kill you."

He dug out a slab of bacon, a tin of beans, and a couple handfuls of ground corn. A glance at the outlaw showed no change of expression; he lay there looking into the fire.

Granger pondered why a man would turn outlaw. It wasn't an easy life, running, always one step ahead of the law—where there was law—hungry most of the time, cold. Finally, he put what he'd been thinking into words. "Why you turn outlaw? Know you come from Missouri, know your folks was hardworkin' farmers. I'd like to know why, 'fore I kill you."

Drago glanced from the fire to Granger, and back to the fire, with a slight hint of emotion in his eyes. "Don't reckon it makes much difference. Might's well tell you. I got no excuses. Like you said, my folks was hardworkin', so hardworkin' I seen my ma when she wuz thirty lookin' like sixty. Just dryin' up, waitin' for a slight wind to blow 'er into the next world.

"Pa worked that hardscrabble farm, worked it hard. Never made more'n a bare livin' outta it. He wa'nt more'n skin an' bones hisself. Broke my heart to see 'em like that. I wuz only thirteen, an' for some stupid reason figured if they'd have more if I left.

"Well, Granger, I did just that. Fell in with a bunch runnin' from the war, an' makin' a livin' off robbin' folks, hardworkin' folks like ma an' pa." He turned his eyes back to his captor. "Don't know of a soul who's gonna give a damn when they hear you killed me. Figure I don't much care either."

"You ever think o' goin' home to see your folks, helpin' 'em do that work that was killin' 'em?"

Drago nodded. "Thought it many a time. Then I'd think they wuz most likely dead, so I kept puttin' it off."

Granger grunted, spread his blankets, threw one of the bandit's blankets over him, and crawled into bed.

Deep into the night, Granger thought of Drago's words until sleep finally pushed his thoughts aside and let the world fade.

The next morning, while frying bacon, he glanced over his shoulder at the outlaw. "How many of those pore miners you kill when you robbed 'em?"

Drago stiffened. "Granger, I wasn't cut from the same bolt o' cloth as Plummer, or Clinton neither." He nodded. "I took them folk's dust, but I never killed none of 'em—not one. Didn't even shoot one of 'em."

Granger finished cooking and loosened Drago's bonds so he could eat. Then he retied him and looked him in the eye. "Why should I believe you? You been ridin' the owlhoot so long you wouldn't know the truth if it jumped up an' bit you."

Drago's face turned red, looked like he'd burst a blood vessel. "Tell you somethin', cowboy, I don't lie, an' when I give a man my word, I keep it. Don't you go 'sinuatin' I'm a liar."

Granger squatted beside the man and chuckled. "Take it easy, Drago. You gonna bust a gut." He waited a moment while the bandit settled down. "Now, I'm gonna make you an offer. You can turn it down if you want. In that case I'll give you a gun an' see can you beat me."

"Gonna be dead anyway from what I hear 'bout you an' that six-shooter. What's your offer?"

"Well, maybe I'm a damned fool, Drago, but I'm gonna ask for your word on somethin'. Then I'm gonna believe you."

He packed his pipe, lit it, and wondered further how to say what he wanted. Finally, he said, "Gonna give you your weapons, a horse, an' head you east. Want your word you'll go back to see your folks, if they're still alive. Help 'em farm that plot o' ground. If they done gone over the divide, want your word you won't ever again take a dime what you ain't earned through honest work. Give me your word on that, you go free."

Hope flickered in the bandit's eyes. "Why you do this for me, Granger?"

Colt held his gaze a long moment. "Reckon I'd give anything to see my folks, but they're dead. For some damned fool reason, I figure there's some good in you, an' I do think your word's good."

Drago studied Granger, then, his face as solemn as a Baptist preacher's at a funeral, he nodded. "You got my word, cowboy. Don't reckon nobody ever seen any good in me 'fore this. I'll work in cow dung up to my chin an' never pull a gun to rob or hurt nobody. Makes me feel right proud a man like you'd trust me."

Granger pulled the knots from the pigging strings. "Pack your gear. Take only your own horse and weapons. I'll keep whatever your partner had on 'im. Now, get gone."

Granger stood in front of the shack and watched until the ex-outlaw, he hoped, disappeared from sight. Then he took his lariat, tied it to the poles that kept the cabin from sliding down the creek bank, and pulled them loose. The shack tumbled once, broke apart, and its pieces fell into the Grasshopper. He was two men closer to seeing Molly.

Molly, now used to walking out her front door of a morning and seeing the five lodges standing only a couple hundred yards from her, pulled an armful of stove wood from the stack Colt had chopped, and returned to the cabin.

Before entering, she glanced at the lodges—men and women scraping hides, drying buffalo meat on racks, children playing games simulating the constant warfare the Flatheads and Blackfeet waged against one another. The Nez Perce, Pend d'Oreille, Shoshoni, Kutenai, and others, had been Flathead allies until small pox decimated the Blackfeet. Now only the Flatheads fought the Blackfeet and Gros Ventre, except during the annual buffalo hunt; then they all banded together as before the smallpox.

Molly had taken to visiting with the Flathead women, and once they got used to one another, they gave her lessons in their language, how to prepare and tan hides, how to dry meat so there wouldn't be hunger during the long, cold months.

She, in turn, found little she could teach them. They had

learned much from the Black Robes through the years; men such as Fathers De Smet, Ravali, Mengarini, Point, and others. They had also known and been befriended by trappers such as Jim Bridger, Jedediah Smith, Colter, and many more who were now legend.

She kept busy, trying to keep Colt from her worries, but at night her thoughts always turned to him. She wondered how he fared. Was he warm, tired, hungry—in danger? And—not the least of her worries—would Colt ever look on her as a grown woman? She'd seen the way other men looked at her, and knew she must be a fairly nice-looking woman. But Colt never looked at her that way.

When Frank Worden would hear of Granger from travelers, he made sure he got the word to Molly where her "steppa" was and how he handled each situation in which he found himself.

Molly soon saw how little the Flatheads were making do with. She at first shared some of the food she had on hand, then more, until her cupboards were getting sparse. But the sharing wasn't all one-sided. There were many times she'd come outside in the morning and find an elk, deer, or bear haunch tied above her door, out of reach of varmints. She'd look from the meat to the lodges, and try to swallow the tears that flooded her eyes. She had grown to love these people who, if they were your friend, would do anything for you.

Little Bear Claw, head chief of all Flatheads, rejected the government's efforts to put them on a reservation at Jocko, wanting to stay in the Flatheads' beloved Bitter Root Valley. Little Bear Claw, whose Christian name was Victor, refused to sign the peace treaty at the Hell Gate Council.

Frank Owen, Indian Agent, was doing all he could to see that the government didn't defraud the Flatheads of their shipments of goods, but the crooked politicians in Washington were making too much money channeling the shipments to friends who sold them. Then they sent cheap trinkets to the Indians, junk the agent was forced to distribute, junk the Indians had not much use for.

Molly made friends with Frank Owen, and his brother,

John, who traded with the Indians, and built the fort carrying his name.

One warm, clear afternoon Molly was carrying a heavy bucket with which to slop the hogs when she saw a rider coming, and by his dress she tagged him as a white man. She threw the contents of the bucket into the trough, went inside, and picked up her rifle.

The rider drew nearer. She soon recognized John Owen. This time he didn't stop to pass the time of day with Little Bear Who Runs. Molly stood her Henry by the door and greeted the gaunt man.

He didn't wear his usual friendly smile. "Miss Tbalt—now, don't get excited. Nothing's happened to Granger, but I thought I should warn you. There's a man at my fort, man by the name of Chet Warren, asking questions about your step-pa. He's not one I'd trust, and the Flatheads won't fight him 'cause of Little Coyote's vision quest. He's told them they aren't to fight the whites. And, of course, the Black Robes want peace for the Indians' sake, knowing they can't win."

Molly had heard of Little Coyote, Flathead seer, medicine man, and warrior. She glanced toward the door and said the coffee was hot, to come on in.

When she'd poured them each a cup of steaming arbuckle, Owen ran his hands through his hair, sipped his coffee, and looked at her straight on. "Reckon what I'm trying to tell you is that man at the fort's trouble, and you aren't gonna get help from the Flatheads unless they see him attack you. Don't know what you're to do."

She toyed with her cup a moment, stared into its bottom, then looked at the trader. "Mr. Owen, reckon I'm gonna have to think on this a while, think what Colt would do in my boots."

"Ma'am, I can stay around here a couple of days, but then I have to get back to the fort." He smiled grimly. "Course since the beaver are about trapped out, and the hide hunters have thinned the buffalo down to almost nothing, there isn't much to trade, but long's I have things the Indians need I'll see they don't do without."

Molly shook her head. "Mr. Owen, I wouldn't ask you to stay. Right now, I'm thinkin' about goin' back with you an' meet this Chet Warren head-on."

Owen's eyes widened. "Oh now, miss, this man's dangerous. He might not cause you trouble where anyone could see, being you're a woman, but to my way of thinking, a shot from the dark, or a knife while you sleep, is not at all beyond him."

She smiled past the fear welling into her throat. "Sir, I been taught by a mighty knowing man how to take care of myself. Don't figure that Warren's any better'n Colt an' me's faced before."

"But, Miss Tbalt, I have to remind you, Granger isn't here to help you."

Molly leaned back in her chair. "On second thought, I may just close my windows and doors and wait for him to come to me." She smiled. "I do thank you, Mr. Owen, for riding all this distance to warn me."

Owen drank the last of his coffee, shook his head, and stood. "Miss, if there's anything I can do at the fort to stop him, I'll do it."

Molly thanked him for his concern and he left. She watched until he slipped below a ridge, then went into the cabin, poured a cup of coffee, and sat staring into the fire. What would Colt have done if he had been there? What could she do? She couldn't go to Fort Owen and shoot the man. She couldn't push him into a gunfight. She couldn't imagine any man being forced to draw on a woman. Then she had the glimmer of an idea. It might work. She thought on it the rest of the day, and into the night. The longer she thought, the more convinced she was that it was a good plan, a plan with which she could protect Colt. If she could help it, no one was going to put the man she loved in jeopardy.

The sun hadn't topped the eastern mountains when she walked to the lodge of Little Bear Who Runs. They stood by his fire and talked. At first he shook his head, then Molly talked harder. Finally, he nodded. She headed back to the cabin and sat to clean every weapon in there. Then she placed them where she could get her hands on them wherever she might stand, except just inside the door.

While cleaning her .36-caliber Whitney Navy pistol, she glanced toward the lodges. The women were busy taking them down and packing to move. Tears flooded her eyes. She was the cause of their moving, the cause of making more work for those whose days were filled with labor. She didn't see Little Bear Who Runs, and hoped he was on his way to Fort Owen.

Little Bear rode to the fort's gate, dismounted, and went inside. Seeing John Owen standing by a bale of furs, he said so all in the room could hear, "John Owen, friend Colt Granger is back. He come in after sun go to sleep, then, this morning he ride to Hell Gate. Say he be back come sunup next day. Say he stay in his lodge maybe two suns till leave again. Say get chance, he see you 'fore he leave."

Owen took Little Bear's arm, led him to his quarters, and closed the door. "Little Bear, you haven't seen Granger. Way I hear it he's only now getting to Virginia City. Besides, there's a man out yonder in that room who heard what you said. He'll attack Granger's cabin. Miss Tbalt's out yonder alone."

The sub-chief looked at Owen. "Woman Tbalt tell me what to say. We take care bad man don't slip up on Woman Tbalt. We signal when he comes. She fight him then."

Owen shook his head. "That girl's either crazy, got more guts than an old buffalo bull, or both." He sat on a stack of bagged flour. Again he shook his head. "Reckon she's a little of both, a little crazy and got a whole lot of guts, enough she might get herself killed." He pinned Little Bear Who Runs with a no-nonsense look. "You be damned sure you don't let that man out yonder get close to her—even if you have to kill 'im yourself."

"She Flathead friend. Not let harm come to her." Little Bear pulled the door open and left. He'd ridden only a few minutes when he spread his hands, palms upward at the side of his horse, his face lifted to the heavens. "Great Spirit, forgive me for making promise not kill white man. This white man bad. Flatheads not kill good white man, kill only bad white-eyes, protect friend.''

He rode back to the area where the lodges had been, careful to stay out of sight of curious eyes. Sun had disappeared behind western peaks when he stretched flat on the ground behind the crest of a land swell to watch the approach to Molly's cabin.

At twilight, Molly stepped outside the cabin door and looked at the now-empty places where lodges stood only hours ago. Her stomach felt as empty as the lodge spaces. Her friends were gone at her own request—fear had taken their place. She closed and bolted the cabin door, then the wooden shutters. She had no doubt the man looking for Colt would take the bait. He wouldn't ride to the settlement to kill Colt. He'd come here where he thought he could bully a defenseless female into keeping quiet, then he'd kill Colt on his return from Hell Gate. Could she handle the task she'd carved out for herself?

She had sat in the dark for maybe two hours when a meadowlark sang a short song, hesitated, and repeated his call to the night. Then Little Bear Who Walks again gave his signal. Molly picked up the Greener, leaned it against the table at her side, and took the Navy in hand.

A few minutes passed before the slow clopping of a horse's hooves approached the cabin and stopped, followed by a knock, accompanied by a gruff voice. ''Anyone to home?''

Trying to keep the quaver from her voice, she answered, ''Who is it? What do you want this time of night?''

''Hear tell a old friend o' mine is hereabouts. Man called Granger. This his cabin?''

She sucked in a deep breath. ''Yes. Colt Granger lives here, but he's not home. He rode to Hell Gate, be back any minute now.'' She wanted to get him in the cabin, but didn't want to seem in too big a hurry.

Again the gruff voice. ''Well now, missy, reckon I'll wait fer 'im. Been a long ride—hate to miss 'im. You gonna invite me in—give me a cup o' that there coffee I smell?

Gittin' a little chilly out here. Could stand to hold my hands out to your fire.''

Molly swallowed the lump in her throat, flexed her shoulders to rid herself of the knot forming between them, and held the pistol out of sight under the table, hoping it looked like she had her hands folded in her lap. She pointed the Navy at the door. ''Latch string's out. Come on in.''

The latch lifted. The door opened inward and a skinny, dirty, whiskered, man stepped through. His clothes were so dirty they looked greasy. He frowned, drawing eyes set too close together even tighter to his nose. He swept the cabin with a look, then settled on Molly. ''Well now, didn't know Granger had 'nough man 'bout 'im to catch a piece like you. Pour me a cup o' coffee.''

Molly sat there, primly. ''Sir, I'm gonna sit right here, my hands folded in my lap, until Colt gets home. Second place, I don't wait on no man but him.'' Her voice hardened. ''Third place, I'm tired of being called a 'piece' by white trash like you. Now, back up to the wall alongside the door an' sit on the floor till my man gets home.''

The man's eyes turned mean. He stared at her, obviously wondering why she was so brave. He stepped toward her, the meanness in his eyes replaced by the same oily sheen she'd seen in Spike Delon's eyes when he talked of raping her.

Fear tightened her chest, her scalp tingled, and, trying to stop him with words, she asked, ''What's your name? You can leave now and I'll tell Colt you came by.''

The man grinned, saliva drooling from the corners of his mouth. ''Name's Chet Warren. No need to tell Granger I been here. I ain't leavin'.'' He took another measured step toward her, then rushed toward the table.

Molly pulled the trigger of the Navy—and missed. She shifted the revolver to her left hand, jumped to her feet, grabbed for the Greener, and knocked the chair over behind her. When the chair crashed to the floor, her fingers wrapped around the barrel of the shotgun.

Warren launched himself across the table and grabbed at her, missing, but his fingers closed around cloth. He ripped down, tearing the bodice away from her breasts. She swung the Greener at his head, again missed, and spun toward the door.

Warren followed in slow, measured strides, as though stalking a hurt animal. Molly whimpered, but the sounds in her throat stemmed from anger. All she could think of was kill—kill this vile, stinking beast. She ran toward the corner, then seeing he could trap her with nowhere to run, she sprinted toward the middle of the room to get the table between them, and barely eluded a clawlike, grasping hand.

She ducked under his arm, reached the table, and shoved it into his path.

He fell across it, but got a handful of skirt and pulled. The force of his tug pulled her toward him, then the material gave way. Her skirt clutched in his hand, he leered at the girl before him clad only in her chemise and pantaloons.

She tripped, fell to the floor, and lay there—vulnerable under his drooling mouth, staring eyes. He stood there a moment staring at her body. It was all the time she needed.

She thumbed back the hammer and pulled the trigger of the Navy Colt still gripped in her left hand, then thumbed back the hammer and fired again. Her first slug took him in the belly, her second punched a black, round hole in the middle of his chest. She pulled the Greener to her side, pointed it toward him, and pulled the trigger. The full load of buckshot took him in the chest.

His eyes lost their lust. Now they stared at her, surprise holding his lids wide. His last look went from her to his chest, to the gaping, bloody cavity where once his shirt had been. A low moan squeezed blood past his throat. She fired the Greener again. This load knocked him against the door. He slid to sit as she'd told him; only now he stared at her through sightless eyes.

The whimpering, mewling sounds in her throat died as her anger died. She placed the shotgun on the table, and with trembling fingers punched a fresh shell into each barrel. While placing the Greener into its rack, she heard running footsteps. She slipped into a robe to cover her undergarments, and again took her weapon to hand.

"Warrior Woman, I come soon's hear shootin'. You all right?"

Molly took note that Little Bear had changed her name to Warrior Woman. Although exhausted from her ordeal, she smiled.

"C'mon in, Little Bear. Yes, I'm all right. Take this trash out and leave it for the coyotes."

Little Bear stared at the bloody remains a moment, shifted his eyes to look at her, then smiled. "Real Warrior Woman now." He took Warren by the collar and dragged him from the cabin.

The next morning five lodges again stood in the pasture.

With the incident of the night before, the return of the lodges, and Little Bear renaming her, Molly took on added confidence. She loved Colt as much as ever, needed him like never before, but now the feeling was within her that she was a woman. She could handle danger without the man she'd chosen as her mate, although he didn't yet know she had her head set on marrying him.

She'd learned to attack. Don't wait for things to come to you—go after them. He'd taught her that, though he had no idea how she'd put it to work—against his enemies, or against him.

The next morning, she asked Little Bear to help her with work she wanted to get done before Colt returned. They agreed on what and how she'd repay him.

That afternoon, Molly on one end of the crosscut saw and Little Bear on the other, they sawed timber cut strictly to her specifications as to length and diameter. She'd wait for Colt to show them how to select and lay the stone for the foundation.

9

GRANGER REINED HIS horse down Virginia City's muddy main street. He was chilled to the bone, and a thin, steady rain dripped from the skies, water flowed from his hat and slicker. He couldn't remember ever being in this country and not being wet, cold, or both.

He wanted a drink, and to talk with Fisk Sanders, find out if any of the bunch he hunted were in town, and if not, where. He needed names, too, although many of that bunch shed names more often than they did their underwear.

He tied his horse to the hitch rack in front of the first saloon he came to, stepped to the boardwalk, stomped mud from his boots, and only then noticed the sign next door: "Fisk Sanders, Attorney at Law." He turned his steps in that direction.

As soon as he came into the office, Sanders stood, came around his desk, and shook hands. "Granger, I thought we'd lost you forever. How you been?"

Granger nodded, shed his hat and rain gear, then looked at the young attorney. "Yeah, Fisk, I've settled over yonder in the Bitter Root Valley. Built most o' my cabin already. Gonna stay there."

"What brought you back to Virginia City?" Sanders

pulled out a chair. "Here. Sit down and tell me about it."

Granger glanced at the chair, wondering if he would stay long enough to get comfortable, then sat. "Fisk, some o' that bunch you didn't get hung are after me. They figure I'm the one caused all their troubles since I was the one what forced Cy Skinner into tellin' who killed Nick Tbalt, then forced Ives to tell who was in the gang. They tracked me to Hell Gate. I killed some there, but there's more. Don't want Molly gettin' hurt, so I come huntin' 'em."

Sanders opened the bottom right-hand drawer of his desk and pulled a quart bottle of whiskey and two glasses from it. He held the bottle up. "Talk you into a drink?"

Granger smiled, then shivered. "Beginnin' to think I was gonna have to show my poor upbringin' an' ask for one. Yeah, I surely could use one to knock the chill outta me." He waited until Sanders handed him his drink, took a healthy swallow, and eyed the lawyer. "Fisk, I need names and wherabouts of any you think might come lookin' for me."

Sanders studied the amber liquid through the side of his glass, then looked at Granger. "Yeah, Colt, there're a few left, but we've not been able to prove anything against them. We're trying mighty hard to do things legal now that we've broken the back of the Plummer gang, but haven't been able to get any solid evidence, so we haven't brought them to trial." He knocked back his drink, shivered, and stared at his empty glass. "Maybe you can shake 'em loose—make 'em do something we can try them for."

Granger chuckled. "Fisk, if I shake 'em loose, they ain't gonna be able to stand trial. You got names?"

Sanders pulled a sheet of paper toward him, spent several minutes writing, then shoved the paper across the desk to Granger. "There's a list I believe fits those who would hunt you. I've not seen but one of them in the last few days, although they might be around somewhere—here, Bannack, or Nevada City."

Granger pulled the sheet toward him, glanced at it, and shook his head. "Could've been in Bannack. Just came from there, didn't see any I knew."

Granger studied the list a moment. The names he read

were known to him, but only two on the list could he put a face to. He nodded. "Thanks, Fisk. This'll help, an' thanks for the drink; it might've saved my life."

The lawyer didn't smile. "You go after them, Colt, it'll take a helluva lot more than a drink to save your life. Good luck."

Granger went from Sanders's office to a saloon reputed to be a hangout for the less desirable crowd. He was a known man in these parts, so when he pushed through the heavy wooden door, he stepped to the side. Because of how bleak the weather was, it took only a moment for his eyes to adjust to the darkness inside. He looked at every man in there, not knowing whether two or three of them were the ones for whom he looked.

No one paid him any mind. The talk centered mostly on Lincoln having signed the bill creating the new Territory of Montana only a few days ago, May 26, 1864. Many in the room argued Lincoln wouldn't have made Montana a separate territory except that the North needed the gold being taken from Alder Gulch to help fight the war.

There wasn't anyone east of the Mississippi gave a damn about the West except what they could get from it. Bannack was named the territorial capital, and Sydney Edgerton the new territory's first governor. Granger didn't care what territory he stood in, or what their arguments were, he had troubles of his own.

He pulled from his shirt pocket the list Sanders provided, studied it, committed the names and brief descriptions to memory, thought to crumple it and throw it away, then changed his mind and stuffed it back in his pocket. He again dragged a slow look across the drinkers. The two men on the list he'd recognize were not in the room. But there were several who scrubbed him down with surly, unfriendly looks.

His temper riding a hair trigger, words formed in his mouth to ask who they stared at. He swallowed the words. He had to get rid of the five men on the list first. He had stepped toward the door when a big burly brute said from the middle of the room, "Cowboy, you got no friends in here. Go back to your own kind."

He stopped. Not knowing who spoke, he aimed his words at all there. "Right particular who I choose for friends. Ain't none in here fits my choosin'." Before more could be said, he pulled the door open and left.

A hard grin crooked his lips when he stepped past the front of the saloon. His mama didn't raise any fools. If he'd chosen to fight the mouthy one, he'd have gotten beaten to a pulp by all in the room who could get a lick at him, or been shot and dumped in a snowbank somewhere. He looked back at the door from which he'd departed, and mumbled, "Smart move, Granger. Don't let 'em pick where you gotta fight. They'll beat you every time." He walked on to Con Orem's Champion Saloon. There, he'd be among friends.

He'd not gotten to the bar before men from every side stood, shook his hand, and said how glad they were to see him. At the bar, Granger saw that the same red-headed bartender dispensed drinks as the last time he was here. "Straight whiskey, Red, water glass full. Take that much to cut through the chill, then when you get a minute I need to ask you somethin'."

Red poured a couple more drinks and walked back to stand in front of him. Granger handed him the list. "Seen any o' that bunch around lately?"

Red squinted, read the list, and stood staring at it a moment longer, then he looked into Granger's eyes. "You huntin' trouble with this bunch, Granger?"

The tall man shook his head. "No trouble. Just figure to shoot 'em when I see 'em."

Red stood there a moment, the shade of a grin breaking the corners of his lips. "No trouble you say. All you're gonna do is blow their heads off. Well, damned if I don't believe you think it ain't no trouble."

He served another drink and came back. "I'm of a mind to not be party to helpin' get you killed, but if I don't tell you, someone will. Yeah, I seen two of 'em in the last week. Don't know where they might be now. The two I seen were Tom Seely an' Jim Custer."

"I seen them two before, but jack up my memory, gimme a idea what they look like. Better'n the one Fisk give me."

Red rinsed a glass, dried it, and held it up to see if he got it clean, all the while obviously thinking what to tell Granger. Finally, he said, "Seely's typical of the moocher you see around low-class saloons—dirty, no shave in a month or two, slim, rotten teeth, long, greasy hair I reckon would be blond if he ever washed it, an' he's got a big dark mole over his left eye, must be the size of a dime. That's how you gonna know 'im."

Granger knocked back his drink, shuddered, and held out his glass. "Sweeten it with a little water this time. Now, what about Custer? Anything special 'bout 'im?"

Red's grin spread. "Yeah, he's big as a bull moose. Tall as you, only outweigh you by 'bout forty pounds. He's a bully. Walks around like the cock o' the walk, pushes smaller men aside an' looks at 'em like he dares 'em to do anything about it. His nose sits off under the inside corner of his right eye, and sort o' flat. Been broke a few times I'd say." He poured Granger's drink, then, all semblance of humor gone, he pinned Granger with a worried look.

"Colt, the one on this list you got to tend to business with is Bill Diamond. He figures himself salty, a gunhand. He's got pale blue eyes, almost white. He's slim, hair's white. You can almost smell the danger in 'im. He ain't old, but that hair makes him look it. Only good thing about 'im, I think he'd want to be lookin' at you when it came down to a shoot-out."

Granger stood thinking of Red's words while the redhead waited on a couple more customers. He figured he already had his hands full, but he needed to know about the other two.

When Red came back, Colt looked him in the eye. "There's five men on that list, Red. What about them you ain't said nothin' about?"

Red sighed. "Hate to tell you this, Granger, but they're the worst of the lot. Mike Gant's smooth, tall, some would call 'im handsome—all muscle and all bad. He'd shoot you from the back, anywhere 'cept head-on, if he couldn't get you in a fistfight—then he'd try to kill you with his hands."

Granger nodded. " 'Bout what I expected of the whole bunch." He grinned. "You ain't made it any easier, yet." He breathed in and exhaled slowly. "Now—you save the best till last?"

"Yep, figure I did. Quirt Clinton. Fat, don't move around much, never bathes, shaves every day though, eats like a hog, belches constantly, got little pig eyes—but behind those eyes he's got a brain that don't never stop workin'. He's smart, Granger, an' totally ruthless. Don't think he'd kill you himself, he'd hire someone to do it. But don't sell 'im short— if he couldn't find the right man to do it, he would. I believe he's the most dangerous of the lot."

Granger frowned into his drink. It would be longer before he saw Molly again. Blood rushed to his head; his throat muscles tightened. "Where does Clinton hang out?"

Red held a bottle over Granger's glass and topped it off. "That's one question I can answer for sure. Said he didn't move around much? Well, he's got a office right here in town. Set 'imself up in real estate. When a miner gets killed 'accidentally,' he always seems to come up with a note owed on the man's claim, or an outright deed to it. Nobody's been able to prove he makes the accidents happen."

Granger pulled a double eagle from his pocket and pushed it across the bar. "Thanks, Red, keep the change. I'll be forever beholden to you."

The big bartender pushed the coin back. "Just don't get yourself killed, Granger. I count you as a friend, and I don't take pay for helpin' friends."

The tall man sat nursing his drink. He couldn't walk into Quirt Clinton's office and shoot him; they hanged people for such. He couldn't question the fat man; that would alert him someone was on his trail. And, putting it all together, Granger realized that Clinton could have been the real brains behind the Henry Plummer gang—and he might be trying to rebuild the gang now that he'd lost Plummer. Granger figured his only choice came down to taking it one step at a time. First track down Seely and Custer. But where should he start?

If Clinton was the boss of most of the trash left in this part of the country, it was an even bet they'd come to him, perhaps not every day, but likely every few days, maybe a week at the most. He decided to find a place from which to watch the fat man's office.

He walked down Jackson Street until he stood in front of the hotel, across from the fat man's office and down about two doors. He went in and told the kid behind the counter he wanted a front room. The stripling looked at the sign-in book and shook his head. "Mister, we only got two rooms on the front, both full."

"Who's in 'em?"

The young man scratched his head. "One's a drummer for the newest things in firearms; he's in his room now—room three. Don't know the other man."

Granger nodded and headed toward the stairs.

At the top of the stairway, he looked down the short hall. The door to his right had a 3 on it, crudely drawn in crayon. He tapped on the door. "Come on in. It ain't locked."

Inside, Granger stared at the drummer a moment. "Well, I'll be double damned. Bill Huxley. What you doin' in these parts?"

Huxley, a man of about Granger's age, stood, grinned, and held out his hand. "Where was it last time, cowboy?"

"Hays City, Kansas. You sold me this here Colt forty-four I'm wearin'."

Huxley grimaced. "Yeah, an' if I remember correctly, you put it to use that very night when that would-be gunny pushed you into a gunfight." He looked at his firearms case. "I got newer, better weapons now."

Granger nodded. "You remember. I couldn't get out of that fight. That's been almost ten years ago." He looked toward the window a couple of times, then back to Huxley. "Bill, want you to do me a favor."

Huxley shrugged. "If I can, I will."

Granger pulled his old handgun and held it out to the drummer. "First off, if you got one in that case, I want one o' them 1860 Colt Army forty-four revolvers. Second, I want you to swap rooms with me. I'll pay your rent for a week if you will.''

Huxley grinned. ''I ain't gonna be here but two more days, and it ain't gonna cost you even those two days' rent. You buy a new Colt from me an' we swap. All right?'' He frowned. ''Care to tell me why you need this room?''

Looking at the case of revolvers, Granger wondered where to start. Finally, he nodded. ''Tell you how it is, Bill. I made a bunch o' enemies since comin' here. They're huntin' me, makin' life miserable.'' He paused, and looked at the drummer, a slight grin crinkling the corners of his eyes. ''Well, you know from before I never took kindly to anybody breakin' up my peace, so instead of lettin' them do all the huntin' I decided to take it to 'em. I need use of the front window in here to see who comes an' goes in the office o' the pig I think is runnin' the show.''

Huxley shrugged. ''You got the room. You don't need to buy a weapon.''

Granger hefted the revolver he'd had his eye on from the first. ''No, Bill, I gotta have this weapon if it fires true an' feels right.''

After hefting several of the revolvers, checking them for balance and feel coming out of his holster, Granger told the drummer to follow him to the back lot. ''I'll fire a couple o' cylinders while we're out there.''

Granger emptied the cylinder twice before he nodded. ''Good weapon.''

Huxley stood at his side, grinning. ''Man, you ain't lost speed or accuracy in the ten years gone by. If I was them huntin' you, I'd be damned wary.''

When they got back to the room, Granger bought the one he'd tried in the back lot, and a spare cylinder. They swapped rooms, and the tall man set up watch on the fat man's office, wondering if Clinton knew he was in town, or if the pig even knew who he was.

Clinton looked across his desk at the big man slouched against the wall. ''Custer, Colt Granger went in the hotel a few minutes ago. He's been askin' questions about you and your partner. I don't like questions about any of us. I want 'im taken care of. Not here in town. It's gotta be done somewhere where you can get rid of the body without anyone finding it until spring thaw. Reckon you and Seely can handle that?''

Custer grinned and flexed his shoulders, muscles threatening to split his shirt. He nodded. ''Mr. Clinton, I'd shore like it better if I could beat 'im to death. Hear tell he killed the last men you sent after 'im. They wuz my friends. But yeah, ain't no problem, me an' Tom Seely'll take care of 'im.''

Clinton let no emotion show in his flat, black eyes. ''Get it done. Don't come back here till you come to tell me he ain't no problem no more.''

Custer tipped his hat and nodded. ''Yes sir, Mr. Clinton. Know you don't want nobody figurin' you had a hand in it. We'll fix 'im right nice.'' He pulled his hat down over his eyes and left.

Clinton sat staring at the closed door. Granger had been a thorn in his side too long. He'd single-handedly wrecked what he had going with Sheriff Henry Plummer. Now Clinton had only dregs to work with, the ones Fisk Sanders hadn't hanged. He swallowed a couple of times, trying to rid himself of the anger building in his throat, his head.

His men tended to think of Granger as a dumb cowboy. Clinton figured him as uneducated—but far from stupid, and as dangerous a man as he'd ever seen. But, to his thinking, Granger had a weakness, one he hoped would be fatal.

From what he'd seen, the tall cowboy barged into trouble without thought. The fat man leaned back in his chair and smiled, his small pig eyes hidden in his fat cheeks. ''Yes sir, Granger, I'll have the men lure you outta town, close in behind you, and you'll find you've bit off more'n you can chew. Yeah, you gonna kill some of 'em, but their kind are expendable. They'll get you, cowboy, then I can get on with my business.''

He wondered if Custer had enough sense to get Granger out of town without being obvious. While thinking, he took out his Remington .41 double-barreled Derringer, checked the rimfire loads in each barrel, and placed it back in his vest pocket. He didn't want to kill Granger himself unless he could set it up to look like the cowboy had attacked him in his office. He checked his watch, noted it was four-thirty, reached in his left-hand desk drawer, and pulled out a bottle for the only drink he allowed himself each day.

Granger watched Custer leave Clinton's office, toe the stirrup, and ride east toward the edge of town. He marked the exact spot from which the muscled man left the edge of town, went downstairs, got his horse, and rode to the spot. Luck rode with him. He'd expected a longer wait, hours or days perhaps, before seeing one of those on his list.

He counted on Custer heading for his sidekick, Seely. That gave him the whereabouts of three of the five he hunted. Custer's horse tracks still trapped light rain when the ex-scout stopped to study them. The ground, too muddy to give a clear imprint of the hooves, gave a trail for Granger to follow. He pulled his Henry from the scabbard and rode with it across the saddle in front of him.

The rain, and the dried-on-the-stem grass, gave off a fresh scent, one he'd never tire of smelling. It spoke of the outdoors, spaces not bespoiled by humans, spaces over which he'd ridden hundreds of miles. Almost unconsciously, he enjoyed the smells. He licked the moisture from his lips and tasted the wide plains, the rugged mountains, the rushing streams—all trapped within the tiny droplets. But his eyes searched every land swell, every break in the flow of the ridges and coulees. Light rain, and windless stillness, gave his ears a chance to catch any sound foreign to the surroundings. His quarry could not be far ahead.

He topped a knoll, and again pulled his horse below the skyline. Custer rode less than a quarter of a mile ahead. He hated the thought of slogging through mud, but he climbed from his horse and led him. Pulling his hat off, he hung it from the saddle horn, and keeping only his eyes above the crest of the knoll, he watched Custer ride over the next rise. The outlaw never turned in his saddle to see if he was followed.

Granger again climbed to the saddle, and careful to maintain distance between them, he rode to the top of the next hill. From there, less than two hundred yards toward the bottom of a draw, he saw smoke curl from a chimney. Custer stood at the side of the cabin, outside a shed made of saplings. He stripped the gear from his horse, pulled his rifle from its scabbard, and reached for his saddle.

Granger fingered the trigger of his rifle, sighed, and lowered the Henry to his side. Shooting a man from hiding wasn't his way. Custer finished with his horse, shouldered his saddle, and went inside.

Colt studied the cabin a few moments, then his eyes focused on the horse shed. Three horses stood under its roof. He prayed the third horse was one used for packing. Another look at the cabin showed windows on every side except where the horses stood. It wasn't going to be easy.

He tethered the Appaloosa back among the trees and, staying below the crest of the hill, crept to the one blind side the log structure showed him. Then, crouched painfully low, he eased around to the back and hunkered under a window. The voice he heard must have been Custer's. He explained what Clinton had detailed them to do. "What we gotta do is find Granger, let 'im see us, an' then lure 'im outta town. One o' us's gotta stay behind; hide in them rocks along the creek bank, don't wantta lead him to this here cabin. The one in the rocks gotta let 'im get close for a sure shot, then empty his saddle. The one who leads 'im outta town can join in the shootin' onc't he gets in range."

Seely's high, thin voice cut in: "Who you figure to sit out yonder in them rocks?"

"Thought you oughtta be the one. You use a rifle better'n me, an' we don't wantta miss. That cowboy's pure roped an' throwed hell when he gets riled."

Granger waited for a third voice to join them; when it didn't he felt sure the third horse was for packing. He nodded, sucked in a couple of breaths, and again crouched low, headed for the cabin's only door—in front.

There, he again sucked in a few breaths and let them out slowly. He checked to be sure the door opened inward, drew his foot back, and kicked the heavy wooden slab. He followed it in, six-shooter in hand. Seely stood by the cast-iron stove. He gawked, then his hand flashed to his side.

Granger thumbed off two shots, and swung his revolver to find Custer. The bull of a man was in midair, halfway out of the side window, when Granger saw him through the thick smoke. He thumbed off a shot before the outlaw disappeared—and knew he missed. He'd fired too fast. He twisted for a look at Seely. The skinny man with the mole over his left eye no longer had a mole. The mole was now a hole.

Granger stepped toward the door for another shot at Custer, then heard the splash of horse hooves in mud. The tall man shook his head. No point in chasing him. He'd be long gone before Colt could get to his horse. He went back to Seely and checked his pockets. He pulled out several small bags of what he judged by their weight to be dust. He stuffed them in his coat pocket, took rifle, handgun, and a gunnysack of provisions, and headed for his horse. No need to track Custer. Granger would bet his prized pony the outlaw would go back to Virginia City and hide among his own kind. Granger would find him there.

It took less time for him to get back to town. Not tracking anyone, he used less care. On the way, he pondered whether to search the saloons the bad bunch hung out in and force a fight with Custer, or wait for a time when he had some of the odds on his side. He shrugged. To hell with the odds. He needed to get back to Molly, needed to finish their cabin before winter set in.

In town, he stopped by Sanders's office. "Get some o' the decent citizens out on the street. Cover my rear end. Gonna get Custer outta one o' them saloons he hangs out in, beat 'im till he shows the white feather, then run 'im outta town—or kill 'im, don't make me no never mind."

"Granger, that man'll beat you to death. He's huge—outweighs you a bunch. Don't do it."

Colt pinned the lawyer with a look that went straight through him. "Cover my back, Fisk. Don't let me have to fight but one man." He spun and went toward the saloon in which he figured to find Custer.

It was almost dark outside, and this time when he pushed through the saloon's doorway and stepped to the side, it wasn't to let his eyes adjust, but because he wanted to have every man in the room under his gaze. The voices, and the pounding of a tin-panny piano, made a constant din in his ears. The smells of stale alcohol, dirty bodies, and tobacco smoke blended to make him want to gag. The feel of evil permeating the room made him want to turn and go back out the door. He stood there.

The piano stopped first. Voices lowered to a hum, then stopped. An ear-splitting quiet settled on the room. Every pair of eyes turned toward Granger. The animosity in those eyes was a physical thing. He could feel the hate. It beat on his taut-nerved body. Hair at the base of his skull tingled. His gut tightened. His stomach churned. He wanted to go back out the door, forget he'd come in here—but he was committed.

"Any in this room touches a gun, I'll kill 'im. I come in here to get a gutless, yellow-livered dog who less'n two hours ago left his partner in the middle of a shoot-out and ran. Gonna get 'im out yonder in the street an' beat 'im to death, knuckle an' skull, no holds barred." His eyes swept the room, then centered on Custer. "Yeah, bastard, I'm talkin' 'bout you. Shuck your hardware, an' head for the street."

"You gonna fight me, Granger? Hell, I done whipped two like you at one time."

The tall man held the outlaw's gaze. "Now's your chance to whip a real man, Custer. Kill 'im—if you can. Now, get rid o' that six-shooter an' your knife. Do it now, or I'll gut-shoot you where you stand."

Granger had never touched his handgun, but all in the room watched his hands and didn't make a move for theirs. He let the bull of a man go out the door ahead of him, then, watching to see that Custer didn't stop outside the door for a cheap shot, he went out. The crowd from the saloon followed.

On stepping from the boardwalk to the street's mud, Granger welcomed the sight of at least two hundred miners,

Fisk Sanders standing with them. They all carried ax handles.

Sanders raised his voice above the shouting, jeering, and cheering mob. "Any here who makes a move to interfere'll get a helluva sore head. Now, stand clear and let them fight."

The bull stood in the middle of the street and flexed his shoulders, and muscles stretched his shirt tight. He rolled his head around to loosen his neck, then walked in on Granger.

The tall, lean man waited, waited until Custer threw a roundhouse right at him. He stepped inside the swing, let it go over his shoulder, and buried a right in the bull's gut. Then he danced back, threw a left that landed above Custer's right eye, and again backed off. The cut over the bull's eye streamed gore.

Custer wiped the blood from his eye with the back of his hand, then bore in. The tall man circled away from the bull's right. Then Custer lurched forward, swung his left, and caught Granger in the chest with it. He gasped, and pain laced his ribs.

Custer could hit with either hand, and either would put Granger down for the count if landed solidly. Colt feinted with his left, drew the bull's guard down, and hit him with his right alongside the chin. He moved back, causing Custer to miss with a sledgehammer right, then went inside and pumped a right, a left, and another right to Bull's body. Custer sucked for air, his mouth a round O. Granger hit him with a solid left to the throat, then again moved out of reach of the stumplike arms.

Custer dropped his arms to his side and rushed. Granger hit him with another right, left, right—but the bull reached him, wrapped his arms around the cowboy's chest, and squeezed. To the tall man, it seemed that all the blood in his body pushed into his head. He kicked his feet out and fell, hoping to slide out of Custer's grip. It didn't work. The bull fell with him.

While falling, Granger tried to twist. That didn't work either. He fell on top, forced his arms up inside Custer's grip, and broke the hold.

He rolled free, got to his knees, then gained his feet. Custer had only reached his knees when the tall man kicked. His boot heel caught the bull alongside his head. He went to the ground, pushed his arms under him, and climbed to his feet. Instead of rushing Granger, he ran toward the crowd from the saloon he hung out in, grabbed one of the men around the neck, spun him so as to have him between him and Granger—then pulled the man's side gun. Before he could get the revolver in line, a shot sounded.

Custer's arm dropped, the six-shooter slipped from his grasp, and a single black hole showed in his right temple. Granger swept the crowd with a searching look. Bill Huxley stood on the edge of it, smoke curling from the barrel of the revolver he clutched in a fist he moved from side to side, covering Custer's friends. "Even one o' you reach for a gun, I start shootin', an' I don't give a damn who I hit. Get back to your slop pit."

Growling like a pack of dogs fighting over a bone, the crowd melted away, most returning to the saloon. Granger went to the firearms drummer. "Thanks, Bill. He had me for sure." He frowned. "Didn't know you could shoot like that."

His hand shaking, Huxley holstered the new Colt. "Granger, if I'm gonna sell guns, I gotta know how to use 'em. Sometimes people wantta see them fired before they lay down their money." His face was several shades whiter than when Granger last saw him.

"You ever kill a man before, Bill?"

Huxley shook his head. "Shot a couple. Never killed one."

Granger took him by the arm. "Come. I'll buy you a drink. Fact is I'll buy you a whole jug if you want it. It'll settle you down some. Ain't nobody likes killin'." He looked at his raw, bleeding hands, and now began to feel the punches Custer had landed, punches of which he'd been unaware during the fight. " 'Nother fact is, I could use a drink myself 'fore I fall on my face."

The walk to the Champion Saloon took almost as great a toll on Granger's strength as the fight, what with the well-wishers clapping him on the back and telling him what a "helluva fight" it was.

A drink might make him feel better right now, but he couldn't rest. Today he'd gotten rid of the two easiest of the five men who wanted his scalp. He had his work cut out for him, and he had to finish the cabin.

Winter would soon be here, and he wanted Molly comfortable before the first snow. Did he dare head back to Hell Gate and hope the other three didn't catch up with him until he and Molly finished the job? He'd have to think on that.

10

GRANGER LAY AWAKE long into the night. He thought of Molly and the home they were building. Thought of the coming winter. Thought of Gant, Diamond, and Clinton, all putting themselves above the law, and each of them setting himself to kill Granger. He tossed and turned, trying to lie so the bruises he'd taken during the fight would pain less. He finally decided that regardless of how he lay, he was going to hurt.

Anger swelled his throat. All he wanted was to be let alone to build a home for Molly, and these three, individually and collectively, had set themselves against him, set themselves to kill him, set themselves to take everything he and Molly had worked for. He turned over, sat on the edge of bed, and stood. He was damned if he'd play their game.

He made up his bedroll, dressed, buckled his gunbelt, and headed for the livery. He looked at the stars and figured it to be about two-thirty. He rode out of Virginia City in the coldest and deepest part of the night.

A wolf howled his song to the stars. Another answered him from the side of the next hill. Out in the open Granger's nerves quieted. His troubles weren't over—the fact was they had only now begun—but from here on he'd fight the best way he knew how. He'd fight the way he'd learned from the Comanche, the Sioux, the Kiowa, and others he'd learned from as both friend and enemy. But the fat man, Clinton, worried him.

How could he fight a man who sat behind a desk, who did nothing but plot, who had others do his fighting for him? Granger figured the fat man would fight, but only as a last resort—then he'd be at his most dangerous, because everything he'd tried would have failed, and he would know that if Granger was to be killed, he'd have to do it himself.

Long in his past, Granger had learned never to underestimate an enemy, but he had to figure some way to get Clinton out in the open. He pondered these problems while he rode. The Appaloosa had set himself a ground-eating gait, and Granger didn't mind. Come every road agent in the territory, he was headed home. He and Molly would finish the cabin.

All that day he rode with a sense of freedom, then in late afternoon a hurting took hold between his shoulder blades. It grew to form a hard knot. He was being followed. How would anyone follow him when he'd left in the deepest night?

He shrugged that question aside. Any of the three could have chosen to watch his every move. Abruptly, he reined his horse up the side of a mountain, then held that course until he crossed a snowmelt stream. He reined the Appaloosa to ride in the waters about a quarter of a mile downstream, then headed back to the trail. He held to the rutted road until he saw the place he looked for, rode past, circled, and came back to it—a dense cluster of aspen from which he could watch.

He tethered his horse and, rifle in hand, went back to the trail side of the copse. He sat there. Purple shadows pushed daylight from the land, bringing the velvety touch of moonlight to engulf him. He sat there another couple of hours, listened to the trembling of aspen leaves, the rustle of night foragers, the burrowing of small animals getting set for the night, and the chuckling of a brook tumbling over rocks nearby. Those were natural noises, ones he expected—it was the unexpected he listened for.

He shook his head. Whoever followed was good. He doubted not that he was followed, but it seemed his pursuer had not been taken in. He went back to his horse, silent as a wisp of wind, took his bedroll off, loosened the cinches, and lay down. If anyone came near, the horse, a careless footstep, the breaking of a twig, would awaken him.

He opened his eyes after what seemed only minutes, and looked through the leaves at the stars. He'd slept longer than he wanted. Only another hour until daylight. He shivered. A cup of hot coffee would be good, but so would a hot breakfast. He dug in his saddlebags, pulled out a strip of jerky, and carved off a piece. Then he saddled, tied his bedroll behind the cantle, toed the stirrup, and rode from the trees while he chewed at the jerky.

The few hours' sleep had eased the hurts of cuts and bruises earned during the fight with Custer. He breathed deep of the crisp air, felt its energy flow through him, and settled in for a long, hard ride. One that would tax his every effort to fool the man on his trail. The knot between his shoulder blades persisted.

He'd tried outsmarting his pursuer, and failed. Now perhaps he could lead him on a chase through the mountains and wait for the bandit to make a mistake.

Clear of the cluster of aspen, he studied the ground for tracks, and saw none. He pondered whether to go home by way of Hell Gate Canyon, or track back through Bannack, from there to Fort Owen, then angle off toward his cabin site. The canyon would give him more room to hide his tracks—but it would help the bandit as well. He'd have more open space going by way of Bannack, but that could work against him, too.

After an hour of riding, headed toward Hell Gate, he abruptly changed his mind. He'd laid down tracks heading for the canyon; now if he could find hard ground, rock to take his horse across, the bandit would be unaware he'd changed course.

He soon found what he looked for. Rains and snowmelt

had rendered a long slab of rock bare of soil. Granger stopped his horse short of it, cut up a pair of jeans, tied the pieces around the Appaloosa's hooves to prevent them scoring the hard surface, and led the horse onto the slab.

The jeans would wear through soon, but would hide his tracks well enough for him to get off the canyon trail. He left the rock slab, and not long after passed through a stand of tall ponderosa pines. A thick carpet of needles lay under them. Granger again stopped, and searched for a way through the trees; then he led his horse into their midst.

About a hundred yards into the pines, he ground reined the Appaloosa, retraced his steps, and looked for soil turned up, or disturbed needles that would mark his route. He found two places where hooves had kicked up soil, and a few others where pine needles looked crushed into the ground.

He repacked the turned-up earth, and sprinkled pine needles over them, as well as over those that showed sign of being stepped upon. Then he again toed the stirrup, and angled his way toward Bannack.

Frequently, he leaned from the saddle to check the wrappings on the Appaloosa's hooves. After a while, he noticed the hoof coverings getting ragged. He removed them and hid them under a low-lying juniper. "Ought to tangle our trail enough to cost him a whole bunch o' time." His horse twitched his ears as though listening to Colt's every word.

He rode past the cabin on the banks of Grasshopper Creek, the one from which he'd pulled the braces. He stopped, and frowned. If Drago and his cohort knew of the cabin, why wouldn't the rest of the outlaws? He studied that question a bit, decided they would know about it, then reined his horse back across the creek, searching for a well-hidden place to make camp. He found it in a great tumble of rocks above where the cabin had stood. He decided to make a stand. He wouldn't lead anyone to his cabin, where Molly might catch a bullet.

Bill Diamond shifted his weight in the saddle and gave the smooth slab of rock a hard look. Before riding onto it, he dismounted and walked a hundred yards or so, studying every inch, thinking Granger's horse would have slipped at least once and scraped the hard surface. He walked another several yards. Still no markings. It took him two or three hours to study the length of stone, about a quarter mile. He walked back to his horse, mumbling, "Damned good horse, prob'ly mountain bred, to not slip even once on that rock."

He climbed back aboard and rode to the other end, where the slab again buried itself under soft soil. There he found no tracks either.

He draped his leg around the saddle horn, built a cigarette, smoked it down to where it burned his lips, then squeezed the fire out between calloused fingers. "Only thing I can figger is, he wrapped them hooves in rawhide, or some such." He chuckled. "Granger, you outfoxed me, but I'll find you, you bastard."

He spent the remainder of the afternoon riding an expanding circle around the rock; then at dusk he made camp, and continued the search the next morning. About time for a nooning, he found what he looked for. He'd learned when soon out of Virginia City what Granger's horse's hoofprints looked like. He dismounted, studied the tracks he'd found, ran his fingers around the indentation, found them dry, and stood. "Yep, cowboy, you done cost me close on to two days. Ain't no hurry though. I'll find you, an' when I bring yore scalp in to Clinton, I'll hold out my hand for the thousand dollars he said he'd pay—an' he damned sure better not go back on his word." He stood and toed the stirrup. "Hell, Clinton, I'd trust a rattlesnake further'n I'd trust you."

Now, with tracks to follow, Diamond kicked his horse into a lope, stopping now and again to make certain he stayed on the tall man's trail. He had no doubt now, that Granger had headed for Bannack. Like Granger, he crossed Grasshopper Creek, stopped, and looked toward the bend in the stream. Only now did he remember the old shack he and several others stayed in on occasion. He thought a while, and nodded. He decided to stay the night in the cabin—him and the rats.

A few minutes' riding brought him to the bank where only

bare earth showed in place of the cabin. "Reckon them poles give out an' let the old shack tumble into the crick." He thought about it a few moments, then decided to camp where the cabin had stood. He tethered his horse on grass fetlock-deep on the flat that tracked the creek bank, brought his bed-roll and rifle to the bare earth, dumped them, and made a fire. He used no care to hide his camp, thinking Granger might even now be bedding down in Bannack.

The tall man looked down on the crude camp the gunfighter made. He picked up his Henry, having already taken care to jack a shell into the chamber, and laid it across the boulder in front of him. He sighted down its barrel, drew a bead on the middle of Diamond's shoulders, shook his head, and eased the hammer down.

Nobody would know how he'd killed the outlaw—but he would, and he'd never again get a sound night's sleep. How then was he to get the job done? He'd checked on Diamond and been told he was swift with his handgun—and hit what he aimed to. Granger figured that if he stood, walked down the creek bank, and challenged Diamond to a stand-up gun-fight, Molly might be left alone in this wilderness. Poor little girl. She'd be as much alone as when he'd taken her off the prairie. But how was he to kill Diamond without having to live with a cowardly act the rest of his life?

He watched the outlaw fry bacon, the smell driving him to the brink of standing, rushing down the bank, six-shooter in hand, and taking what the man cooked. Granger had eaten only jerky for the past few days, and his stomach let him know it. He squatted, carved himself a piece of the dried meat, and began to chew.

While Granger chewed on jerky, Clinton sat at his desk eating the meal he usually had someone from the cafe down the street bring him: country fried potatoes, steak, beans, a large slice of cornbread, a half apple pie, and a pot of hot coffee to wash it down with. He chewed, smacked, and dropped food in his lap, but paid it no mind. His thoughts centered on the one man he himself would kill if he had to.

A couple of days past, and for several days before, he'd seen Granger pass his office window. Each time it was all he could do to keep from shooting him. Now it seemed the tall man had left town—but never mind that; one of his men would get him.

It had been routine for Bill Diamond to come to his office each day. Now Diamond had disappeared at about the time Clinton missed seeing the tall man. He pondered the two incidents, and decided that the slim gunfighter had gone after Granger.

He'd not seen the cowboy draw his handgun, nor had he seen him when he had to shoot at a man shooting at him. But he had seen the thin, white-haired gunman in a shoot-out, and he'd seen none better. Diamond's usually pale, light blue eyes turned almost white when he faced a man. He was a killer.

Clinton smiled and stuffed a huge bite of steak into his already full mouth. Convinced he could buy anything with money, Clinton was certain that the thousand dollars he'd promised Diamond, or Mike Gant, would get the job done. To his mind, Gant might be even more dangerous than the slim gunfighter. Gant would shoot a man from behind, where, through some twisted sense of honor, Diamond wanted to be looking at his man.

His mind went to the thousand dollars. It was a lot of money to pay just for getting a man killed. He frowned, pushed another forkful of food into his mouth, and again thought of money.

Henry Plummer had gotten gold from the miners through robbery and killing. The fat man shook his head. He out-thought Plummer at every turn. He robbed, killed, got the miner's hard-earned dust—and their mining claim, which always sold at a good profit. Plummer just hadn't taken it far enough.

Sitting by his fire on the banks of Grasshopper Creek, Diamond thought about money also. A thousand dollars. He'd never made that much at one time. He'd kill Granger, go back to Virginia City, collect his thousand, and maybe everything else the fat man had, then head for California. Hell, he didn't owe Clinton anything, and he'd been keeping track of what the man brought in, mostly from the sweat of what men like him and Gant made possible.

He smiled, a wintry smile. He would kill Granger for nothing. The cowboy had either killed or caused the death of several of his friends. Yeah, he'd get him, and if everything worked out, he'd take care of Clinton, too.

Finished cooking, he ate bacon from the frying pan, beans from the tin he had put in the coals by the fire, and drank his steaming coffee.

His mind went to Granger. He hoped he could work it so he would face him in Bannack. People would be there to see him do it—outdraw the cowboy, shoot into him, then shoot into him again. His reputation would take a leap forward. Granger had a name for being a right salty gent, but thinking on it, he realized he hadn't seen any of Granger's graveyards.

He spread his blankets, took out his handgun and rifle, dumped the cartridges from them onto the blanket, and commenced cleaning his weapons. Finished with that, he twirled himself a smoke, poured another cup of coffee, and leaned against his saddle, thinking of Clinton and how much dust he must have salted away.

In the rocks above the gunfighter, saliva flowed under Granger's tongue with every bite the outlaw took, and when he poured himself coffee and sat back to smoke, the tall man caught himself packing his pipe. He shook his head. A pipe's smoke had a distinctly different aroma from that of a cigarette, and as attuned as he knew Diamond was to his surroundings he wouldn't chance it. He put his pipe away.

He concentrated on how to get the gunny into a shoot-out without just opening fire on him—and he wanted it to be a lesson to others working for the fat man. *There was his answer.* If he wanted others to learn from Diamond's mistake, he'd have to challenge him where others would see it. Along with that thought, his gut tightened. Was he fast and accurate enough to beat the gunfighter? He swallowed the lump in his throat. He'd never know until he tried. He stood, slipped silently back into the trees, checked his gear, saddled, and headed for Bannack.

He put about twenty miles behind him before he stopped, made camp, and prepared a hot meal. Afterward, drinking coffee and enjoying his pipe, he smiled, wondering if the thought of hot food had influenced him more than setting an example for Clinton's men.

The next morning, after a hot breakfast, with cuts and bruises from the fight healed, he felt better than he had in days.

He rode into Bannack in time for his nooning. Before getting a room, or eating lunch, he visited every saloon in town, made sure the patrons in each saw him and knew who he was. They'd tell Diamond when asked.

He asked for, and got, a room at the front of the hotel, then spent the afternoon sitting at the window watching the street. Diamond should get to town toward sundown.

Shadows stretched long behind the westering sun. Granger stood, and for at least the tenth time checked the loads in his six-shooter, checked that it rode easy in the holster, checked the tie around his leg—and sighed. He was getting antsy, and that was no way to be going into a gunfight. He thought to go to the nearest saloon and have a drink, discarded the idea, and again sat at the window.

The smells of cooking food mixed with dust coming from the street below and wafted to his window—then he saw a slim rider turn into the end of the street. He leaned closer to the pane of glass, watched another moment or two, and again stood.

His stomach churned, neck hairs tingled, and his scalp tightened. This was it. Molly would soon be one man closer to having him come home safe—or he wouldn't be coming home at all.

Figuring the gunfighter would have a drink before getting something to eat, Granger again looked out the window. Diamond reined in at the Last Gulp Saloon, three doors from the hotel. The tall man settled his holster against his thigh, sucked in a deep breath, let it out slowly, did it again, and headed for the saloon.

Figuring Diamond would not have time for a drink before someone told him he was in town, Granger paused on reaching the boardwalk, frowned, shook his head, and turned up the space between buildings. He wouldn't use the front door. He'd slip in the back and let his eyes adjust to the different light, hopefully before anyone saw him.

At the back of the saloon, he pulled on the door. It opened. He stepped into a long, narrow, dark hallway and stood a few moments, letting his eyes get used to the darkness. Then he walked toward a square of light, the sounds of voices, and the smell of stale whiskey coming from the door about fifteen feet in front of him.

Standing in the dark, he studied the room and the men in it before stepping through the doorway. A glance at over half the men in the room showed no one he knew; then his eyes swept along the bar. Diamond was the third man from the end closest to the front door. Granger stepped into the room, stopped at the end of the bar farthest from the gunfighter, ordered a whiskey, knocked back half of it, and stared at the slim, white-haired killer, knowing that a stare can be as physical as a touch.

He'd held his eyes for only a moment on the man he hoped to kill, when Diamond frowned into his drink, looked up, and glanced along the bar. When his eyes came to rest on Granger, they widened, only a bit, but enough to tell Granger he'd surprised the man. Real slow-like, Diamond set his glass on the polished surface and placed his hands palms down next to it.

Granger stood relaxed, and, not taking his eyes off the gunfighter, he motioned with his left hand. "You men better step back a little. I think your friend down yonder's been lookin' for me." Abruptly, his nerves quieted, and he became still inside. It was as though his entire body awaited the deadly moment when gunfire would rip through the room. "Fact is you men better get clear of the bar. Me an' Slim there gonna need some space."

Those at the bar pushed, shoved, cursed, and managed to clear a lane about ten feet wide in front of the long surface.

"Cain't b'lieve you come to me, Granger. You ain't smart

as I heerd. Step out so's all this wood ain't 'tween us.''

Making certain he kept balanced on both feet, Granger eased from behind the curved end to stand in the open. The white-haired killer did the same; then, without looking at the bartender, he said, "Fatso, take one o' them shot glasses an' hold it over the bar." He shifted his words to Granger. "Cowboy, he's gonna drop the glass. When it hits wood—draw.''

Granger gave the dropped glass no thought. He concentrated on Diamond's eyes—they would signal when the gunfighter's brain told his hands to pull iron. Granger had to be both fast and accurate. There would be no second chance, no second shots if the first didn't find flesh.

The gunfighter's eyelids tightened. Granger's hand flashed to his side. Faster than thought, faster than sight, Granger's thumb slipped off the hammer. The killer jerked, the hole above his belt buckle caused him to step back at the same time he fired. The heavy slug whined past the cowboy's ear. Granger fired again. A black spot appeared in Diamond's shoulder. Granger thumbed off another shot at the same time he felt a burning along his thigh.

The slim, white-haired man lay on the floor, another hole in the center of his chest. He tried to lift his six-shooter, but his hand dropped to the thick sawdust. Granger walked in on him, hammer eared back for another shot.

Diamond looked up at him. "Y-you beat me, cowboy. Never figured you could do it.''

Granger stared at him a moment; then, his voice soft, he said, "There's always somebody faster. You use a gun often enough, you gonna die using it." He stood there until the fallen gunfighter quivered, choked on a breath, and lay still. The acrid stench of cordite still curling from the end of his handgun, Granger limped toward the front door before the quiet of the room exploded into a roar. No one offered him a drink. He wasn't among friends.

Once outside, still standing in the light cast by the lanterns inside, he looked at his leg, and found only a slight crease along the outside of his thigh.

He went to the Miner's Rest Saloon next to the hotel—

there he would find friends. And until the word got around that he'd killed Diamond, there would be no backslapping and offers to buy him a drink. He wanted a drink to settle his nerves, then he'd go to the cafe down the street and get something to settle his stomach, and on the morrow he'd head for Hell Gate, pick up Molly, and head for their cabin.

11

AS GRANGER LOOKED at the town of Hell Gate from a distance, a feeling of urgency, the desire to give the Appaloosa his head and let him run, overwhelmed him. He squelched the thought. His horse was as tired as he himself was. But his desire to see Molly pushed concern for the horse aside—almost. He urged the big spotted horse to a lope, while telling himself he was in a hurry only because he wanted to see that she was all right—but telling himself a lie didn't do the trick. He knew he had feelings for her, feelings that weren't proper for an "almost" father. Such a feeling of shame came over him he reined his horse in while he studied on it.

He thought how Molly had looked on the day he'd found her, how she huddled close to Nick for protection, how she shied from him when he rode to their burned-out Conestoga wagon, how once he convinced her and her brother he meant them no harm, only wanted to care for them, she'd placed all her trust in him, and now here he was having feelings for her like she was a full-grown woman. "Damn, Granger, never thought you was such a low-down man. Why that poor little girl would run away if she knowed the thoughts you was havin' 'bout her. Too, every day you spend around her you bring danger right to her doorstep. Any o' them men huntin' you might throw lead an' hit her. Reckon the best thing you can do is get her all set up in a good home, be sure she can make it, then tie your bedroll to the back o' your saddle an' head out.'' Saying it out loud, trying to bolster his resolve, didn't help either.

But talking to himself as though to another person gave him a solution, and he didn't like it. For her own good he reckoned it was the only one. He again urged his horse toward Hell Gate.

Shockley met him at the door. ''Reckon you're looking for Miss Tbalt. Well, she isn't here. Left two or three days after you did. She took the cow, pigs, an' chickens and left.''

Granger stared at him a moment, anger surging into his throat. ''What the hell you mean, she left soon after I did? Thought you was gonna take care o' her for me.''

Shockley stepped back and eyed Granger with a look that had no give in it. ''Granger, don't know how well you know Miss Tbalt, but she's got a mind of her own. When she made up her mind to leave, there wasn't anything this side o' hell gonna stop 'er.''

Granger opened his mouth to give the innkeeper another blast. Shockley held his hand palm outward. ''Now, wait a minute. She's all right. I got somebody watchin' over her, and I been out there a few times to make sure she's doin' good.'' He dropped his hand to his side, stepped back and looked the tall man in the eye. ''Granger, I did the best I could.''

Colt studied Shockley a moment, then his lips quivered at the corners, his eyes crinkled, and he laughed. ''Lordy day, that must've been a sight. You standin' there tellin' that girl she wasn't goin', an' her standin' there, hands on hips, sayin' she damn sure was.''

Shockley grinned. ''That's about the way it was, only she didn't say 'damn.' Don't believe you could've stopped her either.''

Granger nodded. ''You're right, when she gets the bit in her teeth, you might as well give 'er her head.'' He held out his hand. ''Hope you don't hold my temper fit agin' me.''

While shaking hands, Shockley made Colt promise to never hold him responsible for the girl again. Colt glanced at the sun, saw he had plenty of time to reach the cabin by sundown, climbed back on his horse, and left.

He topped the hill above the cabin, stopped, and stared. Five Indian lodges stood not a hundred yards from his front door. "What the h—" He swallowed the last word and spurred the Appaloosa into an all-out run. He left the saddle before the horse came to a full stop, but Molly was there to stop him. She threw her arms around his neck, smothered his face with kisses, then stepped primly back. "Oh, Colt, you're the best thing I've seen in a month of Sundays. I've been lookin' for you for weeks."

Flustered by the greeting, and trying to cover his embarrassment from the grinning Flatheads standing a few paces away, he looked from them to her. "Why'd you leave Shockley's place when I told you to stay there? If I'd a knowed, I'd a been worried sick."

Molly ignored his question and waved to the Indians. "Come on over." She introduced them all around, then looked Granger in the eye. "Gonna tell you somethin', I'd a gone crazy stayin' in that one room alone. Colt, I had to have somethin' to do."

Little Bear Who Runs cut in. "Warrior Woman have plenty to do. She do squaw work, warrior work, all work like you still here. She keep some work for you."

Granger heard nothing Little Bear said after calling Molly "Warrior Woman." The Flatheads—fact was, no Indians conferred that name on a woman lightly. He looked at Little Bear, his lids almost hiding his eyes. "She's Warrior Woman, huh? How'd she earn that na—"

"Oh, Colt, you're gonna be angry again, but I had to do it."

"Had to do what, woman?"

Little Bear, still grinning, placed his hands and arms in a mock shotgun firing position. "She shoot bad white man. Man come take your scalp, Warrior Woman take his." The sub-chief shook his head. "He not take scalp ever again." He waved toward the hills. "Leave him for coyotes."

Granger eyed the skinny Indian a moment, then, trying to push his anger to the back of his mind, he pulled his pipe out, cut shavings from a twirl of rough-cut, packed the bowl, and was about to put a lucifer to it when he saw Little Bear's eyes on the string of twirled tobacco. He held it out to the sub-chief.

Little Bear took his time about filling his pipe, then sat cross-legged in front of Granger and Molly. "Hold council. You not make war with Warrior Woman." His words were not a request.

Colt realized he'd been told how to act. A slight smile broke the corners of his lips. He took Molly's hand and pulled her to the ground with him when he, too, sat. "All right, tell me about it." He listened while the sub-chief told the story of how Owen brought word to Molly that a bad white man was looking for Granger. She opened her mouth several times to add something to Little Bear's story, but Colt squeezed her hand and shook his head that to interupt when one was talking at a council was bad manners. Finally, the skinny Indian nodded. "I have spoken."

Granger puffed his pipe a couple of times, then looked at the sub-chief. "How'd she get you into what happened?"

Little Bear glanced at Molly, and she nodded. "Warrior Woman make war plan, tell me what to do, I do it. Lure bad white man into trap." He grinned. "Warrior Woman big trap."

Granger puffed his pipe a couple of times, then looked at Molly. "What's he mean, you're a big trap?"

Molly told him the whole story while studying the knuckles of her right hand, which was squeezing her left until it felt numb. Then she looked at him. "I figured it was the only thing I could do, Colt. If I'd let 'im go, he'd a gone hunting you. Figured you had about as much trouble as you could handle. Ended up he gave me right good reason to blow 'im in two. He was gonna take me." She watched his face to see how angry he might be at her for acting on her own, and when his eyes didn't turn icy, and the muscle at the back of his jaw didn't knot, she smiled and changed the subject.

"You're gonna be mighty proud when you see what Little

Bear, some of his warriors, and I got done while you were gone. I checked the line you drew in the dirt as to where the rest of our cabin would go, figured how many logs and what size they had to be, then we went into the woods, cut what it'd take to finish our home, and dragged 'em here for you." She waved toward where they'd dragged them. "Know you couldn't see 'em when you rode in, flat on the ground like they are. I didn't think we could do the stone work to suit you, or pick stones you'd like, so you gotta do that."

Again, she studied his face. "You eat yet?"

He shook his head. "Not a bite since breakfast. Got anything you can warm up?"

"Better'n that. I haven't eaten either. Supper's on the stove simmering right now." She looked at Little Bear. "Come on in. You haven't eaten either."

The easy way Molly and the skinny Indian got along surprised Colt. They had not yet told him how the Flathead lodges came to be in front of his cabin. He shrugged mentally. He'd hear that story while they ate.

Molly dished up, and then Little Bear took a plate and sat cross-legged on the floor against the wall while Colt and Molly sat at the table. Granger looked at the sub-chief, and was on the verge of telling him to come to the table when Molly, seeing what he was about to do, said, "Don't, Colt. It was all I could do to get him in the cabin. He's sitting where he sits every time he eats with me."

While they all ate the venison stew, Molly and Little Bear told Colt how the Flatheads had come to be there. When the telling was finished, Granger could only shake his head. "You've made some mighty good friends, Molly."

They finished eating, and Little Bear patted his stomach and stepped toward the door, then looked at Granger. "You want lodges moved? You and Warrior Woman fight together now."

Granger shook his head. "If you'd rather stay here, Little Bear, we'd be happy to have you near us, but if there is somewhere you'd rather be, I understand"

The spindly Indian smiled. "We stay. Help put up Warrior Woman's lodge." Then he left. Granger smiled to himself.

In Little Bear's mind this would always be Molly's lodge.

Granger helped Molly red-up the dishes, hung the pots from pegs in the wall to the side of the fireplace, then packed his pipe and lit it. "Seems like we got us a family, Molly. You could've done a lot worse in pickin' your friends. Them Indians out yonder'll stand fast in a fight, an' we ain't through fightin'. We gonna need 'em."

"Mr. Shockley picked them for us. I'd say he did a right good job of it."

They sat by the fire, Colt smoking and drinking coffee, while Molly knitted. She wouldn't drink coffee at night.

After they went to bed, Colt lay awake long into the night worrying the thought they weren't doing the Flatheads right. The whites were moving in, giving no thought that they settled in the choicest places in this valley which had been used by the Indians for several hundred years. He pondered the justice of it and decided there was none, but if he moved on and left them the land that he'd claimed, chances were whites not nearly as friendly would take his place, and it would get worse.

The railroads were coming, and would bring settlers by the thousands, many of whom would see this valley and go no farther. He'd heard talk the government was going to move the Flatheads to a valley north of there. He wondered how he could make it up to them. He couldn't do anything about those who would ride the rails to get here and take more land, but he could try to help the Indians as best he could now.

The Flatheads would not fight the white man, not because they were afraid—they were among the fiercest of warriors—but because they had been convinced by the Black Robes and trappers alike that they would only cause a loss of their people they could ill afford.

Finally, Colt turned on his side and went to sleep.

The next morning, he and Molly hauled slabs of rock for the foundation of Molly's bedroom. They drove the full wagon to the site and unloaded it. Little Bear, with eight others, several of whom were only about twelve or thirteen years old, stood to the side and watched.

Holding one side of a large slab, Molly looked across it to Granger. "They're good workers, Colt. I paid them for helping me saw and drag logs. I b'lieve they'd like to earn a little money, supplies, or—or whatever comes to mind. I know they have very little to eat." Walking sidewise, sort of crablike, the two of them struggled the large slab into place, then Granger went to Little Bear.

"You," he motioned with his left hand to take then all in, "help move rocks?"

The warrior studied the heavy load a moment. "We help. What pay?"

Granger had pondered that when Molly suggested they might welcome the chance. The Flatheads made war only on their enemies, and they could always use good weapons. Most of those given to them by the Indian agents were of ancient government issue, and Colt had taken several rifles, excellent weapons of the latest design, Henrys and Spencers, from those who came hunting him.

Traders had swapped good rifles for pelts, but, trapping beaver and most other animals, the Flatheads had in the recent past not produced many bales of pelts, and the beaver market had disappeared. Colt motioned Little Bear to wait a moment, then went into the cabin.

He returned carrying a Henry and two boxes of shells. "Help till stone all in place?" He held the rifle toward the sub-chief. The Indian's eyes widened. He looked at the rifle like a man would look at a beautiful woman.

Holding his hands at his side, he shook his head. "We help. You give rifle when we do job."

Granger studied the warrior only a moment. He liked this sub-chief more all the time. "Come on. We'll make sure your young warriors handle only the lighter slabs."

The afternoon of the third day after Little Bear and his warriors entered into the rock-carrying job, Granger noticed a slab he wanted, but a tree had entangled it in its roots. He went to the cabin, got a pick and an ax and chopped at the root system.

After an hour, sweat streaming down his face, Granger dropped the ax and walked a few paces from the tall tamarack. He eyed it from top to bottom and could see no lean to the trunk. He dragged his arm across his eyes to clear them of sweat and looked again. The damned thing stood as straight as it had when he started. He shook his head and went to the horse shed, where he picked up two lariats, put a hackamore on two horses, and saddled them. He went back to the tree and shinnied up the trunk.

When he had gone as far as he thought necessary, he tied the lariats to the trunk, went down, and tied the bitter end of the ropes to the saddle horns.

He urged the horses ahead. "Pull, boys—pull!" The tree leaned a little. He went back and chopped more roots, then urged the horses forward again. This time, with muted cracking and snapping, the larger roots broke loose from the stubborn earth that clutched them. The tamarack leaned, then slowly toppled to ground.

Granger made up the ropes, led the horses back to the lean-to, and motioned Molly to follow him.

Back at the root base, about to pry the stone he'd gone to all the trouble to set free, he looked at the raw, gaping hole the tamarack's root system had left. He frowned, walked closer, then climbed into the hole. Without taking his eyes from the soil, he said, "Molly, come here."

He felt rather than saw her walk to his side. "Look here, little one. Am I seeing what I think?"

She leaned to look, then got on her hands and knees and scooped a double handful of gravelly soil into her hands. "Gold, Colt, richer'n any pocket we found in Alder Gulch."

Holding his face stiff, devoid of emotion, he nodded. "What I thought, too." Then, without another glance at their find, he walked to the rock that had brought the gold to light. "Let's get this rock in place. We'll talk 'bout what we found tonight after supper."

Molly looked at him as though he'd lost his mind, but she put her back into getting the slab out of the ground.

That night, sitting by the fire, Colt drinking coffee, Molly knitting, he sat staring into the dancing flames. He took a swallow and looked at her. "I been studyin' on how that dust got where it is. Way I got it figured is, that stream at the bottom o' the hill must've maybe hundreds of years ago flowed along the base of this cliff we built against, then as it silted in, an' raised the land, the dust settled at the bottom while the land built higher and higher, until it reached the level our home is settin' on." He packed and lit his pipe. "Molly, we're probably settin' here on the richest find in this territory."

She put her knitting needles to the side. "When we gonna start pannin'? We need to channel one of those springs over so we can wash the gravel."

Colt shook his head. "We ain't gonna do neither one. We gonna cover that hole up like we ain't found nothin' "

Her eyes widened. "We're what? You can't mean it. We're gonna just forget what we found?"

He puffed the fire in his pipe back to life. "Nope. We're not gonna forget it. We know it's there. It'll be there hundreds of years from now for whoever needs it, if we don't need it first. Right now we don't need it."

He stood, went to the coffeepot, and poured another cup. "Way I see it, little one, if we let word out what we've found, hundreds of people will flock in here, diggin, tearin' up our beautiful valley, fightin', drinkin', raisin' hell. Don't want that. Don't think you do either." He studied her a moment. "But tell you what. You study on it a while, an' if you say we gonna take it outta the ground, then that's the way it's gonna be."

She nodded. "Hadn't thought of it that way." She grinned. "We'll leave it where it is till we need it."

The next day she helped Colt cover the hole.

Two weeks later, all the rock work completed, and Little Bear the proud owner of a new Henry rifle, Colt got busy with the adze on the logs. This was work he had to do himself, but he told the sub-chief he'd want him to help lift them into place when he finished shaping and smoothing them.

A month later, the cabin completed except for cutting sod and stacking it on the roof, a rider approached. Taking his time, he stopped his horse out close to the Indian lodges, then, eyes squinted, face flushed, he rode toward Granger. Granger studied the man. He was of medium build, with dirty black hair, dark-skinned, and dumb-looking, much like a cow. He dressed like a farmer—overalls, homespun shirt, and heavy, flat-heeled work shoes, all dirty.

Before reining his horse in, he said, "What them damned Indians doing here?" He swung his leg over his horse's rump to dismount.

"Hold it, stranger. Swing that leg back an' put your foot in the stirrup. Out here a man don't step down till asked—an' I ain't asked." Despite his attempt to hold his temper, Granger's face felt hot, his throat muscles tighten. "What business is it o' your's who's on my land?"

"Makin' it my business. My cabin's on south of here about four miles. Don't want no damned Indians livin' close by."

Granger looked the man in the eye, and swallowed a couple of times to squelch his anger, but only felt it cool to an icy calm. "Mister, the Flatheads have never hurt a white man, so it ain't so that what's worryin' you. What's your problem? Too, what's your name?"

"Ike Burrage's my name, an' I don't like no damned redskin what ever lived." A mean, hot look came to his eyes. "And I don't like whites who do."

Granger grinned. "Well now, reckon you made that plain enough. I just didn't understand till now." Still grinning, he moved in close to Burrage's horse and, with a lightning move, grasped the farmer's work boot and upended him from the saddle. "Now, to be polite as I'm usually wont to be, I'll ask you to step down—but I see you done got on the ground."

Burrage, lying on his side, stared up at Granger. "What you do that for? You mean you like them stinking redskins?" He rolled to get up.

"Stay where you are. It'll save some wear an' tear on your face." He put out his foot and pressed the man back to the ground. "Now, I'm gonna tell you how it is. Them Flatheads are my friends. They're stayin' here 'cause I like havin' 'em near me. This is my place an' I do what I like on it, don't ask no damn body what I can do. Have I 'splained it so's you understand?"

Burrage stared, his gaze dripping hatred. "Wait'll I tell my brother Morrie 'bout this. He's bigger'n me by 'bout fifty pounds. He'll take care of you."

Granger still held the farmer pinned to the ground with his boot. "Burrage, you a married man?" Then, not giving him a chance to answer, Granger continued. "If you are, you're on a fast horse toward makin' your wife a widow woman. Hate killin' married men, makes too many orphans." He removed his foot and stood back. "Now, Burrage, get on your horse, and don't never come on my land again. You gotta make a trip into Hell Gate, ride around my place. If you ever make the mistake of comin' here again, them Indians gonna still be here—'less o' course they want to leave, and then it'll be their choice. An' you gonna be leavin' a helluva lot faster'n you rode in. Now, git!"

Granger stood staring after the farmer. He wasn't through with the man yet; he'd be back. He shook his head, wondering how trouble always found him like lightning found a tall tree, regardless how much he wanted to be left alone. Molly saw the scene from the side of her new bedroom.

"Colt, what was that all about? I couldn't hear what you were saying to each other."

Granger pinned her with eyes still cold as a wintry day. "He don't like Injuns."

"Well, a lot of people don't; why didn't you just ask him to leave?"

Granger relaxed. A slight smile broke the hard planes of his face. "Reckon I didn't want him to mis-figure what I was tellin' 'im, so I 'splained it right good.

"Let's get back to work, I seen a couple o' big feathery snowflakes a while ago. Want you settled in 'fore snow flies."

Little Bear and his warriors worked with them until the roof had a double stack of sod on it. Granger had made certain the support for the sod was strong enough to hold a double layer when he used saplings about six inches in diameter under it. And not wanting to build another fireplace, he opened the other side of it so both rooms would catch its heat. He built Molly's bed against the wall close enough so she would be warm. When she moved her bedding and clothes, she was proud as a speckled pup with a new ball. She told Colt at least a dozen times how happy she was.

She had slept in her new room only two days when they had their first snowfall, just a dusting in the valley, but the heavy snow line moved well over halfway down the shoulders of the mountains, foretelling the coming of winter.

Granger worked from sunup to sundown sawing and chopping wood, wanting to get enough stacked to prevent his having to do much of it when deep cold had set in. All the while, he kept a wary eye out for the Burrages. The Flathead lodges still stood, and Ike Burrage didn't seem to be one to forget.

Little Bear and his wife, Antelope Woman, stayed busy digging camas root, a staple food of the Flatheads. Many of the Plains Indians also valued the root for its nutritional content. Antelope Woman showed Molly how to dig it and prepare it.

Then, one day toward the end of fall, Granger set his ax aside and told Molly they would go to Hell Gate the next day. "You ain't had nothin' to look at but me an' them Flatheads for a couple o' months now. Reckon it's time we both visited some other folks. Why, if we ain't downright careful, we gonna be more Injun than white."

Molly tilted her chin. "Don't reckon I find that too distasteful. I like those folks. They're like family, and Antelope Woman is the best friend I've had." She nodded. "But yeah, we can use a few things from Worden's, and it'll be a change of scenery." She smiled. "And, Colt Granger, I might add, you were already more Indian than white when you took us off the prairie."

Clay nodded and returned her smile. "Reckon I could do a whole lot worse. They're good people—spiritual, family-type folks, great warriors and hunters—why, hell, I've seen more whites to dislike than I have Flatheads."

The next morning, Granger told Little Bear where they were going and asked if the Flatheads wanted him and Molly to get them anything. Little Bear's look at the smoke curling from Colt's pipe told the tall man what the warrior would like, but he was too proud to ask. The thin Indian shook his head. Granger knew Little Bear had little money besides the rifle he and Molly had paid him for his help on the cabin, so Colt made a mental note: tobacco for his friend—and anything else he thought he and his people might need. Flour, perhaps, and cartridges for his rifle.

He harnessed horses to the buckboard and they set out. The day sparkled like a precious jewel. The golden leaves of aspen trembled in the sunlight, and up the slopes the mountain mahogany added their brilliant colors to the landscape, and down by the stream, willow and cottonwood did their part, along with the reds of the oak. Granger looked at Molly. "Lord, girl, if the Great Spirit made anything purtier'n this, he kept it for himself." He slanted a teasing look at her across his shoulder. "You reckon we died and went to heaven 'thout even knowin' it?"

She only smiled.

12

GRANGER PARKED THE wagon behind the general store.
They wanted to get their supplies bought and sacked before
socializing. Christopher Higgins told them that Worden had
stepped out. The storekeeper followed them around, sacking
the things they picked as they went. Granger bought Little
Bear Who Runs a couple boxes of shells for his rifle, tobacco, and a Green River knife as a special gift, then asked
Molly if she'd get the things she thought Antelope Woman
would like, and to get her a special gift also.

Molly gave him a pensive smile. "Colt, you've a heart as
soft as mush—sometimes. But, yeah, I thought to get her
something. I know she'd love to have some needles, and I
have in mind something else she'd like." Then, her eyes
twinkling, she put her hands on hips. "You know, we'd best
not come in town often or we'll go broke with you helping
me shop. Lordy day, we might even have to find us another
claim and start panning again."

He chuckled. "Little miss, we ain't spent much of our
cache, an' this here stuff ain't gonna cost us much, an' even
after I find somebody who'll drive us a couple hundred head
of them Durham cattle in here, I figure we'll have a pretty

hefty poke left. 'Sides that, we know where they's a lot more.''

No longer in the teasing mood, Molly laid her hand on his arm. "Yeah, Colt, but I notice you never spend any of my dust, and you won't take any of it to repay you." She dimpled, and cocked her head. "Reckon I'll just have to marry you to get us even."

Blood rushed to Granger's face. "Hush, little one, that ain't no way to talk to your almost-pa. Shame on you."

She only looked at him, shook her head, and went about her shopping. Colt looked at leather goods, fidgeted a moment or two, and asked Higgins if the saloon had reopened. There he'd find all the valley news worth hearing.

"Yeah, only last week, two big freight wagons come in from the coast with Bill Cook's shipment of whiskey and beer. He's runnin' that saloon like one o' those men's clubs back east. Right nice addition to the town, but ever so often some pretty rough customers go there. Go over and make yourself acquainted."

Granger nodded, told Higgins he'd be back to settle up, told Molly where he was going, and left. Outside, he stood on the porch a moment and studied the brands of horses tied to the hitching rails. He recognized a couple of Texas brands, and about three others from Wyoming. Having been a cattleman, looking at brands came as a matter of course to him. Then, too, there was the chance he'd know some of the people from trail drives, the army, or almost anywhere. He figured if they were friendly, it would be nice to see them again.

He stepped off the porch and walked across the dusty, rutted trail. Just on the off chance those Texas men were not friendly, he thumbed the thong off the hammer of his Colt, pushed through the batwings, and stepped aside long enough to see the room clearly. Five men stood at the bar. Granger knew none of them. He sighed. Disappointed. He had hoped to meet a friend.

Cook apparently kept the saloon clean. The smells of sour whiskey and stale sweat were not in evidence, but Colt did catch the aroma of fresh-brewed coffee and tobacco smoke. He went to the bar and introduced himself. As soon as he said his name for all to hear, one of the men—Granger took him to be a Texan by his look—faced Colt. "Granger? Colt Granger? Well, I'll be damned. I rode for Charley Goodnight a while back, an' you wuz one o' the ones we used to talk about sittin' round the fire at night. I hear you're plenty salty."

Granger studied him to see if he was friendly, decided he was, and said, "Cowboy, don't believe everthin' you hear. I've heard some o' those tales, an' didn't know they were talkin' 'bout me. 'Sides that, I never looked for a rep, but got one anyhow."

The cowboy grinned. "Mr. Granger, even if one-tenth o' the stories I heerd wuz true, you're a mix of ring-tailed tornado an' mountain cat." He stuck out his hand. "Glad to meet you."

They shook hands all around, Granger asked for a cup of coffee, and as Western, or sea-faring, men will, they swapped tales, until two men walked in, one a massive man, tall, beefy shoulders, arms and legs that looked like tree stumps. The other man was medium height, still dirty and unshaven—Ike Burrage. The big man with him must be the brother he bragged would beat Granger down to size.

"Well, there's that there Injun lover I wuz tellin' you 'bout, Morrie, the one what told me not to never come on his land agin."

Morrie stood there a moment and looked at Granger, then back to Ike. "Don't see as how that's much of a problem. We'll just ride around him. If he likes Injuns, reckon that's his business."

Ike's mouth fell open; he swallowed a couple of times, apparently trying to swallow anger and surprise. "You mean to tell me you gonna let them Injuns stay there?"

"Like I said, reckon that's his business."

Ike moved away from his brother. His hand dropped to his side. His eyelids slitted. "Well, Granger, my brother's a mite more understandin' than me. You ain't got me lyin' on the ground this time, an' I see you're packin'. Reckon we'll settle this with six-guns."

The man from Texas Granger had first talked with shook

his head. "Mister, don't know you, but less'n you figure to shake hands with the devil in the next few minutes, you'll forget goin' for that six-shooter. Colt Granger could let you get your iron out, pointed at him, an' still kill you deader'n hell before you could squeeze the trigger. If you're smart, an' you don't look to be, you'll let it drop."

Morrie moved to the side of his brother. "Come on, kid, let it drop, I'll buy you a drink."

"Better'n that, I'll buy." Granger stepped forward, his hand out. Ike's hand swept for his holster. He was only moderately fast, but apparently fancied himself gun-slick. Granger moved closer with such speed no one at the bar could be sure he had until his left hand grasped Ike's gun hand and his right swung to the trouble hunter's gut.

Air whooshed from the would-be gunman's mouth in time for Granger's fist to slam into his face. He went down. His shoulders hit the floor first. He grabbed for his revolver— and found himself staring into the muzzle of Granger's .44.

The tall man had swallowed his anger at first; now it took hold of him, choking the breath in his throat. "Mister, you even touch that gun, an' I'll unload this forty-four in your gut. I give you ever' chance to keep that six-shooter in its holster 'thout you losin' face. Now, I done run outta patience."

Ike's face drained of all blood; it shone white as the snow-clad peaks surrounding the valley. He spit out a tooth, licked bloody lips, and let his hand drop to the floor. Morrie had not made a move to protect his brother.

Ike rolled to his side, pushed himself to his knees, and stood. His eyes blazed through slitted lids. "Mister, I ain't gonna never forget this. I'll kill you some way, somehow." He twisted to turn his wrath on his brother. "Y-you jest stood there an' let 'im get away with hittin' me, then drawin' on me 'thout givin' me a chance."

Morrie's voice came out soft. "Little brother, he give you every chance a man could ask for. You brought it to him an' he couldn't let it ride. Count yourself lucky he didn't kill you. I figure I'm lucky, too, 'cause if he'd a shot you, I'd a had to take up yore fight—an' I'm right tired o' doin' that."

Ike stared at his brother a long moment, then spit at his feet. "A helluva brother you are. Pack your gear an' get outta my cabin."

The big man's face softened. "Ike, you was wrong. 'Sides, that there cabin's mine. I set every log in it—done a lot more'n my share o' the work. I ain't movin'."

The smaller brother continued staring a few moments longer. "You don't move, I will." He turned his look on Granger. "Mister, you an' me ain't through." He spun and went out the door.

Morrie looked at the swinging batwings, his face hardened. "Little brother, I hope you didn't mean that last, 'cause if you did, you gonna get me killed, too." His words fell on deaf ears.

He turned toward Granger. "Sorry all this happened, Granger. Don't kill 'im 'less you absolutely cain't get outta it." His shoulders sagged, and he spread his hands in a helpless gesture. "Even then, reckon I couldn't let it lie. I'd have to come after you."

Granger studied the big man a moment. He looked so pathetic Colt felt sorry for him, and found himself liking him. "Burrage, I'm sorry, too. Hate it ended this way—but think twice 'fore you come after me. I'd have to defend myself—don't want that, so think about how he is before you get yourself killed." He faced the bar. "Cook, pour us all a drink."

They knocked back their drinks and Granger shook hands all around, and, after finding that the Texas men were just drifting and intended to stay a while in Hell Gate, he went back across the street to see how Molly was making out.

Higgins folded several yards of a pretty flowered material into a brown paper wrapping, tied it, and asked Molly if there would be anything else. She shook her head. "Reckon that's it. We better head for home, or sundown'll catch us on the trail." She glanced at Colt, then her eyes shifted to his hands, his knuckles. "What in the world happened to your fist? It's bleeding. Your knuckles are all—You've been in a fight."

He stuck his hand in his pocket. "T'ain't nothin'." Then he saw he might as well tell her, or she'd stay after him until

he did. "Ike Burrage come after me." His shoulders
slumped. "Shore wish I could get rid o' one bunch of trouble
'fore more hunts me down." He told her the whole story
while they walked to the wagon.

At that moment, Quirt Clinton was cooking up even more
misery for the tall man. He looked across his desk at the
handsome, cold face of Mike Gant. "We can write Bill Diamond off. He'd dead. Ain't heard one way or the other, but
he left here to get Granger. He ain't come back." The fat
man crushed a sheet of paper into a wad, his fist clenched
around it. "That cowboy's caused me enough trouble. I want
you to find at least four of the best guns here—or in Bannack. Promise two thousand dollars for the one o' them who
brings me proof they killed Granger. The rest get nothin'."

"Hell, Mr. Clinton, you don't need anyone else. I'll take
care of the cowboy, and I'm not dumb enough to try to get
him from the front. He'll die jest as permanent shot in the
back."

Clinton stared at Gant long enough that the suave outlaw's
gaze dropped. "You done had your chance. I want it done
an' done right—but get me the men, an' if you're the one
who gets him, you get the money. All right?"

Gant's eyes hardened; he nodded and left. Clinton stared
after him. He didn't trust the man. He was too smooth, too
educated, too sneaky.

He pushed his ponderous body from the chair, locked the
front door, and went to his living quarters in the back room.
He closed that door and locked it. There, he slid a wall panel
aside, one a person would never suspect was not like any of
the other panels, unless that person saw Clinton move it.

Behind the secret panel, shelves ran from the floor to
above his head, several stacked with paper money, others
loaded with small sacks of gold dust, each shelf labeled as
to how much in gold or currency it held—every bit of it
taken from some hapless miner, or as a result of stealing, or
killing to get property to be sold.

Clinton saw nothing wrong with how he'd gotten his
wealth—he knew to the penny how much the compartment

held: eight hundred thousand, fifty-six dollars. By his thinking, he deserved the money; he was smarter than those he'd taken it from. He slipped the panel snugly back into place.

He sat on his bed and stared at the wall. A whole world awaited him out there. He had money, and money could buy anything. He didn't want fine foods, or liquors; he was a steak, potato, and rotgut whiskey man. Imported suits were for dumb bastards like Gant. Clinton wanted only to buy and manipulate people—people to do his bidding, people who had no conscience about doing in smaller, dumber people. It gave Clinton a sense of power.

But . . . He was trapped. He had no one he trusted to guard him and his money when he left this godforsaken strip of pebbles, sand, and boulders, in and surrounding Stinking Water Creek. He wouldn't trust his own men as far as he could toss one of those mountains—and others would ask questions. He couldn't afford questions. He'd have to put his mind to figuring a way, even though he'd already thought long into each night and hadn't come to a solution. He lay back to take a nap. After that he'd eat—again.

Gant left Clinton's office thinking about money—not food or sleeping, just money. He knew Clinton must have thousands stashed away somewhere, and by his reckoning it had to be in his office or living quarters. The fat man had never deposited anything of value at Dance and Stuart's store; he never went anywhere, except occasionally to the cafe. Most of the time he had his meals brought to him, so the gold had to be where the fat man could see it, touch it, smell it. But how was Gant to find it?

Maybe if he could be the one to kill Granger, when he went to collect from the fat man he could get an idea where he kept his hoard. He intended to get the two thousand offered for the cowboy whether he killed him or not. He'd simply shoot the one who collected it and take it from him. Satisfied he could count that two thousand already in his pocket, he went to the livery and saddled his horse. He didn't know of anyone he'd trust here in Virginia City. He'd find men in Bannack.

Fisk Sanders watched Gant come from Clinton's office, then ride out of town—toward Bannack. He would have given his bottom dollar to know what the two had cooked up. For certain, whatever it was boded good for no one. Many times he'd thought to call the Vigilantes into session, get a rope, and hang the fat man, but his respect for the law prevented that. He had to have evidence that would stand up in court, and he didn't have it.

Yes. He had tried and hanged twenty-two men brought in front of a miners' court, but in their case there had been no doubt they were guilty. He would not again hang a man unless he'd been tried by a duly constituted court of the land.

He wished he could see Granger, for he was certain whatever Clinton and Gant plotted concerned the cowboy, who in Sanders's opinion was hard as granite but honest. When he'd shot the toes off Skinner, he'd been torn with grief for the boy he'd brought to manhood. Sanders found no fault with Granger's hardness; he was a product of the West. He did what had to be done, and had been doing so for years in a land lawless except for that men carried in a holster at their side. It took men like the cowboy to make this land safe for more timid souls.

On impulse, Sanders went to his room, packed trail gear, picked up his rifle, belted on a holster and handgun, which he seldom wore, and went to the livery. It was time he visited old friends in Bannack.

Two days later, he rode into the town where he'd first hung out his shingle to practice law. The last hour on the trail, he'd had Gant in sight most of the time.

The outlaw rode directly to the Last Gulp Saloon, where Granger had met Diamond. Sanders pulled his rifle from the scabbard and followed the smooth gunman to the bar. Before leaving his horse's side, he jacked a shell into the chamber. He had no illusions about his ability with a handgun, but he could handle a rifle with the best of them. Like Granger, Sanders realized he had no friends in the Last Gulp. He felt his hair tingle at the base of his neck. He held his breath as long as he could, to filter out all but a small amount of the smelly, stale sweat and cheap whiskey. The muscles between

his shoulders tightened. He felt fear like he'd not known
before.

Gant knocked back a couple of drinks before looking
about the room, then went to a table at the back and talked
with three men. It was not until then the saloon's clientele
noticed Sanders. "Well, lookee who we got here, boys. It's
that damned lawyer who got George Ives hung." The words
came from a scrawny, bearded man at the middle of the bar.

The young lawyer felt every eye in the place turn toward
him. He glanced toward the door to make sure he had a clear
path of retreat. The same man who had spoken looked from
Sanders to those surrounding him. "What say we show 'im
how a rope feels."

Sanders stepped back, swung his rifle to the top of the
polished surface, and eared back the hammer at the same
time. "Any of you want to try stretching my neck, I believe
a shot would carry through at least two of you from here, so
if you want to make a move toward me, get at it."

Every man there froze. Some held drinks halfway to their
mouths; some had cigarettes ready to light, but held matches
until they burned their fingers; others put their hands flat on
the bar. Sanders sidestepped toward the door, seeing the
whole room but not taking his eyes off the one with the big
mouth.

He had only another step to reach the batwings when the
scrawny one, half-hidden behind another man, reached for
his gun.

Sanders moved the barrel only an inch or so, squeezed the
trigger, and then jacked another shell into the chamber. Two
men at the bar grabbed their chests and fell. Others swept
hands for their sides. Sanders fired again, saw red blossom
from another chest, and, pushed backward through the doors.
He whirled and ran to the corner of the building, where he
looked between it and the next structure, saw the space was
empty, and darted across.

Three men pushed through the batwings at the same time.
Sanders dropped to his knees, aimed, fired, and jacked shells
into the chamber as fast as the muzzle spit out a bullet. Two

men went down; the third forgot what he'd rushed outside for, and bulled his way back inside.

Backing down the street, Sanders came to the Miner's Rest and shouldered his way inside—among friends. Without saying howdy to anyone, he went to the bar, looked at the redhead, and said, "Water glass full o' good whiskey." It took him two swallows to do away with the contents of the glass.

By then, men crowded around him, all asking questions at once. Tom Jacobs, one of his old friends, said, "Hell, Fisk, I didn't know you were a gunfighter. What was that all about?"

Sanders gave him a look he hoped would curdle milk. "Tom, I just found out for sure I'm no gunfighter." He pursed his lips. "Whoowee, I don't ever want to go through that again."

The redheaded bartender filled his glass again. "Tell us what happened, boy. Never knowed you to pull a gun on nobody."

Sanders gave him a sickly grin. "Red, I never have and never will again. I found out a man can get himself mighty full of holes if he isn't careful—and lucky as the only whore in a town full of drovers who have six months' pay in their pockets and want to spend it all—on her." He looked around and, seeing only friendly faces, told them what happened, and why he was there.

"You men watch who leaves town with Gant, write Granger a letter at Hell Gate, and tell 'im who they are. Describe them as best you can. I'm going to ride over yonder to the Bitter Root Valley and see my good friend Colt soon's I quit shakin'. Never knew what it took to stand facing others with guns before. Gotta tell you, I have a lot more respect for people like Granger." He had a couple more drinks, then went to the hotel.

13

GRANGER AND MOLLY gave their gifts to Little Bear Who Runs and Antelope Woman. They sat by the fire outside of the sub-chief's lodge and talked.

Little Bear told Granger the fall buffalo hunt would take place within the week, and he had been elected by the council to be in charge of it. "I must take women back to encampment. They go on hunt to do woman's work. Warriors shoot buffalo." He grinned. "Maybe shoot Blackfeet. Make war during every hunt. White man's smallpox kill many Blackfeet. Flatheads, Shoshoni, Nee Mee Poo, tribe who French call Nez Perce, Pend d'Oreille, Kutenai, and other tribes friendly to our people—all go on hunt together. Fight Blackfeet together. You want bring lodges back here after dry meat and cure hides?"

Granger frowned. It wasn't fair of him to ask his friend to return here when there would be much work at the main encampment.

"Reckon I'd be mighty happy to look out here every mornin' an' see your lodges, but I know there is much to do with your own people. Too, you will miss taking your rightful place at council. No. I reckon Molly an' me's gonna miss you, but stay with your people, an' when you feel like havin' a few pipes with your friend Colt Granger, come on back, pitch your lodges, an' we'll smoke much together.''

Granger saw he'd relieved the warrior, but knew all he had to do was say the word and Little Bear's small band would return. He felt good about that because he'd be lying if he said he didn't feel more secure when he saw the lodges out in front of his cabin.

He stood, took Molly's hand, and pulled her to her feet. Then, in white man's fashion, he shook hands with Little Bear, and got a warm feeling in his chest when the sub-chief said, "You need. We come. Now, gone come sun."

Granger walked with Molly back to the cabin, and once they were inside, she turned to face him, her eyes watery. "I feel as though I've lost my best friend. Looking out there in the morning and not seeing the children at play, not seeing Antelope Woman, or Little Bear, is surely gonna leave a big empty place in my heart. Why didn't you tell them you wanted them back after the hunt?''

Colt grasped her shoulders. "Little one, it just flat ain't fair to ask to give up life with the bulk o' their people.'' He shrugged. "They'd come back, ain't no question 'bout that, 'cause they're that kind o' people. They'd stand by us long's they figure we need 'em, but winter's comin' on an' they got a lot of things to do to get ready for the cold.'' He removed his hat and placed it on its crown on the table, then smiled at her. "Promise you, soon's I figure they need tobacco, sugar, or whatever, I'll send for them—an' they'll come, not for want of me givin' 'em somethin', but 'cause they're our friends. Now, let's get ready for bed.''

The next morning, true to Little Bear's word, come sun, when Colt stepped outside, the lodges were gone. Not even a wisp of smoke showed from their breakfast fires. He would never admit to Molly that he, too, had an empty place in his heart. He took up his adze, pulled a sapling out in front of the cabin, and sliced great chunks from one side. Molly would have as much of her puncheon floor as he could finish by the time harsh cold set in.

Ten days after the Flatheads left, Molly, standing by his

side while he smoothed logs for her floor, touched his shoulder. "Rider comin'."

He stood, told her to go inside, belted his side-gun on, and picked up his Henry. He watched the rider grow from a small speck in the distance to one he could recognize. He frowned. "Damn if that don't look like Fisk Sanders. Now, what would he be doin' over this way?"

Another few seconds and he was sure of his reckoning. He put the rifle aside and walked to meet his friend.

"Fisk, what brings you way over here? Step down. You look tired." He put on a sober face despite wanting to grin. "We got no law here, so won't do you no good to hang out your shingle in Hell Gate. Figure with the big pop'lation they *ain't* got, a lawyer man'd starve to death."

His little joke didn't bring a smile to Sanders's face; instead, he looked Granger in the eye. "Come to warn you, friend. Clinton's put Gant to collecting a few hardcases to come hunting you. Don't know who they are, but some of our friends in Bannack're going to write you and let you know names and descriptions."

Granger stared at his boot toe a moment. "Thanks. All I need is more men wantin' a piece o' my hide." He looked up, smiled, and grasped Sanders by the arm. "Come on in. Reckon Molly's 'bout got our noonin' ready. Know there's coffee in there, an' I'll bet I can scare up a jug if I look hard enough."

"Reckon I can use all three. Fact is, I'll take a drink first." Sanders rubbed his rear end. "I haven't spent this many hours in the saddle since I can remember. Saddle sore won't cover it. I'm sore all over."

Granger chuckled. "You city boys just ain't tough enough for this country." He poured them each a drink, looked at Molly, and nodded. "Reckon this here's a special day. Gonna pour you a drink, too, little one."

While they nursed their drinks, Sanders told them why he'd followed Gant to Bannack, and about the gunfight in, and outside, the Last Gulp Saloon.

"What in the name of heaven you go in there alone for?"

"Only way I could be sure what Gant was up to."

Granger only stared at him, shaking his head.

Sanders took another swallow of his drink, then frowned. "Fact is I'm not absolutely certain even now, but putting two and two together I think it's better'n even odds he was gathering a bunch to do you in.

"Clinton's been heard blaming you for his loss of men, and threatening to get even. Gant's done a number of crooked jobs for him—none of which I could prove in a court of law, but I have no doubts about his guilt." He spread his hands, palms up. "All I'm asking, Colt, is that you be especially careful."

Granger nodded, and Molly jumped up to tend her meal. Granger knew the meal didn't need tending; she got busy to hide her fear for him. The two men sat there amid the smells of cooking food, the scent of pipe smoke and bourbon whiskey, and had another drink.

Sanders stayed with them three days, then saddled his horse. "If I don't get on the road, I'll have all this soreness to go through again. Don't think I could stand that." They watched until the lawyer again became small in the distance. Then Molly placed her hand in the crook of Colt's arm, and they turned toward the cabin.

She looked at him, her eyes swimming in tears. "Will it never end, Colt? I go to bed scared, and wake up with fear for you. I don't know what I'd do if something happened to take you from me."

"Gonna see you don't have to worry 'bout that; gonna make everything comfortable an' safe for you."

She took her hand from his arm and, sobbing, ran into the cabin. Granger squinted at the door as it closed, wondering what he'd said that brought on the tears—it wasn't like her to break down and cry. He went in to comfort her.

Ike Burrage finished tying his bedroll to his saddle, looked across it to see his brother coming, and, not wanting to listen to any maudlin words of comfort, toed the stirrup and rode out. He figured to make Bannack in less than a week. There he would find people who thought like he did.

He didn't know why he'd put up with Morrie as long as

he had—except he'd always been able to count on him taking his part when it came to knock-down-drag-out fighting. His hand brushed the walnut handle of his six-shooter. *He* could handle anyone who wanted to make it handguns. If that bastard Granger had given him half a chance, he'd have blown his Indian-loving head off. Drew on him while he was down, and Morrie doing nothing about it—well, next time it would be different. The farther he rode, the more convinced he was that he was a better man than either his brother or Granger.

His brother. Now there was a milksop if he'd ever seen one. He always found something good to say about people regardless how wrong they were. And damned Indians, pitching their lodges right at a white man's doorstep like—well, hell, like they were as good as a white man, and his brother thinking it was all right for them to do as they liked, thinking it was none of his business. He'd never be able to understand the way Morrie thought.

Three days later, when he rode into Bannack, he'd convinced himself he was better with a handgun than any of the gunfighters who had reputations.

His first stop was in the Miner's Rest. After one drink, he scanned the crowd, noticed they were mostly clean, except those who'd just left their diggings, and, although boisterous, showed others courtesy. He shook his head and muttered, "These ain't my kind o' people." He left, and if pressed, he couldn't have said exactly why he thought the men in that particular saloon were not his kind. He next stopped in the Last Gulp, and immediately felt at home. He didn't question the difference.

A glance at those lined up at the bar showed him men of every shape and size. He swaggered to a vacant spot next to a huge man, maybe six feet, four inches tall, and built like a bear.

"Buy you a drink, stranger?"

The bear looked down at him. "You the stranger in here, little man. Naw, I don't want a drink. I buy my own."

Burrage stepped away from the bar. "First off, mister, this hog leg I got at my side makes me big as you. Second place,

I wuz jest tryin' to be friendly. I'll ask you again. Buy you a drink, mister?''

The big man threw back his head and laughed, a belly laugh that came from the bottom of his chest. ''All right. I'll take whiskey and branch water.'' He glanced at Burrage's revolver. ''You any good with that thing?''

Ike figured he had the giant buffaloed, but felt good having a big man at his side. ''Reckon I never seed nobody any better.'' His glance swept the big man. ''See you don't pack a six-shooter.''

The giant held up a fist the size of a ham. ''Don't need to. This here'll take care of most men, an' kill 'em just as dead.'' He stuck out his hand. ''People call me Swede.'' He laughed again. ''Think maybe 'cause that's what I am, a big Swede. What they call you?''

''Ike Burrage. You ain't heerd about me, but you will.''

The big man took a swallow of his drink. ''Call me Swede, or Johansen, don't make no difference—but talkin' bout you an' that six-shooter, they's a man over in Virginia City lookin' for gunhands. Name's Clinton. You get over that way, stop in to see 'im. Might get a job doin' somethin' you like.''

Burrage signaled the bartender to pour another round. ''Clinton, you say? What's he want done?''

Johansen took another swallow of his drink, almost downed it with the one swallow. ''Ain't gonna say what he's hirin' for, but know he's got a big hate on for a guy named Granger. Might have somethin' to do with that.''

Ike's eyes squinted. How lucky could he get? He looked at the Swede. ''You reckon he wants Granger fixed so's he won't cause nobody any trouble?''

Johansen nodded. ''Sounds that a way to me, an' he's payin' good money to get it done.''

Burrage tried to hide his wolfish grin. ''Hell, Swede, I'd almost take Granger on for nothin'—but I ain't tellin' Clinton that. A man can always use something more to jingle in his pockets.''

Swede knocked back his drink, nodded his thanks, and left. Burrage drank slowly, thinking of what he'd been told.

He caressed the walnut handle of his revolver with gentle fingers. Yep, he could use some extra change, especially if it involved shooting the Indian lover.

When he left the Last Gulp, he glanced at the purple shadows silently pushing their way across the land, and was surprised it had gotten so late. He went to the livery and arranged to sleep in the haymow.

The next morning he'd had breakfast and was an hour toward Virginia City when the sun appeared from behind the mountains. In time for his nooning, he reached the Grasshopper, and had coffee boiling when he heard a horse approaching, then a voice. "Hello the camp."

"Come on in an' step down. Got a pot o' mud jest 'bout ready for drinkin'."

The stranger stepped down and held out his hand. "Ted Benning here, headin' back home to Virginia City. Had a little business in Bannack. You headin' that way?"

Burrage watched while Benning took his cup and cooking gear from behind his saddle. "Yeah, I got some business with a man by the name o' Clinton. You know 'im?"

Benning felt his scalp tighten. He walked to the other side of his horse so Burrage couldn't see and thumbed the thong from the hammer of his Colt, then loosened the cinches so as to let his horse breathe. He looked across his saddle at Burrage and frowned. "Don't know him personally, but hear he's a right wealthy man. Got business with him, huh?" He might as well play it cozy, see what this man would tell him.

Burrage poured them each a cup of coffee. "Yeah, man back yonder in Bannack told me to see 'im. Said he figured as how Clinton might be lookin' for a man good with a gun." He grinned. "Reckon I fit the bill." He patted his holster.

Benning felt himself go quiet inside. So now Clinton was hiring gunhands. He'd better see Fisk Sanders as soon as he got to town. He took out a gunnysack of provisions, ready to slice bacon and put it on the fire.

Burrage shook his head. "Naw now, no need for that. I done sliced enough for the both of us, an' I'll share this tin o' beans with you."

Benning didn't want to be beholden to this man, but didn't want to seem unfriendly; he might learn something of value to Sanders. He grinned at Ike. "Never was any good with a handgun. Always wanted to be, but never could afford practice cartridges." He shrugged. "Reckon the only way I'll ever get any money ahead is pannin' for it. Got me a little claim along Alder Gulch. Ain't gettin' much dust outta it; fact is it's barely buyin' me tobacco an' food, but one of these days I figure I'll hit a rich pocket."

Burrage smirked. "Cain't all o' us be good with a gun—even with practice. I'm one o' the lucky ones."

They ate their meal, tightened the cinches, toed the stirrups, and headed for Alder Gulch, with Burrage bragging about his gun-quick all the way. Didn't either of them mention Granger until just outside of Virginia City, then Ike twisted in his saddle and looked at Benning. "Hear tell Clinton's got a burr under his saddle for a man named Granger who used to live along the gulch. You know anything 'bout him?"

Benning frowned, pushed his hat to the back of his head, and squinted against the bright sunlight. "Granger? Granger? Cain't say as I recollect the name." He grinned. "But then, that ain't no wonder; there's a many a man comes an' goes along Stinkin' Water Crick from day to day."

Burrage nodded. "Reckon that's a fact."

They rode in silence until they parted in the middle of town. Benning reined in in front of Sanders's office and went in.

After shaking hands, the young lawyer, with a slight smile, shook his head. "Didn't think you'd ever have legal problems, Ted. What brings you to my office?"

Benning, always barging into a subject head-on, said, "Fisk, Clinton's hirin' guns, an' from what I could figure, they all gonna be aimed at Granger."

"What makes you think that?"

Benning told him about his meeting with Burrage, told him almost verbatim the conversation they'd had—and he told him his opinion of Burrage. "Fisk, if he's the best Clinton can dig up, he's in deep trouble. The man I met is a

braggart. Hell, Colt'll chew him up and spit 'im out in little
chunks, but there may be others who're not all mouth.''

Sanders toyed with a few sheets of paper on his desk, shuffled them into a neat pile, and looked up. "When I was in
Bannack, I took a side trip. Went to see Colt and warn him.
There're others who are watching and will write him who to
look out for. They aren't gonna catch him by surprise, and
I'd hate to be the man to pull a gun on him. Granger's a curly
wolf from way back. Unless they get him from behind, or attack him in a pack, he'll take care of himself.''

Benning scowled. "You reckon I oughtta ride over to Hell
Gate an' back 'im ?''

Sanders shook his head. "You'd only be in the way. I've
heard Granger talk, and to his way of thinking, a man alone
in a gunfight is better off if he doesn't have to watch out to
not shoot his friends. No. Stay here, and if we hear anything
that might be of value to Colt, we'll write him.''

Benning pulled his sack of Bull Durham from his pocket,
fashioned a tightly rolled cigarette, lit it, and stared at the
floor. "Damn, wish there was something I could do to help
that cowboy. I sure regard him as some sort of a man.''

Sanders looked through the film of smoke at the miner.
"Ted, whether we like it or not, law has come to this town.
Yeah, it often stands in the way of justice, but we have to allow for that, give it a chance to work. The only way we could
help Colt now would be to set the Vigilantes back into operation, and now, without proof, we'd probably hang a lot of innocent people. I don't want that, and I don't believe you do
either.''

Benning shook his head. "No, Fisk, but it sure is hard to
stand by an' do nothing.''

Clinton banked on the very thing Sanders had mentioned—
the lack of proof of any wrongdoing on his part, and the fact
that law would protect him, as it had seemed to in most cases.
The lawless got more protection than those who lived within
the law's bounds.

He looked up when a man of less than medium height,
with trail dust covering him, and needing a shave, pushed

through the front door. One thing he did like was the tied-down holster on the man's right side. "What can I do for you, stranger?"

"Name's Ike Burrage, Mr. Clinton. Man over in Bannack told me you was hirin' fast guns. I'm lookin' for a job."

Clinton studied the dirty man for a long few seconds, long enough that Burrage squirmed. "What makes you think you're fast?"

Ike's face reddened. "Mister, I'm still here. Figure that says it all."

Used to making quick judgments, Clinton pegged the dirty man as a braggart right off. "Don't say a damned thing to me. You probably ain't never been tested. Why you think I'd hire you?"

Clinton's words obviously angered Burrage even more. "Reckon, from what I heered, you an' me want the same man dead. I got good reason to hate Colt Granger. Don't know your reason, but hear you don't like 'im much either."

A slight smile puckered the folds of fat around Clinton's eyes. He looked out of the slits it made. From what he could see of the man in front of him, he didn't think he'd last past one shot in a stand-up gunfight with Granger. Yeah, he hated the cowboy's guts—but respected him as a fighting man. If he had a dozen men like Granger, he figured he could take the whole territory. He didn't know what territory they were calling it today. It had been Washington and Idaho, and some thought of it as Montana Territory. He pulled a sheet of paper in front of him.

"Tell you what I'm gonna do. There's a name on this paper I want you to remember." He pulled another sheet in front of him, a map. "This here spikes out where every claim along Alder Gulch is." He pointed with a fat finger. "The man who owns this claim," he tapped the map, "this claim right here, is the one whose name I'll give you. I want him brought to me. Tell 'im I want to buy his claim. If you get any argument outta him—make 'im disappear. Don't leave anybody around who sees what you do." He grinned up at Burrage. "You do that, an' you got the job huntin' Granger.

You get a thousand dollars when you bring me proof he's dead.''

Burrage swallowed twice, hard. He hadn't figured on killin' anybody but Granger. He looked at the fat man behind the desk. ''I gotta take care o' this miner 'fore you give me the job o' gettin that cowboy?''

Clinton nodded, slowly. ''See you got the picture, mister. You do it my way. They ain't no other way, so take it or leave it.''

Burrage again swallowed. Killing for hate was one thing, but killing a man he didn't know was an entirely different sort of thing. But he was near broke. He had only fifteen dollars in his pocket. He thought on it a few moments, stared at the papers on Clinton's desk, then looked up. ''What you gonna pay me to take care o' that miner?''

Clinton's face took on an oily, satisfied look. He smiled, his cheeks again swallowing his eyes. ''You get fifty dollars if you bring him to me. If you have to get rid of him beforehand, and I get title to his claim, you get a hundred.''

''I got time to think on this?''

The fat man shook his head. ''You give me an answer now,'' a cold, frozen look came to his eyes, ''or you don't walk outta here.''

Ike looked at Clinton's hand. It held a double-barreled hideout gun, and the maw of the muzzles looked big as those on a 12-gauge Greener. He didn't know where the fat man had gotten the gun, he'd not seen him reach for it, but there it was. He sweated. His face dripped with it, and it soaked his shirt; his armpits felt slimy with it. He jerked his head in a choppy nod. ''Yes, sir, it'll be just as you said, Mr. Clinton. I'll have that man here in a couple o' days.''

''Uh-uh. You'll have him here 'fore sundown—today. Unnerstan'? Today.''

''Yes, sir. Yes, sir.'' Burrage backed to the door and left—in a hurry.

Clinton looked over his shoulder toward the door to his living quarters. ''Follow him, Gant. See he don't turn yellow an' mess up his assignment. If he does, you know what to do.''

Gant, with never a word, slipped past Clinton and out the door.

The fat man stared at the closed door, not seeing it. He had nine men he thought he could count on to do anything he wanted done, and then there was Burrage. He didn't like the man; fact was, he didn't like any of the men who did his bidding, they were no more than tools—but Burrage? Clinton shook his head. The braggy little pistolero wouldn't last a week.

His thoughts went to the mining claims. He had but two left. He'd sold twenty of them gotten by theft, or outright murder. Neither means of acquisition bothered him. If a miner stood in his way, and wasn't smart enough to beat him at his game, then he asked for what he got.

He added a column of figures, and nodded. With one or two more claims he should have enough to leave this stinking place of sorry food, bad whiskey, and trashy people. But . . . He'd make certain Granger was dead before he left. He realized he still held the Derringer and slipped it into his vest pocket.

Gant followed Burrage, who went to the livery, where he saddled, toed the stirrup, mounted, pulled his rifle from its scabbard, and held it across the saddle in front of him. Then he rode off in the direction of the claim Clinton had pointed out on the map.

Ike had no feeling he was followed. He was too worried about what he had been told to do, but he needed money. "Thatcher," the name on the paper Clinton held in front of him, had been until now only a name, but he was about to put a face to it.

In the vicinity of the claim, Burrage stepped from the saddle and began questioning men knee deep in the stream, trying to shake every bit of dust out of the creek before it froze over. They shoveled sand and gravel into pans, shook them, and sloshed water over their sides until they had nothing left but the heavier flakes of gold remaining in the bottom.

Finally one of the miners pointed to a tall, thin man at the edge of the stream. "Yonder's the man you asked about.

He's got himself a right nice claim there. He's hit several good pockets and taken a sizable amount of dust from them.''

Burrage studied the thin miner a moment, then turned his attention back to the man who'd furnished him information. ''You reckon he'd sell?''

The man shook his head. ''Naw. Don't see why he would. He's doin' right well where he is. If he sold, he'd only go to another crick somewheres and start lookin' again.''

Ike nodded, thanked the man, and rode to Thatcher. The man looked up from a pan into which he'd only at that moment shoveled more sand and gravel. ''Help you, stranger?''

Burrage nodded and dismounted. ''Yep, if you're Thatcher.'' He looked at the pan, then back to the miner. ''Gettin' much color here?'' At the man's nod, the gunman looked him in the eye. ''Know a man what will buy you out, only he wants to see you 'fore sundown.''

Thatcher was shaking his head before Ike finished. ''Ain't no reason to sell. My wife an' kids have new clothes, a comfortable place to live, and food on the table. No, sir. I ain't about to sell.''

Burrage had hoped it wouldn't come to this. At that time, a tall, thin youngster came up with a tin cup of steaming coffee and handed it to Thatcher. ''Thanks, son. I wuz gettin' right cold.'' He sipped the steaming liquid, pursed his lips, and blew. Then again looked at Ike. ''My son,'' he said by way of explanation. ''He helps me right smart, does his share o' pannin'.'' He shook his head. ''No, sir. I ain't gonna sell my claim to nobody.''

''You ought to at least hear what my boss is gonna offer.''

Again, Thatcher shook his head. ''Ain't interested.''

Ike's face hardened, feeling stiff as cardboard. He nodded, and climbed on his horse. It came down to his second choice. Now he had to kill the man. But what would that accomplish? Thatcher had a son who could take over the claim and do the same work his father was doing, although not in as great a volume as the both of them.

Burrage worried that around a few moments, then decided Clinton wouldn't stop until he'd had him kill the boy, too.

Frowning, he looked down at his rifle; he'd been carrying it across his saddle all the while. He slipped it into the scabbard, reined his horse toward town, then changed his mind. To hell with it. He needed money—but not bad enough to kill a man and a boy for it, a man and a boy he didn't even know, a man and a boy who had done nothing to him. He'd find a job somewhere else. He headed his horse toward Helena. He'd heard it was an up-and-coming town. He looked at the sun, now only a little past noon. He could make several miles before sundown—and he wanted Virginia City as far behind him as he could put it. He'd not unpacked his saddlebags, so he had trail provisions.

After riding about an hour, he sensed he didn't ride alone. His neck and shoulder muscles pulled tight. He had a strange emptiness in his gut. Someone followed. He reined off the rutted road into the woods, thought to sit his horse in the shadows and see if perhaps it was only another traveler, then decided to ride on, but stay to the shadows.

The sun slipped toward the horizon, shadows lengthened, and when only a purple light showed above the western mountains, Burrage drew rein, the feeling of being followed still with him. He'd been riding the side of a mountain; tumbled rocks, some of them as big as a small, one-room cabin, lay along the slope, most held in place by more stubborn boulders that refused to take their place at the bottom. He dismounted and pulled his horse into a sheltered pile of the larger rocks, stripped the gear off, and set up camp. He gathered sticks and firewood, set his fire—and decided to have a cold camp. If things felt right by morning, he'd cook then. While chewing a strip of jerky, he placed his rifle on his blankets and his handgun by the saddle, so that he could reach each of them from where he lay.

Not over thirty minutes behind, Gant studied the tracks of Burrage's horse where they left the trail, and had no trouble following them through the woods. He shook his head. The would-be gunfighter was sure as hell no woodsman. He didn't even have sense enough to cover his trail. Then Gant wondered what had caused the braggart to take any precautions at all. What had made him suspicious?

Maybe he knew Clinton would not let him live if he tried to get out of his agreement. If he suspected he was followed, maybe he'd pulled off to lure the man who trailed him into an ambush. Gant slipped the thong off his six-shooter and pulled his rifle from its scabbard, holding it pistol-fashion in his left hand. He studied every boulder, tree, dip in the path, for sign of a hiding place, walking his horse slowly enough to allow him to study the route ahead.

When the sun dropped behind the western peaks, darkness soon followed. He pulled farther into the trees and unrolled his blankets. This work could be done easier, and safer, by daylight. Before sleeping, he sprinkled branches and aspen leaves around the perimeter of his camp to warn of anyone trying to slip up on him. Then he crawled between his blankets. Satisfied he'd done all he could to maintain safety, he soon slept.

He awakened to a chill, damp morning, long before sunup. Along with the scent of pine and fir, another smell intruded. The faint aroma of woodsmoke. Not what he'd expect from a forest fire, but enough to tell him someone had a fire nearby, a small one, but enough to cook over.

He left his horse tethered, and his camp set up as on the night before. He slipped from tree to tree, stopped behind large rocks, and searched everything ahead that could hide a man or a camp. Then he saw a thin column of white smoke rise skyward from the middle of a large cluster of boulders. Still carrying his rifle in his left hand, Gant pulled his six-shooter.

His look scrubbed down every opening between the rocks, every edge, every top of them, for a man, or rifle—only then did he move farther toward his prey. Finally, he reached the base of the largest boulder, hugged close to its base, and worked his way toward where he knew the fire lay. It came to his sight first, then a pair of boots sitting by spread blankets. His eyes never moved from the blankets. The ratcheting of a gun coming to full cock broke the silence. The sound came from his left. He froze.

14

GANT KEPT HIS hands wide of his guns. "Why hold a cocked gun on me, stranger? I come in peace."

Burrage dropped the rifle to his side, holding it pistol-fashion, still pointed at Gant. "Yep, I cocked it, an' it's got a shell in the chamber. A man comin' in peace don't sneak up on a man's camp. Turn your back to me, drop that rifle, then unbuckle your gunbelt an' let it drop round your feet."

Clinton's lackey did as told, thinking that if he could talk long enough for Burrage to drop his guard, maybe he could get the little Derringer in his vest pocket into action. He'd learned from Clinton that a hideout was some of the best insurance a man could have.

"You come in peace, why you slip up on my camp carryin' a rifle ready to shoot?"

Gant looked over his shoulder. "A man doesn't know whether those he's about to meet is friendly or not. Just thought I'd be ready."

"Who sent you?"

The smooth gunny thought to lie, then decided to bend the truth a little. "Mr. Clinton thought you might get cold feet. He sent me to see if I might convince you to earn the money he's willing to pay. You can't earn that kind of money doing anything else around here. He has some pretty good men working for him, but you impressed him as being a right salty dude. That's why he wanted you to do the job.'' Gant threw in those last words thinking to appeal to the braggart's ego. ''How 'bout me turnin' around and putting my hands down?''

''All right, but step away from your guns, an' stay on that side o' the fire.''

Gant turned slowly, glanced at the fire, and shrugged. ''You have a fire going, so why don't we put on a pot of mud and talk this over?''

The braggart nodded. ''Water's in my canteen. You make the coffee. We'll talk, but there ain't much to say. I done made up my mind.''

Gant poured water into the pot, threw a couple handfuls of grounds in, sat the pot by the fire, and stood back, hooking his thumbs in his vest pockets. ''You gonna make me stand here until the coffee's ready, or can I sit?''

''Sit, but stay clear of your guns.''

Burrage kept his finger hooked inside the trigger guard, still holding the rifle pistol-fashion. To Gant's way of thinking the braggart hadn't relaxed a bit. Maybe when he poured himself a cup of coffee . . .

The coffee finally ready, Gant slopped cold water from the canteen into the pot to settle the grounds, and looked toward Burrage. ''Where's your cup?''

''Over yonder by my saddle. Get it. I'll drink first.''

Gant picked up the cup, thinking that when Burrage poured he'd have to look at the cup to see when it was filled—then would be Gant's chance. He handed the cup to the little gunman and again hooked his thumbs into his vest pockets.

Burrage stooped, poured a moment, then glanced at his cup, but the rifle muzzle never wavered from its bead on Gant. The smooth-talking gunny thought this was his only chance. His finger hooked the Derringer from his pocket and came level, but something was wrong. The rifle in Burrage's hand spat fire and smoke. Gant pulled the trigger, but saw no hole punched into the braggart's chest. He made a dive for his six-shooter, but fell short. His legs didn't seem to have any strength. He landed short of his weapons by five or six feet. He crawled to his knees to try for his handgun, and saw a pool of red where he'd fallen. Looked like blood. His blood. He swung his head to look at Burrage.

The little braggart stood there gazing at him, his mouth hanging open, his face white as those little gumbo lilies he'd seen over in Eastern Montana, then his eyes seemed to have trouble seeing. Burrage's image faded. He tried again to focus, and to reach his handgun, but nothing worked. His knees folded, and he became aware his cheek lay in the dirt. Why did he lie here when he had a man in front of him needing to be shot? The bright morning light faded to a gray—then black.

Burrage stared at the dead man in front of him, a man he'd shot. His stomach turned over. He ran to the side of the camp and retched, then threw up. Killing a man wasn't what he'd thought it to be. Trembling, he went to his horse and saddled up. By then his nerves settled enough for him to think.

Still shaking, he tried twice to loosen Gant's trousers enough to strip the money belt from his waist. Finally he got them loose enough to drag the heavy belt free. He shook it, and whatever it held jingled. It had to be gold coins; men kept other money in their pants pockets. He went through the dead man's pockets, took money from them, a Green River knife, and a couple of brass .44 cartridges. Then he picked up Gant's guns, backtracked him, and took his horse. He collected his own gear and headed for Helena—and beyond, if it took that to forget gunfighting.

Burrage had put several miles behind him when Granger opened the four envelopes a messenger had brought only an hour or so before. He read each of them. They all said essentially the same thing. They were from Fisk Sanders's friends. Each gave him six names, and a description of each of the six Clinton had hired to rid the country of him. Gant's name was on every list. Only one of the letters differed from the rest. It added that two of the men had left Bannack to talk to Clinton, then they headed for Hell Gate Canyon, and would now come through it and head for his cabin. He sighed, a tight feeling in his chest.

He took his Henry from the wall rack and proceeded to clean and oil it, then did the same for his Colt. Molly stood by the fireplace staring at him.

"You gettin' ready to start a war, Colt?"

He glanced at her, then back to his handgun. "Reckon so, little one. I have the names of six men who're being paid to collect my scalp."

"You gonna wait here for 'em?"

He shook his head. "Gonna see if I cain't meet two of 'em in the canyon. Figure I'll stand a better chance there. Most of the men who hung around those in the Henry Plummer gang ain't much for knowin' their way in a stalkin' Injun-type fight. I figure I can out-Injun 'em."

"I'm goin' with you this time, an' I ain't hearin' no ifs, an's, or buts about it. You hear that, Colt Granger?" She didn't raise her voice, but her words came out strong.

He opened his mouth to argue, then clamped it tight shut before he said, "Clean an' oil your weapons. Pack three boxes o' ammunition, an' trail provisions for a week. We'll take a packhorse with us.

"Far as I know, there'll be only the two of 'em comin' through the canyon. When we get back here, we'll have four more to contend with." He gave her a tight grin. "Reckon whatever they're gettin' paid ain't gonna be enough to buy 'em a good funeral."

Molly looked like her folks had just given her permission to go to a country dance.

"What you so happy 'bout woman? We could get ourselves killed."

She gave him a no-nonsense look. "Yeah, but I'm gonna be with you—whatever happens I'll share it with you. That's the main thing, Colt. I just don't wantta be away from you." She smiled. " 'Sides that, I know you can take care of me."

He looked at his revolver, stared at it. Why was it every time they faced a crisis she seemed to think he could take care of anything they faced? Her faith in him made him uncomfortable. He was only human. What if he failed her? Would he leave her at the mercy of some trash who would violate her? And in the canyon there would be danger of Blackfeet. At the very least, they'd make a slave of her, with constant beatings from the women of the tribe. As long as he breathed, he'd never let her be taken by anyone; he loved her too much to think of anyone touching her body unless she approved. His thinking shifted to the two men he hoped to meet in Hell Gate Canyon, two men whose bodies would add to the ground already painted with both Indian and white man's blood.

This was a hard land, a land where a body had to fight for every moment of peace he was likely to get. Yet it was no different from any land in history. Men had fought over land, and the right to live in peace, since small groups lived in caves, and others had fought to establish feudal empires, and still others had sought to conquer vast continents. He looked at Molly. "By my reckoning, them two men will reach the canyon in a day or two. We'll meet 'em somewhere in there. We gonna ride just far enough to find a good place to fort up, an' let 'em come to us."

She ran a clean cloth through her Whitney's barrel, peered down its length, nodded, and put oil on the cloth. "When we leavin'?"

Granger stood. "Soon's we get our bedrolls tied behind our pack saddles."

"We stayin' in the canyon all the way?"

Granger nodded. "We won't have a wagon to cause us problems, but neither will those huntin' me. Saddle up, an' close the door. I'll stay inside, bar it, pull the latch string in, an' leave by our little secret door. I done hid our poke in the cliff's wall so nobody'll find it while we're gone."

They were soon headed toward the canyon. Every once in a while Colt stole a sidewise glance at Molly. Each time his throat swelled with both shame and longing—shame because he saw her as a beautiful, desirable woman, and longing to be able to accept her as grown. Not as his almost-daughter, but as a woman a man could meet without any moral ties.

Mentally, he shook his head. As soon as he could get those who hunted him off his trail and knew she'd be safe, he'd better pack his bedroll and look for new ground. If he didn't, he feared he'd do something he'd be forever ashamed of. He might ask her to marry him, and he was afraid she'd say yes out of gratitude. A man just flat didn't marry his almost-daughter, didn't marry anyone due to gratitude.

They rode in a comfortable silence until they saw the mouth of Hell Gate. The river, set free of constraining walls, spread wider when it entered the valley. The setting sun bathed the hills bordering the canyon's mouth in a golden glow; the few autumnal, needlelike leaves of the tamarack would cling to the limbs until deep cold and snow freed them of the branches. Pine and fir dotted the entrance to the canyon. Molly gasped. "I'll swanee, Colt, this must be the most beautiful place on earth."

He chuckled. "Little one, seems like you say them same words every time we look on this sight."

She bristled. "Seein' it a million times don't make it any less pretty."

"Yeah, but if we get caught in a snowstorm out here away from our warm cabin, you might see it in a different light."

She shook her head. "No matter what, it'll still tug on my heartstrings."

As long as they had had rolling hills in front of them, Colt had ridden relaxed, but now he tensed. They were coming into terrain made for ambush, and he became another man. His eyes constantly scanned the sides of the hills, which in places had been eroded into steep cliffs. Tumbled boulders lined the sides of the slopes, and the deeper they penetrated the gorge, the more they saw heavy timber lining the river's edge and climbing the sides until it hid the remaining daylight like a curtain.

Finally, seeing a shelf about thirty feet above the water's edge, he led them toward it. "We'll make camp on that ledge yonder. Upstream gully-washers shouldn't bother us there."

As soon as they reined their horses in, Molly jumped down and proceeded to set up camp. She spread groundsheets and bedrolls, placed saddles at their head, put rifles and ammunition at the side, and took food from saddlebags.

Colt searched for firewood and started the fire. A glance showed him Molly busy slicing bacon into a frying pan. She'd placed a large tin of beans to her side. He marveled at the efficient way she went about things; whether in her cabin, alongside a dusty trail out on the plains, or here in an Indian-infested canyon, she never wasted a motion. She'd do for any man to ride the river with. He wished he was the one.

The next morning they penetrated the canyon farther. Clouds had rolled in overnight, turning the deep canyon to twilight. Frowning, Colt glanced at the sky, certain that the heavy, leaden overcast signaled snow. He wished Molly had stayed at the cabin, but then he'd have worried for her safety, worried that some of the six who hunted him might have already set their sites on finding him there, and if they found her alone, were they the kind who'd harm a woman?

While riding, Granger pondered how far they should go before setting up to await the coming of those who would do him harm. If they rode too far, they were likely to ride into the two with no warning. He decided to make camp that night in a place they could defend, as well as one from which they could launch an attack. Now, he looked for a stronghold, one which would be sheltered from the weather, for he was now certain snow would fall before night set in.

About mid-afternoon, by his best judgment—it was only a guess because there was no sun to go by—he saw what he wanted: a shelf with a cavelike hollow in its side. Over perhaps hundreds of years the river had carved out the softest of the sandstone and undercut the cliff against which it flowed, at the same time cutting its channel deeper into the gorge, and dropping its water level forty or fifty feet below the cave. Granger had seen places like this down in the New Mexico Territory, where the Ancient Ones had built their kivas. The shelf in front of the cave held rocks the size of buckboards. He nodded. He would put Molly behind one of them, where she'd not likely catch a slug.

He studied the cave a few moments, then nodded again. "Set up camp under that overhang. It's gonna come on to snow right soon. I'll close the cave off so's we'll be right comfortable.'' He took his ax and went into the woods. He cut slim saplings and stood them upright against the over-hang, then wove pine branches between the poles to shut off the outside.

After setting up camp, Molly watched what he did for a while, then obviously getting the idea, she worked at his side until dark shut them down. Colt took his ax inside the cave-like structure and looked longingly at the food Molly had set out, ready for cooking. It took him only a few moments to get a fire going, then he picked up the coffeepot and four canteens, and headed for the river. Having spotted a deadfall a few yards from camp, he thought to wait until after they'd eaten to chop and drag in enough wood to last a couple of days.

Before he got back with the water, large flakes floated gently to the ground. He held out his hand and caught a couple of the white, feathery bits of frozen water, which immediately melted. "Gonna get worse 'fore it get better,'' he mumbled. "Bet them two jaspers ain't gonna be as com-fortable as me an' Molly.'' He checked the wind to be sure it was from upstream, and grinned. They could have a nice fire—and he could smoke his pipe without fear of smoke smell warning the gunmen.

Back in the cave, he stoked the fire to knock the chill off their temporary home, waited until he could rake a bed of coals to the side, then helped Molly fix supper. He thought to stand watch, then decided the men hunting him would be fools to ride the canyon at night. Too, they had no reason to be in a hurry, no reason to believe he'd been warned. He figured to be on the lookout every minute of daylight, but would rest and thaw out during the dark hours. Before re-laxing with his pipe, he collected wood.

He woke several times during the night and threw more sticks on the fire, while pondering the idea of buying himself a watch. He ought to buy Molly one, too. She needed to know the time as much as he did. When he guessed it to be an hour or so before dawn, he stood, put on his hat, pulled on his boots, got the fire blazing, and went to the river to again fill the four canteens they'd brought, along with the coffeepot. He didn't want to get stranded on that shelf with no water, and the gunmen sitting where they had plenty.

After eating, he shrugged into his sheepskin, picked up his rifle, checked its magazine, his revolver, and looked at Molly. "Gonna stand watch. I'll come in ever so often to warm a bit. Want you to keep watch while I'm in here."

She glanced at him, nodded, and said, "Be careful."

When he stepped outside, snow came almost to his knees. Down here in the canyon the wind was quiet, but up above it whistled and moaned through the trees. A slight smile crinkled the corners of his eyes. The men hunting him would surely earn their pay. On top, they'd buck a blizzard. Down here, they and their horses had deep snow to fight.

The two men—Buck Stratford and Chip Bowdeen, as named in the letter—should be easy to recognize, especially Bowdeen, who had a purple birthmark on his right cheek. Stratford, lean and hungry-looking, would fit the mold of many men, but traveling with Bowdeen would spike him out as the second of the two.

Granger again thought through the trail from Virginia City to where he now sat, and decided he might be watching as much as a day too soon, maybe more with the deep snow. If he saw game of any kind, he thought he'd not be taking much of a chance if he tried for fresh meat.

Once during the morning, he went back to the cave to warm while Molly watched. The storm didn't let up; in fact, he thought it got heavier. About sundown, he heard a thrashing through the trees. He tensed, trained his rifle upstream— and waited.

A six-point buck slipped down the embankment, tested the air, and lowered his head to drink. Granger sighted just back of the buck's shoulder and squeezed off a shot. The deer jumped straight up, and crumpled at the water's edge. Before Colt could move toward the animal, Molly rushed to his side, rifle cocked.

"What's the matter? They comin'?"

He shook his head. "Shot a buck. You stand here and cover me in case I misjudged how far they mighta come.

Don't think they're out yonder yet, figure the snow slowed 'em down. But just in case . . .''

He jacked another shell into the chamber and moved down the slope toward the buck. He dressed it where it had dropped, then in two trips took every eatable piece back to the cave. After carving off a couple of steaks, he hung the rest from a limb, high enough that he thought a bear, or mountain lion, couldn't get at it. It would freeze at these temperatures mighty fast. When he finished with the deer, night had set in.

He walked out of their shelter and checked that no reflection of their fire could be seen from either direction. When he went back inside, Molly had supper ready.

They stayed put for three more days, days in which Granger began to wonder if the two had come this way after all. Molly showed signs of getting antsy, wanting to go ahead, or go home. "Colt, let's go ahead. Let's go lookin' for them."

He shook his head. "We'll give 'em two more days. If they don't show by then, I figure the cold an' snow done 'em in, or the Blackfeet got 'em. Don't put much credit to that last, though, 'cause Injuns don't like bein' out in weather like this any more'n we do. Two more days an' we'll head for home.''

Molly had broiled a large roast and they sat eating supper. Colt sliced off another bite, chewed, and swallowed, all the while studying Molly. "Gonna tell you somethin', woman, when they do get here, you ain't gonna rush outside to help me fight 'em like you did when I shot the buck. I'm gonna take 'em on down at the river's edge, and you gonna stay up here behind a rock an' see if you can see anything I'm missin'.'' He swallowed a gulp of coffee and continued. "Be safer that way, safer for you, an' safer for me. You'll see things from here I'll miss.''

The next morning, Granger, lifting his knees high, trudged through the crusty snow to a boulder by the river's edge. He huddled deeper into his sheepskin and turned his eyes upstream, using his ears more than his eyes. With the icy crust on the snow, he figured he'd hear them long before they came in sight, what with the heavy timber growing almost to the water's edge.

He sat there through the morning, and on into the afternoon, not asking Molly to spell him. If they came, he didn't want her down there where she might draw fire. About three o'clock by his best guess, snow still falling, he thought he heard a sound upstream. He eased down to ground level and peered around the rock. Then he heard the crust break again. It might be another animal. He didn't take a chance. A shell already in the chamber, he eased the Henry's hammer back— and waited, now trusting his eyes.

Then, two men came in sight, each leading a horse. Except for the situation, Granger would have laughed. They were the sorriest lot he'd ever seen—bearded, hollow-cheeked, eyes sunk into their drooping heads. The horses, heads hanging, ribs showing through their winter coat, moved one weary leg in front of the other. He had more pity for the animals than the men who led them. He waited until they were within revolver range.

15

THE TWO WEREN'T looking ahead. Heads down, they plodded along, looking about to fall at any minute. Granger stepped around the boulder. "Hold it right there. Move an' you catch lead."

They stopped, staring at him, making no move for their guns. Granger grinned to himself. They couldn't have reached a weapon if they'd tried; rifles in saddle scabbards and handguns buttoned under heavy coats put any firearms out of reach. He studied them, now certain these were the men he had expected. The heavier of the two had a deep-purple birthmark on his right cheek. "What you men doin' out here in this weather?"

Bowdeen answered. "Might ask you the same question. Figure it's as cold there by that rock as it is here. But we're tryin' to reach that settlement they're callin' Hell Gate. If it's any more hell than this here canyon, don't reckon as how I wantta find it."

"You must a wanted to get there awful bad to come through this storm. Ain't nothin' there but a general store, a saloon, an' a couple other businesses. You done 'bout killed your horses, not to mention yourselves."

"Got some 'portant business. Figured if we got there first

we'd make a good hunk o' change. There's others bent on the same business." These were the first words Stratford had uttered since Granger stopped them. Bowdeen's fingers were busy at the buttons of his coat.

Granger's voice hardened. "Tell you waddies somethin', the job you're on's already been tried by at least five others. Them five are either long buried—or runnin' like their tail feathers was on fire. You'd do well to follow their lead." He pinned Bowdeen with a look that would've gone through boiler plate. "You keep fiddlin' with them buttons to get at your gun, Bowdeen, I'm gonna blow your damned head off. You got it?"

The stumpy gunman turned loose the button he fiddled with like it was red hot. "How you know our names, an' how you figure you know what we're comin' here for?"

Colt shifted the Henry to his left hand and pushed his sheepskin back to clear his holster. "Ain't no question 'bout me knowin'. Gonna give you a chance, though. Unbutton your coats so's you can reach your six-shooters. You gonna need 'em mighty quick. I'm Colt Granger."

If he'd hit them in the head with a stick of stove wood, they couldn't look more stunned. "Y-you're Granger?" Stratford stuttered. "Wh-wh . . ."

Bowdeen cut in before his partner could do more damage. "Granger? Seems like we heard about you somewhere. What you got to do with us?"

"That old dog won't hunt, Bowdeen. I knowed you was comin' for me several days ago, you two an' several more. Seems I got only two choices: let you go, or shoot you right now. Reckon shootin' you now is the smartest; then I can set my sights on the rest o' you slime."

"Aw now, Granger. We ain't meanin' you no harm." Stratford's whiny voice implored him. "You let us get to that town up ahead, rest up a couple o' days, then I give you my word you won't never see us again." Neither of them made a move to unbutton his coat.

Granger shook his head and chuckled. "Your word? I wouldn't take your word if you'd tell me that right now we're in the middle of a snowstorm. No way I'm lettin' you go on to Hell Gate. Yep, reckon the best thing I can do is kill you now, else you'll back-shoot me some time or other, or—I can turn you back an' you can hope and pray them spavined horses'll get you back to a town somewhere. One thing for damned sure, you ain't comin' no farther this direction. Now, turn your backs to me, unbutton your coats, drop your gunbelts, then step outta the way an' I'll take your rifles from your horses.''

While unbuttoning his coat, Bowdeen growled, ''Granger, you cain't do this. We'll never make it.''

Colt stared for a moment. ''That's what I'm bettin' on. Now turn around and do like I said.'' He kept his eyes on Bowdeen's elbows. He'd have to crook one of them to make a draw, and if either of them had the guts to try for his gun, Granger's money was on Bowdeen.

The stubby gunman's elbow crooked. Granger drew and thumbed off a shot. He hit where he looked. Bowdeen's coat blossomed red in the elbow. The force of the shot spun him to again face Colt. Stratford's hands shot toward the sky, while he stared bug-eyed at his partner.

''Y-you broke my arm. Gotta see a doctor.''

Granger shook his head. ''No doctor, Bowdeen. Soon's you an' your partner shuck your hardware, he can try an' fix you up for travelin', then you're gonna slope it back toward Virginia City.''

''We'll never make it. We'll freeze to death, an' Bowdeen'll prob'ly bleed to death.''

The cowboy uttered one word: ''Tough.'' He holstered his revolver, hoping one of them would make another try. But all the fight was gone from them. He walked to them and took their weapons, pulled rifles from scabbards, patted them down for hideouts, and walked back to the boulder. ''Move out—now, or I'll shoot your horses an' you can walk.''

He watched until they turned the bend in the river, then he climbed to the shelf where Molly waited. ''They'll never make it, Colt.''

He gave her a cold look. ''Kinda figured it that way or I wouldn't-a let 'em go.'' He walked to the fire and poured himself a cup of coffee, then held the tin cup in his hands to warm them. He had drunk less than half the coffee when a fusillade of faint shots sounded from upstream, along with bloodcurdling yells.

Without a wasted motion, Granger poured the rest of his coffee on the fire, then tilted the remaining contents of the pot on it and watched the steam rise skyward. The yells continued, faint but unmistakable. "Blackfeet. Wonder what brought 'em out in the middle of a storm."

Colt went to their blankets, took Molly's, and wrapped it around her shoulders. "Pull it round your ears too, an' get to the back of the cave. I'll stand watch. Ain't gonna risk a fire till I'm sure them Injuns are long gone."

Molly glanced from him to look upstream. "You reckon they killed those men who were here?"

"If they didn't, them two gonna wish I'd been the one to put 'em outta their misery. Blackfeet can think of more ways to make a man hurt than an Apache ever dreamed of."

Still standing at his shoulder, Molly said softly, "While you had them under your gun, I was hopin' you'd not have to kill 'em. Now I wish you had. No one deserves to die like I know they're going to."

He put his arm around her shoulders. "Little one, if they'd not come huntin' me, they'd be back in Virginia City now, safe and warm. They asked for what they're gettin'."

"Yeah, but it's gonna be mighty hard, harder'n I figure they deserve."

He turned her gently toward the back of the cave. "Now, you get on back there. Keep quiet, an' keep down. Don't want you gettin' hurt. I'm gonna stand here an' see what they're up to if they come this way. Keep the horses all the way in the back."

When night settled in, he kept his eyes focused upstream, and after a while he saw what he'd hoped for—a distant pinpoint of flickering light through the trees. He sighed, figuring they'd made camp, and wishing he knew how many of them there were.

He thought to saddle the horses, and take Molly back toward the settlement, but knowing a horse could break a leg in the rough terrain, or could fall, pinning one of them underneath, he shook his head. He'd rather take his chances here, but he still didn't know what he faced. He thought on it a while, then went to Molly.

"They've gone into camp for the night. Don't know how many, but I do know where they are." He took his blanket and wrapped it around the blanket she already wore along with her sheepskin. "Stay here. I'm gonna snake my way up to their camp an' see what we gotta face come daylight. If I ain't back in a couple o' hours, I want you to stay where you are. Don't make any tracks anywhere. It's still snowin', an' in a short time, maybe a hour or two, ain't nobody gonna know anyone was ever up here. Stay till at least noon tomorrow, an' if they ain't come by, take the horses and get the hell outta this canyon. Head for the settlement. You got your weapons. Use 'em if you have to—don't hesitate."

With another glance at her, he slipped out of camp. The icy crust would make getting close to the Indian camp almost impossible without being heard—unless the Blackfeet continued to celebrate, yelling all the while. His stomach churned with the thought of what those yells would mean for the two white men.

Every step crackled and crunched, even though he pushed his feet past the icy glaze into the softer, fluffy snow, and with each sharp sound his nerves pulled tighter. And with each step he stopped and listened, praying the two gunmen wouldn't die too soon. He chose his route by snow cover. Close to trees, the depth lessened.

At each tree, he stopped and breathed deeply, trying to relax nerves stretched to the breaking point. It did little good, but stopping gave him a chance to put off the probability of getting shot. One thing for sure, if they heard him, he would not lead them back to Molly. Dark as it was, he still could see enough to try and plan an escape up the cliffs. He soon decided his best bet was to stay in the depths of the gorge, and use the trees for cover. The yelling continued.

He figured he'd been moving toward them about a half hour when he rounded a tree with their fire in full view. His breath caught in his throat. He again slipped behind the large pine's bole, and peered toward the fire.

Stratford and Bowdeen, tied to tree trunks about six feet apart, showed signs of having been burned by flaming fagots, and each had been scalped. Their terrified eyes followed every movement of the Blackfeet. One Blackfoot moved to stand in front of the thin Stratford, and his knife slit down the gunman's chest to his stomach, barely deep enough to cause a slow trickle of blood, and made another cut of the same depth about an inch from the first one. Then the warrior from hell slowly peeled the skin from Stratford's chest. The thin gunny opened his mouth to scream, but only a puny mewling came from deep in his throat.

There were four warriors around the fire, each cooking up his own brand of torture. Granger squelched the urge to step into the open and roll shots from his revolver. That action would only have served to give them one more white man on which to work their deviltry.

From where he stood, he checked the camp, trying to spot their weapons. Finally, the only firearms he could see were four 1852 single-shot Sharps 52-caliber rifles. He knew the rifle well; he'd carried one during his first days of scouting for the army. He kept it until he could afford a later model. His nerves loosened enough that his hair seemed to settle back against his neck. If he had to fight them, he'd stand a chance. He twisted to leave, thinking to try and put his feet in the same tracks he'd made coming—if they hadn't powdered over.

His foot found a stick. He tried to pull his leg back before breaking it. Too late. It broke with a sharp, shotlike crack. Abruptly, all sound in the camp ceased. He glanced toward it. There wasn't an Indian in sight.

He put his back against the tree trunk, thinking to blend better with it than out on snow, which gave off enough light to make him an easy target. He stood still, hardly daring to breathe. A shadowy form slipped to a tree not ten feet from him. He waited for the Blackfoot to move to another tree. An instant later, the Indian ran toward another tree closer to him. Granger thumbed off a shot. The warrior fell, pulled the trigger on his Sharps, and rolled over, not moving. But Granger did move, knowing the flash from his handgun had told them where he stood. The tree he picked this time was far younger, with less hiding surface. He stood still, holding his rifle in his left hand, ready to fire, and his Colt .44 revolver in his right, hammer eared back.

He had not long to wait. A Blackfoot moved between him and the fire. He thumbed off a shot, and saw the warrior stagger, stay on his feet, then run behind another tree. Granger found a large boulder close to the river's edge and took up station behind it. Now he'd wait for them to move. From where he stood, he had the first Indian he'd shot in view. He lay still. Granger figured him for dead and shifted his attention to the trees close-by.

Even though they were single-shot, three of those warriors out there looked to have loaded rifles, and even though they were old weapons, and even given the stories white men told one another that Indians couldn't shoot for sour apples— Granger knew better. He'd seen them kill at four hundred yards—and he was one hell of a lot closer to them than that. He tried to meld into the rock. His buckskins, close to the same color as the boulder, would blend with it pretty well. The only thing that moved was his eyes. They never stayed still.

He searched the trunk of every tree for an unusual thickening. Another half hour passed. Nothing moved except the softly falling snow. How many times Colt glanced behind he didn't know, but he made sure the cliff stood close enough that no one could circle and get him from there. He again studied the trees. Finally, he saw one that had a strange hump at the side, a hump none of the pines reaching for sunlight would have. Very slowly, so as to not draw attention to movement, he brought his Henry to his shoulder. When his sights rested on the thickest part of the hump, about where a man's chest should be, he squeezed the trigger. A Blackfoot yelled, pulled away from the trunk, and fell. He didn't even twitch when he hit the ground.

Two down, two to go, one of them wounded, Granger hoped. He shifted his attention to other trees, but not ignoring the snowfield. An Indian could make himself invisible almost anywhere. He thought of Molly back there at the cave, hearing the shots and knowing he was in a firefight. She'd be terrified—not for herself, but for him. He pulled his thoughts back to the here and now. This was no time to be distracted.

He moved to the other side of the boulder and peered around. He didn't like the view from there, but they'd seen the flash from his rifle at the other side. He stayed where he was, jacked a shell into the Henry, and waited. He reached to the back of his belt, felt to make sure his bowie was there, then again studied the trees. After about an hour, he figured they were going to wait until daylight to attack. They knew where he was, and he didn't know their whereabouts. But he also knew the patience of an Indian. They could outwait the average white man anytime. Well, he'd see who was a better Indian—him or them.

Another hour, still no movement, and he was cold, colder then he'd ever been, and his hands felt stiff as old saddle leather. He thought to try for another boulder he saw close to the cliff. He shook his head. Remember, cowboy, you've fought Injuns before. Remember how they usually win. They outwait you. Well, we'll see this time.

When he figured it was getting into early morning, maybe two o'clock, he thought he saw something move out by that old lightning-struck pine. He pinned his gaze on it. After another few minutes a head peered around the bole. He again moved his rifle into firing position, his movement so slow even he wasn't certain the rifle would ever reach his shoulder.

Finally, he had the head in his sights, squeezed the trigger, and watched the Blackfoot with a half head fall from behind the tree. One to go, and he thought it might be the one he'd wounded with his Colt. Still not a one of the warriors had fired a shot. He wondered at that, then decided they waited for a sure shot, knowing they had better make their one-shot rifles do the job. If the remaining warrior got off a shot and didn't put him down, then he had all the advantage. Under other circumstances he might have felt sorry for the Indians. They'd never had a chance—outgunned and out-numbered in most fights.

Daylight came, and still not a sign of the remaining warrior. Granger's stomach growled, reminding him he'd not eaten since their nooning of the day before. But he'd been hungry before, a whole lot more hungry than now. He moved to the other side of the tree, and studied the ground toward where he'd wounded the one Blackfoot. Nothing. He went back to the side he'd left and swept the same area, only now from a different angle. A mound in the snow seemed strange; unless it covered a rock, or a fallen log, he saw no reason for it to be there. He looked at it and tried to see through to whatever it covered. Then, taking an outside chance, he raised his rifle, sighted on the pile, and pulled the trigger. It came alive. The last Blackfoot rolled, came to his knees, sighted down the barrel of his Sharps, and pulled the trigger. Rock chips and fine sand sprayed Granger's face. The bullet whined off the boulder and imbedded itself in the cliff behind.

The warrior worked desperately to reload, but he bled in big spurts from low in his shoulder, and he also had a large splotch of blood high in his side. Granger put his sights on the center of the Blackfoot's chest and waited, figuring that at the rate the Indian lost blood, he'd be dead before he could get the single-shot rifle reloaded.

Finally, the warrior brought the Sharps to his shoulder, stiffened, and fell forward, his face buried in snow. Granger stepped from behind the boulder and walked toward the Indian camp. Bowdeen, Stratford, or both might be alive.

The fire in the middle of camp had burned to slightly glowing embers. He tossed several sticks onto them, squatted, and blew the fire to life. Now that he could see, he piled more wood on the fire and walked to the two white men. Neither appeared to be living. He checked Stratford first— no heartbeat, no breathing. He looked at Bowdeen, only to find the outlaw's eyes, alive eyes, staring at him. Bowdeen might be alive, but he was in a bad way.

Granger cut him loose from the tree, caught his falling body, lowered him gently to the ground, looked around for a canteen, and held it to the gunman's lips. Bowdeen sucked in a ragged breath, then whispered, "I'd a thanked you if you'd killed us back there. Them devils ain't nothin' a man wants to meet up with more'n once in a lifetime."

Granger checked Bowdeen over carefully. The only place he'd been shot was in the elbow, which he himself had done downriver. Granger looked into Bowdeen's eyes. "Ain't nothin' much wrong with you 'cept a need for water, patchin' up a few places where that Blackfoot stripped skin off your rotten hide, an' that elbow o' your'n. A doctor ain't gonna be able to fix that—my bullet went right in the joint. If you was ever any good with a six-gun before, you ain't now. That arm'll be stiff as a poker from now on." He again held the canteen to the bandit's mouth.

Bowdeen drank in large gulps, then moved his head to the side. "Cowboy, you might's well shoot me now as to turn me back upstream to find my way outta this canyon in this weather."

Granger shook his head. "Ain't gonna shoot you. Ain't gonna cut you loose to try to make it in this storm. Gonna take you to Hell Gate, see if anyone there can fix up your arm, then cut you loose." He figured he might live to rue the day he let the stocky outlaw go, but he hadn't the heart to send him out in the storm to perhaps a Blackfoot death, but for certain a freezing one. He bandaged Bowdeen's elbow, checked the camp, and took what keepsakes he and Molly might decorate the cabin with—a bow, quiver of arrows, and a couple of blankets, dirty but washable—then went to each of the Blackfeet. After checking that they were in fact dead, he took their war shields and rifles, then collected the Indians' and the white men's horses. With feed and rest, Bowdeen's and Stratford's horses would soon flesh out again and be usable.

After lifting the outlaw to the back of one of the ponies, Granger headed for Molly. Even though not wounded in a vital spot, the outlaw was in bad shape. He wouldn't last the night if not taken care of. Riding one of the ponies, Colt looked over his shoulder. "Gonna tell you somethin'. You gonna get able to travel, then you gonna get on your horse, an' leave these parts forever. I ever see you again, gonna waste a few shells. Gonna put all six bullets in your gut an' leave you lay. Understand?"

The look in Bowdeen's eyes gave him the answer. Raw fear, along with hate, showed there, but left no doubt the outlaw would head for parts unknown.

Below the ledge on which he'd left Molly, Colt drew the horses in and looked up. "It's all right, little one. Gonna dump this trash down here while I help break camp, then we'll head for the settlement an' see can't we get him doctored some."

It took two days of man-killing, and horse-killing, toil through the deep snow to reach Hell Gate. They found no doctor to care for Bowdeen, but the bartender said he'd fixed a few gunshots before. Granger watched while he dressed the wound, then Colt went through the outlaw's pockets and found a small sack of dust and eight cartwheels. He tossed the bartender a couple of dollars, then went from there to Shockley and arranged for the stumpy outlaw to have a room for one week—no more. "At the end of a week, I want him to saddle up an' ride out."

"Hell, Granger, he won't be able to buck this weather in a week."

Colt grinned. "J.P., you're a businessman. I'm gonna pay you to keep 'im for one week. I took what money he had on him, so he ain't got anything to pay with. You want to board 'im free, that's up to you. I'm takin' his weapons, saddle—everything but one blanket an' his horse. If he gets back to some of his friends, all right, if he don't . . . ," he shrugged, "tough."

Shockley stared at him a moment, slowly shaking his head. "Granger, I don't believe I've ever seen a man with an iron heart before, but I have to say, I'm looking at one now."

Granger's face hardened. "He was gonna take pay to kill me. I coulda left 'im out yonder tied to that sapling, but I give 'im a break—the only break he's gonna get. If he even rides by my cabin, I'm gonna blow his brains out." He nodded. "Yeah, you're right, he's not got much chance of livin' the way I'm sendin' 'im out, but it's a better chance than if he don't steer clear of me." He tipped his hat to the innkeeper and left.

While Granger arranged for Bowdeen to be cared for, Molly bought a tow sack full of odds and ends she thought they might need at the cabin, and the way things had been going, she decided to buy another five hundred rounds of ammunition. When he joined her at the hitchrack, she looked at him. "Bowdeen the last?"

He shook his head. "Almost, but we got one or two more."

16

MOLLY STUDIED THE pommel of her saddle a few moments. Angry blood pushed into her head. She threw him a "tell me the truth" look. "What do you mean, 'almost'?"

Granger pulled his pipe out and packed it, wondering how to answer her, then decided to lay it on the line. "Little one, when I put it the way I did, it was because I honestly don't know." He put fire to his pipe, puffed a couple of times, then, staring between his horse's ears, tried to explain. "We know Clinton's been hiring guns to get rid of me. I've apparently hurt 'im bad in whatever game he's playin'. Don't figure he's got many men left who're willin' to die for his money—one, maybe two, an' then there's him, probably the most dangrous of 'em all, mostly 'cause he's a thinker, a planner.

"I figure to get right busy an' finish the floor in your room long's the weather's this bad. When the weather breaks, gonna bundle you up an' we're goin' to Virginia City. Gonna end this once and for all."

Molly slanted him a look from the corners of her eyes. "That mean we gonna go back to the cabin and live a normal life, bring in a bunch of cows, raise our chickens and hogs, an' buy shells for our guns only to hunt with?"

He chuckled. "Yep. Reckon that's what I mean. Then we gonna accept a invitation to one o' them dances in the settlement, or maybe raise a barn for ourselves an' have a dance in it. Gotta give you a chance to meet some young fellows."

"Don't wantta meet any young fellows. I'm 'bout as happy as I can be right here with you."

Granger swallowed a couple of times, wishing he could make his dreams come true, dreams he was ashamed to admit even to himself. Hell, he almost raised her, made her feel beholden to him—what kind of man would take advantage of a situation like that? "You're only happy, Molly, 'cause you don't know no better right now. You ain't had a chance to get to know any young folks your own age." Before she could give him more argument, he urged the Paloos to a lope. He felt her eyes boring a hole in his back when he rode ahead.

The cold weather held, and they had another snow on top of that already on the ground. Colt hoped it would break soon. He'd finished the puncheon floor in Molly's room, and, enjoying the work inside, he'd gotten well along into putting a floor in the main room. He cut young trees and with Molly's help dragged them inside, where he used the adze to cut a flat surface. Never having liked sloppy work, Granger cut her floor and the one for the main room almost as smooth as though they were made of planed boards. When each sapling was finished and ready to mount, Colt moved his fingers over the surface as though caressing it.

Molly was happy to clean up the shavings at the end of each day. The fact was, having Colt in the room with her where she could see he was safe was something she'd have liked to enjoy for a long while to come—but she knew that as soon as the weather broke, this interlude of peace would end. She sighed. From the long ago memories of her father, she thought of a favorite saying of his: "Everything evens out. You get something and you give something in return. It might be no more than hard work, but you pay for everything you get." Again she sighed. Her father had been so right. She and Colt would pay for these safe times with danger later on. She stood, and helped him place another finished piece into the floor.

He looked at her. "Three more boards, an' I'll have 'er finished so's you won't have to sweep dirt, or draw patterns in it for a make-believe carpet. I want you to be proud of our home."

"Colt Granger, you've never heard me utter one word of complaint about anywhere we've lived." She smiled. "But I'll tell you right now, I'm already proud as that old rooster struttin' out yonder before all them hens. Why I'll bet there isn't another woman in the valley has a nicer cabin than I do."

He chuckled. "Well, now, I wouldn't go so far as to say anythin' like that. There's some right handy folks movin' into this valley."

Her face set in a "no argument" expression. "Yeah, but don't none of those women have a Colt Granger under their roof." She grinned. "At least they better not have, an' let me find out about it."

Only a few nights later, Colt sat in front of the fire and watched Molly set out the flour and pans to start baking. He cocked his head, listening. Water, in a steady sound, dripped from the roof outside. "It's thawing. Better not make up more bread than we'll eat along the trail. We're leavin' for Virginia City come sunup."

Molly stopped kneading the rounded pile of dough. "Must we, Colt? Can't we just wait and let them come to us?"

He shook his head. "You know better'n that, little one. Clinton ain't the kind to do his own killin'. He'll sit back there on his fat rear end an' hire men to come after me. He'll do it till they get me, or he runs outta men.

"The only way to end it is to go after him, and even then I'm gonna have to make damned sure it's all legal-like. Law's comin' to this territory, an' takin' care of your troubles with a gun even right now's gotta be legal. Time'll come when only peace officers and courts'll handle things like that. You an' me, little one, ain't got time to wait for them days." He looked at her straight on. "I'm gettin' that pig offa my tail. Come Christmas, only a few weeks away now, you an' me're gonna be able to sit by our fire in peace an' comfort.''

He had made her a kitchen table by cutting a two-foot-thick slab from a tree that had been three feet in diameter. He then smoothed the top and set it on legs to make a handy sort of worktable.

Now she slammed the dough she'd been kneading to the table and slapped it flat, flipped it, and slapped it flat again. He knew she was taking her building anger out on the dough. He chuckled. ''What's got you so upset, little one? We've lived with this quite a while now. No need to get so angry. I'll take care of it.''

She pinned him with a look. ''*That's* what's got me upset. That tub o' lard over yonder sits in his office an' causes decent folk a bunch o' misery.'' Her eyes blazed blue fire. ''Damn the law, Colt. I'm goin' with you, an' if you don't shoot 'im, I'm goin' to. We ain't comin' back here with anything to worry 'bout on our backtrail. You got it?''

Colt stared at her a moment, his mouth quivering at the corners, his eyes crinkled—then he exploded into laughter that erupted from the bottom of his lungs. Finally, tears streaming down his cheeks, he wiped them with his sleeve, and still choking on guffaws, he shook his head. ''Damn, woman, I sure don't want you gettin' mad at me. But I promise, when we leave Alder Gulch to head for home, we ain't leavin' nothin' behind us that'll ever cause us harm again.'' His voice softened. ''Believe me, little one, I'll take care of it.''

She continued with her bread while Colt thought of this valley they'd chosen to settle in. To his mind, it held riches far beyond the gold they'd sought for such a long while. Soon it would hold friends with whom to visit, and a town where the settlers could meet and socialize. The fact was, when he delivered Bowdeen to Hell Gate, Worden and Higgins had told him they were thinking of moving farther into the valley, closer to the mill.

Worden's friend, Lieutenant Mullan, told him the railroad was close to becoming a reality. The two owners of the general store wanted to shed the ominous name Hell Gate and had decided their new town would be named Missoula, a much prettier name than the one at the mouth of the canyon.

Colt cast a glance at Molly, a glance tender and full of love, one he held for her only when she wasn't looking. In ten years, or so, she might have a right nice place to marry in and raise her children, not his children, which he so badly wanted, someone else's, someone whom he'd make sure deserved her. The thought caused his throat to swell, and brought pain to his heart. But her happiness meant everything.

While watching her finish baking, he cleaned and oiled their weapons.

When she had finished, and cleaned up the mess, he knocked the dottle from his pipe, and got ready for bed.

Fisk Sanders slammed his fist against his desktop. "Damn that unconscionable pig," he said, talking to an empty room. "He's hiring guns to shoot Granger, and I can't prove it. I can't prove he's killing miners for their claims, I can't prove any of his crooked moves—but I know he's behind all the disappearances, all the claim grabs, everything, and he doesn't even leave his office." Then it occurred to him. Clinton would probably have him on his list. He reached in his lower right-hand desk drawer, pulled his gunbelt and then pulled a .44 from it. He'd wear a gun until Clinton was gone from Alder Gulch.

From his office window, Sanders watched the comings and goings of all the riffraff in the prosperous mining town. He wished he had even one man to pose as the type of person Clinton drew to him, a man who could go to Clinton, gain his confidence, find out his plans—and actions—then testify in a court of law as to his guilt in even one murder, one claim takeover. But where to find such a man. Even the riffraff had a code of honor. Then he thought of a name Granger had mentioned the last time he was in Virginia city—what was it, Buck, Buck something or other?

Colt had called the man by name, said he trusted him, said he'd sent him packing, heading for his folks' farm back in Missouri. Was there a chance the big man had stopped to work for enough money to get him home? What was his name, and if Sanders could find him, could he trust him?

He thought about that for some time, then decided that if Granger took the man's word, so could he. That decision left him no closer to finding the man he wanted. If he could only think of his name, he could get the miners to look for him, in case he'd stayed around.

That night, deep in sleep, Sanders's eyes snapped open. He stared into the darkness a moment. What was it that had wakened him? Then his mind focused on what he'd been thinking—or dreaming. "Drago, Buck Drago, that's the name Granger used when he told me of the happenings along Grasshopper Creek." His voice in the stillness of night sounded loud to him. In case he should forget, he threw back the covers, put fire to a lamp, wrote the name on a slip of paper, and tucked it into his vest pocket, the one he'd wear when he dressed come daylight. He crawled back between the blankets and slept soundly.

Sanders wakened, dressed, and went to the cafe before the sun, not yet painting the winter sky to the east with a golden hue, could push night shadows into hiding for the day. Ted Benning, a man Sanders respected and trusted almost as much as he did Granger, frequently ate breakfast in town when he tired of his own cooking. The lawyer hoped this was one of the mornings the miner decided to use the cafe.

He sliced his fork through a biscuit covered with brown gravy, dipped the bite in egg yoke, and put it in his mouth, then glanced at the door. Benning pushed into the room, shivered, removed his sheepskin, and walked to Sanders's table. "Sit with you, Fisk?"

Around his bite of food, Sanders grinned. "Was-going to ask you to do just that soon's I finished chewing this biscuit. Sit. I got something I want you to do if you think it worth-while."

While they ate, then drank coffee, Sanders told Benning what he had in mind. "If you find this Drago, you think it'll work, Ted?"

Benning studied his now-empty plate, frowned, and looked at the lawyer. "Fisk, we got nothin' better. It's sure as hell worth a try. We gotta do somethin'. Another miner disappeared yesterday, broad daylight. He went to his cabin for somethin', an' never showed up back at his diggin's.'' He shoved back from the table. ''I'll get some of the men to lookin' for Drago soon's I get to the crick. Fact is, they's probably some o' us remember him from when we took Skinner outta that cabin.''

Sanders took another swallow of coffee, then packed and lighted his pipe while studying whether Drago would work against men he might have bunked with, traveled with. He might think of it as being a traitor to his own kind. He asked Benning what he thought.

The miner sat there a few moments, frowning. ''Tell you, maybe he don't think on his self as bein' like that bunch. 'Cording to Granger, he sure don't like bein' put in the same stall with liars. If he balks, maybe we can convince 'im he ain't like them others.''

Sanders nodded. ''Maybe, but too, we're taking a chance he'll go right to Clinton and tell 'im what we're planning.'' He frowned, shook his head, and shrugged. ''Hell, that's all we got. Might as well do it—if we can find Drago. He might be halfway to Missouri by now.''

While Sanders and Benning were finishing their breakfast, Clinton sat at his desk, shoveling huge bites of food into his mouth while staring malevolently across the street at the front of the lawyer's office. He had to do something about the man. Sanders had been a burr under his saddle ever since he formed the Vigilantes and rid the area of the Plummer gang. If he'd left well enough alone after hanging the sheriff, Clinton would have considered that Sanders had done him a favor, because it had taken that to put him in charge of running the entire lawless operation.

But now the lawyer's and Granger's meddling had cost him almost every good man he had. Some had left the country out of fear, and some, like Gant, Bowdeen, and Stratford, had simply disappeared. Those three, he figured, had a hard core of greed in them, and would have stuck it out until the job was done on Granger.

While he thought, and stared across the street, he clenched and unclenched his fat fists. Maybe he'd gone after the wrong man first. Maybe he should have taken care of the lawyer, then eliminated the cowboy.

Sanders was here. Here where he could see things that went on in town, here where he heard about the robberies and killings, here where the absence of a gunhand would be noticed. The slim young man might put two and two together. Clinton made his decision: Sanders had to go.

Then, if he had to import a gunfighter to take care of the cowboy, he'd do it. To bring in a hired gun from outside would cost money, savings which he hated to turn loose. He hunched his shoulders over his food. But spending money in that manner would certainly open the door for more claim takeovers—in whatever way he had to do it. His decisions brought on more problems. Who could he get to kill Sanders, and how could he go about getting the best gunfighter, one he could be certain could better Granger? He sighed. If he wanted it done right, he might have to kill Granger himself.

That thought was one he didn't want to consider. He'd kept his own shirttails clean. Stayed out of things such that tracing any of the illegal acts to him was virtually impossible. He wanted to keep it that way. But who could he trust to get things done?

He thought first about gunfighters, ones he knew were good, then thought of a friend in Denver who would know the best available who could get to Virginia City quicker than some of those down Texas or Kansas way. He pulled pen and paper over in front of him.

He wanted a gunfighter who could, before witnesses, outdraw and outshoot Granger. It had to be legal, with nothing traceable to him. He'd find someone in town to take care of Sanders. He again picked up the pen, dipped its point in the well, and began to write.

A full week now, Benning had walked the Stinking Water, searching every face along every claim. He'd made up his mind a couple of days ago that Buck Drago should be far east of Virginia City by now, but he was reluctant to give up. A dozen times, he'd said to himself, ''I'll check eight or ten more diggin's and then tell Fisk the man has gone on through.'' But when he'd looked at every face along those ten claims, he'd shake his head and figure on looking at that many more. Then, early in the morning of the eighth day, wading in water to his knees, he saw a broad back that cut a chink in his memory.

The closer he came to the man, the more certain he was that he'd found the one he hunted. He walked to the front of the man, peered closely at him, and nodded. ''Buck Drago?''

Drago sloshed to the bank and dropped his shovel. ''That's me, an' I don't need to tell you I'm glad for any excuse to get outta that there freezin' water. What you need, stranger?''

Ignoring the big man's question, Benning stuck out his hand. ''Ted Benning here. Been tryin' to find you. Heard you'd headed for Missouri.''

Drago frowned. ''Still headed that way. Stopped long enough to earn some eatin' an' smokin' money. Who'd be that interested in my business?''

Wanting to put the big man at ease, Benning chuckled. ''Ain't me, partner, but I got a friend who wants to offer you a job—one that'll get you outta that water for a while.'' He let his words sink in, and saw that Drago mulled them over. And he saw another thing. Drago was nobody's fool. He thought things over before making a move.

''Got me a job. Almost got enough to hit the trail for home.'' Now a wary look came from his eyes. '' 'Sides, I ain't takin' on no job I'd be ashamed of.''

Benning shook his head. ''The wages you'll earn are as honest as any dollar you get from what you're doin' now.'' He spread his hands at his side. ''At least hear what my friend has to say.''

Drago stared at him a moment, apparently made up his mind, nodded, and walked to a man standing just off the bank. ''Be back in 'bout a hour.''

While they walked back to town, Benning slanted the outlaw a look. ''What you think o' Colt Granger?''

''He got somethin' to do with this?''

''Nope. Just wondered what you thought of him.''

Drago slowed his pace. ''Reckon I can say I like 'im. He's

a square shooter. Ain't many like 'im around." He grinned. "But I'll tell you one damned thing: if you gonna pick your enemies, walk 'bout a hundred miles round that jasper. He ain't one to cross."

They talked until they were on the edge of town, where Benning steered Drago to the backs of buildings along Wallace Street. When they came to Sanders's office, Benning opened the back door, stepped into the dark interior, and nodded for the big outlaw to come in also.

The hinges had squeaked when the door opened. Sanders pulled his Colt revolver and held it under the edge of his desk. Benning, the first to enter, grinned. "Found 'im, Fisk. He was workin' his tail off down the gulch a ways. Didn't take much to leavin' a payin' job to come see you."

The lawyer walked around the desk, his hand outstretched. "Thanks for comin', Drago. Didn't really expect to find you since Granger told me you were going home."

The outlaw studied Sanders a moment, as though trying to figure where this was leading. "Was headed that way, but thought I better make a few dollars to get me across the plains. I give 'im my word, an' I'm gonna keep it."

Sanders nodded. "He said you would, but first I would like you to consider doing something that will help him, as well as me. You'd have to give up the job you now have, but what I have in mind'll pay you more. Then, soon's you finish, and give me your report, you can keep your word to Colt."

"What I gotta do to earn your money, Mr. Lawyer?"

"Sit down and let me explain it to you."

Drago sat in the chair Sanders offered, while Benning poured coffee. Then Sanders launched into what he wanted the big man to do, and why. When he finished, he sat looking expectantly at the outlaw, one he hoped was an ex-outlaw. When the silence had drawn out long enough to make Drago fidget, Sanders prompted him with, "Well, what do you think?"

Drago rolled and lit a cigarette, obviously scrubbing down what he'd been asked to do. Finally he looked from the tip of his smoke to pin Sanders with eyes cold as blue steel.

"You wantin' me to turn on my friends, wantin' me to tell you stuff that'll get 'em hung. I ain't that kind, mister. I ain't gonna spy on men I done sat around a campfire with."

Sanders shook his head. "No, Drago, I'm not askin' you to do that at all. I'm askin' you to spy on one fat pig who uses your friends for his own gain and then if they wind up dead denies ever having known them. He doesn't even see they get a decent burial." He stood and filled their cups again. "The thing is, you never *really* worked for Clinton. He never did anything for you, or anyone else. When he pays a man a dollar, it's after the man has delivered what he asked him to. In fact, from what you've said, you never met the man, wouldn't know him if he walked in the door right now." He walked over and stood in front of the big outlaw.

"Drago, this thing I'm asking you to do will not cause any of your friends harm. You have my word on it—unless they're caught robbing or killing someone, or back-shooting, and then the law will deal with them. The point is, it may give a man like Granger a fighting chance, and from what he told me, you never killed a man, and definitely would not back-shoot one. The men you're protecting are not the ones we're after."

The outlaw stared at Sanders a moment. "Why you think you can trust me? Why you think I won't leave here an' go tell Clinton what you're plannin'?"

Sanders walked around his desk and sat. He fiddled with his tobacco pouch a moment, then looked Drago in the eye. "First, I trust you because a man I admire very much trusts you. Second, I don't think you'll tell Clinton. You're not his kind. But before you give me an answer, I want you to consider the danger you'll be putting yourself in. Clinton will kill you in the wink of an eye if he suspects you. So with those considerations, and if you agree to do what I've asked, tell me how much you'll charge to do it." He smiled. "I want to be sure I have the money to pay you."

Drago stood. "I gotta think on what you told me, an' I gotta figure how much it'll take to get me home with a few bucks to help my folks. An' if I take you up on it, I gotta quit my other job proper. Cain't jest walk out on a man what's payin me.''

That comment engendered more trust in him from Sanders.

17

DRAGO LEFT SANDERS'S office by the back door, cautious to stay clear of Clinton's sight. He had mixed emotions about what he'd been invited to do.

Would he be double-crossing friends, men he'd ridden with, drunk with, gambled with, bunked with? He shook his head, puzzled. Along with those thoughts, pride seeped in, giving him a warm feeling in his chest. Decent people were trusting him to do something to help the community, trusting him to help a friend, even trusting him to have enough sense to carry out the plan. His thinking brought a smile. Maybe he could really do what he'd promised Granger. The feeling of responsibility and respectability flooded his body with a nerve-tingling sensation he'd not felt in years.

Only halfway back to the man he worked for, he decided to do what the young lawyer asked. At the diggings he told the miner he was going to quit, but would not leave him hurting for help, and if the miner wished, he'd stay on a few more days. The miner said no, thanked him for helping as long as he had, and paid him his earnings.

Drago took his money and walked back to town. He stopped in the general store and bought tobacco. He thought to go to the saloon for a drink, but decided whiskey and what he had to do wouldn't mix. He pulled his coat around him and sat on the bench at the store's front, waiting for dark so he could go back to the lawyer's office.

An hour or so after the sun set, he knocked. When Sanders answered, Drago told him to douse the lantern, or close the shutters—they needed to talk.

After only a few seconds, the door swung wide to a lighted office, the shutters closed tight. Drago, although a big man, was light on his feet. Without a sound, he walked to the center of the room and faced the younger man. "Gonna do what you asked, Mr. Sanders. Jest hope I can do it right."

Sanders stared at him a moment. "Be real sure, Drago. You realize this could get you killed. You'll be dealing with a cunning, ruthless man. He'll have no compunction about blowing a hole in you."

Drago grinned. "Don't rightly know what that there cop-uction is, but I'll jest guess it means he ain't gonna give it a second thought if he puts hot lead, or cold steel, into me." He sobered. "Yes sir, I done thought 'bout what I'm lettin' myself in for. Even if he kills me, I reckon I'm still ahead of the game. You see, Granger coulda killed me an' didn't. I already got several days behind me I didn't figure on."

Sanders went to his desk and pulled a bottle from the bottom drawer. "Think a drink is appropriate." He poured a couple of fingers of whiskey into each glass, and handed one to Drago. "How much you think this is worth?"

The outlaw swirled the amber liquid around in the glass, studying it all the while, wondering if maybe a drink now was all right. He hated to take money for doing something he would have done for nothing, considering it was for a man he liked, and to whom he owed his life. But he'd prom-ised that same man he'd head for Missouri, and he had to have a few bucks to travel on. He looked up and locked gazes with Sanders. "All I need is travelin' money, an' I'd shore like to have a few dollars to give my folks when I get home. You reckon two hundred dollars is too much?" He stood there, hoping he hadn't asked for too much, wanting to give his folks something for the heartache he left them with. "If

I'm askin' too much, a hundred dollars ridin' money'll be fine.''

Sanders stared at the floor. He shook his head, then looked Drago in the eye. "Drago, that price is all wrong. Can't have you do it for that."

Drago's heart sank. He felt hollow inside. He had hoped so much he could get home with a few bucks. "Sir, I woulda done it fer nothin', but like I said, I need ridin' money. Now, I done made a few dollars workin' for that man down the crick a ways. So tell me what you can spare, an' I'll do you the best job I can. Figured I wuz askin' too much from the start."

Sanders knocked back his drink, picked up the bottle, and looked at Drago's empty glass. "Here. Let me pour you another." This time, he filled each glass. "Sit, and let's talk about what you're to do." After only a moment, he looked across his desk at the outlaw, lifted his glass to him, said "*Salud,*" and tossed off a goodly part of his drink. "Now, Mr. Drago, we're going to talk money. First off, I wouldn't ask any man to put his backside on the line for the pittance you asked for. If we can bring Clinton to trial and hang him, every miner along the gulch will be beholden to you. I can't go out there and ask the miners for money to get the job done. Someone would be sure to talk. That would get you killed for damn sure. But," he smiled slightly, "I'm sure you know I ride with the Vigilantes, so that's where I'll get the money. I'll call a meeting tomorrow night. I will promise you right now, sir, you'll not ride out of this town with less than a thousand dollars. We'll get it back from the miners once Clinton decorates a hangman's rope."

In the middle of taking a swallow of his drink, Drago choked. "A-a thousand dollars? Did you say a thousand dollars, Mr. Sanders?"

The lawyer sat smiling, nodding, looking at Drago with an expression the big outlaw would never forget, looking at him with the kind of look he hoped to earn from other good men. He couldn't remember the last time tears had flooded his eyes, but they did now. If his folks lived, he could do things for them they'd never dreamed of. He could get Ma a rocker and put it on the front porch where she could sit and watch people walk or ride past out on the road. She might even pass the time of day with some of them. He could—Why, hell, he could make life easy for them with that kind of money.

"Sir, I reckon I'd stand right here an' let you shoot me for that kind o' money if you'd promise to send it to my folks. Yes, sir, now if you don't mind—it's kinda late, an' you might want to get to bed. Let's talk 'bout what I'm s'posed to do."

Sanders frowned, staring into his drink. He knew Clinton was hiring guns to go after Granger, but he suspected the fat man was running low on those he could trust. He also thought that he, himself, stood high on the list of those Clinton wanted out of his way. He took a long time making up his mind about whom he wanted to protect most.

He wanted to protect himself, but he couldn't let Granger get shot from ambush, which was the way they'd have to get him, if they got him at all. He looked up from his drink. "Let's talk about it, Mr. Drago."

"Shore would 'preciate it if you'd call me Buck. I ain't never been called mister by nobody."

Sanders chuckled. "All right, you call me Fisk. Now, let's talk turkey." He went on to explain what he thought the fat man's priorities would be, and told the outlaw he thought Granger would be in constant danger, so he wanted to protect him first.

Drago shook his head. "Reckon I cain't agree with you on that. Here you are sittin' right under Clinton's nose where you can see a lot o' what's goin' on. I figure he'll want to get rid o' you, then take his time gettin' rid o' Granger." He knocked back the rest of his drink and grinned. "I got a idear. Why don't we wait an' see who he wants me to shoot, if'n he takes me on, then we can do some more figurin'?"

Sanders smiled. Already the big man showed he had a brain. He nodded. "Good thinking, Buck. First, though, let's see if you can infiltrate his organization."

Drago's grin was almost as big as he was. "You keep usin' them big words like that infil . . . whatever you said, an' you gonna get me so befuddled I ain't gonna know what to do."

Sanders held up the bottle. "Want another?"

Drago shook his head. "Better get outta here. I ain't gonna try to see you less'n I got somethin' I figure you ought to know, somethin' that won't wait."

"Good." Sanders opened his desk drawer and took out a small bag of dust. "You need eating money?"

"Naw. Reckon I got enough for that. Let's wait till I get the job done. I'll slip outta the back door now, an' see you when I need to."

For the first time in months, Sanders felt good. The big man went silently to the door, opened it, and disappeared into the night. He'd never trusted a man of Drago's background before, but for some strange reason he'd put his and Granger's lives in the outlaw's hands, and felt good about it.

The next morning, before sunup, the big outlaw ate breakfast at the cafe down the street about a block from Clinton's office. Enjoying the smell of frying bacon, fresh-brewed coffee, and pipe smoke, he dawdled over the meal, thinking of what he had to do, but mostly watching the front door of the office where he was certain the fat man manipulated men for his own gain. Now all he had to do was go in there, gain the man's confidence, take steps either to prevent a crime, or to get the evidence Sanders wanted that would stand up in court. Before going down there, Drago wanted to see what kind of men went in and out of the man's office. Chances were, he'd know some of them, and might find them a source of information.

When finally he'd seen three men enter and leave, he stood, payed his bill, and headed for Clinton. His stomach felt queasy, his back muscles ached, and he found it hard to swallow. Settle down, he told himself, Clinton's got no reason to figure you for anything but what you've always been—a outlaw.

Even though he was going to see a pig, he'd shaved and had a bath before leaving his room at the cheap hotel, one he thought he could afford. Maybe being clean would not set well with the fat man, but like he'd told Granger, Buck Drago liked to stay clean.

On reaching Clinton's office, he raised his fist to knock, and instead reached for the door handle. This was an office; he'd seen no one else knock. He pulled the door toward him and went in. Clinton sat behind his desk, staring through fat-encased eyes at him. "What you want?"

Drago removed his hat and held it at his waist. "Want to talk with you, Mr. Clinton. Hear you're hirin' men who can use a gun. Reckon I fit the bill. Been usin' one 'bout ten years now."

Clinton's fat cheeks swallowed more of his eyes until he looked at Drago through slits. "What would I be hirin' a gun for? I got no enemies. Where you hear this yarn?"

Drago wondered how he could explain where he'd heard, then decided on the truth. "Over Bannack way. Man named Tom Seely told me he was 'bout to make a pretty good haul for gettin' in a gunfight with a cowboy goin' by the name o' Granger, an' killin' 'im." He shrugged. "I had dealin's with Granger before, an' got no reason to do nothin' but hate 'im. He killed a couple friends o' mine. Fact is, I worked for Plummer, an' Granger wuz a big cause of gittin' that bunch to get broke up." He shuffled his feet a couple of times, then said, "Seely ain't gonna do the job fer you. He's dead."

Clinton settled his bulk more comfortably in his chair. "Dead, huh?" He shook his head, his jowls hurrying to catch up with his face. "Shoulda known better, ain't many around good enough with a side gun to get the cowboy." He scrubbed Drago down from head to feet with a look the big man thought missed nothing. "What makes you think you're good enough to beat the cowboy?"

"Don't figure I am, but I need money, so I ain't p'ticular where I shoot from—front, side—or behind." There, now he'd laid the bait out for Clinton to snap at it. He waited a few long moments while the fat man obviously studied what he'd said.

Squirming deeper into his chair, Clinton finally said, "Gotta have time to think about what you said." He pinned

Drago with a look. "An' you might's well know now, I'm gonna check you out. If you don't pass, you the one's gonna die. Come back to see me in a couple o' days."

Knowing he'd been dismissed, the outlaw put his hat on and left. Whew, he thought, a man could get killed by saying one word that didn't fit. But this was one time he was glad for the company he'd been keeping. There wasn't a one of Plummer's gang who wouldn't give him good marks. He'd better stay clear of Sanders's office; the wrong person seeing him go in the lawyer's office would certainly give him a short ride to boot hill.

He'd gone only a short distance up Wallace Street when he came face-to-face with Granger, who had a pretty girl on his arm. Granger squinted at him and said, "You promised me . . ."

Drago, never slackening his pace, said out of the corner of his mouth, "Don't say nothin'. See Sanders. He'll tell you what's goin' on." He continued walking, wondering what the cowboy was doing in Virginia City, but awful glad he'd had the chance to say a few words before anyone could see they had met before.

Granger escorted Molly into Sanders's office and stuck out his hand. "Howdy, lawyer man, need to talk with you."

Sanders nodded to Molly, then looked Granger in the eye. "You show up at the most inopportune times. What the devil are you doing here now?"

He grinned. "Damn. Glad to see you, too, Fisk. Why you so happy to see me?"

Sanders shot him a sheepish grin. "Aw hell. I have something going on that might get your neck stuck out a mile. Glad to see you and Molly. Sit and I'll tell you about it."

Granger shook his head. "First, tell me why Buck Drago said to see you. I met 'im out on the street. 'Fore I could say much, he said for me to see you. Okay. I'm seein' you."

Sanders nodded. "That's what I'm going to tell you. Drago told me he'd promised you he'd head for home when you didn't shoot him over yonder on Grasshopper Creek. I talked him into postponing that trip. Talked him into doing something for me—and you.'' Sanders went to the coffeepot and poured them each a cup. "Fresh-brewed," he said. "Now I'll tell you what's in the mill." He started with his and Benning's idea, told them what they'd decided, told them about finding Drago, and how they thought to accomplish getting Clinton into court. Finished, he sat back and stared at Granger. "Now tell me what you're doing back here."

Granger shook his head. "I come to kill Clinton—legally, or illegally. I'm tired o' lookin' over my shoulder. Now that you come up with a plan to get 'im legal like, I'm willin' to give it a chance, but I ain't waitin' long."

A faint, whimsical smile breaking the somber contours of his face, Sanders nodded. "Good. We have to give the law a chance to function. This may be the one best chance we'll have to get Clinton, and if we find him guilty—he's gonna hang."

Sitting primly in a chair facing the lawyer, Molly eyed him. "Sounds like you already sentenced him, Fisk, but then, I have, too. I told Colt if he didn't put lead in that pig, I would. So this kind of justice better work right fast, 'cause I wantta get home in time for Christmas. It ain't very far off now."

"Yes, ma'am. I think, even with giving you folks time to ride back to your valley, we'll have this taken care of, then we can all get on with our lives."

They had stood to leave, when Sanders cautioned. "Don't, for any reason, let anyone see you have anything to do with Drago. It'll get him killed, spoil our chance to legally get Clinton, and maybe get you and me a burial plot, Colt."

His face feeling like leather, Granger promised. They went from Sanders's office to the hotel. They'd not had a chance to secure rooms when they ran into Drago on the street. Now, Granger put Molly's bedroll beside her bed, looked at her, and shrugged. "We'll give this a chance to work; it'll give us time to get some shoppin' done. After you get gussied up, go ahead and shop. I got some to do myself."

He dumped his gear in his room, looked at his Henry, picked it up, and took it with him. Walking along the street, glancing at stores he already knew were there from the time he and Molly had spent in this town, he almost passed a ladies ready-to-wear, then stopped and pushed through the door. A lady looked up from showing a customer some sort of foofaraw. She came over and offered to help Colt.

"Well, ma'am, don't reckon I know what I'm lookin' for." He thought a moment, then realized the clerk probably knew Molly. "You remember Miss Tbalt?" At her nod, he said, "I'm sorta lookin' to get her somethin' for Christmas. Ain't made up my mind yet what she'd like. You ever see 'er fingerin' any o' these dresses with a 'wantta have you' look?"

The lady laughed. "No, sir, if I remember Molly very well, you'd probably have to hog-tie her to get her in a fancy dress." She frowned. "But I'll say this, down deep inside of every woman, there's a desire to look nice. Let's see if we can find something she would be proud to wear." Granger wanted to tell her Molly always looked nice, but he swallowed the words.

The clerk remembered Molly's size, so they looked at everything in the store in that size that Molly might like. Granger didn't see anything he particularly liked, and left, saying he'd be back if he didn't find something elsewhere.

He roamed the town, saw a lot of things he was told women treasured, but didn't find a thing that took his fancy. Finally, he admitted to himself that he had no idea what he was looking for. He decided to have a drink over at Con Orem's saloon and think about it. There, he'd be among friends.

Weaving his way through the foot traffic, horses, freight wagons, buckboards, and stray dogs—all cluttering the rutted, muddy street—he reached the side Orem's saloon faced—across and down the street about fifty yards from Clinton's office. He stepped to the boardwalk and a man, not of the type who favored the working class, deliberately pushed a shoulder into Granger. Not wanting trouble, Colt apologized. "Sorry, mister, wasn't lookin' where I was goin'."

The giant of a man stood back a step and eyed the cowboy. "You're used to shovin' your weight around, ain't ya. Or shootin' the toes off'n a man what ain't holdin' a gun." He backed up another step, his right hand brushing the well-used holster at his side. "Well, mister, I got a gun."

Granger went quiet inside. He didn't want to kill this man, who might even be one of those looking to collect Clinton's thousand dollars. He saw the heavy shoulders, massive chest, and arms built like tree stumps, and gaged his chances of whipping him. "Mister, I want no gun trouble. If you gotta beef with me, we can settle it with fists. You look like you've had your share o' knuckle-an'-skull fights."

The man grinned. "Yeah, I can whip yuh, but that ain't gonna hurt long's Ives's feet did. I figger to blow your damned brains out—dead lasts longer'n a whippin'."

Thinking to take the brute by surprise, Granger smiled. "You gonna take that thousand dollars Clinton's promised for my hide home with you tonight. That what you got in mind, scum?" Anger pushed into his throat. "Ain't no corpse ever spent a dime, so I'm waitin' to see can you manage it."

While talking, he stepped toward the bully, swung from his waist, and sank his fist into the man's gut above his belt buckle. The man bent at the waist, gasping for air. Granger clasped his hands and clubbed the giant behind the neck, forcing his face down into the knee Granger brought up.

The man went to the ground, flat on his face. He crawled slowly to his feet, his mouth drooling blood and his nose slewed off to the side, dripping gore. His gun apparently forgotten, he rushed at Granger. The cowboy stepped to the side, swung his boot at the man's shin, and tripped him, throwing him off the boardwalk and into the hitching rack.

Granger watched while the brute unfolded from the rack, kicked a length of sawed timber holding the hitching bar up, wrung it free with his hands, and took a slow, deliberate step toward him. The giant pulled the board back and swung it at Granger's head. He jumped to the side, then stepped inside the piece of wood, sank a right blow into the huge man's gut, and a left to the already broken nose. The bully dropped the board.

Wild with pain and anger, the giant rushed Granger, grabbed him in his huge arms, and squeezed. He butted the cowboy in the forehead at the same time. Lights flashed behind Granger's eyes. If he went out now, the brute would kill him. He lifted both feet from the ground and dropped, breaking the giant's hold. He hit the ground, rolled away from a kick, and gained his feet. Then he waded in, swinging with both fists. A right and a left to the soft gut, a right to the giant's mouth, another left to the gut, then he measured the brute for a knockout punch. If it didn't work, he was really in trouble. He brought his right up from his knees and clubbed the brute over the heart.

The huge man's mouth opened, sucked for air. His face purpled. Granger opened his fist and swung the flat of his hand into the giant's throat. He felt the windpipe crush. Granger stood, holding his face expressionless, watching the bully try desperately to get air into his lungs. The effort was futile. Air would never pass through his crushed throat again.

For the first time, Granger became aware of the crowd. He swept them with a glance. Some cheered, others looked on with awe, and yet others fingered the walnut handles of their revolvers.

Granger's face felt stiff as sun-baked cardboard, and his forehead hurt, his entire head hurt. He squared off toward those standing together massaging the handles of their handguns. "You trash got any ideas about them guns you're packin', go ahead. Reach for 'em. I'll bury you in the same hole I throw this garbage into."

Those he'd addressed stared another moment or two, then turned and drifted toward the saloon they frequented, muttering to each other. "They had a notion, Colt, they sure had a notion."

Granger whirled to find Benning standing beside him. The miner locked gazes with him. "What would you have done if they'd gone for their guns?"

Still feeling as though his face were made of plaster, he eyed his friend. "Reckon they'd need a bigger hole." He walked to the man he'd killed, stripped him of his belt and holster, went through his pockets, and found a couple bags of dust. He handed the gold dust to Benning. "Give it to the sheriff. He can find somebody to bury this trash. I'm gonna finish what I started—gonna get a drink.''

In Orem's saloon, he had no trouble finding friends who wanted to buy him a drink. After wringing the subject of the fight dry, they wanted to know what he was doing, how he liked the Bitter Root Valley, how Molly was getting along, and what he was doing back here at the gulch. He nursed two drinks while he answered their questions—all but the one about why he'd come back to Virginia City. Time would answer that.

Clinton watched the fight from his office window. The fat blob followed, and mimicked, every swing, cursing and damning his hired gun for not going for his revolver and killing the man he hated above all else.

When finally the fight ended, he thought a moment to make sure there was no way they could trace the dead man to him. He felt no pity for the man who had just been killed. His only feeling was that the man was a damned fool. He shrugged—no one could prove a thing.

To make matters better, his letter to Denver would be there by now. Another week would give Snake Muldour time to have found a gunfighter, and also give the gunman time to get here. After Granger filled a hole in boot hill, or perhaps before, he'd have Sanders taken care of. Then it would be over—finished, and he could get on with his business.

He went back and melted into his chair, every ounce of his blubber molding itself to the contours of the solidly built piece of furniture.

He frowned. That man Drago looked capable enough to get rid of the meddling lawyer, and he looked in need of money. Clinton nodded to himself. The man he'd sent to check the big man out should have that done by the time he'd told Drago to come back. He smiled. Everything seemed to be falling into place. He pushed against the arms of his chair, and on the second try stood, went to his back room, unlocked the door, and again counted the rows of carefully stacked bags of gold dust. Some men got their kicks from women, whiskey, and cards. He looked on them with contempt. Gold—gold was the real boost a man needed.

The next evening, the man he'd sent to check Drago out slipped into his office. Clinton didn't ask him to sit down, or offer him a drink. The man stood in front of his desk.

"What'd you find out?"

The skinny outlaw nodded. "He's what he says he is. He rode for Plummer, hit hard times when Plummer got his self hung, then his partner got killed over on the Grasshopper, he escaped from the posse chasin' 'em without bein' recognized, come over here an' worked for day wages. Workin' for that kind o' money didn't work. He told some friends o' his his hands didn't fit a shovel." He nodded. "Reckon he's what he says he is. What you want 'im for, boss?"

Clinton gave the man a hard look. "That ain't none of your damned business." He took a small handful of bills from his wallet, put them on the desk in front of the man, and told him to keep quiet about what he'd done and who he'd done it for.

18

AFTER DARK, THE day after he had his report on Drago, Clinton snapped the lock on his door and waddled toward the back room. A knock sounded. He took his Derringer from his vest pocket, went back, and stood to the side. "Who is it?"

"Drago here. Come after night set in. Figured you'd want it this way."

Clinton grunted with satisfaction. Maybe this man had enough sense to keep him out of trouble. He unlocked the door, and quickly closed it behind the big man. He still held his pocket pistol, and still pointed it at Drago. The man was an outlaw. Despite what he said he was here for, he might be bent on robbing him. He laboriously walked back to his desk, placed the small gun on it in easy reach, and told Drago to sit.

He studied the big outlaw long enough for Drago to wonder if he'd found something about him to cause distrust. "You want a job, huh? Don't care what it is, that right?"

Drago nodded. "That's right. Ain't been p'ticular till now. Don't see no reason to change."

Clinton toyed with the gun, twisting it around in a circle on his desktop. Through the folds of fat around his eyes, he pinned Drago with a look. "We talked 'bout you goin' after Granger. That's changed. He may be the one I'll send you after when you get the first man—if he ain't taken care of by then." He looked at a coffeepot on the stove in the corner. "Get us a cup o' coffee, an' I'll tell you what I want done." His demanding tone ruffled Drago's feathers.

But, despite his feeling, he went to the coffeepot, his cheeks and neck hot with angry blood at being ordered around like a dog. Mentally, he shrugged. What difference did it make? Well, yeah, it made a difference. It made him even more sure he was doing the right thing for Sanders. He took the two cups back to the desk. "All right, Mr. Clinton, what you want done?"

Clinton took a swallow of coffee, then eyed Drago and without preamble said, "Want you to kill Fisk Sanders. He's gettin' in my way."

Drago acted as if dumbfounded, then shook his head. "That's gonna take some doin'. That man is knowed all over the territory. Anythin' happens to him, the Vigilantes'll be madder'n a bitch wolf who done lost her pups."

"You sayin' you don't want the job?"

Drago shook his head. "No, sir. Ain't sayin' that a'tall. What I am sayin' is, that's gonna cost you some money. What'd you figger to pay for a job like that?"

Clinton's hand shook. Drago thought it might be from anger. He'd already gauged the fat man as not liking obstacles. Clinton studied his desktop a moment, then looked up. "A thousand dollars ought to take care o' you pretty well,"

The ex-outlaw shook his head. "Ain't no way. Granger, or any ord'nary man, a thousand'd be good, but a man well known like Fisk Sanders? Nope, to my way o' thinkin', two thousand would be cheap."

Clinton hesitated only a second, then nodded. Drago knew in that instant that Clinton would kill the man who did the job for him, and wouldn't be out a cent. "Two thousand it is. How long you figger on takin' to get it done?"

For a few moments, the big man made a show of thinking about it. Frowning, he studied his hands folded in his lap, and still staring at them, he said, "Prob'ly take at least two weeks. Have to check out his habits, see where he goes, and when. Then I'll pick a spot to get it done from."

Clinton's face flushed. "Two weeks? You any good, you ought to take care o' ten men in that time."

Drago made as if to rise. "Get yourself another man. I work real careful like."

The fat man took the bait. "Now, don't get all in a huff. Sit down." His face puckered in what might have passed for a smile. "I like a man who's careful. Be best for us both. I was just tryin' to see if you really was the man to do the job." He nodded. "You got it. Now let's see can you produce."

Drago relaxed inwardly. He didn't know what he would have done had Clinton not stopped him from walking out. "You want me to come by ever' once in a while an' tell you what's goin' on?"

Clinton shook his head. "Be best if you ain't seen comin' in here. All I want outta you is when you finish the job, bring me proof you done got rid o' that meddlin' bastard. Then, come here at night an' get paid."

Drago thought: Get paid? Yeah, with a slug from that little hideout pistol the fat man toted. He stood. "Next time I see ya, you'll be free of that skinny little shyster." He grinned as he said it, and walked to the door. "Better lock this door after me—ain't no tellin' who might like to get in here." Quiet as a shadow, he stepped out and pulled the door closed behind him. The lock clicked as he walked away.

Drago walked a little over a block down Wallace Street, crossed it, went between two buildings, and walked back the way he'd come. When he was in back of Sanders's office, he tapped lightly. The door opened a crack, obviously letting Sanders see who was there, then it opened enough for the big outlaw to slip in. He grinned. "See you got the habit now of closin' your blinds. Noticed that from across the street."

Fisk didn't say a word. He walked to his desk, took out his bottle of good whiskey, and poured two glasses full. He handed Drago his drink and looked expectantly at him. "Get the job?"

Drago nodded and grinned. "Yeah, an' you're the target. Figured it'd be Granger, but Clinton acted like he had that taken care of by somebody else, didn't say who."

Sanders toyed with his drink a moment. "That worries me. Far as I know there isn't a man in the territory who can handle our friend in a stand-up gunfight."

Drago took a swallow, frowned, and said, "We both know a bullet in the back don't call for nothin' but a good rifle shot—but Clinton's done tried that, so what does it leave?

Sanders squinted across the table. "A hired gun? Somebody from outta the territory? Somebody not known hereabouts?" He nodded, answering his own questions. "Could be. He's tried everything else, but bringing in a gunfighter from outside will be expensive."

"Yeah, Fisk, but s'pose he don't figger on payin' out no money. S'pose he thinks to kill whoever does anything for him. I b'lieve that's what he thinks to do with me. I asked for two thousand bucks to get rid of you, and he didn't bat an eye. Told 'im it'd take me 'bout two weeks to set things up to kill you. He didn't like takin' that much time, but when I started to walk out, he backed off an' give me the job."

"Why two weeks?"

Drago scratched his head, took a swallow of his drink, and put it back on Sanders's desk. "Don't rightly know, Fisk. What I wuz figgerin' wuz, if he's got somethin' planned to get rid o' Granger, it'll happen in that time, an' I gotta do some thinkin' 'bout what you an' me's gonna do to make 'im b'lieve I disappeared you for good."

Sanders stood. "Stay here. I'm going to fetch Sheriff Neil Howie. He'll need to know what we're doing."

Drago felt a shiver go up his spine. He'd never had much dealings with the law, and those he'd had were unpleasant. "We gotta do that, Fisk? He might be another Plummer. Can we trust 'im?"

Sanders nodded. "He's honest, a good man, you'll like 'im. Stay here, I'll be right back. Pour yourself another drink."

The lawyer closed the door behind him, and the ex-outlaw stared at the half-full bottle on the desk. He reached for it, drew back his hand, and settled back in his chair. If a sheriff was going to be sitting in this room with him, he wanted his thinking to be straight.

The people with whom he now associated brought a smile to his face. He really was getting to be respectable. A lawyer, a sheriff—hell, next thing he knew he might be going to Sunday morning preaching and dinner on the grounds. Well, that wouldn't be all that bad; he'd enjoyed that sort of thing before he left home.

He stood, slipped the thong off the hammer of his revolver, grunted, and thumbed it back over. He had to begin trusting people; besides, Sanders said the sheriff was a good man. If the young lawyer said it, it must be so.

He thought about what to do about Sanders and came up blank, but he had to think of something to make the fat man believe him. Then it occurred to him that whether Clinton believed him or not was beside the point if the crooked claims broker had it in mind to kill him regardless of the outcome.

He had no chance to think about it further. Sanders returned, bringing with him a man of about thirty-five years, tall, tanned, and boyish looking. After introductions, Fisk poured them each a drink and sat.

They told Howie what they planned, and had in fact already set in motion. When they finished, Drago sat forward. "Sheriff, it ain't Mr. Sanders here I'm worried 'bout. Figger I can keep him alive. It's Colt Granger we gotta keep from getting' bushwhacked."

Howie smiled. "Why're you so concerned about Granger?"

Drago looked at Sanders, then back to the lawman. "Gonna tell you a story, Mister Sheriff. When I get through, you might have it in mind to arrest me." He felt his face flush. "Fact is, reckon they's a lot o' men out yonder less deservin' of bein' put in jail than me, but you gotta know 'bout me."

He told Howie his story, told him about Granger, and his promise to the cowboy about going home. "Figgered to keep that promise, Sheriff; still do if it's in your thinkin' to let me.''

Howie frowned, his face stern, and shook his head—obviously trying to look serious—then he smiled. ''Hell, Drago, you think Fisk would lead me into something like this without telling me who I was dealin' with?'' His smile widened. ''But, big man, I'm glad you told me yourself.'' He pulled his sack of Durham from his shirt, twirled a cigarette, and lit it before continuing. He squinted at Drago. ''You really think you can keep our lawyer friend alive?''

''Reckon so, bein's I'm the one selected to do 'im in.'' He shrugged. ''Reckon he's a lot safer than I felt when you walked in here with that star on your chest.''

Apparently seeing the long ash building on Howie's smoke, Sanders pushed an ashtray across his desk toward him. ''As I see it then, we have to do something about keeping Granger from getting boxed in.''

The sheriff looked at them. ''Men, there's not one damned thing I can do so long as it's a stand-up gunfight Clinton has planned for him. Of course we don't know that's what it is. The only thing I can do is wait and see.''

In a sleazy little office in the middle of Denver, Snake Muldour again read the letter from Clinton. There were several gunfighters close-by, but most of them had made their reputations by shooting young cowhands who'd come in for a night on the town. And he didn't believe all Clinton wrote. This Granger must be pretty good with a gun, or his fat friend wouldn't have had to go out of the territory to find someone good enough to face him.

Muldour knew that a man not being a known gunfighter didn't mean a thing. There were many men, both fast and accurate with revolvers, but not seeking a reputation, who weren't known outside their own settlements. Too, Clinton had not said how the gunfighter he sent for would be paid, but had said he'd pay two thousand when the job was done. Muldour thought about that for several minutes. The old idiom about there being honor among thieves didn't hold with him. He wouldn't trust the fat man as far as he could throw the building he sat in.

He shrugged. He'd collect his fee for finding whoever he selected, from whoever he selected, and let Clinton and the gunfighter argue about pistol wages.

He carefully went over a list of names he kept at hand, names of men who didn't quibble about what kind of job they were asked to do. Finally, he put a finger on the name of a man who'd worked for him several times, a man who always got the job done, but the only one on the list who had pride, a man who would insist on a fair, face-to-face gunfight: Branch Doty.

Muldour looked over his shoulder at a small, ratlike man sitting against the wall behind him. "Find Doty. Tell 'im I want to see 'im *muy pronto*."

The rat scurried out while Muldour again studied Clinton's letter. Still looking at it, he drank a couple of cups of coffee while waiting for Doty to show.

About to put Clinton's message aside, thinking the rat had had trouble finding his man, he looked up and saw Doty walk in. He was about thirty years old, a slight, erect man, clean-shaven, dressed in neat tan range clothes—Muldour thought he'd be considered handsome by women.

"You sent for me, sir?" His eyes never shifted from Muldour's.

Unlike Clinton, the mining broker always played it square with men he sent out. He flipped a hand toward a chair across the desk from him. "Have a seat, Doty. Got something you may want, but I'll tell you straight out, I don't trust the man who wants to hire you." He leaned forward. "What I'm saying is, if you take this assignment, get your money up front—at least half of it—and when you go back to get the rest of it, go in with your revolver in hand. I wouldn't put it past him to shoot you and strip the front money off your corpse."

Doty grinned. "Why you always give me the easy ones?" He sobered. "Tell me about it—who he wants, where, the whole thing—then I'll tell you whether I'll saddle up an' head out."

Muldour read him the letter. "Now you know as much as I do. Except I know Clinton. He's a pig, literally. Where most men have some interest other than money and food, he doesn't—and he doesn't care how he gets either one." He sat back, then leaned forward and on impulse said, "If you take the job, you can pay me my retainer fee when you get back. I don't know how good this Granger is with a gun. I don't know what Clinton's beef is with him. If you're interested enough, he says right there in that letter he's willing to pay you two thousand dollars. When can you let me know if you'll take it?"

Doty shrugged. "I'm not doing anything right now, and with winter coming on, reckon I better pack my gear and get goin'." He stood. "Virginia City, Montana Territory?"

Muldour nodded. "See you when you get back."

Doty laughed. "Assuming I get back." He left, with Muldour staring at the door, feeling dirty—nasty dirty. He had to get out of this business. The people for whom he usually procured gunfighters were ranchers looking for guns to help fight range wars. Doing anything for Clinton made him feel like slime.

Branch Doty, an ex–Confederate cavalry officer, had caught a minié ball in his right thigh and been discharged. He'd come west, was good with a gun, and drifted into gunfighting. The limp caused by his wound soon disappeared—but the pain stayed. He thought of himself as a man of honor. That opinion was what caused him worry while packing his gear. He knew nothing of this man Granger, but since leaving Muldour's office, and having had a little time to think on the job he'd agreed to, he had begun to think it sounded like Clinton was the sort of man he should be going after, rather than Granger. He shrugged. He'd not taken money yet, and when he got there he'd make up his mind—besides, he was getting tired of Denver, and had not seen that Montana country.

He thought to take what became known as the Bozeman Trail, then changed his mind. The Bozeman was shorter, but far deadlier. The Lakota seemed to take exception to white men crossing their hunting grounds, so Doty headed farther west, along the Oregon Trail, then cut north toward Virginia City.

After taking a well-worn trail north, and about to begin looking for a campsite, he saw the tracks of heavily laden wagons cut deeply into the trail ahead of him. He climbed from his horse and on hands and knees studied the tracks. He grunted. The wagon sign was only a few hours old. He toed the stirrup and rode to the top of the next hill. Far in the distance dust rose, covering what he might have seen had the trail been muddy. He studied on the distance a moment and decided to catch them the next day. He'd been without company for several days now, but couldn't catch the wagons by dark. He made camp.

The next day, about mid-afternoon, he rode alongside the last of fifteen wagons in the train. "Howdy, mister, y'all mind if I ride along with you? I'm getting rather lonesome for someone to talk to."

The bullwhacker looked from Doty, to his tied-down holster, then to his horse and packhorse. "Don't make me no never mind, stranger." He chomped at his tobacco cud a moment, spit, and said, " 'Nother gun'll be welcome. We done had more'n a mite o' trouble in the past with bandits takin' our wagons an' all that's in 'em." He spit again. "Course, if you're of a mind to take what we're carryin', you ain't gonna live long. We got extra guns on this trip."

Doty laughed. "Mister, I find more trouble by accident than I'm wont to face. No, sir, I only want your company." He cast a questioning look at the leathery man walking beside his team of oxen. "You look like you been doing this a long time. Doesn't all this walking get mighty tiresome?"

An amused glint came to the bullwhacker's eyes. "Well, sir, I reckon my feet don't get near as tired an' sore as yore rear end sittin' up yonder in that saddle all day, for days on end." A belly laugh exploded from the bottom of his chest. "Days on end," he slapped his thigh, "by gum, I never thought o'it thataway, but that's 'zactly what it is—days on end. Yore end." He laughed and slapped his thigh again.

Doty grinned. "Reckon you're right about that, but to each

his own. Don't think I could get used to traveling by foot.''

He climbed back in the saddle and rode forward, stopping at each wagon and making the acquaintance of the man swinging the bullwhip.

He noticed the first and second day that they seemed wary of him, but by the end of the third day they had accepted him. When they found he was headed to Virginia City, as they were, they loosened up and talked of the town, and people they knew and liked there. Doty liked the men he traveled with: rough, uneducated, hardworking men, men who he judged would be particular about those they called "good people.''

The third night with them, seated by the fire after supper, he brought the conversation around to people he'd heard of in the town. "Any of you men ever hear of a man by name of Granger, or Clinton?''

The first man he'd met eyed him a moment. "Well now, I reckon we all done heered 'bout both o' those two.'' He squinted sideways at Doty. "You know them men?''

Doty shook his head. "Never seen either of them. Heard their names down Denver way. Thought to look 'em up when I get there. Be nice to start out with knowin' a couple of people in a new town.''

The bullwhacker chomped his cud a couple of times, then pinned Doty with a hard look. "Mister, one o' them men's a right nice one to know—that's Granger. Now, I ain't sayin' as how you can push 'im around—fact is I ain't got the guts it'd take to try—but long's you treat 'im friendly I reckon he'd make the kind o' man you could ride the trail with.''

He chewed his tobacco a couple more times, then spit. "Now that other'n you mentioned.'' He raked Doty with a look from head to toe. "You look like a right nice young feller. That other one ain't the kind no self-respectin' citizen like you would want anybody to figure you was tied in with.'' He squinted at Doty. "Mister, that Clinton's nothin' but pure trash, an' he ain't one to trust no further'n you could see 'im even if you wuz half-blind. No sir, ain't nobody in that town likes Clinton but some o' the bunch what does dirty stinkin' jobs fer 'im, an' I ain't sure they like 'im, they jest like the money he pays 'em.''

The bull session broke up after a while and Doty went to his blankets. For some reason he felt dirty, and the bull-whacker's description of the two men in Virginia City had everything to do with the way he felt.

Lying in his blankets, he thought about himself. He scrubbed himself down hard. At one time he'd been considered a gentleman. Now the people from his past with whom he'd been accepted, as ''their kind,'' would likely ignore him if they met on the street. A gunfighter was tolerated only as long as someone needed his services. From what he'd heard, Granger, even though he was a man one had better be wary of crossing, had not earned the name ''gunfighter.'' He might have been one somewhere else, but not in the Montana Territory, and Doty felt a surge of respect for this man who had in some way escaped the taint—and his reaction lowered his self-esteem even more. His thoughts went to Clinton.

He'd not heard one good word about the man all described as a crooked pig. Doty frowned up at the star-studded heavens. Why had he come on this trip? Why had he taken up the gun for a living? Was it too late for him to turn back, make a new life for himself?

19

NOTICING THE PACKAGES Molly brought to her room each time she went out, Granger decided he'd better get busy and find her something she'd like. A dress was out of the question. He'd been in every ready-to-wear shop in town. He either wasn't sure he liked the dresses he looked at, or wasn't sure he'd get the right size.

He walked aimlessly along the street, came to a goldsmith's shop, and on a hunch went in. Molly didn't wear jewelry, but there might be something in there she'd like. Then he saw the watches and remembered when, during the fight in the gulch, he had thought to get her one. He looked at everything the smith had in his case, but kept coming back to a simple, locket-style watch with a black grosgrain ribbon to hang it from her neck.

Colt asked the jeweler what he thought about replacing the ribbon with a chain. The man tried several with the watch, and shook his head. "Mr. Granger, I think the chain takes away from the beauty of the watch." He smiled. "Of course I'd like to sell you a chain, but that's what I think."

Granger again held chains up to the watch and couldn't make up his mind. "Tell you what. Gonna let Molly make up her own mind. Gimme the ribbon an' chain." Before he left, he bought her a wide hammered gold bracelet to go with the timepiece, put the bracelet in his inside coat pocket, and dropped the watch in his side pocket.

On leaving the shop, he came face-to-face with Drago, and walked by him as if he didn't exist. He went to Orem's saloon, and as soon as he ordered a drink, Red told him he'd heard Gant was dead, shot by some drifter name of Ike Burrage. No one bothered to look for the killer.

His face expressionless, Granger mentally went over the list Sanders had given him. Clinton he now had to worry about, and if the young lawyer didn't get the pig in court soon, Granger figured to take the law into his own hands. As long as Clinton lived, he was a threat because he'd hire his killing done, and there were always men looking for money they didn't work for. Neither he nor Molly could go on this way.

He looked up when Red poured his drink. "Thanks. That narrows it down to Clinton."

"Be careful, cowboy. Know you can take care of yourself if you see the man comin' after you. It's them you don't see you got to worry about."

Granger shrugged. "I come over here to deliberately kill a man. Don't know as I ever done that before. But Sanders says to wait, give the law a chance. Well, I figure to do like he says, up to a point, then if I have to break his door down an' blow that fat bastard's brains out, that's what I'm gonna do."

Red made a swipe at the polished surface in front of Granger, then pinned him with a look. "Give Fisk a chance. He knows what he can do, and he can work a jury like nobody I ever seen."

Colt nodded. "All right, but if we get Clinton in court, an' they turn 'im loose, I guaran-damn-tee you he'll never get back to his office."

Red gave him a hard-faced smile. "Fair enough. Ain't a jury in the territory gonna find you guilty for doin' it your way."

Colt had one more drink and left. Out on the street, he walked aimlessly past stores, the livery stable, reached the

outskirts of town, and turned back. When again approaching
the livery, he thought he saw a glint of sunlight off metal.
He slowed his pace, wary that it might have been a weapon
of some sort. He grinned to himself. He was jumpy as a bride
on the first night of her honeymoon—not that he'd ever been
with a bride, but he reckoned that was the way she'd feel.

He saw the flash of light again, and stopped. Jumpy or
not, he'd lived this long by not being careless. On impulse,
he twisted, drew his .44, and ran toward the stable. The sharp
crack of a rifle sounded, then he felt a tug at his coat. While
running, he fired two shots at the door of the haymow. In
the back of his mind he was aware people on the street were
running for doorways, alleys—anything to get out of the line
of fire.

He came up flat against the livery wall, then ran to the
back, hoping to catch the ambusher. No one ran from the
stable. A glance along the back showed only the closed double doors. He couldn't go barging through them; he'd take
lead for sure.

Silent as a still night, he moved down the wall to the other
side. The window into the hostler's quarters stood only four
or five feet away. Squatting, he crab-legged his way to hunker under it.

If he stood and showed himself in the opening, he might
catch a face full of bullet. He took off his hat and, holding
it on the end of his revolver barrel, pushed it above the sill.
It didn't draw fire. But the gunman might be waiting to see
his eyes.

He thought on that a moment, and, figuring the gunny
could not aim the rifle and fire as quickly as he could get a
look inside, he went to the other side of the opening, swept
the room with a lightning glance, and dropped below the sill.
Although there was not much light, there had been enough
for him to determine that the gunman was not in the room.
He climbed through the window and slipped toward the door
to the stable.

A look for metal hinges showed that the door hung from
leather straps. They shouldn't make noise on opening, but

just in case, he lifted on the door to take weight off it, and pulled toward him. No noise.

He hesitated to step through the opening. Once in the runway of the stable, he'd be in plain sight of anyone in there—if the gunman looked his way. He pulled in a deep breath and let it out slowly. Smells of leather and horse droppings came to him, but the breath did little toward calming his tight stomach, or pushing the taste of fear out of his throat.

He clutched his revolver in a tight fist, the hammer drawn back. He let the door sag on the straps and slipped into the long, dark space between stalls. His gaze searched the side he could see, but two blind spots remained: the side on which he stood and the loft. He was certain the bullet aimed at him had come from above. He settled on looking for the gunman there.

Searching for a ladder, he found it in the middle of the row of stalls, then continued looking. He couldn't go up that way and poke his head into the haymow without having at least half of the loft out of his range of sight. Against the wall in the back he found another way to gain the upper level: rungs nailed to a support stanchion. He sighed. He might get shot, but from there he'd be able to see who threw lead at him.

He'd never slipped up on a Comanche camp any quieter than he went to the back ladder. He looked up, hoping there wasn't a door over the opening at the top—and lucked out. Often a door in the floor would have junk on top of it, things that would be noisy if disturbed.

He tested each rung to make certain it supported his weight, and if it made noise. With each upward step his nerves stretched tighter, seeming on the verge of snapping, but then they told him he still had a way to go before reaching their limit.

The yawning hole at the top seemed all too inviting to help him meet his maker—but it was the only way. Then, less than halfway up, he got another idea. He carefully lowered himself back to the ground and shadowed his way to the farthest, darkest corner of the runway, where he sat holding his .44 across his knees. His man had to come to ground sooner or later, and he could wait. He'd played this game many times.

He sat there wanting to smoke his pipe. His rear end went to sleep. He shifted his weight. His neck got stiff from looking up. He rolled it around on his shoulders. Suppertime came and went. Hunger didn't bother him. He waited.

Finally, a scraping, as of a boot sole, sounded, close to the middle ladder. He focused his attention there, and the door at the top opened. A head came through first, swung around as though looking to see if anyone was there, then pulled back into the top. A grunt, then clothing scraped the wooden floor, and feet came through the opening, followed by jeans with a rifle dangling down the side of them; then the rest of the man appeared, his rifle hung from a finger attached to a stiff, unbending arm sticking out straight from the shoulder. The man moved his good arm to a rung, clasped it tightly, jumped down, and grabbed the next rung with the same hand, until he reached the bottom. When his feet touched the ground, he turned and stared straight into Granger's eyes.

Even with a crippled arm, the man swung the rifle in a smooth arc and fired. The bullet knocked Granger against the wall. He slipped his thumb from the hammer of his .44. A red splotch appeared on the man's shoulder.

Watching the gunman slam back against the base of the ladder, Granger eared the hammer back again. This time he made sure his shot went for the gut. He fired, then eared back the hammer and put a second shot into the man's gut. Then he walked to him. "Knew I shoulda killed you over at Hell Gate, Bowdeen, an you gonna wish a thousand times I had. Gonna sit right here an' watch you die. Anyone comes to help you, I'm gonna kill them, too."

The gunman stared up at Granger from eyes filled with pain, fear, and hate. "You cain't do this, man. For God's sake—help me."

Granger only stared down at the man.

"C'mon, Granger, you ain't no Blackfoot, you're a white man. Help me."

Granger punched out fired shells from his .44 and punched in good ones. He picked up Bowdeen's rifle, pulled his revolver from its holster, and walked to the other side of the runway, where he put his back against the wall and slid to the ground to watch Bowdeen hurt.

His ribs smarted like a mule had kicked him. Not taking his eyes off the bushwhacker, he ran his hand over his shirt, felt blood, and slipped his hand inside. His fingers found only what he thought might be a crease under his arm. Puzzled, he ran his fingers over where he felt the most pain, winced, and did it again. Felt like a broken rib. He'd look at it back at his room.

Running footsteps sounded outside, then more circled the stable on both sides. "You, in there, you're surrounded. Throw down your weapons and come out. This is Sheriff Neil Howie speaking."

Granger looked from the stable door to Bowdeen. "Don't figure this in your favor. I ain't lettin' nobody get a doctor for you till you take your last shiver an' die." He turned his face toward the big double doors. "Howie, Granger here. One o' us is too close to dead to walk out, an' I ain't comin' out till this'n with me ain't with me no more. Come on in if you want. Ain't nobody gonna shoot a sheriff."

The stable doors swung wide and three people came through them. The sheriff walked to Granger. "What happened, Colt?"

Granger led him through the whole thing, then, staring hard-eyed at the lawman, he said, "Don't a one o' you get a doctor. I'm gonna sit right here an' watch that slime hurt till he dies."

Howie shook his head. "Knew you were a hard man, Colt, but you can't do this, it's inhuman."

Granger nodded. "Figured it that way. He's gonna die anyway. I know where my shots went. He's another one o' them wantin' to collect Clinton's filthy money. Deserves what I'm givin' 'im."

The two who'd come in with the sheriff stood gawking at Bowdeen. One of them asked, "Want me to get a doctor, Howie?"

Before the lawman could answer, Granger cut in. "Wait. I got a idea. Tell Bowdeen you'll get a doctor if he levels with you why he shot me, an' who's payin' 'im.''

Howie only now looked at Granger's bloody side. He squatted. "You hit, Colt? Bad? Why didn't you say something?"

"Ain't bad. Do like I asked."

Howie frowned at his friend a moment, then nodded and went to Bowdeen. With a wave of his hand, he motioned to his side the two men who had come into the livery with him, and said, "Listen to what this man has to say, and remember it. You gonna have to tell it in court."

He looked at Bowdeen. "I'll get you a doctor on one condition. Tell me why you tried to bushwhack Granger and who's paying you. You lie, and you'll stay here like he wants you to, hurting and bleeding until you're a dead man."

Bowdeen stared at the lawman a moment, then puckered his lips and spit on Howie's boots. "Ain't tellin' you nothin'. Gonna die anyway."

The lawman's next words told Granger what kind of man they had for a sheriff. "Yeah, Bowdeen, you're gonna die anyway, but we do it Granger's way and you're gonna suffer the miseries of seven different kinds of hell. Tell me what I want to know, I'll get a doctor, he'll give you some sort of medicine to kill the pain, and you can cross the divide in some sort of peace."

Bowdeen sucked in a pain-filled breath. "Go to hell, lawman."

Granger couldn't help but feel admiration for the outlaw, then pity, when Howie continued, "Gonna tell you how this works, scum. The pain's gonna get worse. Gangrene's gonna set in, and when it does, your body's gonna turn black— then the pain's gonna get so bad you'll beg me to give you a gun, or blow your brains out myself." He glanced toward Granger. "Now I'm gonna go sit with my friend till you start whimperin'."

One of the men who had come in with Howie stepped toward the door.

"Where you goin'?"

"Aw hell, Sheriff, I'm going to get a doctor. We can't let this man hurt any more then he is.''

Howie pointed at the ground by one of the stalls. "Sit. We're doin' this like Granger said." Then, by way of explanation, he said, "Depend on it: justice will be served by doing it his way." Though obviously reluctant to follow the sheriff's instruction, the man did as he was told.

The five men sat silent, but four of them had eyes only for the wounded bandit. After a half hour, sweat poured down Bowdeen's face; he held hands tight against his stomach, and despite obvious efforts to squelch it, he moaned. The sounds increased until they were a steady mewling sound deep in his throat. He nodded. "I'll tell, Sheriff. Send for a doctor."

Before the doctor arrived, Bowdeen told them everything he knew about Clinton's offer of a thousand dollars for Granger's scalp, as well as a rumor he'd heard of another two thousand for killing Fisk Sanders.

The doctor examined the bandit, shook his head, and pulled a bottle of laudanum from his valise. "No point in moving him. This'll ease his pain until he goes." He looked at Bowdeen. "Nothing I can do for you. Drink this." Then as an afterthought, he said, "You're going to die. You would if I'd gotten here as soon as it happened." From the outlaw, he went to Granger, and dressed his wound despite his protest he didn't need it. Then he picked up his little black bag and left.

The sheriff instructed the two men who'd witnessed Bowdeen's words to not leave town, that he thought everything would be settled in a couple of weeks, to pack weapons, and to keep quiet about what they'd heard for their own safety, because if Clinton would hire men to kill, he'd certainly put them on his list if he knew what they'd been told. He let them leave.

When the two cleared the door, Granger nodded. "Reckon that 'bout wraps it up."

Howie shook his head. "Don't think Fisk's gonna be satisfied. He's gonna want more than one man's word. Better wait until we see what Drago comes up with." He stared at Granger's coat a moment with a puzzled frown. "How'd that bullet hit right over your heart and yet cause only a crease?"

Colt felt his ribs. "Been wonderin' that myself." The back of his hand rubbed something hard when he withdrew it from his shirt. "Oh damn. Molly's present." He pulled a badly bent gold bracelet from his inside coat pocket. "Looks like it's really hammered gold now, don't it?"

Howie grinned. "You got two choices, cowboy: you can go back to that goldsmith and have 'im fix it good as new— it'd take 'im only a short time to do that—or you can give it to Molly like it is, tell 'er how it happened, and I'll bet she'd treasure it forever."

Granger gave him a sheepish grin. "Aw, figure it'd worry her if she knew how it happened. I'll get it fixed."

Granger glanced at Bowdeen. The outlaw lay slumped against a stall, his eyes droopy, almost asleep. "Looks like that laudanum's workin' pretty good. He ain't gonna last much longer. Want me to stay with 'im till he's gone?"

Howie shook his head. "We'll both stay, then I'll get somebody to fix 'im for buryin'. After that, we better see Fisk, let 'im know what we have."

Two hours later, Bowdeen shuddered, drew a last, gasping breath, and died. Another hour and the two men sat at Sanders's desk. They told him what had happened, what they'd found out, and, like the sheriff had thought, Sanders said he wanted more. He wasn't going to see Clinton go free.

"Fisk, he ain't goin' free no matter what happens. I'm gonna see to that. Fact is, if I had my druthers, he'd go out a whole helluva lot harder'n Bowdeen."

Sanders stared at the two of them, then reached into his bottom drawer, took out three glasses and a full bottle of whiskey, and poured them each a drink. After they'd all packed their pipes, lit them, and taken a swallow, the lawyer smiled slightly. "Give me time, Colt, give me time. It'll all work out."

"Yeah, if they don't put you in your grave first—an' me alongside."

Buck Drago thought for days, and most of every night, how he could make it believable he'd gotten rid of Fisk Sanders for good. Every plan he came up with, he thought long about

it, trying to see if he could punch holes in it—and he even-
tually did. On this night, despite the chill in his room, he
sweated. He was not a man who knew how to walk around
an issue, or plot how to keep people from figuring the truth,
but tonight differed from the rest. He thought he had a fool-
proof idea, one that wouldn't get him killed while saving
Sanders hide—but put Sanders's safety first. He turned the
plan in his head until he was certain nothing could go wrong.
He'd see what Fisk thought.

20

DRAGO LOOKED AT his watch: two-thirty, cold and dark.
He lay there a few minutes dreading getting from under the
covers—but Sanders needed to know his plan. Any delay
could be deadly. If he put off seeing him, he'd have to wait
until night again before he dared risk going to the lawyer's
office. He pushed the covers back, dressed, and went out.

At his second knock, feet, sounding like they were shoved
into oversized slippers, shuffled on the other side of the door.
"Who is it?"

"Drago here. Need to see you."

"Damn, man, you know what time it is?" Sanders's voice
sounded tired.

"Yeah, Fisk, I know, but this cain't wait till dark comes
agin." A scraping of wood on wood, and he heard Sanders
lift the bar from the door.

Hair tousled, face haggard, red long johns drooping from
his shoulders, Sanders opened for the ex-bandit to enter.
"This better be important."

Buck grinned. "You gonna feel better if you put the coffeepot on, then I got a plan to try on you." Not waiting for
his friend to put the coffee on, he threw wood on the fire,
poured water into the pot from the white enameled pitcher

at its side, dropped a couple handfuls of grounds into the water, and sat at the kitchen table.

With a sour look, Sanders said, "Make yourself at home, Buck."

Drago looked innocently at the lawyer. "Thank you, I already did." He rolled a cigarette, then looked at Sanders. "Gonna tell you right at the beginning, I done scrubbed this plan down every whichaway, an' the only thing I can see goin' wrong is, we gotta let two somebody elses in on it: a man we can trust what ain't known to Clinton, an' the other one we all know, but he's gotta be in on it in order to save your life—an' tie Clinton up in a package we can take to court." He listened to see if the coffee boiled, then sniffed to see if he could catch its aroma. It hadn't started boiling. "Now, here's the plan."

They talked, and at several points argued. After about four hours—talking, drinking coffee, and again looking at the places Drago's plan might come apart—Sanders nodded. "Think it'll work, my outlaw friend."

"Ex-outlaw. Remember, I'm headed home when this is all finished." He glanced at the window. "Daylight's 'bout to come on us. Better get outta here 'fore somebody sees me what shouldn't."

Sanders nodded. "Let me know about a day ahead of time when we want to get this plan of yours under way. In the meanwhile, I'll set it up with the two men we gotta include."

Drago patted his stomach. "Reckon I'll go to the cafe an' get breakfast 'fore I go back to bed." Straight-faced, he added, "Course they's some o' us gotta work today." He left before Sanders could answer.

Branch Doty shrugged into his sheepskin, thinking this was the coldest, most miserable country he'd been in. He looked down on Virginia City, with Alder Gulch winding past it, and even with the cold, there were what looked like hundreds of people milling about in the street, and the creek and its banks had men strung along their length. Busy town.

He'd soon see what kind of people he dealt with. First, he wanted to meet the man he'd come to face in a gunfight, see what kind of man he was, see why this man Clinton had sent out of the territory for someone to take care of him. Then he wanted to see Clinton. The way Muldour described his client left a lot of questions in Doty's mind about why he'd ridden so far on a quest about which he had serious doubts.

He rented himself a hotel room and asked for hot water— as soon as possible. When it came, he shaved and dressed in his best black suit. He reached for his gunbelt, thought a moment, decided to leave it in the room, then changed his mind. He didn't expect to see anyone from his backtrail, but he intended to see Clinton before going to supper. He didn't know why that should call for a weapon—but just to be safe he buckled it on. Right now, he thought to go to the best saloon in town, have a drink, and listen to the talk going on around him.

His first stop was the general mercantile store, where he bought a tin of tobacco and asked the whereabouts of a saloon that served good whiskey. The proprietor pointed him to Con Orem's Champion Saloon.

When he pushed through the heavy wooden door, like most men in the West who had things on their backtrail, he stepped to the side long enough to study every face in the place. Satisfied he knew no one in the room, he went to the bar, ordered a drink, and nursed it while listening to the talk around him.

Most of what he heard centered on the War Between the States. The sympathizers were about evenly split between the North and the South. He wanted no part of their conversations, which he'd found frequently ended in a fight.

He stood next to a slightly built man wearing a suit. The man eyed him a moment and, apparently not wanting to drink alone, or maybe just wanting company, pointed to Doty's drink. "Buy you a drink, stranger?"

Doty smiled. "Why yes, sir, but only if you'll let me reciprocate."

Fisk Sanders nodded. "Sounds fair enough." He introduced himself while shaking Doty's hand. "What brings you to this out-of-the-way place, Mr. Doty?"

A chill went up the gunfighter's spine, then he figured the

question was innocent enough. He smiled. "Well, sir, I think it's obvious I'm not a miner, but I am interested in cattle. Thought to go out to the Oregon country around the Willamette Valley—never been there, but hear in addition to farm country a man might find good range in the higher valleys."

Sanders nodded. "Might. In fact I hear the Durham breed does right well out there." He frowned, obviously thinking. "Seems like I remember a friend of mine who's thinking of bringing in Durhams to his place up in the Bitter Root Valley, not too far from Hell Gate. Maybe you'd like to talk with him about that country. Don't know that he's been out there, but he'd be a good man to meet anyway. Nice man. You'd like 'im. His name's Granger, Colt Granger."

Doty's emotions went to war with each other. Granger, Sanders had said was a nice man, and he'd like him. Hell, he didn't want to like him. He knocked back his drink and ordered them another. "Where might I meet this fellow you mentioned? Granger, I believe you said."

Fisk nodded. "Right. But you just missed 'im. He comes in about this time every day for a drink. If you're staying a day or two, drop in, I'll introduce you."

Doty nodded. "Yes, I think I'll lay over a few days, get the trail dust outta my nostrils. See you here tomorrow?"

Sanders nodded. "I'll be here."

Doty walked to the cafe. Used to the Denver restaurants, he found this establishment rustic, but surprisingly clean and neat. He seated himself at a corner table, from where he could see everyone in the room, which was full except for one other table.

Across from him sat a tall man, well built and handsome by men's or womens' standards. Sitting with him was a young woman, only a few years younger than the man, tall, with features a little too strong to be called beautiful, but pretty as any woman he'd seen. They conducted themselves like people by whom in days gone by he'd been befriended. He thought he'd like to know them. Almost all who passed their table stopped to chat.

He continued to scan the area. Most of those he saw were obviously miners, to judge by their rough dress and weath-

ered features. In the back next to the kitchen sat a man different from any in there. Fat, slurping his food as though at
a hog trough, spilling it down his shirtfront, he belched with
about every other bite. Doty noticed how pale the man's skin
was, as though it had never seen the sun. The sight of him
made Doty's skin crawl, made him feel dirty to know there
was anyone in his world that filthy and evil-looking. He
stood and walked around the table to another chair so he
could eat and enjoy his food.

The proprietor came for his order. His ride into town, the
weather, and the drink before dinner had made him ravenous.
He ordered steak, eggs, biscuits with butter and honey, and
coffee. Before the owner could walk away, Doty pinned him
with a look. "Who's the hog sitting in the back? Hope he
doesn't come in here often; he'll ruin your business. I had
to take a chair facing away from him so I could eat."

Jim Turnbull, the proprietor, gave Doty his own name, and
offered that people called him Bull. He didn't turn to look
at the fat man; instead he shrugged. "I gotta serve whoever
comes in here. I'm lucky that one don't come here often. I
have a boy takes food to his office. He's got a office here in
town—name's Quirt Clinton."

Doty thanked Bull and waited for his dinner. After seeing
Clinton, he wondered stronger on what he'd gotten himself
into. He'd met a man who had nothing but praise for
Granger, and now that he'd seen Clinton . . .

Granger and Molly rose early. They'd decided that according
to what Sanders had told them they had time to renew ac-
quaintances. They spent the day walking along the gulch,
shaking hands, and passing the time of day. After leaving
the claim they had once worked, Molly slanted Colt a look.
"How long you gonna wait, Colt? You saw that pig in the
cafe last night. All he does is plot ways to cheat and steal
from others what they work hard to get."

He took her elbow and helped her over a large boulder.
"Tell you what, little one, I figure it'll all be over in less
than ten days. You notice that man sittin' across from us in
the cafe last night. I figure he's a right dangerous man.

More'n that, I figure he's the one Clinton sent for to gun me down.''

Molly frowned. "Why you think that? I thought he looked like a nice man—sort of a gentleman.''

Granger nodded. "B'lieve you're right. He might be both o' them things you mentioned, but there are them who are nice, an' who are gentlemen, who'll pull a gun quicker'n scat an' kill you just as fast. Many of them left the North or South, an' come out here lookin' for somethin' better. Some of those are naturally good with weapons, an' found on gettin' out here there's a market for their talent. The only thing I hold against 'em is they take money for shootin' people. We don't have many of their kind here, mostly because they ain't no people warrin' against each other.''

He stopped to pack and light his pipe. "Now, take that gent you think is so nice. I got 'im figured as one who would only draw on a man who was lookin' at him. An' I figure he'd give the other man better'n a even break." He shrugged. "Don't know as he's the one after me, but I got the feelin' we gonna find out right soon. I noticed 'im studyin' everybody who came an' went in the cafe—not just a glance, but he checked 'em over pretty good, like he was measurin' what they were capable of gettin' done in a brawl.''

Molly studied him with a worried frown. "Seems like you did a little measuring yourself.''

"Yeah, little one, that's the way I stayed alive this long. Cain't break the habit; fact is this would be a bad time to let down my guard.''

They finished their stroll, and got back to the hotel at about three o'clock. "I'm gonna take a bath, then read a while. What're you gonna do?''

Granger thought a moment. "Think I'll bathe, then go see Fisk for a few minutes. Probably stop by the Champion for a drink before we have supper. Be back here 'bout six. That okay?''

"Fine with me, Colt, long's I know what time to be ready.''

An hour and a half later, Granger sat sharing a drink with

Sanders in his office. "Anythin' new happen since we talked?"

Sanders nodded. "Quite a bit if my thinking is straight." He leaned forward. "I believe things are beginning to fall into place. First, Drago came up with a plan I think'll work toward getting Clinton hung, and I think the gunfighter the fat man sent for, if he sent for anybody, is here in town."

A slight smile crinkled the corners of Granger's lips. "Bet you a drink I can describe the man to you." He leaned back and took a swallow of his drink, then described the man he'd seen in the cafe the evening before.

"You meet this man, Colt? What name did he give you?"

"Naw. I ain't met 'im, just seen 'im in the cafe. How's my description fit who you're thinkin' of?"

Sanders shook his head and cast a surprised look at Granger. "You nailed him right down to a tee. His name's Branch Doty—you're gonna meet 'im when we go down to Champion's for that drink I just lost to you. He's posing as a cattleman, so make like you accept what he tells you at face value."

They sat silently for a few moments, then the lawyer knocked back his drink and eyed his friend. "Colt, I hate like hell to admit it, but I liked Doty. I think he's a straight shooter, but picked the wrong way to make a living."

Granger raised one eyebrow, and allowed himself a slight smile. "Don't feel bad, old friend. I've met several gunfighters I liked—as long as they didn't come gunnin' for me. Fact is, there're places in this country where people call me a gunfighter—but I never took pay to kill a man."

Sanders shoved back from his desk. "Let's go meet the man who came to kill you, if we've got 'im pegged right. I'll tell you Drago's plan later."

A few minutes later they stood at the bar. Doty hadn't arrived. Granger bought a bottle, telling Fisk he'd taken advantage of his hospitality long enough, that now it was his turn to furnish the drinks. They went to a table close to the back wall and sat.

Sanders looked toward the door and then turned to Granger. "There's our man." He stood and went to meet him. "Come on back. Granger's back yonder at a table."

When Sanders introduced them and they shook hands, Granger noticed a hard callous on Doty's thumb pressed to the back of his hand. A man got a callous like that from slipping his thumb off the hammer during hours of practice with a revolver. He had Doty figured right. He poured the gunfighter a drink, motioned to a chair against the wall, and invited him to sit, but he, too, took a chair where he could see the room.

They talked cattle, mining, gambling. Granger didn't get the feeling he was being interrogated, but instead the feeling that he was having a conversation like he would with any man. He told Doty what he knew about Durham cattle, and what he'd heard about the Oregon country. After a couple of drinks, he knocked back the rest of one and stood. "Promised Molly I'd be back to take her to supper. Better go." He shook hands with the gunfighter, telling him he was happy to meet him, and left.

Doty watched until he went out the door. He faced Sanders. "Nice man. You're right, I like him." He smiled. "But I have the impression he'd be the wrong man to cross." He hoped Sanders would take the bait and talk about Granger's capability with a gun.

Sanders nodded. "I'd say your impression is right. I know I'd not like to rile him, but as far as being dangerous, he may have been at one time, but since coming here he's had no reason to show other than friendship, to those who want it. Around here, we let a man's past stay buried. I think that's the way it should be."

Doty felt self-hate well up in him. Damn. Why had the two men he'd met, one of whom he'd been hired to kill, turned out to be men with whom he'd like to be friends? He worked the conversation around to the night before. "Although I hadn't met him, Granger and a pretty girl sat across from me in the cafe last night." Without much effort, he put on a disgusted face. "And I could have enjoyed my meal a lot more had there not been the most evil-looking hog of a man sitting toward the back. In fact, I've seen hogs eat with more polish."

Sanders nodded. "Sounds like you saw Quirt Clinton. He's our local bad boy, although if he knew people thought of him that way, I imagine he'd be surprised. I'm certain he thinks what he does, and the way he operates, is because he's smarter than most."

Doty studied his drink a moment, topped it off with the bottle Granger had bought, and, dreading the answer, asked, "Is what he does illegal? If so—you're a lawyer—why hasn't he been arrested and brought to trial?"

He held his gaze on Sanders's face when he asked the question. Sanders looked hesitant to say anything, then apparently pushed his doubts aside, and pinned Doty with an honest look. "Gonna tell you straight, Branch. I want to do things legal here, want to take our problems to a duly constituted court of law, want to get good solid evidence that'll stand up during a trial." He knocked back his drink, poured another, and shrugged. "Everyone along the gulch knows Clinton is paying killers to get rid of hardworking miners, so he can take their claims and then sell them. I won't go into how he's getting it all done, but you can bet everything you own he's doing it." He packed and lit his pipe, then slammed his fist into his palm. "I can't get the evidence. Any witness whose testimony I look forward to turns up dead—or missing."

Doty sat there wondering if he'd sunk so low as to do the bidding of a man obviously held in contempt and despised by all decent people.

Never having taken others' opinions without looking at all the facts and then making up his mind, he decided he'd see Clinton, talk to him, try to ferret out what the fat man was doing. But the hard fact was, he'd ridden several hundred miles for this job, and though he was far from broke, he could use the money. He and Sanders talked a while longer, then Doty stood. "Maybe if I have supper now I can avoid the time the fat man eats."

Fisk smiled. "Not much of a gamble, Branch. He usually eats in his office." He still sat after Doty left. He poured another drink, realized he was mildly drunk, and figured to hell with it. He'd not been drunk in a long time; fact was— never.

He'd deliberately told Doty the way he, and others, thought about Clinton, wanting to see his reaction. It had done him no good. The gunfighter had sat poker-faced all the while. He wondered if he'd told him too much. Would he tell the fat man what he, Sanders, suspected? What would Clinton do?

A mental shrug dismissed his worries. What more could the fat man do? He'd already hired a man to kill him, and he'd bet the gunfighter had been brought in to take care of Granger. He pushed his drink aside, pushed the bottle along with it, and decided come daylight to leave for Bannack. He had to see a man there to help set up Drago's plan. The ex-outlaw would take care of things on this end.

When he left the saloon, the sky had darkened. Fisk glanced worriedly at the heavy gray clouds, and hoped another storm stayed away until he could make his trip. He glanced down the street toward Clinton's office, wishing he could get Granger to make the trip with him. The cowboy knew more about surviving in this country than most would ever learn. He decided to try and meet him at the cafe.

Drago sat in his room, wishing he could use Granger in his mission, but knew he couldn't. He didn't dare let anyone see them together. He stared at the bare wall of the room and thought to go to the saloon for a drink. He didn't want one, but that was the only way he could be around people. He realized abruptly that he was lonely. Recently he'd been around people he liked, and he wanted more of their company. He stood, thinking to go to the livery and talk to the old man who ran it. He'd eat later.

The big door opened hard against the wind. Drago opened it only enough to squeeze through and into the dark livery runway. He walked back to the room the old man slept in, and let himself in. "Howdy. How's my horse doin'?"

The spindly old man glanced his way. "Doin' right well, but don't figger you come down here to see 'bout yore hoss." He cast the big man a sly look. "You come down here for company. You're 'bout as lonesome as I am, an' you don't like settin' round no saloon sloppin' up rotgut whiskey. Right?''

Drago frowned, having not realized he was that transparent. His frown slipped into a grin. ''Reckon you threw that calf an' got 'im hog-tied right nice.'' He glanced at the coffeepot. ''You got anythin' in that pot?''

The old man nodded. ''Hep yoreself, I got a full cup right here. Tried stickin' a pitchfork in it while ago to see if it had any body to it. It et the tine right off'n that fork.''

While pouring his coffee, Drago glanced around the room. In his spare time the liveryman made coffins. There were a couple stacked one on top of the other back in the corner. Drago glanced over his shoulder. ''You been right busy makin' these here buryin' boxes lately?''

The spindly one frowned. ''Yep. An' you know what? I cain't figger it. They's a whole bunch o' miners gettin' killed, men what you wouldn't figger to be careless enough to buy the farm the way they're doin'—some shot, some drowned, some brought in with their heads bashed in.'' He shook his head. ''Cain't figger it.''

Drago thought to throw out some bait. ''Well, them gettin' killed is good luck for that man Clinton. He ends up with most o' their claims. Makes right good money offa sellin' 'em.''

The old man took the bait. ''Goshding right he does. Makes a man wonder how much of it's luck, an' how much was made to happen.''

That's what Drago needed to know. Now he thought he might lay it on the line for the coffin maker. No. He'd better not. He'd better let the old man know what he thought about Clinton. No again. He'd better go a little slow. Too, he had time. Sanders had to make his trip to Bannack first.

The big man and the skinny one talked a while before Drago stood. ''Shore did enjoy talkin' to you, old-timer. Sorta like to stop by again.''

''Why, goshding it, I'd be right hurt if'n you didn't. All I ever get in here is 'Build me a box to fit this'n,' or, in case it's a hoss, 'Feed 'im grain, rub 'im down, an' water 'im.' ''
He took a swallow of his coffee, and grinned. ''Them I'm

buildin' the box for don't do no talkin', an' them hosses, if
they ever do any talkin', I'm gonna give up this job an' head
for parts unknown.''

The first couple Sanders saw in the cafe were Molly and
Granger. Without being invited, he pulled out a chair and
sat. Granger grinned. ''Well, damn, Fisk, why don't you pull
out a chair and have supper with us.''

Sanders didn't feel like cracking a smile. ''Don't feel like
observing the amenities tonight. Gonna make a long, cold
ride over to Bannack. Start early in the morning if it doesn't
set in to snow. Thought to ask if you thought Molly'd be all
right here alone, if you'd go with me.'' He grinned, knowing
it was sheepish. ''Fact is, I'd feel a lot safer with you siding
me. Don't know whether Clinton hedged his bet and hired
another man to do the same thing he hired Drago to do.''

Granger looked a question at Molly. She nodded. ''I'll be
all right, and I'll feel better knowing you're looking after
Fisk.''

Their supper came and they settled in to eat. After butter-
ing a biscuit and putting honey on it, Granger slanted Fisk
a look. ''You notice it's comin' on to snow?'' Without waiting for an answer, he said, ''Gonna be a blowin', howlin'
damned blizzard if I read it right. Wind's already picked up
more'n a mite.''

Fisk swallowed the bite he'd been chewing. ''Colt, I
thought to make this trip before the clouds rolled in. I have
it to do. I'm not setting myself up as the Alder Gulch savior,
but I believe I'm uniquely qualified to do what has to be
done to get rid of Clinton's evil. I have to go.''

Granger looked from Sanders to Molly. ''Little one, if
anything happens to us, you have the cabin, you know where
the gold stash is, we got friends in the settlement, and among
the Flatheads. You can shoot better'n most men I know, so
you take care.'' He drank a swallow of water. ''Now, gonna
tell you somethin'. Whatever happens, I think this is gonna
end it. Clinton won't dare come after you if we ain't around.
Too many men what'd string 'im up for even thinkin' to
harm you.''

Molly stared at him a moment. "You'll both be back. I figure you could lead Fisk into the jaws of hell and bring 'im back.'' She smiled. "Somethin' you gotta remember, too—next to you, Fisk Sanders is some sort o' man. Don't reckon there's anybody in the territory who could best the two of you.''

Granger nodded. "Sort 'o the way I figured you'd take to us leavin' you, but I'd like to say one more thing. If you find yourself needin' a friend, you ain't gonna do much better'n Buck Drago.''

A frown puckered her brow. "You've taken quite a liking to that outlaw, haven't you? Well, if you trust him that much, and I need any help, I'll take your word for it. We better get to bed now. You men have a hard tomorrow coming.''

The next morning, Granger awoke to just what he'd predicted. Wind howled about the eves, snow swirled and danced down the frozen street, then sheets of it shut out all before his eyes. Before going to the cafe to meet Sanders, he went by the hotel he knew Drago stayed in, wakened him, and told him to watch after Molly. Then he told him what he and Fisk were about to do.

The big outlaw stared at him a moment. "Sounds bad out there, Colt. You take care, an' don't worry 'bout Miss Molly. Ain't nothin, or nobody, gonna bother her.''

Granger pulled from his pocket a couple bags of dust. "Fisk give me this in case somethin' happens we ain't here to pay you.'' It was actually his dust, but a white lie here and there never hurt anything.

"Aw now, hell, I ain't earned that yet. You keep it till I do.''

Granger shook his head. "We trust you to earn it. This is just in case somethin' happens. Both o' us want you to take somethin' home to your folks.'' He tossed the two bags to the bedside stand, and when he turned to leave, he'd have sworn the big outlaw's eyes were swimming in tears.

"You take care, you heah.'' Drago's words followed him out the door.

An hour later, using all the trail smarts he'd ever had, Granger kept them in the right direction. They'd pulled blan-

kets from their bedrolls, draped them over their heads, pulled
hats down over them to keep them in place, and buckled
gunbelts around them at their waist. Under the blankets, each
wore a sheepskin and two shirts, along with two pair of trousers.

Granger slanted a look across his shoulder. "Ain't gonna
make many miles today, but I figure we mighta got outta
Virginia City without Clinton seein' us leave. Course, 'fore
the day's done, he's gonna miss seein' people go in an' outta
your office. then he's gonna know somethin' ain't right."

His face blue, his teeth chattering, Fisk said, "Be too late
by then. Don't believe anybody's gonna catch us in this
storm."

Wind gusted in great puffs, then settled to a faint breeze,
allowing Granger to see the trail. During the gusts it swept
the rutted, hoof-marked road clean. Colt remembered a blowdown about fifteen miles from the gulch. He figured to find
it, if he could find the old lightning-struck pine close to
where they'd have to pass. Snow came in squalls, heavy,
then light, but the drifts built regardless.

He looked at the sky in vain. No way to tell the time when
you couldn't see the sun, or at night the stars. He wished
now he'd bought himself a watch when he'd bought Molly's.
He hated to have Sanders dig under his blanket and coat for
his timepiece, but he asked anyway.

"Three-thirty. You thinking to stop soon?"

"Reckon so. These horses done had 'bout all they can
handle for one day."

Fisk chuckled. "Yeah, and you can put me in there right
along with them."

Another hour and it set in to snow in earnest. They had
to get off the trail—or get lost and waste hours finding where
they were the next day. Granger looked at Sanders. The man
had guts. He hunched over, now holding his saddle horn, and
what Colt could see of his face was almost black. He
frowned. He had to get his friend to shelter—or he wouldn't
have a friend.

As soon as he had the thought, the old pine showed
through the blowing flakes. Granger kneed his horse against

the side of Sanders's pony and urged him over. In only a short time he found the blowdown snuggled close to the base of a cliff.

He climbed from the saddle, certain every joint would break if he tried to bend them. They were so stiff they hurt like nails were being driven into them. He stood by the side of his horse hanging onto the saddle horn. When he could move, he staggered to the side of Sanders's horse, reached up, pulled his friend from the saddle, held him a few moments, then eased him to the ground.

Before making the campsite tight against the weather, he built a fire and pulled Fisk close to the cliff. He next cut and wove branches from live trees into the pine's skeleton to break the wind, then cut saplings and leaned them against the cliff to seal off the weather.

21

THE SHELTER SNUG against most of the wind, and with little snow filtering in, Colt turned his attention to Fisk. He looked down at the young lawyer, now beginning to get color back in his face. "You all right, Fisk? Coffee's on, an' I'll start supper soon's I get some warm liquid in you."

Sanders moved his lips. Nothing came out, but on the second try he said, "You're one helluva man, Colt Granger. Most men woulda died out yonder. You had enough left to take care of me, make a fire, a shelter, an' cook."

Embarrassed, Granger felt a surge of blood flush his face. "Aw hell, I been doin' this since I was just a button. You could, too, if you'd been brung up doin' it." He busied himself making a broth by slicing thin strips of jerky into boiling water. When it was ready, he spooned it into Sanders until he'd taken in a coffee cupful. Then he got down to the serious cooking: bacon, beans, hardtack. They'd both share in those things.

The next morning, the snow had stopped and the wind had lessened to a dead calm. Granger poured Sanders a cup of coffee, and studied his face for frostbite. "You feel up to goin' on? We can rest here another day if you figure that'll get you ready for the trail."

"We'll go on. Hate it I couldn't keep up, Colt, but I'm okay now. We got a job to do."

By midday the clouds had given way to a distant, cold sun. The lack of wind, with sunlight, made it seem warmer. They rode into Bannack soon after the last rosy glow in the west, too late for Sanders to see his man. They rented rooms, went to supper, and turned in.

The next morning they looked for Bert Colgan, a hardcase, with a shady past behind him—but a man who owed Sanders a favor. And according to Fisk, Colgan paid his debts. He described the man to Granger before they separated to look in different parts of town. For Sanders's own safety, Colt took the rough part of town.

He stopped in a saloon, let it be known he looked for Colgan, and moved on to another. In most places the customers gave him dirty looks, but since his gunfight with Diamond, word had spread he was no man to cross. They left him alone.

The fifth place he stopped, the Last Gulp, a man sidled up to him. Granger knew at once he'd found his man: tall, bone-thin, with muscle and sinew stretched over his frame, large nose, and Texas eyes, light blue behind lids permanently squinted from looking into the sun. "You lookin' for me, stranger?"

"If you're Bert Colgan, I'm lookin' for you. If you ain't, I ain't."

"This friendly talk, or gun talk?"

Granger grinned. "Friendly. Fact is I'm a friendly sort o' man."

"That ain't the way I heard it, an' I ain't just talkin' 'bout here. Down Texas way, I heard you still had the bark on, wore yore shirts out from the inside."

Granger's grin turned into a laugh. "Hell, Colgan, anybody'd believe that would run rabbits an' bark at the moon on a dark night."

Colgan pulled at his nose. "Reckon I can put the thong back on my six-shooter then. What you want?"

"A friend of yours wants to see you. Fisk Sanders needs

a favor right bad. We can probably find him in the Miner's Rest.''

''Sanders needs a favor?'' He pulled at his nose again. Colgan nodded. ''That man needs a favor, he don't have to ask. I'll do it.''

Granger raised his eyebrows. ''You better find out what he wants first, it might get you a six-foot hole in the ground.''

''Don't make me no never mind. I'll do it. Let's find 'im.''

It didn't take but a moment in the Miner's Rest to find the lawyer. He was surrounded by old friends. He looked up when Colgan thrust a hand through the crowd. ''Well, I'll be damned. Bert. How you doing?''

Colgan gave him a sour look. ''Doin' fine till I heard you wanted to see me. Ever' time I hear them words, trouble soon follows. What you need?''

Sanders pushed through his throng of friends and took the hardcase's elbow. ''Let's get a drink and go to a back table. Got somethin' I want you to do.''

At the table, the first thing the lawyer wanted to know was did Colgan know Clinton, and when the answer was no, he nodded and said, ''That's good. Now, here's what I need.'' He explained in detail what he wanted Colgan to do. ''Now, if you don't want to do it, don't feel bad. This is dangerous. I won't blame you one whit if you turn me down.''

Colgan glanced at Granger, and pulled at his nose. A slight smile crinkled the corners of his eyes. ''He does this to me ever' time, an' he knows all the while I ain't gonna say nothin but yes to him.'' He again pulled at his nose.

Sanders shook his head. ''Thought by now you'd a pulled your damned nose off.'' He studied Colgan's shiny red beak. ''I don't believe it's any longer'n the last time I saw you.'' He held his hand up for the bar girl to bring another round. When the drinks came, he leaned across the table. ''First off, I'm gonna pay you for this job. Second, I want you to buy yourself a twelve-gauge Greener, get the barrel sawed off to about ten, maybe twelve inches, then come to my office in Virginia City. Use the back door and don't let anyone see you.'' At Colgan's nod, Sanders added, ''Be there in four days.''

Standing at his window, Clinton had seen Granger and Sanders leave town headed toward Bannack. Snow fell, but lightly. He studied on it a moment, thinking if he could find a couple of men good with a rifle he could settle all his troubles. He glanced at the sky, thought it was coming on to blow, and shrugged. If his nemeses went to Bannack, they'd surely head back within a couple of days. That gave him time to find men.

That night he went to the cafe, and from there to the saloon, a thing he seldom did.

The fat man waddled to a seat at the back of the room, sat, and studied those in there. He spent about twenty minutes sipping a drink before Hoppy Costeen came in, stopped inside the door, looked at the men at the bar, and then swept the tables with a glance. When Clinton saw Costeen's eyes rest on him, he signaled him to come over. He hated for people to get close to him, but he needed this man. ''Sit an' have a drink.''

They had talked only fifteen or so minutes when Costeen stood. ''Don't get in any hurry. When you find another man, leave tomorrow, that way you can catch them on the way back.'' Costeen nodded, went to the bar, and pulled another man aside.

They could have been twins—squat, beefy in the shoulders, small heads set on thick necks—except Costeen had one leg shorter than the other, and limped badly.

The two talked a few minutes, had a drink, and left. Clinton sat back, frowning. If those two stupid bastards had enough sense to carry off his instructions, his troubles would be over. If not, he still had Drago and the gunfighter from Denver, but the two he'd now hired might save him three thousand dollars—if he had to pay it.

Clinton made as if to stand, then sat back. A man he'd not met walked to the bar. A gentlemanly man, but the way he wore his gun in a plain leather undyed holster, tied low on his thigh, added to the fat man's opinion of him. He wondered if the man might be the gunfighter he'd sent to Denver for, but he had mixed emotions about hoping he was the one. The man looked like he'd not be one to try to beat out of his promised pay.

Four days later, Granger and Sanders crossed Grasshopper Creek on the way home. The cowboy looked at the lawyer. "Fisk, I got a feelin', don't know what brung it on, but I got a hurtin' 'tween my shoulder blades. That feelin' always signals trouble's 'bout to happen. Get your rifle out an' hold it 'cross your saddle horn."

Sanders asked no questions; he simply did as Granger directed. Granger rode around a stand of timber, stopped, and peered at a pile of tumbled boulders. He didn't like the way they sat close to the trail, so he nudged his horse to ride out of rifle range, and when his paloos turned to head in the direction he'd been kneed, it saved Granger's life. A bullet whined past his ear, then the sharp report of a shot.

He leaned over his horse's neck and kicked him into an all-out run. Sanders taking his cue from the cowboy at his side. Two shots followed them. They rode into a stand of tall ponderosa pines, left their saddles, and hunkered behind the trunks of two large trees. "Hold your fire, Sanders. We'll wait 'em out. You watch downtrail. I'll take the other end. Don't b'lieve they gonna leave—they want our hides."

They had held their positions for about thirty minutes when Sanders, squatting, straightened his legs, then went to his knees. Granger knew how he felt, how stiff a man could get holding one stance for a long period, but he didn't move. If he could get some idea where in those rocks his attackers were, and could see a way to Injun up on them, he thought to do it. He didn't cotton to staying in these trees until nightfall; it was already cold enough to freeze the horn off an anvil.

Not wanting to take a shot until he was certain of a hit, he stared at one side of the pile of boulders, slowly moved his eyes over every inch of their edges, checked the spaces between them, and paid special attention to the bottom of each rock, where it rested on the ground. There he thought a man might lie flat, and try to get off a shot before drawing back behind protection. Then he got an idea.

In barely more than a whisper he said, "Fisk, fire a couple of shots in that opening between those rocks on your end. I'll take the one over here. Fire when I say 'go.' . . . Go."

Granger fired, levered a shell into the chamber, then did it again. A groan, and curses, came from the pile. Granger grinned. Rock fragments and ricocheting bullets could make a man right uncomfortable. They sat tight another thirty minutes, then Colt told Fisk they'd try the same thing again.

When he'd fired his second shot, not waiting to hear whether they'd hit anything, he sprinted for the end of the rock pile, thinking the gunmen would be too busy trying to stay low, out of the way of bits of rocks and lead, rather than looking for an attack.

He made it to the end of the pile of boulders without a shot being fired. He went flat on his belly and snaked his way around the largest of the tan sandstone Goliaths, some larger than a house. He moved forward a few feet and stopped to listen. Voices grumbled on the other side of the rock, every word clear. "Damn, Costeen, didn't figger on nothin' like this. That fat bastard said it'd be easy—ain't nothin' easy 'bout them two. They acted like they wuz 'spectin' us. Let's get outta here."

"Nope, ain't goin' nowhere, Barnes. They's five hunnerd apiece sittin' over yonder in them trees. Go ahead. I'll collect your dust an' spend it myself."

To Granger's ears, it sounded as though Barnes thought it over a moment, then said, "Aw hell, I'll stay."

Granger edged farther around the boulder, enough to look on the other side. Each gunman hugged the rock behind which he stood, their faces pressed firmly against the rough surfaces. Granger thumbed the hammer back on his .44, and the ratcheting sound caused each of the two to whirl toward him.

The one Granger took for Barnes swung his rifle toward him, and pulled the trigger too soon. The shot went over his head at the same time the bullet from Granger's revolver went into his throat. Blood spurted. No longer worried about

Barnes, Granger eared the hammer back for a shot at Hoppy Costeen, but the gunman stood, hands grabbing for the clouds.

"Drop your hardware an' step away from it." The gunman dropped his rifle and his gunbelt then stepped back against the boulder. Granger yelled for Sanders to come on in. When the lawyer walked around the rock, he stared at the gunman on the ground. "I didn't even know you'd left that tree you hid behind."

"Yep, an' collected you one varmint to take back to the gulch. Figure it's been a long time since we had a hangin', an' them people over yonder prob'ly gettin' right bored without some sort o' entertainment." Granger holstered his six-shooter. "Hold a gun on Costeen while I find their horses. We can make a few miles 'fore sundown." He slanted a look at Sanders. "You figure to call the Vigilantes to a meetin' soon's we get back?"

Sanders nodded. "No point in feeding this swine—costs money. We'll hang 'im 'fore sundown tomorrow."

Granger gave him a cold smile. "You're learnin', Sanders; you're sure as hell catchin' on right fast."

The next day, mid-afternoon, Granger and Sanders led their prisoner between the rows of weathered buildings bordering Wallace Street. Men started lining the street when they saw what the two men led on the end of a rope.

Clinton watched from his office window. As soon as he could identify who they were, and who trailed behind, every ounce of flesh on his body quivered, blood surged to his head. He picked up the chair in front of his desk and slammed it against the wall. "Nobody, no-damned-body can do anything right." His breath came in great choking gasps. He waddled to his chair and fitted himself into it, thinking he'd better be careful, calm down; he could have a stroke. With shaking hands he poured himself a glass of whiskey.

After a while, he settled down. His thoughts went to the dapper man he'd seen in the saloon a few days before. He had no doubt but what the man was a gunfighter, but was he the one he'd sent for? He couldn't go to him and ask.

He'd have to wait, but if he was the one, why hadn't he contacted him?

Then there was Drago. Now that the meddling lawyer was back in town, he'd better get ahold of the outlaw and set his plan in action. He thought of the two men, and came up with the same answer. He'd have to find a way to get rid of them after they did their jobs. To shoot them here in his office would cause questions he wasn't prepared to answer, but it might turn out to be the only thing to do. He could always claim they tried to rob him. Damn! Why couldn't things go smoothly?

He sighed. He needed a man like Gant, a man he could send on errands—he'd have to go back to the saloon and find a man. He could pay him a pittance and then he wouldn't have to leave his office until he wanted to.

That night in the saloon, he found himself another lackey, not of Gant's quality, but one who would do his bidding. Then he saw the gunfighter standing at the bar. He had to be the man, but again Clinton pondered why he'd not been contacted. Why would the man wait? Why hadn't he come to him, made his agreement, gone out, picked a fight with Granger, shot him, tried to collect his money, and left town? He sat staring at Doty's back until the gunfighter turned, looked at him, then came to his table.

"You've been staring at my back for quite a while now, stranger. Is there something you want of me?"

Surprised that the man had sensed he was being looked at, Clinton stammered, then said, "No, I want nothing of you. Why you ask?"

Doty stared at him, a cold smile breaking the corners of his lips. "Yeah, you want something, but perhaps this isn't the time or place to talk of it. I'll come to your office tomorrow afternoon. We'll talk then." He turned and went back to the bar. Clinton had felt as though a ghost walked up his spine when Doty flashed him that cold smile. This then was the man he'd sent for—and he might be as much danger to him as he would be to Granger. He felt as though he'd looked into the eyes of Satan, and felt fear like he'd never felt before.

Doty smiled to himself when he got to the bar. He'd seen that fear in the fat man's eyes, and felt satisfaction. He'd disliked Clinton the moment he saw him in the cafe the other night, then in the saloon that dislike had been reinforced, and now, although he never allowed himself to hate a man, his feeling approached that emotion. He finished his drink and went to his room.

He stretched out on the bed and thought of the man he'd come to kill, and the man who wished to hire him to do it. Then he pondered why Clinton would fear him. If the fat man intended to deal with him fairly, he had no reason for fear. Hmmm, now that was something to think about. Did Clinton fear being found out? Did he in fact intend to deal fairly with the man he hired? Was he afraid Doty would not be able to accomplish the job, or would talk? Doty kicked those thoughts around until tired of them, then turned over and went to sleep.

Sanders did as he'd said. He called the Vigilantes to a meeting in the basement of Kenna and Nye's store. They tried Costeen, found him guilty, and sentenced him to hang before sundown that day.

Before the meeting broke up, an idea that had been trying to form at the back of his mind became clear. He held up his hands to stop anyone from leaving. "Men, I'm going to ask you to defer carrying out the sentence until we question Costeen." He looked at the gunman. "Who hired you to come after Granger an' me?"

Costeen, steely-eyed, stared back. "Ain't tellin' you nothin', lawyer man. You done decided to hang me, so get on with it. Or," his face took on a sly look, "you promise not to hang me, I'll tell you what you want to know."

Sanders shook his head. "Tch, tch. You obviously don't understand. You see, we have Granger here, who really knows how to hang a man—like he did George Ives, slow and easy. Took him at least thirty minutes to finally let that killer strangle."

He packed his pipe while some of the Vigilantes rolled cigarettes and others cut off fresh chews. "Costeen, you tell me what I want to know, something I can take before a court of law, and we'll let you live until after the trial of the man we really want. At his trial you'll be the star witness. You don't tell us, before all these witnesses, and you're gonna be a corpse by sundown.''

One of the men in the crowd said, ''Hell, Fisk, you let 'im live that long, it'll give 'im a chance to escape. I'm for hangin' 'im right now.'' A grumbling of agreement ran through the committee.

Sanders held up his hands for silence. ''Listen, men, the one we really want is the one who's caused so many of you to die or get robbed. I say it's worth a chance to let Costeen live long enough to bring the other to trial.'' He puffed his pipe to life. ''Now I don't want any of you to mention the man's name we're after. I don't want it said we put that man's name in Costeen's mind.''

He looked at the bushwhacker. ''You gonna take the extra few days of life we're offering?''

Hope flickered in the depths of the gunman's eyes. He shook his head only slightly—then obviously changed his mind. ''It wuz Clinton,'' he blurted. ''He wuz gonna pay me an' Barnes five hunnerd apiece to bushwhack you an' Granger. Said it'd be easy.''

Sanders smiled his satisfaction. ''You gonna stand before a jury and tell them what you just told us?''

Costeen nodded.

''Don't nod. Say you're gonna play it our way.''

''All right! All right! I'm gonna tell 'em just what I done told you.''

Sanders looked at Granger. ''Take this garbage to the sheriff. Tell 'im I want a guard on him day and night.'' When Colt left, along with the other men, Fisk slumped against a bale of jeans. He needed more than one witness against Clinton. He needed Drago to testify. They would still have to carry out their plan to turn the case into an airtight one.

The next afternoon, Doty walked to Clinton's office and let himself in. The fat man sat behind his desk, thumbs hooked in his vest pockets. "Took you long enough to contact me. Why?"

Doty gave him that wintry smile that had chilled him so the first time he'd seen it. "You and I had better get something straight right from the beginning, Clinton. You don't own me. You don't tell me what to do or when to do it. I traveled a long way to do a job for you. Other than that, specifically, you don't have any hold on me—understand?"

Clinton sat back against his chair, his face red. He was not used to being talked to this way, but he needed the services of this gunfighter. He would put up with his insolence until payoff time. "Yeah, I understand. All I want outta you is a good smooth job, not in any way traceable to me." He sat forward. "Now, do *you* understand?"

The smile never left Doty. "Yes, but there are a few minor items which must be cleared up before I agree to anything. First, I want half of the two thousand right now—the other half when I finish the job."

Clinton felt his face flush. If he was going to ever hate a man more than the lawyer and Granger, this gunfighter was fast earning that privilege. He stared through his folds of fat at Doty. "You're strugglin' under a misunderstandin', gunfighter. I don't pay for nothin' till I get exactly what I ask for. You kill Granger out where everyone can see, come to me, an' I'll have your pay waitin'."

Doty stared at the fat man a moment through those cold eyes, then turned to leave. "Where you goin'? We ain't through talkin'."

Over his shoulder Doty said, "Yeah, we're through. We do it the way I said, or I head back to Denver."

"You mean you done rode up here, an' are gonna let a little thing like when you get paid stand between you an' two thousand dollars? You'd turn around an' ride back without gettin' a red cent?" Doty reached for the door.

"All right. I'll give you a thousand now, an' the rest later." Clinton figured, What difference did it make? He would take it all back at the big payoff, and he was certain the gunfighter carried a pretty hefty poke of his own while traveling. He smiled inside. That arrogant bastard would, in the end, contribute to the Clinton retirement fund.

Doty faced him. "Count it out, slow like. And understand, I'll do this my own way, in my own time." He counted right along with Clinton, and when all the money lay on the table, he reached with his left hand, shuffled the bills together, folded them, and stuffed them in his pocket. He didn't turn his back on the fat man until he'd closed the door behind him, and stepped toward the cafe. He wanted a cup of coffee.

The first man he saw upon entering the cafe was Granger, who waved him to sit at his table. Doty pulled out a chair and sat while the cowboy motioned the proprietor to bring another cup. He felt like a hypocrite, sitting drinking coffee with the man he'd just accepted money to gun down.

A slight smile crinkling the corners of his eyes, Granger said, "You an' Clinton get your business taken care of?" Then, not waiting for Doty to answer, he continued. "Somehow, Doty, I cain't see you havin' anythin' to do with that hog. You're from a far better background than him. Yeah, maybe you come on some hard times at one time or other, but I figure you never took a dollar you were ashamed of— till now."

Hot blood rushed to Doty's face. "Didn't know I would get a sermon when I sat. Reckon I better leave."

He stood, but before he could step away from the table, Granger looked him in the eye. "How much am I worth to you dead, Doty? An' if you happen to outdraw, an' outshoot me, will you be able to sleep very good from then on? I like you. Think maybe you feel the same 'bout me, but figured the first time I saw you, you were the one he sent for."

Doty pulled his chair back and sat. He looked into his coffee cup, then in a quiet voice, he said, "I suppose I have slipped a lot further'n I thought. When a man can spot me for a hired gun, my face, all of me, must have hardened to the point I don't appear to have a conscience." He looked up into Granger's eyes. "Yeah, Colt, I'm the one he sent for. I had no idea what kind of evil piece of cow dung he was until I walked into the cafe the night I first saw you. I've been scrubbing myself down with some mighty harsh thinking since then. Now I've taken his money—and I don't want to meet you, in the street, in a saloon, anywhere." He took a swallow of his coffee. "Know it sounds like I turned yellow, but that isn't the case. If we were on opposite sides of a cow war, or any honorable squabble, I'd face you in a minute, despite having a strong liking and respect for you."

Granger toyed with his cup, ran his finger around its edge, sat it back from the table, and shook his head. "Hell, ain't it?" Then he pulled his pipe out and took a long time to tamp the tobacco and put fire to it. When he looked up into Doty's eyes, the gunfighter saw pain there. "You really got it to do, Branch? The least can happen is one o' us won't walk away, the worst is we'll both die. I cain't believe that kind o' waste is right. People like you an' me are needed out here in this country. Our time will be over one o' these days, but in my belief that's a long time in the future." He dropped his gaze to again stare into his cup.

"I got it to do, Colt. I took his money." Doty shook his head. "Can't welsh on this. It'd be worse than welshing on a bet."

Granger sat back and smiled, sadly. "Reckon if it's gotta be, that's the way it'll be." Their supper came and they ate in silence, an uncomfortable quiet.

Deep into the night, Granger, Drago, and Bert Colgan sat in Sanders's office. The lawyer looked at them. "You men understand what to do? We don't want anything to go wrong with this; it may be the only chance we'll have to nail Clinton legally."

Drago nodded. "One thing we ain't talked 'bout. I figure it'll be downright necess'ry for the fat man to know I done took on a partner. Think maybe tomorrow night I better take Colgan over there an' tell Clinton 'bout 'im, an' we ain't gonna charge 'im no more'n he's already said." He grinned. "Fact is, I figure we gonna play hell gettin' to keep a dime o' that money—if he has his way."

Sanders sat forward. "That's why I want both of you to go in with those sawed-off Greeners. The man has no honor. He'll kill you in an instant. I don't want it to happen, but get the information we need first of all, then be sure you protect yourselves.''

"You can be right sure of that, Fisk. Right now, make sure you leave town day after tomorrow where ever'body can see you. Me an' Colgan'll leave a few hours after.''

Sanders looked at Granger. "You've been mighty quiet, Colt. Everything sound good to you?''

He nodded, and gave them a thin smile. "Yeah, sounds good, but by the time you get back, Doty an' I might've already met.''

22

ALL THREE STARED at him. Drago cursed. "Ain't there no way to stop it? You want me to side you? Hell, we ain't gonna lose a man like you, no matter what."

Granger cocked an eyebrow, smiled, and shook his head. "Well now, sounds like you done got me dead an' buried." He sobered. "Fact is, we also need men in this country like Doty, and the bad thing is, we may be fast enough, an' accurate enough, that we'll both die." He looked at Sanders. "That brings on somethin' else: if it don't end the way we want—see that Molly is all right."

Sanders never broke his gaze. "Colt, you didn't need to ask, you know we'll make sure she's all right."

Granger squirmed a moment. "I reckon I never met a man I just flat didn't want to shoot, when I knew I was gonna have to look at him over the barrel of a revolver. He's a helluva man."

For the first time Colgan said his piece. "Granger, you go into that fight thinkin' thataway, an' you gonna buy the farm for damn sure. Work up a hate for him, man. You gotta."

The meeting broke up soon after, none of them feeling good after hearing Granger's words.

● ● ●

Soon after midnight the next night, Drago and Colgan tapped on Clinton's door. Each wore long sheepskins that hung almost to their ankles.

His hair tousled, face puffy from sleep, the fat man opened the door a crack, then pulled it wide enough for the two to enter. He held a handgun on them. "What you want this time o' night? Told you I didn't want to see you till you'd done what I asked."

Drago mummbled, "Cold out." He shivered and glanced at the revolver in the fat man's hand. "You can put that away. Figured I'd better let you know I done took on a partner," he grinned, "with no increase in pay for the job. Another thing, Sanders is makin' a trip to Hell Gate tomorrow. Figured to leave ahead o' him, catch 'im on the trail, shoot 'im, an' bring 'im back across his saddle. Tell folks we found 'im lying in the trail."

The fat man studied Colgan a moment, then looked at Drago. "How long you know this man?"

"Me an' Bert here grew up together back in Missouri, rode with some o' them Kansas raiders till things got too hot fer us, then we come on out here. He wuz one o' Plummer's men over in Bannack, same as me."

Clinton continued to study Colgan another moment or two then nodded. "All right. Long's you know there ain't gonna be another copper in it for either o' you."

'Oughtta be back in a day or two. Gotta find a good place on the trail to shoot from. Lot o' people figure that lawyer man for a soft dude, but I'm here to tell you he's hell with a long gun. Seen 'im tree a whole saloon full o' men in Bannack a couple months ago." Colgan grinned. "I wuz one o' them."

Clinton grunted, belched, and pointed at the door. "Get the job done. Now, don't want to see either o' you again till I know Sanders ain't in my way no more."

As soon as they were out of earshot, Colgan grinned and clapped Drago on the shoulder. "You notice he didn't think nothin' of us wearin' these long coats? Course it's gotten downright cold out, so most'll be puttin' on their warmest." He cocked his head to the side and gave Drago a look.

"Didn't know you was such a good liar, Drago. That stuff 'bout you an' me growin' up together, ridin' with the raiders. Whew! Remind me to never believe nothin' you say from now on."

Drago frowned, hoping the cold snap lasted a few more days, but of course this time of year the weather wasn't likely to get any higher'n five or ten degrees. He thought they should pack their trail gear before going to bed, and he put those thoughts into words.

Packed and ready to go, Drago looked across his saddle at his new friend. "Figure we might's well head on out, build us a good fire, fix coffee, an' settle in to wait for Fisk. He oughtta be where we agreed on by noon."

Colgan shook his head. "Sure do go through hell for that lawyer man. Didn't think to be sleepin' on the cold ground when he asked me to help 'im."

Drago chuckled. "C'mon, man. Figure I know you right well by now. You'd a done this for him without pay, an' in the middle of a blizzard, same as I would." Abruptly, his thoughts turned to Granger. "Sure wish we could protect that big cowboy somehow or other."

Colgan toed the stirrup. "You figure that big man a special friend for some reason. You gonna tell me 'bout it?"

"Yeah, I'll tell ya, soon's we get a fire built an' coffee boilin'."

Sitting in a cold saddle, hunkered into their long sheepskins, not talking, they came on the place where they'd agreed to meet Sanders, a place well protected by large boulders and surrounded by a heavy stand of pine.

The sky lightened to a dull gray before they had a fire going. Colgan glanced at the clouds, jabbed a thumb toward them, and growled. "Looks like yore blizzard we'd ride through for Sanders ain't too far off the mark."

Drago only shrugged, then glanced from the sky to the fire. "Reckon we rode right on into breakfasttime. You gonna cook, or you want me to?" A few feathery flakes floated to sizzle in the fire.

Colgan stared at the flames a moment, then, sober as Drago had seen him in the few days they'd known each other, he said, "Well, figure I might's well get used to yore cookin'. Reckon if you think you could stand me ridin' at yore side I'd like to partner up with you, go back to Missouri an' help yore folks git that there farm to payin'." Still sober, he continued, "Course along the way I'd figure on doing my share o' the chores."

Drago choked on the lump in his throat, swallowed hard, and stared into the murky light. He'd hoped for something like this, but didn't figure he'd known Colgan long enough to saddle him with a quick decision. He waited so long to give the hardcase an answer that Colgan broke into his thoughts. "Well, heck, Drago, it wuz only a thought. Don't feel obliged to take me on. I figured bein' as how you ain't gonna ride the owlhoot no more, an' I damned sure ain't, we might ride together."

Drago sputtered. "Now, you ain't gonna weazel outta doin' yore share o' the chores that easy. You're danged right you're gonna cook, build fires, fight Injuns—whatever comes our way—an' when we get home, you gonna see does yore hands fit a plow."

After that tirade, the two stood there grinning at each other until Drago felt foolish. He stuck his hand out and Colgan gave him as firm a handshake as he'd had.

Grinning like two boys who'd skipped out of a watermelon patch with the largest melon in the field, and the owner of the field yelling and shaking his fist at them, they went about fixing breakfast. After they'd eaten, Drago told Colgan the story of how he met Granger, and why he was quitting the outlaw trail, and most of all that he'd promised to go back to his folks. Then while waiting for Sanders to show, they sat and talked about crossing Indian country. The snow got heavier.

The sound of a horse broke into their conversation. With only a glance at each other, they grabbed their rifles and melted into the trees.

Sanders rode to the fire, glanced at the meat cooking, and said, "All right, you two, c'mon out. It's me."

When they walked to the fire, the lawyer sat and dished up a healthy helping of food. "If you think I'm gonna ride across my saddle all the way back into town, think again. We'll stop in that thicket at the creek's edge an' get me fixed for viewing." He sliced a huge bite of venison, put it in his mouth, and chewed before continuing. "That old codger at the livery got a box ready for me?"

Drago nodded. "Everything's set. That old man despises Clinton most as much as we do." He looked at Sanders's horse. Then, letting a slight smile crinkle his lips, he said, "Glad to see you brought a bedroll, Fisk. Ain't no room in my blankets for a skinny lawyer. We gonna wait till tomorrow to go back into town."

Sanders looked the ex-outlaw up and down, shook his head, and frowned. "Nope, I don't see a thing that'd make me want to share a blanket with you."

They loafed about the camp until supper, ate, then turned in. When they woke, a foot of snow was on the flats, and it was still coming down. Mid-morning they broke camp, and about four hours later they rode into the thicket outside of Virginia City.

Drago hoisted Sanders so that he lay across his saddle, and tied his hands and feet to cinch rings. Then he climbed on his horse, and they rode into the trail, almost at the end of the street. "Sure hope this works," Drago growled to no one in particular.

Despite the heavy snow, a crowd started gathering as soon as they appeared between the rows of stores lining the street. Those along the street soon numbered in the hundreds. Someone yelled, "Who you got there?"

Colgan yelled back, "Fisk Sanders. Found 'im out on the trail, deader'n last year's garden. Froze stiff, too."

Hearing the word pass from man to man up the street, Drago quickly led the three horses into the livery before any nosey citizen got too close and determined the whole setup was a ruse. The spindly old man swiftly closed the double doors behind them while they led Sanders's horse to the back of the stable and cut the lawyer's hands and feet loose.

As soon as his feet touched the ground, Sanders looked toward the doors. "Think it worked?"

"Ain't no doubt about it, Fisk. Me an' Colgan both heered

folks all up an' down the street talkin' 'bout it. They already talked lynchin' whoever done it. I told 'em I'd be out in a few minutes to tell 'em where we found you, how you'd been shot—the whole story. Told 'em nobody could come in here till after the sheriff come in and got a good look at you.''

They put Sanders in the pine box the old man had made for the occasion, folded his hands across his chest in case someone sneaked a peek through the cracks between the boards, and sent Colgan to get Sheriff Neil Howie.

Howie had been waiting for them to return to town, so it took Colgan but a few minutes to find him and bring him back to the livery.

Clinton watched the street from early morning. He'd dragged his chair over to the window so he could watch in comfort. When three horsemen, one tied across his saddle, rode into the end of the street, he stepped out on the boardwalk, and the word passed from man to man soon reached him. The young lawyer, Fisk Sanders, had been murdered out on the trail. Two men had brought him in, one from Bannack, the other recently from here on the gulch.

The fat man hitched his trousers up on his gut and grinned until his fat cheeks closed his eyes to slits. Finally, he thought, he'd found someone who could think, and get a job finished. A shame he couldn't keep such a man in his employ. He pushed back into the room, closed the door, and pulled the Derringer from his pocket. He took the two loads from it and pushed fresh ones in. Probably nothing wrong with those he removed, but a man should never leave anything to chance. Now he was ready for the big dumb outlaw and his partner. No. Not quite. He went to his desk, pulled his .44 from the top drawer, reloaded it, and put it back within easy reach. He didn't expect Drago and his partner until well after dark and, he told himself, they had no reason to suspect him of treachery. Now all he had to do was wait.

Down the street in Molly's hotel room, Granger stood looking at her. ''I been tryin' to tell you, little one, I cain't get outta this gunfight. You been out here long enough to know a man might's well leave the country if he shows the white flag. I cain't do that to you—or me.''

"You like Doty, why must you shoot him—or worse, why you gonna let him shoot you? Talk to him once more, Colt, get him to thinkin' straight.''

Granger shrugged. "That's the trouble, he is thinkin' straight. He's thinkin' of a code gunfighters live by. If he backs down on this, they ain't room enough in the West to hold 'im.'' He again shrugged. "Same goes for me.''

She squared her shoulders, clamped hands on hips, and pinned him with that look she always gave him when she'd not stand for any argument. "Colt Granger, you do like I said. Go down to the Champion—that's where he'll be—go down there and give it another try. He may see reason this time.''

If it hadn't been such a serious subject, Granger would have laughed. Instead, he gave her a jerky nod and left the room. He shook his head—she was the damnedest spitfire he'd ever known. He'd give everything, anything, to be able to take her as his wife—but he'd raised her from a spindly little filly. It just wouldn't be fit.

Before going down the stairs, he bent and tied his holster to his thigh.

Out on the street, all the talk was of Sanders's killing. People gathered in clumps, all talking of getting together a posse and hunting the killers. He hoped they wouldn't do that. In the snow they'd soon find where the two men met Sanders, and a smart tracker would know the two men who'd brought Sanders in were the ones with him out on the trail. Although, even if they formed a posse, the whole thing should be over before they could get back. Then the truth could be told. Too, as hard as it snowed, the tracks from where they camped should be covered. He headed for the Champion.

He pushed through the door, letting a gust of wind and powdery snow in with him. He saw Doty standing at the end of the bar, staring sullenly into his drink. Granger walked to his side. "Buy me a drink, Mr. Doty?''

"Don't treat me like a stranger, Colt. I've stood here for

hours trying to think of some way to get outta this." He
spread his hands in resignation. "Not one damned thing has
come to mind." He signaled the bartender to bring them each
a drink.

Granger waited until his drink sat in front of him, then
said, "Why not just saddle up an' ride out?"

Doty looked into his eyes. "You know I can't do that. I
took his money."

"Give it back. I'll give you what he paid and you're off
the hook."

Doty smiled, a sad smile to Granger's thinking. "If I
didn't know better, I'd think you were afraid. I wish by all
that's holy you were." He knocked back his drink. "No, I
don't mean that. I wish there were some honorable way for
us to call this off." He pounded his fist softly on the bar.
"Whoever made up this code of honor we live by? He's the
one who deserves shooting."

Granger snorted. "He prob'ly did meet his end in a shootin'." He downed the remainder of his drink, asked Doty if
he'd like another, and when the gunfighter declined, he
shrugged. "Well, reckon this's it. It'll still be light outside
about five o'clock. That time all right with you?"

Doty nodded, and Granger said, "See ya then."

On the way back to his room, Colt turned the situation
over in his mind. Everything he did seemed to have a point
of honor messing things up somewhere in it: he had to fight
Doty—honor—he couldn't marry Molly—honor—he couldn't
go down and shoot the fat pig—honor, and law. Hell! Things
might be better if he let Doty beat him. He thought about
that a while. That might be the answer. Honor would be
served in every case that way.

When he got to the second floor of the hotel, Molly stood
outside her door holding a gun patch in her hand. "How'd
it come out?"

"Way I thought it would. Neither of us can afford to back
down. What you holdin' that patch for? You cleanin' yore
rifle?"

She gave him a jerky nod. "No matter how you an' Doty

come out, I'm gonna go down there and kill that slimy bastard that caused all this.''

Granger shook his head. "That's not the answer, little one. Let Fisk do it his way.''

She shook her head. "Nope. Gonna do it my way.''

Colt knew that in her frame of mind, to argue would be useless. He reckoned it about twenty minutes of five. He looked into her eyes. "If things don't work in my favor, you know where our cache is, you know who our friends are, an' you know how much I've been honored to have you for my almost-daughter. It's meant everything to me.''

She gasped and, her eyes swimming, made as if to come into his arms. He couldn't bear such, and spun on his heel and went into his room. Inside, he leaned against the door breathing hard. He straightened, pulled his .44, and checked the loads. He added one to the empty chamber on which the hammer rode, slipped it into the holster, and eased it, then waited to hear Molly's door close, and hesitated. Her soft sobs came through the thin walls to him. His first thought was Honor be damned. He came within a hair of opening his door, going to her, and telling her he'd let himself be branded a coward. He stood there a moment, his hand gripping the doorknob. He shook his head. He couldn't do it. He opened the door and walked to the stairs.

Drago, Colgan, Sanders, and Howie stood in the middle of the liveryman's sleeping quarters. Sanders looked at Howie. "You think you can hear what they say inside that room, Sheriff?'' Howie nodded. Sanders turned his eyes on Drago. "You think now is the time? You sure you don't want to wait until dark to collect your money?''

Drago nodded. "Might's well get it over an' done. Waitin' ain't gonna 'complish nothin' but give me more queazies in my gut. I know the fat man's gonna welsh on payin' us, an' that will be a whole bundle o' trouble.'' He looked at Colgan. "How you feel 'bout it, partner?''

Obviously to cover his nervousness, the hardcase grinned. "Long's you an' me got them sawed-off Greeners under our coats, reckon we ain't got nothin' else to do but end this whole thing. Hope we can end it with a hangin', but if not, an' Clinton don't kill us, it'll be over and done with anyway.''

Drago took his long coat from a peg in the wall and turned to Sanders. ''You gotta stay here, hid, till this is done, Fisk. Clinton might see ya, an' that'd ruin the whole show.'' He shifted his eyes to Howie. ''Sheriff, reckon it'd be best if you went on ahead o' us, walk on by Clinton's office, then come back an' squat under that front window o' his'n.''

Howie smiled. ''Looks like you're running the game, Drago.'' He looked at his watch. ''Twenty minutes till five. I'm gonna move out now, walk the street like I would when making a regular inspection, and after I see you two go in, I'll come back to his window.'' He stepped toward the door, looked back, and said, ''Good luck.''

Drago and Colgan pulled their long coats around their shoulders, arms inside, each man holding a sawed-off Greener in his right hand. They buttoned the top button of their coats, looked at Sanders, and made as if to leave. Drago stopped and turned toward the lawyer. ''We look like we got these shotguns under these coats?''

''Can't tell a thing. Bless the two of you.'' Fisk's words followed them out the door.

The walk to Clinton's office was only a couple of blocks, but due to the time of day, the aroma of cooking meals and wood smoke permeated the air—enough to remind Drago how hungry a man could get if he missed a meal. He paused three or four times to explain to people what had happened on the trail, and how they found Sanders. Miners and townspeople gathered in small groups, all still talking of forming a posse. To put them off, he told them dark would fall before they could get to where they'd found the lawyer. ''Lead you out there come daylight. Have a better chance of trackin' 'em—if the snow ain't already covered the tracks.''

They walked to the fat man's door and knocked. In only a moment footsteps sounded the other side of the wooden panel and the lock clicked. Clinton peered around the door's edge. ''What the hell you doin' here this time o' day? Told you I didn't want nobody knowin' I had anything to do with you two.''

Drago growled, ''You don't want that, you better let us in. Most ever'body in town can see us standin' here.''

The door swung wider, and when they stepped in, Drago saw Howie come around the corner of the building and hunker under the window. Inside, the ex-outlaw looked at the hardcase and saw that Colgan had as much trouble with the close, hot smell in the room as he did. It reminded Drago of rancid bacon he'd had once. The smell came from Clinton's fat, unwashed body.

''Come on in.'' Clinton walked to his desk, eased his bulk into the chair, and opened his desk drawer. ''What you want that cain't wait till after dark? Ain't gonna pay you now an' have you go to a saloon flashin' a bunch o' money.'' He rested one fat hand on the edge of the open drawer, the thumb of his other hand stuck into his vest pocket.

Talking louder than he normally would, hoping the sheriff could hear, Drago looked into the eyes of the fat man. ''Mr. Clinton, you done promised us two thousand dollars, one thousand apiece, if we'd kill Fisk Sanders. Well, he's down yonder in the livery. We brung 'im in across his saddle.'' Drago grinned to himself; not a word of what he'd said was a lie. ''Now we figger to get our money an' leave town 'fore dark.'' He talked, but his eyes never left the fat man's hands. He had not a doubt but what at least one, maybe both hands would hold a gun in the next few moments.

An oily smile creased the fat man's face. ''Yep, that's what I promised you, an' I seen you bring 'im in. Reckon it's time for payday.'' He reached into the drawer as if to take money from it. His hand came out filled with a revolver; his other pulled a Derringer from his vest.

As ready as Drago was, he was too slow. Each of Clinton's weapons blossomed flame while Drago rotated the Greener up. A hard blow hit him in his left side, knocked him backward, and twisted him from his target. He pulled the trigger of his shotgun at the same time he heard the twin bellow of Colgan's scattergun, the two shots sounding almost as one.

He straightened, turned toward the fat man, and pulled the

other trigger. Clinton was already dead when Drago's second shot reached him. He figured he could hold both fists side by side and shove them into the cavity Colgan's two shots had put in the fat man's chest. He watched a hole open in Clinton's stomach from his shot, and stared, wishing the fat one still lived to suffer from the gut shot.

It was then the pain hit. He bent at the waist, grabbed his side, pulled his hand back, and saw blood, a lot of it. Colgan ran to him. Howie broke through the door and ran behind Colgan.

"C'mon, big man, come over here and lie on the desk." The sheriff's voice soothed, while he tried to steer Drago to the back of the room. He looked across his shoulder at Colgan. "You hurt?"

Colgan shook his head. "Let's get my partner taken care of." He hovered over the big man like a mother hen.

The sheriff lowered Drago to the desk. "Find the doctor."

Though hurting like he'd never believed a man could hurt, Drago pushed against Howie's hands. "Ain't stayin' in here with all the stink that bastard put in the air. Get me outside. Think a couple o' my ribs're broke." The sheriff helped him from the desk and obediently turned and led him to the door. "You hear 'nuff to know he wuz guilty?"

The sheriff nodded. "Heard it all, big man. Damned shame we couldn't hang 'im, but the town'll know the many things of which he was guilty."

Up the street only two blocks from Clinton's office, Granger glanced at the Regulator clock behind the hotel clerk's desk: five o'clock. His stomach churned. His neck muscles pulled on his shoulders and head, causing both to ache worse than he'd ever thought possible. He checked the thong holding his holster to his thigh, eased his Colt in the holster, and stepped toward the door.

On the boardwalk, about to step into the street, the sounds of two shots came to him. He hesitated. Revolver, his mind tagged the first one subconsciously, then the single roar of a shotgun blast—then two scattergun blasts close together, a moment, and another shotgun blast. He frowned and shook his head. Too early for Drago and Colgan to have gone to

Clinton's office. He thought it might be some drunk blowing off steam, and hoped no one had gotten hurt. He stepped into the street.

People still lined the trail talking about Sanders's murder. He raised his voice. "You people clear the street. Gonna be a gunfight." Before he could repeat his warning, men and women scurried into stores, alleys, behind freight wagons—anywhere for shelter, and from where they'd still be able to see the fight. Granger looked up the street, then down it. Doty stood about fifty yards from him. He looked relaxed, confident. The tall cowboy hoped he looked the same—then, abruptly, all fear, all emotion, drained from him. His nerves stilled.

He squared his shoulders. He stood ready. In short, measured steps, balanced on the balls of their feet, the two walked toward each other, fingertips brushing the handles of their side guns.

Approaching the gunfighter, Granger stared into his eyes. Now they were separated by only twenty feet, then fifteen. Each stopped. Granger didn't want to draw. He was doing exactly what Colgan had warned him against. He couldn't work up a hate against this man, a man he'd come to respect and like as much as he did Sanders.

Almost as if slowed down somehow, Doty's hand swept for his handgun. Granger's six-gun came to his hand as though it jumped from holster to hand. He squeezed the trigger—but pulled off at the last moment, a moment when he heard the buzz of Doty's shot go by his ear. The tall man lowered his revolver to his side, and saw Doty's arm drop to his side at the same time.

A load lifted from Granger's aching shoulders. His headache stopped, his shoulders relaxed, his stomach calmed. Doty smiled. "Couldn't do it, Colt. You couldn't either. I heard your slug pass my ear."

Granger stood there, wanting to grin, wanting to hug the slender gunfighter. Instead, he said, "Reckon you know we'd've both been dead. It was that close."

The ear-shattering silence up and down the street erupted into cheers, people running from doorways, alleys—all con-

verging on the two. Then came the backslapping offers to
buy them drinks. One man yelled to them through the noise,
"Cain't let good men like you two die! We need you!" He
had a jug in his hand and shoved it toward them. Doty pulled
the cork, took a long swig, and handed the bottle to Granger.

It was then Molly ran into Granger's arms. She kissed him
square on the mouth. He didn't turn his head. She pulled
from his arms, hugged Doty, and stood back, hands on hips,
feet planted in the crusty snow, tears streaming down her
cheeks, choking out her fear and happiness. "God bless both
of you." She looked the gunfighter in the eye. "Branch, I'll
love you forever for not taking my man from me."

Branch grinned. "Ma'am, we'd have both been lying here
in the street if we'd not realized at the last moment we
couldn't do it." His grin widened. "Know it isn't proper for
a young lady, but how would you like to join us for a drink
in the Champion?"

Molly again had that no-nonsense look. "Proper-snopper,
I don't care what anyone says." She turned her eyes to Colt.
"You better not start givin' me that stuff about not being
old enough. This calls for a celebration."

Colt grinned. "Never had it in mind to tell you nothin'
right now, little one." He threw his arms about the shoulders
of both of them and headed toward the Champion.

Seated at a table in the back of the room, Colt poured
them each a drink, but cut Molly's short of two fingers in
the glass. She reached for the bottle and brought the level of
whiskey up to what showed in their glasses, looking at him
all the while, daring him to object.

Before they could lift drinks in a toast, a burly miner ran
into the saloon. He yelled, "Hey, listen. Quirt Clinton's been
shot. Them two who brought Fisk Sanders in done killed that
fat bastard. One o' them, the one what's been workin' round
here the last few weeks, took a bullet. Don't know how
bad."

Granger knocked back his drink, put his glass on the table,
and stood. "Goin' down there. Buck might need help." He
ran from the saloon, Molly and Doty on his heels.

Before they got to Clinton's place, Granger saw Drago,

the sheriff supporting one side and Colgan the other as they brought him out the door. The doctor stood to the side. "Put 'im down here. Spread his coat and I'll check him before we take him to his room." Then, kneeling in the snow at Drago's side, talking to himself, the doctor said, "Gotta see where he took the shot, stop the bleeding, put some o' that greasy concoction the Shoshoni woman gave me on the wound, get him bandaged and in bed." He cast an irritable glance at Colgan. "If you'd give me room to breathe, I could take care of him better."

"Damn, Doc, is he hurt bad? He gonna be all right? Don't let 'im die, Doc, he's my partner."

The sawbones shook his head. "Dammit, man, give me room to work. He'll be okay if I can get him taken care of." He opened Drago's shirt. The bullet had gone all the way through. With two fingers he pushed gently at the sides of the front hole. Drago gasped. The doc nodded. "Couple of cracked ribs far as I can tell. Clean the wound, bandage him tight, and he'll be all right."

Granger stared at Howie. "What the hell you bring 'im out here for? Why didn't you keep 'im in there where it was warm?"

"He wouldn't stay in there. Said the place smelled like a rotten buffalo corpse he smelled once." The sheriff smiled. "I had to agree with him. It stank." He held out a padlock to Granger. "I found this, and a key for it, inside. Snap it through the hasp on the door. We'll come down and see what we can find inside tomorrow."

Granger locked the door, then waited for the doctor to finish with Drago. He helped Drago to his feet and, with the big ex-outlaw leaning heavily on him, headed for the hotel. He looked over his shoulder at Colgan. "Go stay with Fisk till I can get down there. We'll tell 'im the happenin's—then we got a bigger job o' tellin' this town what, an' why, we done all we done."

Grimacing with pain, Drago turned his head and whispered to Granger, "Colt, reckon Doty's gonna let the gunfight go now Clinton's dead? Yeah, he took his money, but seems to me he oughtta let it go bein' the pig's dead."

Granger chuckled. ''We done shot it out, Buck—we both missed.'' The chuckle turned to a belly laugh. ''Once I get you tucked into bed, and get ahold of Sanders, I'll tell you about it.'' He looked at Molly. ''You mind stayin' with Drago till we can all get back to his room?''

With tears in her eyes, Molly said, ''Colt, I'm so happy right now I'd baby-sit a grizzly bear, but with this big man I figure it'd be a pleasure. We'll be there when you get back.''

23

GRANGER FIGURED CON Orem's Champion Saloon as the best place to let the town know Sanders was alive, and about Sanders's plan to get evidence against Clinton that would hold up in court, and how Drago, Colgan, and Doty fit into the plan. He didn't intend to tell them his and the gunfighter's face-off was the real thing—until they both decided at the last moment they couldn't shoot a man they liked and respected.

Granger, Colgan, and Neil Howie went in together, and had almost finished their first drink when Sanders slipped through the back door. At first, the crowd stood ready to lynch the four of them for the cruel hoax. When they explained why they'd done it, and bought the house a couple rounds of drinks, the atmosphere thawed. Granger held up his hands for silence. "Men, all your troubles ain't over, but I'm here to tell you, with Clinton dead they ain't no troubles you got you cain't handle all by yoreself. Now, I'm gonna have one more drink with you, then I'm goin' to my room an' get some sleep."

On the way out, Howie told him he'd like him to be at Clinton's office the next morning after breakfast, about seven, and they'd all go through the fat man's papers and such together. "Bring Doty with you. I'll tell the other three. I don't want anyone but those of us involved in this thing to be there."

Molly awaited Granger when he got to the hotel. "Can we go home now, Colt? We've already been gone longer'n I ever again want to be away from our cabin."

He took one of her shoulders in each of his big hands. "Little one, I figger it'll take one more day to get all this straightened out. So what do you say to leaving for the valley day after tomorrow?"

"I've got my Christmas shoppin' done." She smiled. "We might need a extra packhorse to take it all."

Granger grimaced. "I done bought a bunch o' stuff, too. You reckon we might do better with a buckboard?"

"I was gonna ask if we could, but thought you might not want to."

"Well, dang it, woman, all you ever have to do is say what you want an' you know we'll do it."

She looked him straight in the eye. "If you mean that, there's one thing I'm gonna say later, after we get home, an' I'm gonna hold you to your word."

"Tell me now."

She shook her head. "Nope, it's kinda private. I don't want no one seein' you get mad at me."

"Damn, woman, you're the most exasperatin' human I know." He turned toward his room. "Now I prob'ly won't get a wink of sleep all night for worryin' 'bout what you got cooked up against me."

The next morning, all but Drago and Colgan met in the cafe. "Didn't plan it this way," the sheriff said, "but it works out better. Soon's we eat, you reckon we could get Colgan to sit in for Drago? They've partnered up, so he could probably speak for the big man."

Granger grinned. "Bet you a dollar Drago'll be there—if Colgan has to carry 'im." He was right.

The hardcase and the ex-outlaw stood shivering in front of Clinton's office when they got there.

Colgan volunteered to build a fire in the stove while the rest began to inspect the sleeping room and office.

After about an hour, Sanders stood in the middle of the floor, brow puckered. "You know, men, I talked with Dance and Stuart, and they tell me Clinton never stored any of his gold with them. Don't know whether he had much to store, but when we searched his body he had no money on him. It stands to reason he had some cash, somewhere."

Granger stopped pulling drawers from the fat man's desk and looked up. "I can tell you right now, they ain't a damned cent in this desk, an' from them papers we looked at we knew he had titles to minin' claims, an' had already sold a bunch o' them. I done almost tore these drawers an' the sides and back apart—they ain't nothin here."

His eyes showing pain, and his face pale, Drago sat in a chair close to the stove. "Shore wish I was of more use to you men, but I gotta say right now, I jest cain't move around much. Ain't goldbrickin' on you."

Granger chuckled. "C'mon, Drago, I figger you're restin' up to help us tear down that wa—" He frowned. Why not?

"What wuz you gonna say, Colt? You stopped mighty sudden. You got a idear?"

Granger nodded. "Might not be nothin', but it's sure worth a try."

"What's worth a try? I'm ready to try anything." Sanders's eyes scanned each wall, and returned to the tall man.

Granger pushed his hat to the back of his head. "What I was gonna say, just jokin' o' course, but now that I think on it, maybe it ain't so crazy . . ."

"Well, dammit, what isn't so crazy?" Still standing in the middle of the floor, Sanders pinned Granger with a look that would have penetrated cast iron.

"What I was gonna say was, why don't we tear down that wood wall he's got back there? Don't see no reason for that wood to be there. Clinton wasn't one to decorate a room unless the decoration had some use."

While he talked, Sanders had slowly nodded. "Believe you might be right, cowboy. Let's do it."

They walked to the back room, to find Howie and Colgan tearing the lining from suit coats, ripping pockets from trousers, and looking as though they were doing it to show their dislike for the fat man.

"You can stop that. Granger had a better idea. Let's tear down that wall back yonder." While he talked, Sanders picked up a hammer they'd brought with them, put the claw behind a board, and pried it loose. That's all it took. The board fell to the floor, and behind it one row of recessed shelves showed, stacked with bags of dust, silver dollars, and paper money. They made short work of removing the remaining planks.

Sanders called them in to sit around the stove. "That money we'll turn over to the territorial government." They all nodded. "But first, it is my belief we should see that justice is done." At their questioning frowns, he smiled. "We all know that once a politician gets his hands on money it has a habit of getting spent on pet projects, most of them to further the politician's career. Now, I'm saying let's take care of those who made this possible, and those who were hurt by Clinton."

"What you sayin', Fisk?" Granger packed his pipe and lit it.

Instead of answering him, Sanders went to the desk, took a quill in hand, dipped it into the inkwell, and looked at Drago. "How much was Clinton to pay you and Colgan?"

"Two thousand dollars, one thousand apiece."

Sanders turned his eyes on Doty. "How much to kill Granger?"

"Two thousand."

Sanders wrote a while, then said, "I promised you, Drago, a thousand from the Vigilantes to help Granger and me get evidence on Clinton. You got the evidence. He didn't live long enough to get tried, but that's not your fault. We'll pay you anyway." He glanced at Colgan. "We'll pay you a like amount; you helped make the plan work. That's two thousand apiece for you two."

He frowned, again dipped the pen in the inkwell, and looked at Doty. "Seems you got only half of what he promised you. We're gonna pay you the other half for not shooting our good friend, Granger."

He looked at Granger. "I figure you've had a couple hundred dollars out-of-pocket expenses comin' over here—so have I. Howie, if Granger and I get two hundred, so do you. The rest goes to the government, and we're lucky there, because this month, December, the legislature approved moving the territorial capital from Bannack to Virginia City. We'll turn it over to them as soon as you men get what was promised to you, regardless the source."

Granger studied a moment the smoke coming from his pipe. "Fisk, you cain't do this. They find out, it'll be hell to pay."

"I intend they find out." Sanders grinned. "Fact is, I'm gonna write it all down, get each of you to sign the paper as to the amount paid you, and turn the paper over to the authorities along with the total amount we found behind the wall, less what we're getting. If they want to do something about it, I'll spread the word to the miners. We've saved their bacon. They won't stand for any political legalese against us."

Sheriff Howie smiled, shook his head, and said, "If all lawyers thought as you do, we could soon do away with them, as well as the kind of work I do. But then, I was told once upon a time, by a very knowledgeable judge, that the law and justice had no relationship. Here we've had justice, but sure as hell not much law."

"That judge told you the facts, Neil, and maybe sometime in the future we'll be tied to the law, but not here and now." Sanders counted out sacks of dust, put them in separate piles, then pushed a pile toward each man. "Help me count the rest so I can write my letter to the authorities."

About to move from the desk, Granger stopped, held up his hands, and swept them with a look. "Hold it. I b'lieve I got a better idea 'bout that money. It'll take longer, but I reckon it'd be a whole lot fairer."

"Let's hear it." Sanders sat back in his chair. "I'm not much for givin' money to the government."

Still standing, Granger looked at each of them. "All them papers we been lookin' at, well some o' them people might still be alive; if not, we oughtta be able to get ahold o' some o' their folks. That money rightfully b'longs to them.''

When they'd torn Clinton's desk apart, Granger had set two bottles of whiskey against the wall. Sanders picked them up, pulled the cork from each, and motioned the five men to again sit. He handed a bottle to Drago on his left and Howie on his right. ''Drink from the bottle, not them glasses. Clinton mighta had rabies.'' He picked up a sheaf of papers and riffled through them. ''I think Granger's right. How do you all feel about keeping the money I've given you and dividing the rest up, as evenly as possible, and sending it to the people who own it.''

Sheriff Howie smiled. ''Just who the hell's got time to seek out them people? It's gonna take a lot of time.''

Sanders nodded. ''I thought of that. I'll take on the job for a fee, and those owners, or heirs, I've not found at the end of a year, we'll turn their share over to the territorial legislature. I think my fee of five hundred a month will be fair.''

They all nodded their agreement and took a swig from one of the bottles to seal the deal.

Drago patted his pockets. ''With this here money I reckon me an' Colgan'll head east in the mornin'—if it's all right with y'all.''

They wished them luck. Granger then said he thought as how he and Molly would head back to Hell Gate. ''We gonna take Doty here with us if he figures to give up the gun. Figure a man like him'll own half the Bitter Root Valley in a few years.''

Doty made as if to unbuckle his gunbelt. Granger grinned and shook his head. ''No. Reckon you better keep wearin' it for self-defense. You notice that's the only reason I wear mine.''

Sanders stood, took a drink, and passed the bottle on. ''I'll give each of you an accounting when the money's all been disposed of.''

They all said in unison, ''Don't send me no damned paperwork.'' Then they left, and Sanders locked the door behind him.

• • •

It took Molly and Granger, riding a buckboard, with Doty leading a packhorse, ten days to get back to the valley. Doty went on to the Indian Agency to file for squatter's rights.

Colt busied himself getting the cabin finished the way he and Molly had dreamed it. Christmas came and went. Molly oohed and aaahed over her watch, as did Colt over the one she'd given him. Much of what Molly bought in Virginia City was for her friends the Flatheads. She and Granger made a trip to Little Bear's lodge to deliver their gifts.

It got harder with each passing day for Granger to be near Molly, seeing her move around the stove preparing meals, sit by the fire at night knitting or sewing, or scrub the puncheon floors he'd built into each room. He'd long since stopped her from the backbreaking labor of cutting stove wood, and helping build the barn, storage house, and corral, and other outside work. But it was inside—where he was close to her, could smell her clean woman scent, see the grace with which she moved while doing her chores, or feel the way she would touch his arm while talking—that his resolve weakened to be a proper man, to not let her know how he felt, to not admit to her that he was less than the man she seemed to think him. He would not take advantage of any feeling he might have generated in her from his raising her and Nick. He had taken to staying outside as much as possible, keeping a distance from her.

He told himself hundreds of times she was not his real daughter, told himself to go ahead and tell her he loved her, but he could not bear the thought she might reject him, or, worse, accept him out of obligation. Hell, she wasn't beholden to him for anything. She'd been a full-fledged partner in all they'd done. Why couldn't he accept things as they were and enjoy them?

He was standing at the corral, hunkered into his sheepskin, watching the horses, when he felt her walk to his side. She placed her hand on his forearm. "Colt, what's the matter? You've put a fence between us, you're distant. Ever since we came back from Virginia City, you've grown further from me." She took her hand from his arm, turned her back to the corral rails, and leaned against them. She looked into his

eyes. "Have I done something wrong? Are you angry with
me? What's the matter?"

He shook his head. His voice soft, he said, "No, little one,
I'm not angry 'bout nothin'. You sure ain't done nothin'
wrong. Maybe it's me. Maybe I got cabin fever." He
shrugged. "Hell, I don't know. If I could tell you, I would."

She stared at him a long moment, her eyes swimming, then
spun and almost ran to the cabin. He watched until she closed
the door. He scanned what they had built together—none of
it worth having without her. A huge emptiness filled his
chest. Why couldn't he just reach out and take her into his
arms? Because he'd never know whether she truly loved him,
or loved him only for what he'd done for her and Nick. It
was then he made up his mind. He was only making her
miserable by staying here. Perhaps she would be better off
if he left.

The next morning, he saddled his horse, took one of the
other horses for a pack animal, rolled his bedroll, shoved his
rifle into its scabbard, and was putting his gear on the packhorse when she came to him.

In a quiet voice, she asked, "What are you doing, Colt?
Are you taking a trip, maybe to the coast for cattle?"

He faced her. "Nope, little one, I'm leavin'—for good."
He motioned to the cabin. "You're right comfortable here,
got good friends, got money. I'm leavin' you my share of
dust what we got from the diggin's, an' under that tree out
yonder they's plenty more if you ever need it."

She stood looking at him, tears running in rivulets down
her cheeks. "Is it me? You gotta see what's on the other
side of the hill? If it's that, I'll go with you." She waved
her hand to include the cabin and their land. "All them
things you talked about don't mean nothin' to me. Fact is if
my partner ain't part of my life, don't nothin' mean anything."

He took her shoulders in his hands. "Don't cry, Molly,
please don't. No. It ain't you—Yes, it is you. You see I'm
doin' this for your own good."

"For my own good." She sniffled. "For my own good?
How can that be when you're my whole life?"

He pulled her into his arms, kissed her roughly, then kissed her again, this time gently, letting his heart, his pent-up love, show in the caress his lips gave hers. He released her, stepped back, and looked at her, knowing all of his feelings showed in his eyes. "There. Now do you see, little one? I love you, have loved you since I first took you from your burned-out wagon." He shook his head. "I love you, an' ain't gonna have you less'n you love me, too."

She clamped her hands to hips and pinned him with that no-nonsense look. "Colt Granger, I been tryin' to tell you every way I knew how, for oh-so-long. I been tryin' to show you in the little things I could do for you. I've done everything I knew to show you. That's what I've been meanin' to tell you. I have loved you ever since I knew what it was to be a woman and want a man, my man—you. You gonna marry me, Colt, or you gonna let it be with us just partners?"

He grinned, pulled her into his arms, and whispered, "Will you settle for both?"